THE KINGDOM'S CROWN

KATHRYN MOON

This is a Reverse Harem Fantasy Romance and is not suited for those under the age of 18.

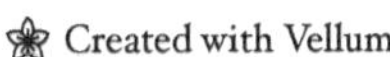 Created with Vellum

To my pack babes,
Lana, Chloe, Crystal, and Aleera

CONTENTS

1. Bryony — 1
2. Thao — 13
3. Bryony — 21
4. Bryony — 31
5. Bryony — 39
6. Aric — 51
7. Bryony — 65
8. Cresswell — 73
9. Bryony — 85
10. Bryony — 99
11. Cosmo — 113
12. Bryony — 119
13. Wendell — 129
14. Bryony — 139
15. Thao — 149
16. Bryony — 163
17. Owen — 175
18. Wendell — 187
19. Bryony — 197
20. Bryony — 211
21. Bryony — 221
22. Bryony — 235
23. Bryony — 245
24. Daniel — 255
25. Bryony — 265
26. Bryony — 277
27. Bryony — 285
28. Bryony — 295
29. Bryony — 311
30. Bryony — 319
Epilogue — 331

Also by Kathryn Moon 335
Acknowledgments 337
About the Author 339

THE KINGDOM'S CROWN

INHERITANCE OF HUNGER
BOOK THREE

BY KATHRYN MOON

1.
BRYONY

"**I**s that a note to Griffin? Bryony, it hasn't even been a day since we left," Wendell chuckled, leaning in to watch me scribble quickly against the rocking of the carriage.

"I know, but I was so busy with Lady Prudence that I barely got to—Oh!" I hissed as the carriage jostled roughly and my pot of ink toppled, spilling across the page.

Cosmo and Wendell both leaned in to help me as Thao snorted from the opposite seat.

"I think correspondence can wait for us to rest for the night, little muse," Cosmo murmured, his lips twitching as he took my writing desk away and Wendell disposed of the ruined page.

"I just wanted to suggest to Griffin that she might—"

"The hawk will have schemes of her own," Thao said, cocking an eyebrow.

I hummed and glanced out the window. That was probably true. Griffin had only winced when I'd proposed a caper to unite my somewhat fractured thieves' court. It seemed diplomacy was more complicated when it came to rogues.

Owen and Daniel passed us on their horses, laughing easily with one another, their cheeks flushed with the cold weather.

"I like him better than I expected, although I'm not sure I can say why," Wendell murmured, watching with me as the two men passed.

"Would it have something to do with how ridiculously huge his—"

"Thao!" I cut him off with a gasp and a laugh.

Thao only shrugged and smirked at me. "If you'd mentioned it earlier, I might've been more understanding when it came to you finding yourself unexpectedly taking him for a ride."

"That had *nothing* to do with it!"

Cosmo had his mouth covered with his hand, a poor attempt to hide his laughter, and Wendell was not so subtly kicking at Thao's shin, but our prince was piled with blankets and didn't seem to notice.

"If I hadn't seen for myself how well you take him, I would've sworn it wasn't possible for him to fit," Thao continued, so obviously enjoying teasing me.

I blushed, which was absurd after all the acts I'd committed with these men, and resisted the urge to lunge at Thao and cover his wicked mouth. I knew where it would lead, which was perhaps Thao's aim.

"Mmm, I had my reservations about Daniel, but that *was* an attractive show," Cosmo said, nodding to Thao, who took the statement as a victory.

Wendell wrapped an arm around my shoulders and bundled me into his side. "Ignore them, love. They're just jealous."

Cosmo chuckled, but Thao's mouth dropped open in offense.

"That you don't get to enjoy him yourself, of course," Wendell added, grinning at Thao, who hmph'ed.

"Well I have you, my darling, and you are certainly adequate," Thao said tartly.

"I suddenly understand the need to protect you all from your own statistics," I said on a sigh. "Daniel's cock had next to nothing to do with why he is my Chosen now."

Cosmo's knee nudged against mine. "Ignore us. Anyway, Thao is just nervous for tonight."

Thao's eyes widened, and he shot an utterly betrayed look in Cosmo's direction.

"Are you?" Wendell asked, voice bright with surprise.

We'd made it down from the mountain, leaving the Winter Palace in the care of Lady Prudence and Sam, and the thieves' court with Griffin, and we were on our way to Wendell's family home to rest for a day. As eager as I was to see my grandmother in the south, there had been a tender tentativeness in Wendell's suggestion that we stop there for a night. One that left me certain of how much it would mean to him to see his family again after being so long away in Mennary.

It was only now occurring to me what this brief visit might mean for Thao as well, who had never met his lover's family before.

Thao shied away from the question, trying to find something else of interest within the carriage and failing. "A bit," he admitted, and both Wendell and I froze at the two words. From Thao, they revealed a great deal. "But the focus will be on Bryony, so I can relax into the background."

You hate blending into the background, I thought and resisted saying. I glanced at Wendell, who was wearing a soft smile that Thao refused to notice.

When Thao and Wendell had joined my Chosen, they'd belonged solely to one another in heart. It was more equal now between us and even Cosmo, but Thao and Wendell had meant so much to one another for so long and lived with it secretly. Which meant that whether he liked it or not, I was going to find a way to thrust Thao into focus at some point during the visit.

"I think my mother is equally flustered over both of you. The Popes have never hosted royalty."

"I hope they aren't going to too much trouble," I said, frowning.

All three men scoffed at the idea, and Wendell squeezed my hand before I could object again. "I did my best to reassure her that you are very humble and agreeable and of all your loveliest qualities," he said, leaning in to press a kiss to my forehead and another to the tip of my nose. "I doubt it did any good."

"Speaking of new Chosen," Cosmo started.

"I thought we'd moved on from that—"

"How is Cresswell? I have trouble reading the pair of you," Cosmo said.

I groaned and Wendell shifted, letting me hide my face against the soft sweater he was wearing, his hand soothing over my back.

"I hardly know," I mumbled. "I thought we'd reached some moment of understanding days ago, but he's barely touched me since. He takes his position very seriously and seems to be under the impression it leaves no room for us to be together."

"You could remove him from your guard," Thao said with a shrug.

I lifted my head from Wendell's chest and shook my head. "It isn't that I haven't considered the idea, only that it seems cruel. It means a great deal to him."

"As much as I want you to be happy with him, I'm relieved he's coming with us to the south as your guard," Cosmo said softly. "I'm not sure there's anyone I trust with that duty as well as him."

I nodded and sighed, glancing out the window as if I might see Cresswell passing by. He was probably at the back with Aric. "Unfortunately, I feel the same."

"We will find a way to make time for the two of you to come together," Wendell said, twisting a finger through a loose curl over my shoulder.

"I should think two tigers and a mage ought to do as well as one head guard in protecting you," Thao said, nodding.

"I object to violence, but I am very handy with a chisel," Cosmo said lightly.

I smiled to hide the sting the words conjured in my chest. Cosmo seemed to either have reconciled himself to my killing Emory, or was able to effectively ignore the memory. I wasn't sure the same could be said of myself, the man's face appearing in my thoughts at the oddest moments.

I wanted to put Emory and his death behind me, but I was too aware of the weight of the future. Camellia had tried to leave Sam in my court in a poorly considered assassination attempt. Sam had proved too happy to be liberated from my sister, but what if the next arrow she sent in my direction was sharper? We were headed south to the castle, where I would be in regular proximity to the dangers she posed, not just to myself but to my Chosen. She'd already attempted to force Owen to fuck her once, what if she found another opportunity to do the same to him, or Cosmo, or Daniel, or any of my men?

Whether Camellia was the direct threat, or she found another vessel, I was afraid Emory's blood was not the last I would wear on my hands.

"Bryony," Wendell murmured, and I startled, realizing all their gazes were fixed to me.

I shook myself and forced a smile. "I think an unconsummated love affair is the least of my worries, really. Cresswell and I will find our moment."

❦

THE POPE ESTATE rested in the heart of the Highminster Woods, just south of where the foothills seemed to roll to a weary stop. We'd only rested for a brief picnic, and it was very late and the woods were dense, but the modest manor home we approached glowed sweetly within the canopy. A pair of servants appeared in the doorway before we rolled to a stop, and they hurried down the small front steps to meet the carriage and take our bags.

"This is very pretty, Wendell," I said as Thao and I crowded the window to peer up at the house.

Daniel had joined us in the carriage, taking Wendell's seat, who moved to squeeze in with Cosmo and Thao.

"It's not Danser Hall but—"

"But it's probably in a great deal less debt," Daniel answered to Wendell wryly.

It was smaller than Danser Hall, but also less austere. Rose trellises rose up along the front facade of the pale brick, and even though it was too late in the year for any blooms, the greenery gave the place a pleasant wildness.

"It looks every bit as you described," Thao said, his usual energy subdued.

A figure appeared in the outline of the open door, tall and feminine, and Thao jerked back from the window suddenly.

"There's Mother," Wendell said.

The rest of my Chosen, including Cresswell, appeared in front of the carriage door, and it was Aric who opened it for us, Thao stepping out and handing me down. My mage looked weary and windswept from the long ride of the day, and a sharply cold cheek rested against the top of my head as I leaned into him.

"I know I said we shouldn't spare so much time here, but I'm relieved at the thought now," Aric grumbled softly.

"You know you *could* sit in the carriage," I whispered back, restraining my laugh as he let out an offended grumble. Aric was far too opposed to luxury for his own good.

"Wen!" the woman on the stairs cried as Wendell's long frame ducked out of the carriage.

Wendell's mother, Miriam Pope, rushed down the steps of her home and across the grassy drive as Wendell jogged to meet her. He bent as she rose to her toes, enveloping him in a fierce hug. It was too dark to tell if her hair was a lighter shade of blonde than Wendell's, or if she had his blue eyes, but it was obvious in their embrace her own joy and relief at seeing her son again. Wendell lifted his mother off her toes briefly, the pair of them laughing as he set her down just as quickly.

My heart ached at the sight of them, a strange kind of jealousy rising up inside of me.

"Bryony?" Aric asked, and I smoothed my expression.

"It's nothing," I said quickly, not wanting to explain the source of my discomfort.

Wendell's mother kissed his cheeks twice before they settled, her smile catching some of the light from the lamps in the manor windows. He stepped to her side, and Miriam's hand rose to rest over her chest. She was every bit as elegant and beautiful as her son, with creases in the corners of her eyes the only clear sign of her age.

"Oh, excuse me, Your Highness—"

"No, please!"

"It is such an honor to-to have you all visit here. And to—" Her words failed her, and Wendell's arm wrapped around her shoulders as she beamed up at him.

I moved to join them, and Wendell's hand squeezed on her shoulders, thankfully keeping his mother from falling into a curtsy for my sake. "It's my sincere pleasure, Mistress Pope. And please, call me Bryony."

Wendell and his mother released bright laughs at the same time, hers a little panicked. "You'll have to forgive my mother when she can't help herself, love," Wendell said, turning his smile back to his mother. "Have you driven Cook mad rearranging the dinner plans a hundred times yet?"

"I—maybe a bit. Speaking of dinner, I went ahead and asked

for suppers to be sent up to the rooms we prepared for you. I'm afraid accommodations are a little tight—"

"It's fine," Wendell and I said at the same moment.

I had the oddest impulse to step in closer, to claim a hug from the woman with the same ease that Wendell had, but her nerves were obvious and she leaned into him for support. Thao joined me, one hand cupping over my shoulder, and Miriam's eyes widened.

Not even Wendell could stop his mother from the low curtsy she fell into then. "Oh! You must be Prince Thao. Wen always had such wonderful things to say about you and how at home you made him feel in Mennary. I am so grateful to you and so happy the both of you were Chosen!"

Thao answered the curtsy with a deep bow, and Miriam flushed and nearly tottered over until Wendell pulled her up. "I can assure you the praise is mutual and I've long looked forward to meeting you as well, Mistress Pope."

Thao's gallantry met awed silence, and I took the opportunity to introduce the rest of my Chosen.

"Please come in, you all must be so tired from the traveling," Miriam said, her wide eyes flicking back and forth between Thao and I as she clung to Wendell's arm and he guided her toward the doors.

"Father?"

"Oh, he said he would make it to your arrival, but he fell asleep immediately after his—"

"His port," Wendell finished, chuckling. "Glad to know that hasn't changed."

Cosmo and Thao joined me on the way in as I drank in Wendell's family home. It was more modern than the Farraque estate, with larger windows to look out into the woods, and there was something sweetly comforting about the space. The carpets were a little worn, and ample bouquets rested on every available surface, overflowing with greenery that looked as though the mistress of the house had arranged them herself.

This is what a lovely home must look like, I thought, thinking of scenes and settings from the books I'd read. If I'd been a heroine in a novel instead of a princess, this might've been the hall where

I'd greeted guests at a dinner party, and that might've been the staircase I raced down as a girl.

Miriam Pope's eyes slid in my direction, a self-conscious flinch in her gaze. "It's not mu—"

"It's beautiful," I said quickly.

"It reminds me of Wen," Thao said, making our lover blush.

"It's late. You should join Father. I can see our party gets settled in," Wendell said. "Tours and longer introductions can wait for the morning."

It was an awkward procession up the stairs with Miriam trying to excuse the little faults she kept discovering in her home. Wendell had the best luck with reassuring her, and Owen, who declared in his most sincere way that the manor made much more sense in its size than the Winter Palace.

Wendell sighed and gave me a sheepish grin as his mother retreated into her room, and he led us further down the hall. "I warned you," he whispered.

"She's lovely and every bit as kind as you. I hope she'll be more comfortable with me in the morning, but either way, I'm glad we're visiting here so she gets to see you," I said.

"I'm afraid the more charming you are, the more flustered she'll be. Come, let's find these suppers waiting for us," Wendell said, taking my hand.

❧❧❧

THAO'S FINGERTIPS stroked absently over mine as we both lay awake. The only sounds breaking through the silence of the house were Wendell's deep breaths.

"Is he asleep?" Thao whispered in my ear. I nodded, the pair of us staring at the silvery outline of Wendell's profile, his lips parted and hair mussed over his forehead. "Are you as nervous as I am?"

I thought over his question. I wasn't very nervous about meeting Wendell's parents; I was...unexpectedly uncomfortable. I didn't really know how to be easy with Wendell's mother the way he was, and she certainly didn't know how to be easy with me.

"Not sure," I said, pushing back against Thao's chest with my shoulder.

"Wen wants to introduce me to them, to tell them about our tigers."

"You're afraid they'll disapprove?" I asked. Thao was silent in answer. "Is he?"

"No."

"Then trust him, he knows them best."

"Will you join us? If it goes poorly, you might distract from the tension."

I scoffed and smiled, rolling away from Wendell to face Thao. He was murky in the dark room, and I wiggled closer until our noses bumped. "I will not," I said softly, stroking my hands over his bare chest.

The Popes' beds hadn't been made for a princess and her Chosen, so my other men were sleeping in separate rooms. Thao had barely fit in with me and Wendell in Wen's former bed. I hadn't expected the distinctly *wrong* feeling of us all sleeping apart, but it was there, itching at me as if I wouldn't find comfortable sleep without all the excessive heat and chorus of snores I'd grown used to.

"If it were your family—"

"They didn't approve," Thao whispered. "The continuation of our line was paramount. There was no allowance for same-sex couplings. Not public ones at least."

"I suppose the same might've been true for me," I murmured, and Thao hummed, his lips grazing aimlessly against mine. "You know that even if Wendell's parents have reservations, it won't change anything, right?"

Thao was quiet for several moments before speaking. "It may not change his feelings for me, but I would hate for it to change his feelings for them."

Thinking of the way Miriam had embraced her son on our arrival, I both understood Thao's fears and doubted the need for them.

"I know why I am awake, but why are you?" Thao whispered.

"I'm afraid of everything that comes next when we return to the south. And it feels strange not to have the others in here and..."

Wendell sighed in his sleep, rolling over, and Thao and I both fell quiet.

"You sleep best when Cosmo or Aric holds you," Thao whispered, smiling as my eyes widened. "Don't worry, the rest of us aren't offended. Go on."

I kissed Thao briefly and then withheld my giggle as he rolled me out of the bed and lightly onto the floor. Wendell's room was wonderfully cluttered with books and maps and stray pieces of paper that I thought his mother must've been dusting all this time, and I shuffled carefully for the door, grabbing up my robe from a chair and peeking out in the hall.

Directly across from the bedroom door stood Cresswell, his eyes meeting mine immediately, head cocking. The lamps were turned low in the hall, and there was another guard, the young Stanley Piper, stationed at the top of the stairs.

"What are you doing up?" Cresswell asked, frowning as I shut the door behind me and crossed to his side.

"Do you really have to be on duty tonight?"

Cresswell's frown deepened, but I thought I caught a slight flush in his cheeks as I reached up and pressed a fingertip against the corner of his mouth, trying to push it up into a smile. His eyes flicked in Stanley Piper's direction, and when I followed his gaze I found the young guard now standing with his back to us.

"You know how much I appreciate your dedication to protecting me—"

"Bryony—"

"But I really think we need to negotiate on the terms. I'd rather you were guarding me closely while I was awake and able to enjoy your company," I said, smiling. "If you insist on guarding me in my sleep, it would be much more fun if you were in the bed too."

Cresswell's snarl was soft and velvety, and his lips were curled up of their own accord now. He checked on the other guard once more before I suddenly found myself caught in his arms and trapped against his chest. Cresswell ducked and his lips found mine before I'd gathered a breath, their press firm and trapping, holding me tight. He breathed into the kiss, content with the embrace, and my body melted into him, tension uncoiling and eyes growing heavy.

When he pulled away, I was too subdued to demand more, even with the Hunger simmering.

"I'm willing to consider your terms," Cresswell said, obvious pride in his faint smile and laughter glittering in those cool eyes of his. "But first you will have to sleep."

He lifted me off my toes, and I was only able to make one small huff of protest before he was kissing me again. Cresswell's lips were wonderfully soft and full, his kisses demanding and thorough. I was aware he was using them now not as a seduction but as a distraction, but I couldn't care enough to protest.

A door creaked and the light from the hall vanished, bedsheets rustling.

"I have no objection to this, but I'm not sure there's room on the bed."

Aric.

Cress pulled away from the kiss, and I blinked in the dark.

"Whussgoin' on?" Cosmo grumbled sleepily.

"Not quite sure," Aric answered.

And then Cresswell set me back down on my feet, the backs of my thighs bumping into the edge of a mattress. "Her Highness has come to sleep," Cress said, kissing my lips once more gently.

"Wait, I—"

"And so have I, but here on the floor."

I tried resisting Aric and Cosmo's arms as they bundled me up to tuck me between them, but Cresswell's kiss had acted as a kind of drug, and I was finally feeling the exhaustion of the day.

"Not on the floor," I managed.

"I'll be fine, Bryony," Cresswell said, his voice dropping to a growl. There was a rustle and a faint sparkle, and then Cresswell's shadow was enormous and clumsy, nudging the bed with a creak out of his way as the bear settled down to the floor by the bed.

"Well, I can honestly say this is a first for me," Aric grumbled as he and Cosmo wrestled the blankets up over me.

"Cress, are you really going to be comfortable like that?" I whispered.

"More comfortable than he'd be trying to fit in the bed with us," Cosmo said, cuddling me into his chest and wrapping his arms around me.

My only answer from Cresswell was a chuff of breath and a glittery blink of an eye before his head ducked down below the edge of the bed.

"Didn't expect a bear to smell so decent," Aric mumbled, joining Cosmo in tangling up with me. And damn him, but Thao was right. I fell asleep within a happy, peaceful minute, all worries of the south fading under the chorus of breaths that reminded me of the beat of waves on the shore.

2.
THAO

Wendell had always described the home he'd grown up in as like something out of a children's story. In Mennary, children's stories were full of jungles and animals making wicked bargains and children outwitting their kidnappers. Apparently, Kimmerian stories were of tricksters sitting on wood stumps waiting to lead travelers astray and young women going on long adventures and mysterious cottages that never appeared in the same place twice.

The woods of the Pope estate did have a kind of magic to it, especially this time of year. I'd never been anywhere where the trees changed color to mark the seasons, and the effect of the falling leaves sparkling between sunlight and shadow when a wind struck stopped me in my tracks. It was almost worth the sacrifice of good weather.

I shivered and tugged the collar of my coat up, frowning at the way the wind was able to sneak through every weave of fabric I wore. I was not so privately relieved we were returning south as winter was hitting. Bryony and the others appeared delighted by the snow already coating the mountains, but Kimmerian winters struck me as having a very bland color palette and terrible temperatures.

"Suppose you don't get much in the way of cold weather where you're from."

Douglas Pope was a typical Kimmerian gentleman. He was tall and broad like Wen, with thinning hair in shades of rust and gray, and a much rounder stomach. His cheeks and nose had been red when he'd appeared at breakfast to take great pains in complimenting Bryony as she tried to eat her jam and toast, and they remained red now out in the cold of his woods.

"Not like yours, no," I said, nodding.

Douglas Pope nodded too until we both fell into silence again. We were outside under the pretense of hunting with Daniel and Wendell, but I was suddenly wishing I'd stayed back with the other group, regardless of Wendell's imploring look. I could've been napping by a fireplace, listening to Bryony try and coax Miriam into ease, or wandering the other side of the woods with Cosmo and Owen, waiting for the inevitable parade of wildlife to join us.

I hope the two parties don't meet, I thought aimlessly, not sure how Miriam Pope would take a number of rodents joining our dinner party under Owen's invitation.

"Mennary has to deal with monsoon season," I found myself saying, for no clear reason.

Douglas grunted, and Wendell shot me an encouraging smile.

"I suppose rain is as good an inducement to stay indoors as snow," Daniel said in a small attempt at support. He was, apparently, not entirely useless.

"Ah, there!" Douglas hissed, lifting his rifle and pointing into the trees.

I saw it too, a large stag, and I held my own gun in my hand, but I didn't bother raising it. I wasn't a good shot, and I didn't have the heart to hunt for sport.

Daniel raised his own to aim, but either he was very patient or he was only miming. Douglas Pope fired, and I grimaced at the thunderous bang. The stag leapt and took off running, unmarked.

"Good effort," Wendell said, and his father grunted.

"Well, this way your mother won't try and change the menu at the last minute," Douglas said with an easy chuckle. "Come on, we'd better get in before His Highness freezes."

I opened my mouth to object, but Wendell rushed ahead. "You mean it's time for your afternoon pipe."

Douglas grinned, clapping Wendell on the shoulder and flashing me a wink. "Wen's always been too clever. Not certain where he gets it."

"He always spoke very highly of his professors," I said without thinking.

And by some miracle, Douglas Pope only laughed, raucous and delighted. "Glad to know my money went to some use for all that schooling."

I sighed and fell into step behind Wendell and his father, Daniel scuffing a gloved hand over his twitching lips. Wendell's parents were as sweetly humored as their son, but I hadn't yet found the same sharp intensity he kept hidden under his polish in either of them and it left me floundering in how to behave.

"I think I'll go and see if I can track down Owen and Cosmo," Daniel murmured to me, passing me his gun.

"Just remember it gets darker faster in the woods," Wendell warned him.

"And Miriam has a grand affair planned, what with—" Douglas gestured vaguely at me. "You know, royals filling up the house."

Daniel nodded and jogged for the trees.

With the guns passed to the groundskeeper, we entered the manor from the veranda, a servant hurrying to help us out of our coats until they looked buried beneath the layers. Miriam Pope appeared, her cheeks flushing sweetly as her husband and son both moved in to kiss her cheeks.

"Her Highness—"

"Mother, please, call her Bryony."

"—went out with that...oh, I've forgotten his name," Miriam said, frowning. "The old one."

Douglas scoffed. "He was younger than me, I should think."

"Aric," I said.

"Yes! Thank you! Her Highness and Aric went out to find the others," Miriam said. "Oh and the handsome guard."

Which meant it was only me. "Perhaps I should go and join them so the three of you—"

"Wait, Thao," Wendell said, brightening and stepping away from his mother to move to my side. "No, actually, I'd love for the four of us to sit down together."

Miriam bit her lip and smiled tenuously, and I was sure she would've preferred if I left them to their time together without me.

"As long as you don't mind my little routine," Douglas said, heading for the pair of doors leading to the large study.

"Do you think Her High—"

"Bryony."

"—Will dress very finely for our dinner tonight? I did tell Joan I might need her to freshen my hair for the evening," Miriam murmured.

"The princess is very informal and a little bit of a wild beast," I said, making Miriam's eyes widen and Wendell laugh. "If we are very lucky, she will return from the woods without mud on her skirts or twigs in her hair. But you may need to prepare yourself to dine with a very pretty and well-mannered animal."

"Oh, dear. I've been making too much of a fuss, haven't I?" Miriam said, but she was smiling and she seemed to relax.

"Don't mind what he's said. Bryony is every bit as anxious to please you as you are to please her," Wendell said. And then his hand found mine at my side, our fingers tangling together. "Now I promise this won't take long, but I really do want to grab this moment with you and Father."

Miriam hummed and nodded, following after her husband to the study as Wendell's fingers squeezed around mine.

"Quit looking as though you're about to face an army," he whispered, leaning in and resting his forehead against mine.

"Are you sure this needs to be done?" I asked, gaze flicking back and forth between the open study doors and Wendell's face.

"I'm sure that it will mean a great deal to me to tell them," Wendell said. "And I think it might to you as well."

"There is always a letter," I muttered, but I followed as he tugged me toward the door.

Miriam had already found a seat in an armchair by the fireplace, and Douglas was packing a small pipe with dark tobacco, his eyes lifting and pausing on our linked hands. He blinked, stilling in his movements before setting the pipe aside, a slight frown on his lips as he crossed his hands over his stomach. Wendell guided me down to join him on a small couch.

"I've been so eager for you both to meet Thao for such a long time, and I regret that this is such a short visit," Wendell began.

I wanted to compliment the Popes on their son or their home

or their hospitality. Wanted to speak on all the warm stories Wendell had told me as we'd fallen in love in Mennary. My tongue was glued to the roof of my mouth as his parents stared back at us, a little furrow of confusion between Miriam's eyes and a cool understanding in Douglas's.

"There's always been more I've wanted to tell you about my friendship with Thao, but it didn't feel right to put it in a letter," Wendell said. I glanced at him and found him every bit as bright and hopeful as he had been arriving here at his former home.

"It is so good that you both were Chosen by Her Highness," Miriam said brightly.

Wendell's grin was sheepish. Bryony had chosen us more out of mercy than desire at the time, and solely for the reason we were sitting across from Wendell's parents now.

"We were very lucky," Wendell murmured.

It struck me then that I was giving him this burden of confession. He didn't seem to mind. He was certainly more excited than I was. But Wendell deserved more than my silence at his side, and his parents ought to know how much I valued their son.

"Your son has taught me a great deal since we met. Of friendship and respect, how to support someone in deed rather than only words. He has shown me the best and worst of my pride, and I have taken great pleasure in learning every wonderfully generous, intelligent, and kind facet of him," I said slowly, gazing at Wendell, speaking every word of truth and knowing that whatever came next, it was worth the happy flush in his cheeks. "I love Wendell, far more deeply than I knew was possible before meeting him."

Miriam Pope sniffled, a handkerchief conjured from her sleeve to dab at her eyes, a wavering smile on her lips. Douglas Pope, however, remained frowning. He didn't appear angry, but he certainly wasn't as touched by the sentiments as his wife.

"And I love you," Wendell said, bowing his head to me, stopping just shy of a kiss.

"And the princess?" Douglas asked.

Wendell frowned and turned back to his father, blinking. "Bryony?"

"What will you tell her of all of this?" Douglas's question

sparked obvious concern in Miriam's expression, and all four of us sat up straighter.

"Bryony was aware from the very start, and we are every bit her Chosen," Wendell said, shrugging. "But it doesn't change the fact that Thao and I... How important it was to me that you know what Thao means to me."

"Wendell and I love the princess, but for myself, I don't know that I would've been capable of such a depth of feeling without Wen first teaching it to me," I said.

Miriam sighed, her smiling returning. "Oh, that's lovely. Isn't that lovely, Douglas?" she added, a little more sharply.

"And you fulfill your duty to the young woman?" Douglas asked, eyes narrowing.

"Douglas!"

"We do," Wendell said, but the happy flush narrowed into darker twin spots of embarrassment.

Douglas Pope eased back in his chair, returning his attention to his pipe in his hand. "Ah well, that's all right then, isn't it? Long as there's no offense to the crown, you might do as you like."

Wendell stiffened, and Miriam stood up from her chair.

"Prince Thao, I wonder if you wouldn't help me pick out a bottle of wine for our dinner?" she said.

Wendell was simmering at my side, and I hesitated briefly, wondering if I shouldn't stay with him to hear whatever came out next. But I had faced my father alone in Mennary when he discovered my relationship with Wendell. At the time, I'd felt the shame firsthand and carried it on my own shoulders. If I had to sit through the same conversation today, I would've been more ashamed of my father than myself. I glanced at Wendell who nodded firmly and then I stood, offering Miriam my arm, although it was she who led me out of the room, a low murmur of voices rising at our back.

"I am happy, you know," she said as we stepped into the hall. "I always was. It was exciting for Wen to receive the ambassadorship so young, but Mennary is such a long ways away. When his letters began to arrive, they were lonely at first. A mother can tell. And then you appeared in them. And then they were full of you."

"I felt the same. Wen erased a great deal of the isolation I'd been raised with," I said.

Miriam beamed up at me, washing away some of the awkwardness of the study. "I am so glad you all decided to visit. I've wanted to meet you for so long."

She paused outside of a narrow service door, squeezing my arm and turning to face me.

"Thank you for taking care of my son, Your Highness."

"Thao, please," I said, bowing a little and making the older woman giggle. "The care was mutual."

"Now, I think we ought to pick one of Wen's favorites for dinner. I suppose as Chosen, I won't have many more opportunities to see him."

I hummed as she opened the narrow door and lit the lamp for the stairs down to their cellar. "I wouldn't discount it yet. Bryony is very conscious of our comfort and feelings. She would never deny Wendell time with his family."

Miriam brightened further at that. "I shall have to learn to say her name then, I suppose."

I worried briefly over how Wen was handling the remnants of conversation with his father, and then realized we'd already been given their blessing. Douglas Pope might not be as fond of his son's romance with me as he was of knowing Wendell was in good favor with the Kimmerian crown, but he hadn't tossed me out on my ass.

"I think we'd better choose a red for the roast," Miriam said, and I hurried to follow her down the stairs.

3.
BRYONY

"More wine, Your Highness?"

"Oh, no thank you," I said, shaking my head at the servant who had jumped forward to answer Miriam's offer. "The dinner was absolutely wonderful."

Miriam settled happily, and Wendell's hand found mine under the table, squeezing gently. Miriam had managed to stutter out a 'Bryony' earlier in the evening, but she quickly shifted back to my title. My Chosen and I were squeezed around the table with the Popes and two other older noble couples with nearby estates, including Sir Weston and his wife, Hermania.

There were more servants and deference to the evening than I'd dealt with since the castle had hosted an event in the capital, and I hadn't realized how used to our simpler life in the north I was until suddenly thrust back into the pomp of gentry.

"You would've enjoyed the show, Douglas," Sir Weston said, leaning back in his seat as he retold the story of my barging into the council meeting, his elbows brushing against Aric's, who looked positively constipated after the length of the evening. "Her Highness was every bit the queen as we haven't—Well, you reminded me a little of the dowager queen, Your Highness."

A year ago, I might've been appalled at the comparison, but now I only smiled and dipped my head. I would need my grandmother's ferocious command to make it to the throne.

"I'm afraid it will take more than a good speech at an interrupted council meeting to make the kind of change Kimmery needs to see," I said.

Sir Weston nodded, picking up his own wine glass. "You go to speak with your mother, I take it?"

My grandmother's current illness wasn't widely known yet. My mother had wanted to wait for my return to make the announcement, and there'd been a letter waiting here at the Popes' when I'd returned from the woods, reassuring me that my grandmother was holding on, remaining on bed rest.

"I'd like for her to be aware of everything I've learned with my time away from the capital," I said. "My mother loves this kingdom deeply."

Sir Weston's eyes slid away, his head still nodding but with less enthusiasm.

"You must look forward to seeing your sister, Camellia. My sister Nancy and I can barely stand to be parted," Lady Evelyn Ashley said, and her husband huffed gruffly. "Lord Ashley is so tolerant of my getting to see her a great deal. We should always be visiting one another if we could."

"Not sure sisterly love always extends so sweetly amongst the royal families," Lord Ashley chuckled. He'd taken every offering of wine Miriam Pope posed until they'd no longer been issued. "Wasn't it Queen Rose who had Princess Gardenia shipped off to some ruinous palace at the western border until she might be married away?"

"She died before the marriage," Sir Weston said gravely, swirling his wine in his glass.

I looked between the men. "You both know a great deal of my lineage."

"It was common before your great grandmother's time for the noble families to keep a record of the queen's line. Births, marriages, deaths," Douglas Pope said with a shrug.

"Banishments," I added and watched the men shift uncomfortably. As if I might be unaware of the ugly competition between two princesses for a crown.

"Ladies, I hope you might join me in the sitting room. I have been longing for a decent game of cards, and it is never as much fun with Douglas for I always know how he will play his hand," Miriam said, the men all rising from their seat to see the women out.

"I hope you won't mind my absence from your game," I said, rising too. "I was hoping to have a word with the gentlemen.

"I can take your place," Cosmo said quickly, meeting my gaze and nodding at my grateful smile. He would charm the women and also keep them from gossiping together through my discussion with the men.

"Are you sure it's safe?" I whispered to Wendell as the bodies shuffled around the table.

"Lord Ashley and my father have no political ambitions, and they take Sir Weston's advice in most matters. And we know he is on your side," Wendell said, arching an eyebrow.

"I suppose that means no pipe and whiskey," Lord Ashley grumbled, not quietly enough after all his drinking.

"By all means," I said, catching the words. Of the three men not part of my Chosen, I trusted Lord Ashley the least, and it might be better if he remembered less of the conversation about to take place. "I don't want to interrupt your routine together, only speak a little more with you."

"Let's move this to the study so dinner can be cleared away," Douglas said. *And so the servants aren't all listening in*, remained unspoken.

Daniel offered me his arm, his muscles tense beneath my tight fingers. It was a gamble to approach any political topic with these men, but we already knew Camellia had her mouth to the council's ear—if not elsewhere, I thought darkly—and I couldn't be the innocent and naïve girl who'd left the capital on my return. I needed solid allies, and I needed them speaking in my favor.

My Chosen were my shadows in the hallway as we moved, quiet support, their energies almost tangible at my back. Wendell's studious and careful nature weighing the coming conversation, Thao's confidence shoring me up to hold my chin high. Owen's devotion and utter faith in me, Daniel's steady commitment to serve me and his growing affectionate interest in belonging. Cresswell appeared from the shadows in his crisp uniform, warm tawny skin glowing in the lamplight, his eyes watchful over my head, ready to defend me at every moment. And Aric, a little bored, a little tempted, a little disgusted with himself for the finery of the evening, and every bit as loving and constant as he'd proved himself to be in the past month.

Daniel led me to the couch in the study, and I held his arm, coaxing him into sitting with me, Owen happily taking the other side of me. Cresswell remained at my back and Aric moved to lurk near the windows, watching the scene from afar, as Thao and Wendell both grabbed chairs near me. Lord Ashley was busy helping himself to the whiskey, but Sir Weston and Douglas Pope both sat near the fire, facing me immediately.

"I take it from your visit to our council meeting that you don't intend for the council to hold the same influence it's been privileged with in the past century," Sir Weston said immediately. He looked easy, untroubled by the notion, but I didn't want to take that for granted.

"I don't believe it would be possible for a queen to rule a kingdom single-handedly. The council is of great value to Kimmery," I began.

"In theory," Aric said softly from the window, before ducking his head in apology to me.

It was a bit of an act, actually, Aric playing my rude and outspoken Chosen. He *was* my rude and outspoken Chosen, but in this moment he had my permission to be so.

Douglas huffed and raised his glass to Aric. "No offense, Weston. You know how highly I think of you."

"And you know how poorly I think of many of my peers on the council," Sir Weston said with a shrug. "No offense taken. Your Highness, I do wish you would feel comfortable here in this company."

"I only wish not to be mistaken. I have no intention of doing away with the council. I am not greedy for control. I am simply *desperate* to do well by Kimmery," I said.

And this was my role for the evening, the heartfelt young woman only thinking of others. Sir Weston might've seen through it, he'd witnessed me sharp and demanding in front of the council, but it was a kind of shield against Lord Ashley or even Wendell's father's opinions. If my experience with the council had taught me one thing, it was that some men didn't appreciate a young woman having her own strong mind. I was learning from Wendell that a lot of diplomacy had to do with pretending to agree with a person while tricking them into agreeing with you.

I sometimes related to my mother's disinterest in ruling and understood how the responsibility of the crown had been shuffled into the council's hands.

"Some control will have to be seized," Weston said with a shrug. "Thomlinson and Roderick won't cede, you know. Not while they have other ears to bend to their own purposes."

Those ears being my mother's and Camellia's.

"Her Majesty has sincere love for her people. She has a great deal of confidence in Kimmery. Perhaps more in the council than I have though," I said carefully.

Lord Ashley snorted, taking the responsibility of rudeness out of Aric's hands for the moment.

"There is a curious phenomenon in the queen's line. Two princesses is a rare occurrence, and not once has there ever been two heirs remaining when it was time for succession," Sir Weston said.

"How often has it been avoided?" Wendell asked leaning forward. "We've been attempting our research in the Winter Palace, but the library there was obviously stripped before our arrival."

"Three times that I recall," Sir Weston said.

"Five, at least," Lord Ashley said, noisily dragging a chair in our direction. "The queen's line is a bloodthirsty lot."

I blinked, staring at my lap and imagining the pattern of blood on my fingers I'd worn after slitting Emory's throat.

"Gregory, watch your tongue. Excuse him, Your Highness," Douglas said, glaring at his friend.

"My family does have a remarkable history on the battlefield," I said calmly. "Although I was unaware of such a pattern between princesses."

"There's been no outright declaration or notation, Your Highness. Just a tendency toward sudden illness taking away one of the heirs," Sir Weston said, but he grimaced in acknowledgment of the obvious implication.

And my grandmother's sudden illness? I glanced at Aric, who was already looking back, and he nodded briefly. He knew exactly what needed to be learned when we arrived in the south.

"The council has remarked on my own sister's ability to rule, should my mother choose to pass succession over me," I said, turning back to the gentlemen. "I would not object to any choice my mother might make, but I do have my concerns about Camellia."

"To be frank, Your Highness, I have not seen any intent from the queen's line to ensure such equality and care of the people of Kimmery until I met you. If this promising interest of yours was missing from your sister, it wouldn't be a surprise to me," Sir Weston said.

"I believe Camellia would certainly be happy to let the council carry on as they have been," I said. I turned to look at Wendell, who dipped his head at me in agreement. "That's not my only concern, however. There are...rumors regarding my sister."

And here was the real goal of the evening.

"Have you heard of Paul Kent?" Daniel asked the men softly.

Douglas frowned and shook his head, Sir Weston remained watching me, and it was Lord Ashley who drew a sudden breath.

"Jeremy Kent's son? Ah, indeed, the one the young princess wrung out like an old rag. And not the only one from what I've heard," Lord Ashley said with a dark chuckle.

Owen's fingers squeezed around mine. Here it was. The one concrete crime we could possibly prove against Camellia.

"I had not heard there were others," I said softly, leaning forward to catch Lord Ashley's glazed gaze. "It is my hope something might be done for the men. Some kind of justice."

"Oh, there'll be no justice for Thomas Gensley, Your Highness. He killed himself as soon as he was strong enough to finish the act."

My blood chilled, but there was a strange kind of energy running through me too. Another name. Another man my sister had harmed, and this time so thoroughly... And now I needed to pull Lord Ashley's threads and see what else fell out.

❧

CRESSWELL TOUCHED my arm just outside of the room I was sharing with Aric and Cosmo, and I ushered them in ahead of me.

"Come walk outside with me?" Cresswell said.

It was the dead of night, the ugly conversation from the study wandering late into the evening before we'd all learned too much to be able to stomach another word. I was glad Cosmo had been entertaining the women instead, had missed the chilling claims Lord Ashley made against my sister. He was the only one of us wearing a smile as we'd said goodbye to the two older couples, and Sir Weston and I had exchanged a grave and dangerous glance.

I looked into the dark bedroom, and Aric nodded at me. "Go on, princess. Get some fresh air. You can sleep in the carriage tomorrow."

Cresswell's hand slid to mine, and together we tiptoed back down the stairs, his eyes seeing through the dark halls better than my own. He led us toward the back left of the house, through the kitchens, and out into a small courtyard with lines strung up to a post, waiting for tomorrow's laundry.

"Why outside?" I whispered.

"Being out of doors calms me and I..." He trailed off, looking back over his shoulder at me.

"And you calm me," I said, squeezing my fingers around his hand.

The moon was full, although shrouded behind thin clouds, creating an almost lamp-like glow above us, just enough light to see our way into the trees.

"You've been so low since you got that letter from your mother. Not that I'm surprised. Except I don't think it's just your grand-mother's illness upsetting you," Cresswell said, pulling me closer. I leaned gratefully into his warm side as we walked, smiling as his arm draped around my shoulders.

"I thought I went to the north to discover the truth about Kimmery, and I suppose myself, but now I wonder if I wasn't hiding there."

"If you hadn't been in the north, the legislation against shifters would've passed."

I nodded.

"And Aric might be dead," Cresswell said.

My heart panged at just the thought, and I slid my own arm around Cresswell's waist to clutch at his side.

"I would be in the army."

I stopped, and Cresswell stopped with me. The shadow of the

house was broken by the trees around us, and we were entirely alone but for the soft activity of the woods. I turned to face him, and his hands moved to my shoulders. This was the first time we were really alone together since he'd kissed me, and the distraction of passion was tempting in the moment. The Hunger wasn't really present, chased away by the disturbing evening, and I couldn't decide if that made me shy or more eager to take advantage of being alone with this man.

One of Cresswell's rough hands moved up to my throat, tipping my head back, and I was sure he would kiss me again.

"What would you say to the idea of purchasing a boat?" he asked.

My lips parted, and my mind went blank with confusion. "A boat?"

"Mm. Large enough for the others, I suppose. And we all got aboard and...left."

"Left Kimmery?"

Cresswell nodded, the tiniest curl in the corner of his lips, but his brow furrowed with a frown. "I worry for what comes next, Bryony. I can guard you physically, but I can't protect you from the sacrifices and decisions you'll have to make to become queen."

I released a weak and wobbling sigh, and Cresswell's arms circled me as I leaned into his chest, so solid he could take all my weight and weariness in the embrace. "I know," I said, turning my cheek against the dense wool of his uniform. "But I can't leave shifters to be enslaved and magic to be trampled and...and whatever Camellia might make of the Hunger or of Kimmery."

Cresswell grunted, unsurprised, and his head bowed, warm breath cascading over the top of my head. "You would've made a very daring pirate."

I barked a laugh against his chest and leaned back in his hold, turning my face up to his. "What an idea! I shall have to make a daydream of it when things get very bad."

Cresswell frowned, and I regretted reminding him of what was coming, so instead I rose to my toes, pressing my lips to his. My hands reached up between us to hold his jaw, ignoring the way he stiffened at the first touch of the kiss and waiting for his acceptance. It came with a low note in his throat, something between a growl and a groan, and his arms tightened around my waist.

I sighed as Cresswell returned the kiss, his tongue sweeping across the seam of my mouth and then his lips sliding apart to fit against mine.

Ah, the Hunger was on her way back now.

"Cresswell," I breathed in invitation as his mouth slid away to kiss a path to my jaw.

"Not a chance, Bryony."

"But—"

"It's freezing out. And none of those fools ever bed you properly."

I blinked at that, grinning and pulling away to catch his eye. "What on earth do you mean? I'm properly bedded plenty."

"How many of your Chosen took you to bed behind closed *doors* to make love to you the first time?" Cresswell asked, eyes narrowed.

I opened my mouth to correct him and then stopped. The pond, the library, the carriage... Oh! Aric at the—no, it was his desk first, wasn't it?

"Thao and Wen—"

"That was a curtain and you had a whole handful of men listening in. I remember. *Vividly*."

I blushed and let out a nervous giggle. "To be fair, those locations weren't really anyone's fault but my own."

"There's a lack of restraint."

"Ohhhh, you have entirely too much restraint, Guard Stark," I grumbled, but I snuggled into his chest again to hide my smile. "Fine, take me in to bed."

"Not tonight, Bryony," Cresswell said softly, pressing a kiss to the shell of my ear. I started to object, but he cut me off. "When we get to the capital, I will choose a few more guards who I think can be trusted along with Piper and Brummer. When I know you're safe, then I will be yours."

"You *are* mine," I corrected, glaring at him. "You should've been at dinner tonight. I hate that there's still some distinction that leaves you on the outside."

"I don't mind the outside, really. It gives me a better view,"

Cresswell said, loosening his hold on me, pushing us back on a loose path through the woods.

I huffed and followed his lead. "I find it very galling to know that I can't make a man as passionate for me as I am for him."

Cresswell's laugh was rough, his head ducking quickly to nip at my throat before pulling away again. "I promise you, Bryony, my passion will exceed yours. But not tonight," he said before I could press.

I was briefly glad that Cresswell was a shifter and couldn't be as influenced by my Hunger's magic because it was suddenly very tempting to test that iron restraint of his. I leaned my head against his chest and let him guide me through the woods, a slow loop around the property and back to the kitchen door until my steps dragged and my eyelids were heavy. When my nose and fingertips were cold from the night, Cresswell lifted me into his arms and carried me inside.

4.
BRYONY

"Y ou're glaring."

I shook myself, drawing up a smile as we neared the village of Lambden. There was a glitter on the horizon, Kimmery's shining capital, but we had a full day's ride before we reached the edge of the city, and I had the part of the princess delighted to return home to the south to play.

I glanced at Aric where he rode his chestnut stallion next to me. Crescent, my own ride, was trotting impatiently down the road, annoyed at having to behave for so long on the journey south.

"You're glaring again," Aric said, chuckling.

I huffed, and my smile was a grimace. "I can't help it. I keep thinking of all the towns we've just left."

"It isn't really these people's fault," Aric said, and he laughed again, raising a hand in surrender as I glared at him. "I know, princess. Can't believe I'm saying it either."

"I know it's not their fault, I'm just..." I sighed and closed my eyes, lifting my face to the sun. It still felt like fall here in the south, and as much as I missed winter on the mountain, the warmth was welcome for the ride.

"It reminds you of everything that's wrong," Aric said nodding. "If it's any consolation, all I've seen on our ride so far was how much good you've already done for the north. Lots of work yet to be done, of course."

At last, my smile was sincere, and I reached a hand across the gap for Aric to take in his. "Thank you."

Aric turned to Cresswell riding ahead of us. "Stark, what do you say to allowing the princess to walk about in the village?"

"I say no."

I laughed, but Aric's lips pursed in a stubborn frown. "She had her freedom at the festival."

"And let's all remember how that turned out."

"She's at her best when she lets them know her," Aric answered.

I bit my lip to fight my grin, watching Cresswell's shoulders rise and fall with a heavy sigh. When his head turned, eyes searching for mine, I sat up straighter. "Aric has the magic to protect me, and I have you," I said.

I didn't beg as I had for the festival. Walking through the town did sound nice, but it also sounded like another delay. I was reluctant to arrive back at the castle and all the trouble waiting for me there, but also knowing it was the inevitable destination just made me want to get the whole journey over with.

"Three shops," Cresswell said.

We hadn't announced our journey south or informed any of the villages we'd passed through of our coming, but the word seemed to travel and there was usually a small crowd watching us as we passed through.

"We could take lunch in one of the—"

"No! Three shops, that's it."

Aric smirked and winked at me.

The villagers were trickling out of their doors as we reached the edge of the main road, where houses grew closer and shops with bright windows crowded together. I smiled and waved as I would've done from a carriage with my mother when she was in the mood for an excursion. The gazes staring back at me were cheerful and curious, none of that slow judgment I'd received in the north. These people were already happy, satisfied with my role above them, tickled by my passing by their homes and businesses.

I slowed Crescent as we neared one business, a bookshop with bryony vines climbing over the brick, framing the foggy dusty windows with white flowers.

"Here please," I called to Cresswell, ignoring the delicate gasps of the crowd as I jumped down from my saddle, straightening my skirts as my Chosen trickled out of the carriage and off their horses to surround me.

"A bookshop, princess?" Aric asked.

"I've never been in one," I said, shrugging.

Aric frowned briefly and then jumped ahead to push the door open for me, smiling as my eyes brightened at the scent of ink, parchment, leather, and glue spilling out to the street. I could stall returning to the capital for another hour.

One hour became two as I lost time browsing the spines of new and familiar books, forgetting about the faces still peering through the glass. Owen talked Cress into sending one of the other guards to a bakery for hand pies, and by the time we left the village, I was too deep in a new story to remember any anger or anxiety.

❦

THE DIN of cheering faded as the trellis gates to the castle were pushed shut, my own eyes closing against the vision in front of me. The pale peach brick glowed brightly, hundreds of windows glittering with candlelight, carefully manicured flowering vines twining up the corners of the castle.

"It will be all right, Mistress," Owen murmured, drawing me back from the window to lean against his chest.

"Strange to think of the last time we were here," Cosmo said, still watching our approach to the castle. "Daniel, were you at the choosing?"

"I arrived late, somewhat intentionally," Daniel added sheepishly, shrugging at me. "I was in the line on the stairs when we were finally dismissed."

Thao and Wendell were riding, so it was only the four of us in the slow-moving carriage. I rested, trying to find peace in their aimless conversation, wishing it could drown out the torrent of thoughts in my head.

Camellia had wanted Sam to kill me. She had tried to force herself on Owen. My grandmother was dying, seemingly all of a sudden. My mother had confidence in me, but also in the Council, and probably Camellia, and possibly anyone who asked it of her.

"I don't even know where we'll be sleeping tonight," I said

sitting up, blinking at Cosmo's frown. "A princess with Chosen usually receives a new suite."

"We'll be sleeping together, just as you like it," Owen said.

"That exactly, even if we're in a terrible pile on top of one another," Cosmo said, his expression softening.

I was more afraid that my men would be given their own rooms surrounding mine and they might find themselves gradually drifting away with the afforded space. Wouldn't it be more pleasant for them to be able to sleep without a half dozen other men surrounding them?

You don't mind it, why should they? I thought, and I smiled just as the carriage slowed to a stop.

An unfamiliar footman opened the carriage door, but Cresswell appeared behind him a moment later, watching with sharp focus as I was handed down. There were a great number of castle officials I knew vaguely all waiting around our party of travelers, and I wondered if I imagined the way they counted the men around me, their gazes assessing as I moved to Cresswell and took his arm. It wasn't the usual place for a princess and her guard to stand together, but Cresswell was more than that and I wanted it known from the start.

"Welcome home, Your Highness." It was Lady Amelia Goddard, my mother's lady-in-waiting, and she was falling into a deep curtsy, her dark head bowing and the others in front of us quick to follow suit.

Was this still home? It didn't feel like it.

"Your mother is waiting to receive you in the great hall," Amelia said, rising. She was older than my mother and very quiet, more severe than I would've expected my mother to favor in her company, but she followed like a shadow. Unlike some of the women in the castle, I had never once caught her staring longingly at any Chosen, or indeed any man. "And if I might introduce Miss Ophelia Goddard, my niece. You should've taken your own ladies with you to the north, but there was such a great rush. It is your mother's greatest hope that Ophelia will be a dear companion to you, just as I always aim to be to her."

Miss Ophelia Goddard stepped forward. She was about my age or younger, with glossy black hair and a great deal more spirit to her step than her aunt's. She curtsied again, but was unable to tear her eyes away from the men surrounding me.

No. She would not be dear to me.

I'd learned enough of my Hunger in all of our recent troubles to know that the animal jealousy rising up in me was as irrational as it was irrepressible. One day of Ophelia appearing and examining my men, and I would claw the poor girl's eyes out. We might've been friends once, but I didn't have that kind of control at the moment, at least not with my tension so high.

"I find myself in little need of a lady-in-waiting. Perhaps Ophelia might be better suited to my sister's court," I said, forcing a gentle smile. It was only stalling, I would have to take ladies-in-waiting eventually, it was expected. But absolutely not tonight, and absolutely not this girl.

Amelia and Ophelia both paled at the suggestion. "Perhaps, Your Highness," Amelia said, and with one look at her aunt, Ophelia retreated back into the crowd of castle staff.

"I'd hate to keep my mother waiting, and we have been traveling for a long while," I said, too much energy running through my sore body. Hunger gnawed at me, both physical and magical. I hadn't had much time with my Chosen while we traveled, and I'd been too mentally occupied to think of it. Now, irritated by Ophelia's staring at Owen, I was fighting the urge to drag my men to a bed and claim them all over again. It was absurd and inconvenient, and I was still so *tired*.

"Of course, Your Highness," Amelia said, curtsying again and making me wince with all her bobbing.

As soon as the staff parted to make a path, I marched forward, glancing back in a reflex to make sure all my Chosen were with me. Owen's eyes were on me, and he smiled brightly as I looked at him, soothing some of the bite of jealousy. We passed Ophelia, and her eyes remained down this time, color high in her cheeks. I felt a little bad for dismissing her so suddenly, but it was as much for her sake as mine. I didn't need to waste my time fighting off the Hunger's territorial impulses, and she didn't need me snapping at her unexpectedly for admiring men who I knew were perfectly worth admiring. It was just that I preferred to be the only one to do so.

I knew my own way to the great hall, but Amelia insisted on hurrying to keep up with us.

"I believe the dowager queen arranged your new suites above your old rooms. There was some renovation. She said you liked your view," Amelia said, her voice thin from keeping up with my rushing pace.

My steps stalled briefly at that. I hadn't even known my grandmother had noticed, although I supposed she found me reading in the windowsill of my rooms often enough.

"Is it true you and your Chosen only had two rooms in the Winter Palace?"

"We had an entire palace. But we only really needed the one bedroom for ourselves," I found myself saying.

Amelia's eyes widened, an unusual openness on her face as she stared back at me. "That's unusual. Your mother has always preferred to sleep alone."

And Camellia slept with men littered about the floor and furniture around her.

"Well, your bed is spacious enough, and you may rearrange as you please, of course," Amelia continued.

"Oh good, more rooms for art studios and mage's studies," Thao said at my left, squeezing my hip and drawing a smile out.

"And a closet for all your sweaters," Cosmo tossed back.

"An indoor stable for Owen too, of course," I murmured, just to make the others laugh.

Amelia stared at us all as if we were a puzzle. We reached the doors of the great hall, two guards in all their bright armor stationed outside. Their eyes flickered over Cresswell and his uniform, dusty from traveling, but quickly drifted away again, used to not taking notice of curiosities in the castle that didn't concern them. One knocked, and a female voice echoed from inside.

"Her Royal Highness, Princess Bryony, and her Chosen."

The doors opened, and my breath caught. I had left the Winter Palace more beautiful than I'd found it, but it was in a soft and organic kind of way. There was nothing like the prismatic shine and glitter of the great hall by candlelight, the floors polished until they were almost mirrors, the actual mirrors bouncing light in every direction. It was a small royal secret that all of the glass lining the wall was ever so slightly tilted toward the thrones, just enough so that much of the flickering candlelight turned softly in my mother's direction.

My mother, and Camellia.

I should have but hadn't expected to find my sister waiting for my arrival too. And if I had imagined it, it would've been some kind of debaucherous scene. An orgy on the dais perhaps.

My mother sat serenely on her throne, or rather, she sat in the lap of a man on her throne, her cheek against his temple, her eyes heavy lidded with either satisfaction or slumber. She was smiling before I even entered, and the expression didn't grow or falter as I stepped forward with my Chosen.

"Oh, Bryony. I'm so glad it's you," Mother said.

It didn't really sound as though she'd been expecting me, let alone that she'd requested me to greet her here, which meant...

My eyes turned to Camellia next. Her collection of men had grown, her harem now twice the size of my mother's and at least three times the size of mine. I recognized a few men from the Winter Palace, but even more so, I realized that some of the familiar faces were now gone. Igor was missing, and another whose name I didn't know. She smiled at me, but it was a sour expression on her face, and her fingernails were digging into the shoulder of the man at her feet as if she was bracing against some physical pain. She was fighting the Hunger, I realized. The cravings held her that fiercely.

She thinks she's more powerful because she has more men, more Hunger, I realized. I was beginning to wonder if it wasn't the opposite.

"How is Her Majesty this evening?" I asked after my Chosen and I had delivered deep bows to my mother and sister. "Any changes in her health?"

"It's just terrible, Bryony, it really is," Mother said, eyes growing glassy and face turning into her Chosen's cheek. "The doctors say there's no hope of recovery. It's just buying time with her now. I'm so glad you returned. It was so wrong of you to stay so long away from us."

My jaw tightened, my head dipping to my mother. Out of the

corner of my eye, Aric shifted uncomfortably, gloved hands clenching at his side.

"I'd like to see her," I said.

"Oh, not tonight, darling," Mother said, brightening. "She's sleeping, surely, and you and your Chosen should see your suite. It really is quite pretty. I gave some advice on the finishing touches myself."

I wondered if that meant I'd be barred from seeing my grand-mother, or only if my mother didn't understand the same urgency I felt, but I nodded again, taking a breath before trying to find the right way to leave the room.

"Sister, it will be such fun here again, now that you are back," Camellia said, forcing a grin as she rose from her throne and stepped down from the dais.

I swallowed and shrugged, trying to smile while that darker version of the Hunger rose up in me, the one that called for blood, for my sister's as she approached with slow steps. The air around me buzzed, and I didn't know if it was my magic alone, or if Aric was fashioning some kind of barrier.

"Kiss my cheek," Camellia said softly, baring her throat as she turned her head to offer her cheek. "I have missed you."

It was a taunt, this false surrender of hers, a farce of affection to appease or disarm my mother. Camellia certainly wasn't expecting *me* to be fooled. I leaned in and rested my cheek to hers, holding my breath against the overwhelming scent of jasmine covering something more sour and animal.

"At one point while you were gone, I thought I might never see you again," Camellia said softly.

Because you meant to have me killed, I thought.

"I will never falter in my duty to Kimmery," I answered, holding my sister's gaze as she stepped back. Her lips were chapped, and her eyes were bloodshot. She'd given herself over to a force of magic, and I wondered if she even realized how little control she really had.

"It is so good to have you home again, Bryony," my mother said, but her lips were against her Chosen before I could answer.

5.
BRYONY

"Well, that bed will certainly fit us all," Wendell said, head tipped as he stared at the expansive platform curtained with gauze that would serve as my bed.

Really, it was far too large. It could've accommodated two Owens sleeping foot to head with its depth alone, let alone the amount of room it would afford my Chosen to spread out. A man at one end might as well be sleeping in another room as one on the other end.

"You have spent too much time with Aric if you look that troubled by luxury," Thao said, brushing a lock of hair over my cheek.

We'd afforded the palace staff enough time to settle our trunks into the rooms, and my Chosen were exploring the suite as I was meant to be relaxing. I was failing at my task. The room was certainly designed for comfort, even without the enormous bed. There was a circular, pillowed bench where we might all gather together, a rich collection of couches and low tables. Most beautiful of all, facing the bed, was one wall almost entirely overtaken by dark bookshelves with glass doors, my favorite romances thoughtfully arranged inside, alongside old framed landscapes I'd painted and decorative trinkets. The colors of the room were rich and heavy, with the occasional hint of floral. Someone had obviously taken a great deal of care with the space, but there was a tidy organization to it that didn't sit right.

It wasn't the lush chaos my magic had created at the Winter Palace, organic and whimsical and strange.

"I just...the bed at the Winter Palace was just the right fit to have you all close," I said, frowning at our new bed. "It was cozy."

"Just because we have a larger bed doesn't mean we won't all be crowded around you," Wendell said, kissing the top of my head. "Come, let's get comfortable."

I leaned into him as he helped me out of the heavy layers I'd been wearing for traveling. The room was more than warm enough, even with all the doors hanging open to the rest of the suite. Owen appeared from one, his expression bright and dazzled.

"Never seen a place so big. How much of the palace have they given us?"

"More than we need," Daniel answered, entering from a door on the opposite side of my new bedroom. "There are more bedrooms than there are Chosen."

"Bryony will be expected to add to us over time," Wendell said softly, and he pressed a kiss to the corner of my frown.

"For now, we will make use of the rooms as we see fit," I said quickly, strangely troubled by the idea of adding more men to my Chosen. I certainly wasn't about to go through another choosing ceremony. I'd gotten lucky the one time, but it was obviously a system not built for someone like me. "I wonder if anyone will stop me from seeing my grandmother tonight."

"As much as I understand your impatience, it *is* late for a sickbed visit," Wendell said. "It will be better to let her rest and speak to her tomorrow."

"I haven't had a single note from her since we heard from my mother," I said softly.

My men all wore matching sympathetic expressions, and I felt a little guilty at the sight. I was concerned for my grandmother's health, but I was more concerned about the implications. Who was running Kimmery now without my grandmother's influence? Certainly not my mother.

The others returned at the same moment, Aric and Cress together from one direction, and Cosmo from another.

"I've already heard from Head Guard Amos," Cress said with a wry smile. "I've been demoted to your personal guard. I've made the request to keep Piper and Brummer, but appointments are up to Amos."

"How does he seem?" I asked.

Cresswell shrugged. "Fair, I think."

"If he were aligned with your sister, he likely would've sent Cresswell packing back to the north," Aric said.

Cresswell's gaze held mine, our thoughts probably in the same place. If anyone tried to remove Cresswell from my service, he would only immediately join my Chosen.

"I'm going to join the others now, we should go through the suite and the palace," Cresswell said.

"Oh, Cress. Please stay."

His boots echoed on the polished wood floor as he crossed the open room to me, bending and resting his lips against the top of my head, his breath ruffling my hair and warming me. "Not tonight, Bryony. The more confident I feel in knowing how to keep you safe, the sooner we'll both have what we want."

I bit my lip as he left. He was testing my patience, but it gave me a pleasant, bubbling feeling, knowing where it would all lead.

"Would you like to see what I've discovered? I think it may cheer you up a little," Cosmo said, bouncing on the balls of his feet in a shadowy doorway.

"Is it anything like what we discovered our first morning at the Winter Palace?" I asked, thinking of the spyglass that Wendell and Thao had found in the room next to mine.

"It is not," Cosmo said, laughing. "Cresswell will have to keep his eyes out for that sort of thing. But this, I think you'll appreciate."

Wendell tossed my jacket on the bench, and Owen joined my side, an arm thrown over my shoulder as we all moved to follow Cosmo. The hall he traveled down was dark, only the occasional candle illuminating the narrow space. There were doors open farther down on the right into the various rooms and bedrooms that had been allocated for my Chosen, but Cosmo stopped at the first door, gesturing an arm in for me to lead the way.

I paused at the sound of rushing water and then stepped into the dark room. There was a candelabra on a low side table and the view of the sky and sea at night through the large window ahead of me, but what immediately drew my eyes was the long, low pool on my left. It was half as big as my bed, which meant it was still plenty large enough for me and all my Chosen. At the back, near the tall tiled wall, was a cascade of water which seemed to come from nowhere at all and filled the pool.

"*This* is what southern magicians spend their magic on?" Aric scoffed, stomping forward to glare up at the water.

"Aric, I won't let you ruin this for me," Thao said, already tugging his layers of sweaters off, eyeing the steam rising from the water with a greedy gaze.

My first laugh in hours bubbled up as Wendell and Cosmo hurried to join Thao, while Aric stood puzzling at the water.

"It seems to be almost on a cycle. I suppose they just refresh the magic as it wears down," Aric muttered to himself.

Daniel's hands came to the laces at the back of my dress, pulling them free for me as I grinned and watched Cosmo intentionally kick water to hit Aric's pant leg.

"Are there any other charms?" I asked Aric.

He shook his head and then wobbled a hand in the air. "Well, there were. But to be honest, royal spying charms aren't nearly as interesting as the ones spies come up with. I got rid of all of those as I passed through. It's safe, princess." His lips twitched as he turned and watched Daniel and Owen peel me out of my dress. "I suppose I've seen *less* useful uses of magic."

I arched an eyebrow, stepping out of my skirt, fully nude, with a half dozen pairs of eyes on me. "You won't refuse to use it out of protest?"

"My morals were never that high, let's be honest," Aric said, flashing me a wolfish grin and then making quick work of his clothes.

Cosmo stood up from the pool, which sank down several feet into the floor, to take my hand and help me into the water. It rose high up my waist, the floor sloping down and then back up again. Wendell was standing under the rushing water, his hips just high enough for me to get a teasing glimpse of dark blond curls and an inch of his length. Cosmo floated with me in his direction, and I gasped as something soft and dense brushed against my foot, before a bright orange tiger surfaced in the water, sharp teeth grinning at us. Thao shook himself, and I giggled as the droplets sprayed against me.

He stood, the tiger vanishing and replaced with my golden and dark prince. "We have waterfalls like this in Mennary. There is one in the palace gardens that we played in as children," Thao said, moving to join Wendell under the stream, it splashing beautifully against them, their profiles outlined by the water. "And Wen and I played in it by moonlight."

Thao reached a hand out to me, and Cosmo pushed me to float in his direction until I reached Thao. The waterfall misted the air as I grew closer, and I moved shyly forward.

"This is just what you need tonight, Bryony," Wendell said, turning so that I had to slide between them.

I gasped as the water struck my arm, heavy and almost reminiscent of the strike of a fencing blade. But the pressure elongated, becoming soothing, pounding at my tight muscles. I moaned as I stepped fully under the water, turning to angle it onto my shoulders and sighing. It was almost as good as when Owen would work his fingers into my muscles after I finished sparring with Thao.

Gentle hands cupped the back of my thighs, and I opened my eyes to find Daniel sinking down in the water before me. "I used to spend days swimming. Let's see if I can still hold my breath as well," Daniel said.

He slid under the water, and Thao and Wendell braced me between them with my arms over their shoulders, their mouths landing on my throat as Daniel found his place between my thighs.

"It was a long journey south, princess," Aric said, stepping into the water, holding my eyes as he skimmed his hand through the water, bubbles popping up on its surface, my favorite faint scent of violets rising on the steam. "Take tonight for yourself."

I might've protested, but Daniel's lips already held me in thrall, gentle and slippery beneath the water. The spiraling tension of the journey unwound in the bath with my Chosen. There would be many days of fighting and positioning and planning ahead, but here, with them, I could surrender myself. They were my Chosen and I had claimed them and made them almost like property to myself and my Hunger, but I was in their control during moments like these, relieved to be used and shared and cradled back into bed when they'd had their fill and I'd had mine several times over.

⚘

ASIDE FROM MY NEW SUITE, the castle was as I remembered it, vast and beautiful, often quiet. There were fewer courtiers in winter, with even less now that my grandmother was on her sickbed, and the halls were remarkably empty as I passed through with Cresswell at my side, the rest of my Chosen still arranging the extra rooms in our suite to their liking. We'd delivered strict orders to the guards that no one, including my sister, was permitted entry to the suite while I was gone, and I tried not to think of what might happen if the guards couldn't be trusted.

"Where do you and the others sleep?" I asked Cresswell.

We were on our way to my grandmother's tower, my hand tucked into the crook of Cresswell's arm. I didn't miss the way guards in the hall took brief glances at us. Guards in the castle generally remained almost like statues, shuffled into the corners of rooms where they were less likely to catch the queen's eye, or the Hunger's attention. I could vaguely recall my mother pulling one of the guards away from his station at a ball once, the pair of them disappearing together, but it wasn't a common occurrence, and most of the guards we passed weren't much to look at.

"I took a room in your suite," Cresswell said. "The others have beds in the guards' wing. They got word this morning that they're to continue to report to me."

"That's good news, isn't it?"

Cresswell nodded, thoughtful as ever. "Seems to be. I plan on getting to know Head Guard Amos better if I can, but for now, he seems to be interested in doing his duty to keeping the queen's line safe, no special alignments with either you or your sister to consider."

"You could sleep in the main bedroom, you know," I said, bumping my hip against Cresswell's.

"I don't like to sleep while you and the others are. It leaves you too vulnerable."

"You have to sleep sometimes, don't you?" I asked, trying not to laugh. I was worried he really might try and avoid it altogether.

"I sleep while you are...occupied with your Chosen, and the others are on duty," Cresswell said, lips twitching.

I couldn't restrain the laughter now. "You sleep while we're fucking?"

"It's easier than standing outside the door and listening," Cresswell growled, ducking his head but stopping himself before he snatched a kiss from my lips.

We turned a corner and reached the doors of my grandmother's suite, two guards stationed outside the doors.

"Princess Bryony to see the Dowager Queen Violet," Cresswell called as we approached.

One guard knocked lightly on the door, turning to speak through in answer to some murmured question.

"The dowager queen will see the princess and only the princess," the other guard answered.

"No—"

"Cress, it's all right," I said, squeezing Cresswell's arm gently. He frowned down at me, and I nudged my hip against his again, letting him feel where my blade rested, still charmed to warn me of danger.

"I'll be right out here," Cress said.

I nodded and stepped forward as the doors opened. An old man stood inside, eyes a little milky but smile soft.

"Come in, Your Highness," he said, with a brief and shallow bow. "I'm Hector, one of your—"

"Grandmother's Chosen," I finished for him, nodding and examining the man. He was tall and broad-shouldered, although somewhat stooped with age, one hand wrapped around the top of a cane. "I recognize you, I think."

Grandmother had retired a great deal of her Chosen not long before Camellia and I were of age to take our own, but I knew a few remained. The doors shut behind me, and Hector sighed a little, gesturing across the sitting room to another door.

"I'm sure Violet might prefer to receive you in here, but we're trying to keep her resting as much as possible. It's good that you're here, she's been very impatient to see you."

He moved swiftly, a slight wobble in his walk, and I wanted to pepper him with questions. Why was he one of the Chosen who remained with my grandmother? How ill was she? What were her symptoms? Why hadn't I heard from her personally instead of just my mother and her ladies-in-waiting?

I paused in step as the door to the bedroom opened, bracing myself against the heavily perfumed and smoky air, frowning at the stark darkness. The curtains were all closed, and there was only a single candlestick lit near the door, leaving the large canopied bed on the other side of the room in murky shadow.

"Heck, what's all the coming and going about?"

My heartbeat stammered at the first notes of her voice, but I frowned at the weak tremor running through the words.

"You have a visitor," Hector answered brightly.

"Heck!"

I stifled my laugh at her bark of outrage and moved forward into the dark.

"Peony, that had better be you and not your ghastly daughter again."

"Ghastly daughter, I'm afraid," I answered, strangely gleeful.

My grandmother gasped, and then let out a series of shocking, gasping, shredded coughs. I rushed forward to the bed at the sound, afraid my teasing might've just killed the dowager queen, but she recovered with a few squeaking wheezes of breath.

"I'm sorry, I—"

"About time you showed up. Vincent, light another candle for goodness sake, it's like a tomb in here. What on earth took you so long? Were you trying to *miss* the main event? If so, I am pleased to disappoint you."

Vincent, another of my grandmother's Chosen, a very hand-some and notably younger man than Hector or my grandmother, appeared by the flick of a match, lighting a candle by the bed. The glow brightened, and even through my damp eyes, I caught the wince of my grandmother at the flame, until it was shaded by an opaque lamp lense.

"Are you blubbering? What for?" Grandmother snapped at me.

I was not blubbering, I was just a little teary-eyed. "I am prac-ticing my mourning," I said instead, and Hector chuckled behind me as my grandmother scoffed.

She'd grown so frail so quickly, or so it seemed in the wavering shadows, with her bundled up in the tall bed, surrounded by pillows and silk quilts, a little bonnet covering her hair.

"We visited with Wendell's family on our way south," I explained. "And then last night when we arrived, they told me I shouldn't see you. Mother wanted me to wait for us to come together—"

"That's the council in her ear. They think you've influenced me or I've influenced you, whichever tips Peony in the direction they want her fretting." Grandmother's hand twitched in my direction, and I reached out to her. I remembered her grip around my wrist as she snatched novels out of my grasp to drag me off for a lecture, and it was hard to believe these trembling fingers could ever have been responsible for such force. "I'm sorry I didn't see the cage our line has built for itself before now, but your mother seems far too content and—"

Grandmother's words halted, her body seizing and trembling. Hector pushed past me, and together he and Vincent pulled my grandmother upright as she began to release wracking coughs, her breaths stolen on strangled gasps. I stood and stepped back, my hands clutching at the waist of my gown as I held my own breath and waited for my grandmother to recover.

Gradually, the fit released her, Grandmother growling weakly as her Chosen moved her slowly back into the pillows. Vincent brought a glass of water to her lips, and my grandmother glared at him as he smiled back patiently. There was something else too, she was annoyed with him, but mostly with her own body, and there was a softness flowing between the two of them, between Hector as well. These were the Chosen who loved my grandmother, really loved her as my Chosen loved me.

"Grandmother, what happened?" I murmured.

"Took ill after a dinner party," Grandmother muttered with a scowl.

I pursed my lips. "Poison?"

"Perhaps."

"Perhaps?! Isn't that... Shouldn't you *know*?"

Grandmother sighed and sank into her pillows, eyes closing for a moment, and I wondered if she wasn't planning on answering me. "I've been poisoned before. Long time ago. It wasn't so successful then. To be quite frank, Bryony, I *am* old—"

"But—"

"And when I returned from the north, I...I dismissed some of my Chosen. Most of them." Hector's hands slid over the sheets and clasped around my grandmother's. "I didn't have much Hunger left in me anyway, and not all of them made very good company," my grandmother said primly.

"And without the Hunger..." I trailed off, freezing at the implication. "What exactly is wrong though? Why aren't the doctors helping?"

"Her lungs are taking on water. They don't know why, only that it's coming on quickly and nothing they or the mages can think of to do seems to be working," Hector said.

"They think my time is up," Grandmother growled, but her voice squeaked with effort. "And perhaps it is."

"Vi," Vincent chided softly.

"You could have my magic! I have plenty," I said, reaching out.

My grandmother only twitched away from me. "The magic isn't working, Bryony. What Hunger I have left is doing what it can for me, but it will run out."

She ignored her Chosen, her eyes fixing to mine, and I sat down at her side again, the weight of truth landing heavily in my bones. This was more than just a plot against me. This was age and ill health and the nature of our magic.

"And the poison?" I asked. She couldn't be just...dying, surely?

"We couldn't prove it, but Head Guard Amos launched an investigation that turned up next to nothing. A footman who conveniently vanished from the castle in the night, no doubt paid off and sent packing on a ship out of the country," Vincent said softly.

I remembered my conversation with my grandmother before she left the north when I said I was uncomfortable with the mandatory nature of the Chosen. If my grandmother was failing now because she didn't have those men here... "Grandmother, you didn't dismiss your Chosen because of—"

"I dismissed them because I wanted to," my grandmother snapped. "Bryony, listen to me. This is important. It is easy enough to wrest control from your mother. Too easy. She is soft-hearted, I think. I should've pushed her more, but I...thought I had the kingdom in hand. She is inclined to you as her successor, but she will only agree with you on changes to Kimmery as long as you are the voice in her ear."

I nodded, I had guessed as much already. "She has Camellia and the council there now, but I'll find my way," I said.

Grandmother frowned, and her hand covered mine gently. "The council has to be changed."

"Of course," I began.

"No, listen. All your convincing will go to waste when they talk her out of your decision in the next moment. The council has to be changed, and so does Kimmery's ruler." My breath caught, and I started to shake my head. "You are a little young, I know, and Camellia will not make it easy for you, nor the council. But your mother doesn't have the heart to fix the kingdom, let alone to see the problems. She will pass on the crown as I did if she can be convinced it will give her fewer burdens, and she won't stand in your way as I did with her."

I searched for words, but none made their way to my tongue. This conversation felt so final. My grandmother was resigned to her fate and with hers, mine. To take the crown, now, not just wait for the time to come. I knew my grandmother was right, I'd known as much almost since the beginning of this journey, but it didn't make the obstacles I faced feel smaller. If anything, they grew monstrous in my mind. The council. Camellia. Taking the throne.

Queen. I had to become queen. Not eventually, but *soon*.

"Your Chosen, do you trust them?" Grandmother asked.

"With my life," I said without even having to think about the words.

"With Kimmery?"

I paused then. I trusted Aric, Wendell, even Thao with Kimmery. They understood the weight of a kingdom on my shoulders. Daniel had come to me as a spy for the council, but he'd made a horrible one, and I knew where his loyalty lay now. Cresswell's duty to Kimmery was mixed up in his love for me now, but the two weren't unrelated. Owen's devotion was so deep, he would never go against my wishes, but Cosmo...

Strangely, of all my Chosen, Cosmo was the one most likely to defy me if he thought it was done in defense of me, or at least my heart. But no, that would never send him to the council's side or to Camellia's.

"Yes," I said, holding my grandmother's eyes.

"Good. Perhaps your strangeness served you better in this," Grandmother said, lips twitching.

I laughed, but there was a note of panic in the sound.

6.
ARIC

Roasted ducks glazed in orange and ginger. Meatballs smothered in a rich cream sauce. A mountain of roasted vegetables, spiced and salted. Pork chops and golden potatoes. Egg tarts topped in delicate greens.

Enough wine to drown a village. Enough food to feed one too.

The longer I stared at the feast, the less appetite I had for the food and drink. I'd thought our meals in the north were rich and sumptuous, but they'd always been well considered in portion and Bryony had made sure that the staff ate as well as we did.

This was...waste and decadence all at once.

She warned you, I thought. Bryony had warned me when I'd given up my life as bar owner and King of Thieves that my position as Chosen might leave me trapped in the fineries I resented, but I'd failed to imagine the real scope of a royal dinner.

"Ohheeeee!"

My eyes automatically flicked toward the sound and then away again just as quickly. If the feast wasn't bad enough, the way it was disregarded by more than half the table was equally offensive. Camellia was on the floor with three of her Chosen, and Bryony's mother, the *queen*, was seated at the head of the table, her head back and mouth parted, and two of her Chosen presumably keeping her occupied under her skirts. Magic buzzed in the air, but it was eaten up by the lovers just as quickly, creating an irritating kind of friction against my skin.

I glanced across the table to where Bryony was sitting, curious to see her reaction. It was as if she was in an entirely different room. Or no, not quite. She was studiously eating a tart, her eyes down, but she was wearing a fallen expression, similar to the one she'd returned to us with after visiting her grandmother. It made me itch to go to her, to pull her into my lap and scratch my rough chin against her neck to make her giggle. Except that display would be a little too similar to her family's antics.

"I know what you're thinking, but just eat so she has one less worry on her mind," Cosmo whispered in my ear from my left. Owen sat on his other side, and to my right was one of Camellia's Chosen, guzzling wine and ignoring the towers of food in front of him.

Thao and Wendell sat on either side of Bryony, with Daniel near another of Camellia's Chosen, who was openly sleeping.

"More!" Camellia cried out, voice ragged.

Heat tugged at me, and I stiffened in my chair, throwing up a guard of magic almost unconsciously, shocked by the ease of the act. The man at my right groaned, whimpered almost, and slid out of his seat, crawling reluctantly in the young princess's direction.

Bryony's movements froze, her body trembling with tension, eyes finally lifting from her plate to glare in her sister's direction, green fire in her gaze. I leaned forward, putting myself in the way, and found it easier to smile than I expected, rewarded with the slow sigh that lowered Bryony's shoulders.

I was angry, I hated sitting at this table, stuck with the role of forced audience to the younger princess's performance, but so did Bryony. Her anger was palpable, and even that prickling bite of her Hunger snapping at me was more welcome than the dizzy torrent from her sister or mother.

"It's not meat on a stick, is it?" I asked, making Thao flinch by lifting what I supposed was a quail from a pile, jiggling it by its leg.

Bryony blinked and then snorted, shaking her head. "Unfortunately not." She glanced briefly up the table before turning her face away, color on her cheeks. "Royal dinners aren't... They're not so common," she said softly. "I usually just ate in my room."

"With your ladies?" Thao asked.

Bryony shook her head. "I didn't have ladies. With a book," she said, smiling to herself.

Thao opened his mouth and then shut it again, looking to me. Alone? Is that what she meant? That she usually ate her dinners alone in her room with a book?

"When we were young, sometimes Camellia and I ate with a nursemaid or one of our tutors," she added, taking another bite of her tart, not noticing the way we all stared at her.

The suite had a private dining room and I'd sneered at the room, thinking it unnecessary at the time I'd found it, but now I looked forward to dinners there. It would be like we were at the Winter Palace again, but more intimate. With this hint of how Bryony had grown up, I wanted to fill her dinners with conversation and company.

There was a moan from the head of the table, but already I'd learned not to look. Chairs squeaked, and a feminine laugh echoed as footsteps rushed away. On the floor, Camellia's cries grew louder.

Bryony's expression shuttered again. "There is music after dinner, but no one will notice if we're here or not."

It was tempting to try and find a way to make her smile again, maybe a little dancing. But it was more tempting to get away from the scene around us, and I suspected it would do Bryony more good.

❦

THE CASTLE WAS ORDERLY, easy to map in my mind, rooms defined by the rare treasures decorating every surface. A little light thieving in the castle might go unnoticed, and it could do a wealth of good in the north.

Bryony would *probably* forgive me.

But my role of the moment wasn't rogue, but mage. I was hunting through the castle for the royal mages, trekking up and down floors of courtly rooms, libraries, meeting halls, even down into the relatively empty dungeons. It wasn't until I accidentally tripped my way into the guard's quarters that I was able to get directions.

The mages' study was in the heart of the residential wing. After a moment of confusion, it began to make sense. Camellia stuffed her Chosen up with her Hunger, creating a constant loop of attraction, but Queen Peony seemed to let hers float about as Bryony had before learning control. By putting their studies beneath the queen's quarters, the mages provided themselves with a constant supply of power.

It was clinging to the ceiling, pale and soft, not quite as potent as Bryony's magic. A little airy like the mother. Did the nature of magic relate to the personality of the woman who created it? The thought made me smile. Bryony was a little like her fencing sword —light and elegant, flexible, unexpectedly powerful and sharp when challenged—but she was more precise than her magic, which was wild and somewhat sensual.

No, she's that too, I reminded myself, conjuring a picture of her twisting in the sheets of her bedding, chasing pleasure even as she tried to squirm away from it.

There wasn't much decoration here in the hall. Already in our suite, Bryony's magic had begun to work its way into minor details of the room, unraveling the orderly elegance and fashioning it into whimsy. Either the mages were gathering every spare scrap of the queen's power, or hers didn't have the same clever creativity as Bryony's.

I raised my hand to knock on the broad double doors and then hesitated. Did I want to ask permission to enter and risk being denied?

My lips twitched, and my hand dropped to the door handle, trying to twist, only to find it locked. Easily dealt with. I traced a quick sigil over the lock, magic flying readily from my fingertip, and listened to the tumblers turn and thunk. The handle twisted easily under my grip, and I leaned in to shoulder the door open.

The air inside the room was stiff, lamps turned up high and windows shrouded in heavy dark curtains. It was immediately clear where the queen's magic was going. At the center of the room was a massive crystal prism, throbbing with light, shimmering without cause. The most outrageously enormous and well-charged conduit I'd ever seen in my life, my dreams even.

Doors remained open on either end of the room, but there was no one here watching this prism, and I hesitated in place, almost afraid to step forward. Bryony's magic that she'd shared with me tugged me in the direction of the prism. It called magic, like to like, and I closed my fist at my sides, holding on tightly to what I possessed.

There was no furniture in the room aside from tables in the corner, and none of the trinkets other mages might use to collect power—gold coins and shells, fine gemstones cut into rings. Of course there wasn't, anything else would've interfered with the vacuum of the prism.

I stepped softly closer, moving in a slow circle around the object. It was resting in a gold stand, branches extended around the facets of the prism, pinching it between the ends like an egg held in a bird's claw. It was about a foot off the ground and as tall as my waist. Every step I made, the light changed and shifted inside, as if my eyes were playing tricks on me. Or the prism was.

This was what powered waterfalls in our bathing pool, what made the palace floors shine and the chandeliers glitter and the fires roar. This was also what held magic captive, preventing it from being so easily accessed outside of the castle.

"Who are you?"

I spun, stepping away from the prism and facing the older man leaning forward on his cane, glaring at me over the glasses perched at the end of his nose. He looked more like a solicitor than a mage, dressed in a careful black suit coat and brightly polished shoes. From the other doorway, papers rustled and footsteps clapped closer.

"Aric Martin, Chosen," I said, the title a little odd on my tongue.

"You can't come in here," the second man said, and I was surprised to find him so much younger, closer to Bryony or Owen's age. He was slight with a full beak of a nose and hair so light, it reminded me of Sam, wispy and too long around his ears.

"I'm also a mage," I said.

"Where's your certificate?" the old man asked.

"Well, I haven't got it on me, have I?" I didn't have a certificate at all, not that they needed to know that.

"I have. He has," the young man said. "You've got magic in your fists, and you're not wearing a conduit ring. He's untrained, Nathan."

"I can see that, Kenneth."

"Are you two the only royal magicians?" I asked them. The

prism was a constant presence in the corner of my eye, pulsing and pleading for my magic.

"Don't answer," Nathan, the older magician said.

My eyebrows rose at the obvious suspicion. "You had a Leftman's locking charm on the door. It isn't hard to break."

Kenneth squawked and slammed his door shut on me, but Nathan only tilted his head. "You'd better come in, I suppose. He still has trouble with Leftman's. Prefers Bundry's."

I scoffed, glancing back at the other door. Bundry's lock was child's play. A good lock pick could break it, let alone any mage with basic skill. Weren't royal magicians meant to be powerful? I turned again and followed Nathan into a crowded office. He remained at the door for a moment, staring at the prism, before slowly shutting it behind us.

"Make me a cup of tea."

I frowned at the older man, watching him drift toward a large but old fashioned armchair with bald patches on the velvet. He sat down and cocked one eyebrow at me, tipping his gnarled hand in the direction of a teapot resting on a table.

This was the kind of instructional magic I'd avoided learning when I first discovered my talent. A pot of tea? When people were starving and sick? Eventually, I discovered that the principles in the charm reappeared later in more significant workings, ones with meaning.

I moved to the table, smiling and studying the scraps of paper with scribbled notes as I set about the magic. Pulling humidity from the air to supply water in the pot. I added a spoonful of tea from an open tin and deftly pocketed a note on balancing magical frequencies to examine later. My hands cupped around the chipped and cracked porcelain of the pot, held together with magic no doubt, and I created heat to warm the water and steep the leaves.

There was a mug on the far end of the table, stuffed with another note, and I called it over with a manipulated breeze. Nathan's breath caught, and he bit off a grumble as I swept the note—this one was more scientific and a little beyond my knowledge—into another pocket, and cleaned out the mug with a rinse of hot water.

"This is why mages aren't meant to be Chosen," Nathan muttered as water steamed from the teapot, and I strained the leaves as I poured his mug.

"I don't understand," I said, taking the mug to him.

He reached for it, eyeing the color, taking a deep sniff, and only frowning more deeply with every detail. "You have too much access to the source," he said, eyeing me warily.

I searched the floor and found a stool buried under a pile of books. Nathan didn't reprimand me when I moved the books, but he huffed as I helped myself to the seat.

"Because I don't use conduit charms to hold—" I didn't want to say Bryony's name. He probably knew exactly whose magic I used, but she was more to me than magical theory and a power source. I suddenly regretted showing off my skill with her power. "To hold power?"

"You're unmeasured. You spent twice the magic you needed on every one of those acts."

"The tea is too hot? Too strong?" I asked.

Nathan scowled at his tea. "It's a perfect cup. I think you know that. But no one needs magic to brew a cup of tea."

"Oh, and they need it for a luxurious bathing pool?" I laughed and narrowed my eyes at the older man, glancing briefly around the room. He was obviously scholarly, but also nervous, secretive. That prism was stuffed with magic, not because this man was using it for himself. He was hoarding power. "And you know about the source?"

"*You* know about the source!" he tossed back, leaning forward, a little tea spilling over the brim of the cup onto the floor. "That's another reason why mages aren't meant to be Chosen. And why mages aren't meant to be self-taught. To do as they please with any kind of instruction they can get their hands on!"

"If no one is meant to know about where Kimmery's magic comes from, why all the talk about the queen's line and—"

"*Prosperity*," the old man hissed. "It's not a very clear word, is it? Could mean plenty of things. None of them necessarily magic."

"I don't understand why it matters either way, if I'm honest."

"It's too much. It's too much power running about," Nathan

muttered, leaning back into his chair, head shaking and eyes trailing away from mine.

I frowned, running through his words, through the fragments I'd read on the notes strewn about.

"Unpredictable. Dangerous! Might end up doing anything, in anyone's hands. Might hurt someone," Nathan continued.

My mouth opened and then shut again. The royal mages were *preventing* magic being released? And even more disturbing was the fact that Nathan's words sounded a little too similar to the one's I'd thrown in Bryony's face when I discovered her Hunger. I'd been wrong in that argument—on *many* points—and the Hunger had more or less demonstrated that it posed more danger to Bryony than it did the general populace or any inexperienced magician.

"What does a royal magician do?" I asked. Aside from choke Kimmery's magic inside of a conduit the size of a boulder.

"It really isn't any of your business. You shouldn't even be here." Nathan was growing agitated again, taking a gulp of the tea I'd brewed and then grimacing as he remembered how it had ended up in his hands.

"I was only thinking I might be able to assist—"

"Assist? A Chosen?! That's not—you're not... We don't need any extra hands around here as it is. We're running the castle, we're not some experimental busybodies from the universities. Certainly not self-trained mages."

His words were winding in all the wrong directions, and he gave up his chair to pace around the room. The pulse of the conduit on the other side of the wall was tangible and tempting, overwhelming even, and I wondered what kind of toll it took on a magician who worked next to that drum of power every day.

"Magical janitorial staff," I murmured, eyeing the spines of books, memorizing the titles.

"Get out."

I looked, and the older man was vibrating, glaring down at me. If I were a mage in his position, I would've hated the work. I suspected he *did* hate it. I hoped he found the purpose of that conduit as unnatural as I did, but either way, I'd pissed him off properly, ruffled his tidy feathers, and it was time to go. Nearly.

"One last question," I said, ignoring his glare. "The princess said there's been no luck healing the dowager queen with magic. Why not?"

"You can use magic to heal a wound certainly, or cure an illness. But the dowager queen's magic is the illness," Nathan said, frowning.

"Her magic is poisoned?"

"It's running out. She's too ill to feed the Hunger, so the Hunger feeds on her. She knows what's wrong with her, believe me, Chosen," Nathan said.

"But then the queen or Bryony—"

"No! No. It has to be her own. Trying to force magic in would only do more harm. It creates friction, you see, after it leaves the source. We can use a little magic here and there against her symptoms, nothing more."

I frowned, disturbed by every bit of this news. Bryony tried to resist her Hunger sometimes and we'd seen how it hurt her, but I'd always imagined it would just lead to her lashing out and demanding sex eventually, not that she might resist it to her own death. I needed to know more of her nature if I was going to keep her safe.

I stood, bowing briefly, distracting him from the easy lift of a book from the floor which I slipped into an inner pocket of my coat.

"Apologies for the interruption in your busy day. I'll see myself out."

Nathan didn't move to the door, but he followed me every step of the way until I was out in the hall. The main door slammed shut behind me, and I turned, listening to the locks fasten in place again, smirking at the heady flare of magic. Well, that certainly wasn't Leftman's charm now. Poor Kenneth would never find his way out.

⚜

"So the conduit will take my magic too?" Bryony asked, trailing her fingertips in the fountain pool.

Owen had remembered Bryony liked the rose gardens and

sweet-talked her away from her grandmother's bedside and outside for the afternoon with the rest of us. She sat between Daniel and Cosmo, the latter sketching the pair as Daniel's fingers flirted with the lace overlay of Bryony's skirt.

I didn't like the steady small frown Bryony had been wearing for days now. She looked a little tired, a little bored, but mostly tense, all her muscles bound up tight like she was constantly bracing herself for an attack. She'd relaxed a little by the water, but not enough to reassure me—or the rest of her Chosen, based on their watchful expressions—that she wasn't entirely miserable here in the castle, but my news regarding her grandmother's health had draped a shadow over her eyes.

"If you let it loose, probably. If you and I are containing it, it doesn't seem a problem, but..."

Bryony's lips curled up, but it wasn't a real smile. "But I make more than we really need."

"Be fanciful with it then," I said shrugging. "Direct it to our furniture, your dresses. Owen's old shirts."

"I like my shirts fine," Owen said from the hedge border of the garden where he was collecting an audience of chipmunks and seagulls and one pale fox.

"You said stones and seashells make good conduits?" Bryony asked, brow furrowing and spine straightening. "And coins?"

"For small workings, yes."

"Why don't I charge those? We could send them north. Or to minor magicians."

"Very clever, princess," I said grinning. I leaned forward on the bench across from where she sat at the fountain and tugged on her skirt until she met me halfway.

"Ah, well there goes the sketch," Cosmo said with a sigh.

"What will we do about the conduit?" Bryony murmured as I brushed my lips over hers.

"The mages are drawing on it," I said, trying to distract her from the problem with delicate kisses, resisting the laugh in my chest as she started to tip in my direction. I caught her by the waist and drew her onto my lap, relieved to see the pink in her cheeks and a genuine smile curling her lips. "Breaking it would be dangerous, and I can understand its purpose in general. A store of magic is wise for a kingdom."

"But it's hoarding everything," Bryony said, tracing the outline of my mouth with her fingertip.

I nodded. "It's a less urgent problem, but it's good to know about it early."

"Thank you for snooping," she said, and I tightened my hold on her waist as she kissed me. She pulled away, holding me in place with a gentle touch on my chin. "What did you steal?"

"A few notes. A book," I said, shrugging.

Her eyebrow arched. "And?"

My jaw ground as I glared back at her, but she only laughed. "Some sort of gold wreath off a wall."

"Wicked thief," Bryony said fondly, gifting me with another kiss.

A throat cleared at a distance, and I bit at Bryony's lips as she pulled away. There was an older female servant hovering nearby, Wendell, Thao, and Cresswell moving closer to our cluster.

"Her Royal Majesty is holding dinner in the grand dining hall and—"

"And Her Royal Highness is occupied for the evening and will be unable to attend," I snapped.

"Aric," Bryony gasped.

"But—"

"Unless of course, it's a demand," I said, glaring at the servant. Not that they deserved my ire.

Despite Bryony's claims that royal family dinners were rare, we'd been called to one every single night since we'd arrived earlier in the week. Queen Peony made no effort at conversation during the dinners, and Camellia took it as an opportunity for blatant sexual performances. And all through the meal, Bryony remained stiff and unhappy, moving her food around her plate and responding to her Chosen tentatively. I wasn't sure whose idea the dinners were, but I'd had enough.

"N-no," the servant said, blinking.

Bryony's cheeks were red and she gaped at me, but she didn't correct me and she didn't really look angry. The servant scuttled away, and Bryony's tongue flicked out over her bottom lip.

"I'm not sure you should've refused," she said.

"For your sake, I am sure."

"I think he was right to say no. One refusal won't hurt, and your sister puts me off my appetite. I think she's the one arranging the dinners just because she knows it bothers you to sit through them," Thao said, drawing Bryony's attention.

She squeaked as I rose and lifted her with me, setting her down on her toes. "But what shall occupy me instead?" Bryony asked coyly.

The others grinned at the thought of dragging her off to her suite, but I had a better idea. Well, not better, but something I thought might do Bryony's low mood more permanent good.

I'd thought my princess spoiled and privileged when I first saw her seated on her throne in the great hall months ago. She was stiff and determined to have her own way, defying her grandmother to add me to her Chosen. I'd assumed it made her like her sister, and I couldn't have been more wrong.

Bryony had been lonely, I suspected. Lonely and searching for some sign in us, the men of the choosing ceremony, that we might understand her or she us. She and I were learning to understand one another, but it was obvious that being back at the castle reminded her of the neglect of her childhood.

"We're going to the seashore to gather shells and stones," I said.

Bryony's eyes widened, a bright little light flaring in her green gaze.

"Wait," Thao said, our brief alliance evaporating. "Isn't it colder by the water?"

"Collect your sweaters and scarves, my love," Wendell said to the prince, grinning.

"I haven't been to the shore in ages," Bryony murmured.

"It's all right, isn't it, Stark?" I asked, turning to a frowning Cresswell.

He sighed and shrugged. "I suppose so. Better track down a few extra hands."

"There is a secret tunnel, you know. Right to the shore," Bryony said, already bouncing a little on her toes. "It can be damp, but it'll make a nice shortcut in and out of the palace."

"Come on then, princess. Lots of work for you to do for your next project," I said. It would be playing mostly, digging through the sand and chasing the waves on the shore, but she was in need of a little peace and joy for the afternoon. I caught her hand in mine and dragged her back to my side before she could race to her rooms to dress for the trip. "And lots of magic to make tonight," I rasped in her ear.

Bryony laughed, turning and nipping my jaw before dashing for the door, making Cresswell curse and chase after her.

7.
BRYONY

I smoothed my skirts once more, Cresswell and Guard Piper at my back as I hesitated outside of my mother's suite.

"We're sure Camellia's not going to be there?" I asked softly, my hand squeezing around Cresswell's arm.

"Aric said his tracking charm has her in her suite with her Chosen," Cresswell said.

I hummed and nodded, knocking on the door, a feminine call to enter answering. Cresswell's hand moved mine from his arm, and he offered me a brief smile before nudging me forward.

"It's just a room of women," he said. He wanted to laugh, I could tell. And I wanted to tell him how dangerous a room of women could be, at least mentally if not also physically, but I didn't want Cresswell overreacting.

I took one deep breath to steel myself, and then opened the door and stepped inside. My mother's sitting room was full of bouquets, overflowing vases spilling out orchids and roses and anemones and always peonies, fresh from the capital's best hothouses. A low table took up the majority of the center of the room, covered in trays of confections and pastries, pots of tea and cups of steaming chocolate. And on every settee and in every chair, rested a woman in a fine gown.

My mother was dressed in blue velvet, even wearing rings and a jeweled necklace. Her gaze was clear as she found me at the door, a bright smile on her lips. "There you are, my darling, come and sit with me!"

A dozen women's heads all snapped in my direction. Amelia and her beautiful niece Ophelia were sharing a settee, but the rest of the faces were unfamiliar. Most were young, around my own age or a little older, and a few had older women at their sides like Ophelia did, probably mothers or aunts with some royal connection to help them gain the position of my lady-in-waiting.

"The guards can stay out in the hall," Amelia said.

"No," Cresswell and I said at the same time. Amelia's answering expression was somewhat sour. That was twice now I'd refused her.

"I think Bryony is a little partial to her handsome guard," my mother said, sweetly teasing.

I twisted in my seat on my mother's couch to find Cresswell behind me, standing and blushing, and I grinned, leaning briefly into my mother's side. "Very partial," I admitted happily.

All around me, the women in the room tittered like birds, scratching at me. The jealousy that had stabbed at me the night of our arrival wasn't quite as potent here in my mother's sitting room. I didn't have to contend with a room full of women admiring my Chosen this time. But I still understood why I was here. I was expected to grant the favor of prestige to a few noble houses by choosing companions for myself.

I knew my mother's ladies-in-waiting managed my mother's meals and her choice of dresses, and even occasionally her correspondence, so that she might carry on lovemaking with her Chosen. My grandmother's managed more of the social events of the castle—balls and state meetings with the council—and soon that task would be passed onto my mother's women. I had too much on my mind to worry about planning balls, so help might be appreciated in that area, but I could dress myself without an extra opinion easily, and I planned on taking a personal interest in my own meetings with the council rather than leaving it to someone else to manage.

"I am so happy to have my daughter home again, and with such handsome Chosen!" my mother cried with a clap of her hands and a tender smile aimed in my direction. "And while there is no blessing to our line like finding our Chosen, I have always taken great comfort in my ladies, Bryony. It would reassure me so well if you were to choose a few for yourself."

I forced a smile for my mother, which was sufficient because Amelia stood and bowed to us both.

"If I might begin with the introductions, Your Majesty."

"Of course, Amelia, please."

I watched, my hands folded in my lap, fingernails digging into my own palm, as Amelia moved to Ophelia first, the pair simpering and smiling as if I hadn't already roundly rejected the suggestion.

Cresswell stood behind me, towering in a room full of ladies on low settees, and I paid attention to the gazes that wandered in his direction. I knew the claw and bite of the Hunger's jealousy was irrational. I trusted Cresswell and all my Chosen in their faithfulness to me. What I didn't trust were the familiar family names of Amelia's introductions. These women were all related to council members, and ones whose alliances I knew went to Thomlinson and Roderick.

Did they really think I was so gullible or so accommodating that I would let their daughters and nieces into my court to spy on me and my Chosen or worse?

"Miss Nora McCallum," Amelia said, about to move on quickly, even as I perked up. Here was an ally.

"You met my brother, I think, Your Highness," Nora said, jumping in before Amelia could introduce the next girl.

Nora looked very young, as if she'd been yanked out of finishing school abruptly or had only just graduated. Her skin was pale, as a lady's ought to have been, but I liked the bright freckles dusting her cheeks and the wrinkles on her skirt where her hands had been clutching the fabric nervously.

"I did, yes, although we didn't get to speak as long as I might've hoped," I said. I'd met her brother, the viscount, at the council meeting. He was familiar with Griffin, and Owen had pointed him out to me as two-natured. I wondered if this young woman was as well.

Nora beamed, her smile a little crooked and her shoulders easing. She was younger even than Camellia, I suspected, and I wasn't sure what kind of help she could be in planning dinners and correspondence. She looked as though she would rather be running through a field or still playing with her school friends. And it somehow reassured me. She was an ally, yes. She might be a friend too.

"I never get to speak with Jack as long as I hope to," she said. "He is always running about somewhere on business."

"As gentlemen are wont to do," another girl murmured with a roll of her eyes, a trio of friends around her snickering as if they had been cued for the sound.

"What was your favorite subject in school?" I asked, ignoring the other women.

"Not quite a subject, but I preferred music, Your Highness."

"You play?"

"I do, and compose a little," Nora answered, and new huffs of irritation rose up from the other girls.

"How fascinating! You will have to tell me more and play me a few of your own pieces," I said, and then I turned and held Amelia's sharp gaze before nodding my head for her to continue.

Nora's cheeks were pink, her lips pressed firmly together, hiding a triumphant smile as all the other young women glared at her from beneath their lashes. Well, I had found one lady at least, even if she was still a girl.

Amelia had barely begun to introduce Katherine Oberlin of Packsen when the door to the room opened and a young woman tripped over the threshold and into the heart of the room. Her dark brown hair was a mess of untamed curls, which obscured her features as she stumbled onto the carpet, tracking mud into the room. Her hem was dirty, and when she swept her hair out of her face, there was another spot of mud on her cheek.

"So sorry—"

"Oh, honestly, go and change," Amelia snapped. "Your Majesty, I apologize for—"

"Morgan Weston, Your Majesty," the young woman said, blushing, but sinking into a low wobbling curtsey before me and my mother. "I apologize for arriving so late, but the invitation barely made it to the estate."

Amelia winced, and I wondered if the letter was meant to arrive at all.

"Sir Weston's daughter?" I asked.

"Yes, Your Highness," Morgan said, rising a little and winking at me.

My mother laughed and waved Amelia away. "It's fine really. I like your eagerness, Miss Weston. Please, have a seat. You look out of breath."

Morgan rose, still a little unsteady in her curtsey, and spun. She scanned the room quickly, and I caught the wolfish grin as she went and squeezed herself between two of the girls who'd been laughing at Nora. Morgan leaned in close to one who stiffened, color rising high on her neck and cheeks.

"Hello, Gretch," Morgan murmured, smirking at the girl, and then relented, pulling away and helping herself to coffee and cake.

I didn't know if she'd been flirting with the other young woman or antagonizing, but either way, I had made my decisions on who my ladies-in-waiting would be.

I looked up, a genuine and wicked smile spreading across my lips, and the bitter stony look on Amelia's face was as defeated as I was victorious.

❧

"WHAT ARE you going to do with ladies-in-waiting?" Cresswell asked as he escorted me back to the suite.

"I haven't the faintest idea, but at least they will be ones I like," I said.

Amelia and my mother had tried to wheedle me into choosing another girl aside from Morgan and Nora, but Mother had given up easily and eventually lost patience with Amelia's urging. My new ladies-in-waiting were being shown to their quarters at the far edge of my own suite, and Cresswell was escorting me back by a longer route, Stanley Piper following far behind.

"And trust?" Cresswell asked.

"I think so. Not as I trust you and the others. But their families appear to be on my side and..." Nora's brother was a shifter. Owen would be able to tell quickly if she was as well. I didn't want to *blackmail* the young girl into loyalty, but at least I had a weapon if I needed one later.

I frowned at my own line of thinking and then startled as Cresswell wrapped an arm around me.

"Sorry, I was just—"

"No! I like—you're welcome to," I rushed out, catching his

hand before it retreated and pulling it back about my shoulders. Cresswell was stiff and awkward, but I leaned into his side and looked up at him. "You know you are. I've been waiting for more."

"Bryony..."

"You're not allowed to change your mind."

He huffed, fighting a smile. "I would if it were that easy. It took enough focus to keep you safe in the north, but there are so many different kinds of threats here. Some I don't even understand," he said, the smile fading away quickly. "Piper and Brummer have some idea of who might be trusted in the guards but—"

"Danger won't evaporate conveniently, Cress," I said softly. "I think I am in for a lifetime of opposition. The council has had their hooks in Kimmery for too long to give up, even if I win the crown. You will have to learn to love me around the threats."

Cresswell frowned, his arm around me guiding me closer to the wall as a maid appeared in the hall, her head tucked low and steps quick in our direction, hands fisted around the handles of a tea tray. Cresswell's lips parted to speak, brow furrowed, and my steps faltered.

Scorching heat ran down a line against my hip, my eyes widening. The dagger! I kept my gift from Aric on me at all times, to the point I'd nearly forgotten its purpose, but it was blazing now, warning danger.

"Sir!" Piper cried out.

The maid—harmless, tiny creature as she appeared—swerved suddenly, the tea tray clattering to the floor, porcelain shattering and drawing my eyes down. I had my hand on the hilt of my dagger, drawing it from its sheath, at the same moment Cresswell reacted instinctively to the shout, shoving me to the wall and pinning me there with his tall broad frame.

There was a soft screech from the other side of Cresswell, and he buried a grunt of pain in my hair. His arms squeezed me in place as I tried to buck free, breaths panting into my hair.

Piper's steps thundered on the tile of the hall, and Cresswell shouted, a yelp really, before groaning again, his body shuddering.

"Cresswell, let me—"

"No," he said through gritted teeth.

I tried to squirm out from between him and the wall, my heart hammering and my throat squeezed tight.

"Cress!" I cried.

Above me his face was ashen, eyes squeezed shut and lips pressed to a firm white line. He'd been injured, stabbed by the glint of silver I'd seen in the maid's hand before he'd thrown me to the wall. His body was acting as my shield, but the knowledge he'd been harmed only made me burn with anger.

There was a feminine roar of frustration and then more slapping footsteps as the maid raced away. It was too late for her, I could hear Piper fast behind her, but I ignored them both as Cresswell sank against me, his weight heavy and beginning to droop.

Hunger was sharp in my palms, and a month ago I would've worried about hurting Cresswell, but I knew better now. I dropped my dagger back in its sheath, and my free hand tore away at the buttons of Cresswell's uniform, wrestling under his jacket and searching his back. I whimpered at the hot wet rush of blood I found and swept my touch against him until he groaned. The wound, one of them at least, soaked my palm as I pressed down, and I followed Cresswell to his knees at the first jagged pulse of magic.

8.
CRESSWELL

Bryony's magic was fire under my skin, a pain worse than the stab of the maid's little dagger. I hadn't been paying attention, too busy thinking of the invitation in Bryony's words to really process the tight set of the small woman's shoulders. I arched as another lightning pulse rushed into the muscle of my back, groaned as blood and flesh sizzled. It was as if she were branding me. No, cauterizing the wound.

"I'm sorry, but you shouldn't have taken that in the first place. I could've knocked her aside myself," Bryony rushed, her voice soft and a little breathless in my ear. "Oh stars, she's left the knife in."

I tried to hold Bryony in place, but the flex of my arms pulled on the wound where the knife was still embedded in my shoulder, and Bryony wrestled out of my grip easily. "There could be more," I squeezed out, words ragged.

"Then I will kill them," Bryony snapped, slipping out of my arms and scooting on her knees to face my back.

I nearly swallowed my own tongue as she pulled the knife out, an excruciating and unapologetic yank of the weapon from where it was buried, my vision going white as my fingers tried to dig into the wall to hold onto my sanity.

"Piper has her," Bryony murmured, the screams of the woman buried slightly under the white noise ringing in my head as Bryony applied her palm to the second stab wound, flooding it with her horrific magic. "Cresswell, what were you thinking?"

I wasn't. If I had been, I would have lunged for the woman, not Bryony. I could have caught her, twisted the knife out of her hand before she'd hurt either one of us, but all I'd known in the moment of Stanley shouting for me was that Bryony—not my duty, the princess, but *Bryony*—was in danger.

The ringing in my head grew louder, drowning out Bryony's rapid chiding, magic scalding me from the inside out, right up into my brain. The bear rumbled, and I realized a moment too late that it was taking my place in the hall.

"Oh!"

I growled, sniffing blood on the air, the stress of the woman, the sharp pinch of anxiety and sweat. My view narrowed to two points, the pretty young woman with my man's blood on her hands, now leaning against the far wall, and the predator a few yards away, thrashing in another man's grip. That was my kill.

Bryony scrambled up from the floor, racing to jump in front of me, stained fingers diving into the fur around my shoulders. "Cresswell, no! No, come back. Piper has her, and she needs to be questioned. See? See, other guards are coming. I need the man right now, Cress."

Petting a bear was a useless gesture. More an irritation than soothing really, but my man's brain recognized Bryony's effort as her touch combed through my fur. She leaned fearlessly into me, her cheek against mine, even as my snarl was open, hot breath and fanged teeth far too close to her throat.

I came stumbling back as a man, the threat my bear form posed to Bryony its own kind of alarm in my head. Her magic had done its work, a faint ache left on my back, nothing more, and I gathered Bryony against my chest as I watched over her head as two guards helped Piper subdue the woman.

I knew what I should do in the moment—take Piper's place and join the others, find Head Guard Amos and question the woman. And I knew what I wanted too.

And fuck it, they weren't so different. I would take what I wanted.

I scooped Bryony up off her feet, ignoring her shout of protest.

"Piper! Find Amos. I'm sending Martin and Farraque down to join you," I called, marching swiftly down the hall. Aric had his own techniques in inquisition, and he would help the guards get the information. Daniel would be able to sort through it better.

The maid's uniform wasn't quite right, and I suspected she wasn't really castle staff.

"Got it, sir. Brummer's in the suite," Stanley said. "I can send Humphries here with you too," he added, nodding at the one guard who wasn't busy restraining the woman. Humphries was one of the men Stanley trusted. I could leave him at the door and Brummer inside, and it would be enough.

"You aren't going yourself?" Bryony asked, keeping her voice quiet and for my ears only.

I shifted her in my arms, ignoring her hmph of annoyance. "Do you want me to?"

I ducked down a side hall, looking for a faster route back to the suite, watching Bryony bite her lip and shake her head slowly. "No. I want you close. I want to speak with her myself too. But later."

"Later," I agreed, my voice lowering.

Bryony's cheeks turned pink, and she leaned her head in, resting it against my temple, her lips just barely grazing my skin. "I'm still angry with you for jumping between us."

"Doesn't change that I'd do it again."

"I'd better learn to hold more magic," she said, more to herself. "You know, I could be walking. You're the one who was injured."

I grunted and clutched her closer.

"Cresswell," Bryony murmured, voice low and lips brushing back and forth over my skin with little turns of her head. "Where are you taking me?"

"To bed, Your Highness." There was no use keeping the growl out of my voice—the bear in me wasn't satisfied with being denied the right to attack. The sound made Bryony shiver in my arms, and her teeth nipped softly at my cheek.

"Why now?"

She was pressing kisses on my temple, my cheek, even my earlobe, damp light touches to tease me. I suspected her questions were teasing too, but my focus was narrowed on the turn of the hall that would lead to a back door into her suite.

"We'll have to get you a new personal head guard," I said, ignoring her question.

"I don't want anyone but you."

There was another meaning to her words that sent blood rushing to my cock. "You'll have me, Bryony. Closer than ever."

Humphries, obviously aware of what was brewing between Bryony and me, hurried ahead of us to open the narrow door. We entered the study Aric had claimed for his own and found the man scribbling at a desk, five books open around him. His head shot up at our entrance, eyes narrowing immediately.

"What's happened?"

"Put me down now," Bryony said, patting my shoulder.

"Assassination attempt. She healed me." My voice rose over the screech of Aric's chair as he leapt up. "I want you and Farraque to go down and find Piper and the others in the dungeons. Make sure the interrogation isn't muddled."

Aric's expression tangled, mouth opening, perhaps to argue with me, and he took one long step forward. I squeezed around Bryony as he reached out for her, my hackles rising, and then Aric paused and took a slow breath. His palms turned out, and he stepped forward again, face smoothing.

"All right," he said slowly, watching me as he approached.

He wanted the same reassurance that I did, to know Bryony was safe and whole, and I had to restrain myself from snatching her out of his reach. His hand stroked her shoulder, and she leaned away from me to accept his soft kiss on her lips.

"There's a bedroom with only one entrance around the corner," Aric said, catching my eye.

I nodded. "I know the one."

"Better not tell the others yet, or you'll have—"

"I know," I snapped, losing my patience.

Bryony's lips twitched, and she sank back into my chest, soothing the snag of frustration in my chest. Aric nodded and eyed the guard over my shoulder.

"Want me to ward the door?"

I wanted him to *leave*, but he was right. We had Piper's word that Humphries was trustworthy, but the entire castle staff were unknowns. I nodded and let Aric lead the way through a hidden door in a bookcase, down a side hall and to a small private room. He flicked his hand, and the fireplace flashed into life.

There were no windows in the room and only the one door we'd entered through. I turned, and Aric remained on the other side of the threshold, a knife out and scratching marks into the frame.

"Bryony will be the only one who can open the door while she's inside," Aric said, brow furrowing with concentration.

"Is that something you could make for the queen?" Humphries asked.

Aric and I exchanged a look, and he frowned. "Not without using the queen's magic," he said without looking back at the other guard. I thought it might've been a lie, but at the moment, I didn't care one way or another. Aric was making Bryony a safe room, one that would be powerfully useful in the future if we needed it. *If* we could convince Bryony to hide. That would be the real battle.

"Don't stay trapped in here all day. The others will hear about the attack and go into a panic," Aric said, finishing his work and stepping back, a slow smirk growing over his lips. "But enjoy yourselves in the meantime."

Bryony snorted, and Aric swung the door shut.

I didn't wait another moment. The bed was only a few feet away, and I crossed the space with two steps. I didn't know what color the walls were, what pattern the tiles made on the floor. I didn't care about the fire or the furniture, although the massive mirror hanging on the wall opposite me was worth noting. All I could really see was the woman in my arms, smiling up at me with perfect understanding in her eyes.

"If I'd thought an assassination attempt would break your restraint, I would've—"

I stopped her teasing with my mouth over hers, feasting on the lips I'd been denying myself for weeks, sucking on the wicked tongue that taunted and tempted me. Bryony moaned and arched beneath me, her arms circling around my shoulders, hips bucking into the air and searching for mine. My arms still cradled her, pushing her across the bed, my knees bracketing her hips as I followed above her.

I pulled away as she began to whine, fighting my grin as she gasped for breath. The fire made her golden and bright, and now I saw that the bed was blue velvet, a dark contrast for all her gleaming shades.

"You won't change your mind?" Bryony asked, a little narrow line appearing on her brow.

She was probably right to ask. I hadn't objected to becoming one of her Chosen lightly. I wanted to be the one responsible for Bryony's safety because she was the most precious piece of my life now. As her guard, she'd been mine in a way she didn't belong to any of the others. My responsibility. My princess. My duty.

I wasn't sure I would be able to entirely surrender that role to someone else, but Piper had proven that my focus was already too close to Bryony to guard her properly. I'd gladly put myself on the sharp end of a knife again, one hundred times, regardless of Bryony's objections. But just in case she couldn't save me next time, I was going to make sure I died knowing the full force of Bryony's love, and sure that she knew mine.

"I'm your Chosen, my princess," I said, slipping one hand out from under her to smooth the line on her forehead. I dipped and caught her lips, gentling the kiss, settling my weight on top of hers to pin her to the bed. Bryony's sigh was sweet in my mouth, her legs trying to part beneath me, still trapped by my knees on either side.

I knew a torturous amount of detail about Bryony's sex life for always placing myself outside of it, and I knew how impatient she was with her Chosen. I'd heard her demands and pleas, her cries of pleasure and triumph. I knew exactly how often and quickly she got her way.

So I ignored her urgent wiggling, kissing her in languid strokes and sucks until she trembled for breath, savoring her whimpers as I followed the muscle of her throat with my teeth and tongue.

"Cresswell, *please*!"

She huffed as I returned to her lips, growled into the kiss, thrashing a little beneath me and then slowly melting again.

"Interrogations take hours, Your Highness," I said before sucking on the corner of her jaw. "We might as well too."

"Don't you dare," Bryony gasped.

I stroked my hand up her side, cupping her breast through the fabric of her dress, squeezing it roughly, and grinning at the long groan that fell from her lips. I would make her repeat every wicked sound I'd ever heard through a wall.

"I can't stand your patience."

"You are spoiled," I answered, pushing myself up on my elbows, pleased to see her laugh.

"Maybe a little." She reached between us, unfastening the buttons of my uniform, frowning at the shirt she found beneath. "Can't you be terrible without our clothes on?"

I had a feeling I would be a great deal less able to resist Bryony's demands if our skin was touching everywhere, but it was hard to argue the suggestion when I wanted to unwrap her and feel her writhing against me.

"Undress me then," I said.

Bryony's huff was irritated, and she sat up, pushing roughly against me until I rolled on the bed, still sitting up and now with her over my lap. Her hands were eager, lips pursed with concentration as she wrestled me out of my coat.

"Oh!" she said, and I stiffened at the note of distress before following her gaze back over my shoulder. In the mirror we were reflected, deep red stains soaked into the torn fabric of my shirt. She tugged roughly on my shoulders, and I helped pull the shirt off over my head.

Her hands were hot on my skin, mapping my back, and I leaned in to suck on her pulse.

"There are still scars," she said, throat arching for me, hips rocking over mine as she rubbed the healed wounds of the knife on my back.

"Some might be from the army," I said, shrugging and helping myself to handfuls of her ass through the dense volume of her skirt. Her eyes fluttered shut, lips parting, and she ground herself against me.

"Give me your cock," she said, breathy and sweetly cajoling.

I grinned. The friction was too muffled between all the fabric, but I had a pretty view of her breasts swelling with every gasp and her throat flexing with her swallows. When I ignored her order, Bryony growled and sat up on her knees, frowning down at me. She reached for her own dress, and I caught her hands, shaking my head.

"You have to finish undressing me first," I said.

The Hunger's magic was buzzing, and for a moment there was a dark look in Bryony's eyes. Chosen were meant to obey, to satisfy their mistress when she demanded it, but I'd seen the way Bryony occasionally bent to the others, giving them control over her pleasure, and I'd witnessed the dazzled expression she wore after, how loose and tender and flushed she looked.

Bryony jumped down from the bed, hands on her waist and gaze flashing as she examined me from head to toe, planning her attack. I wanted to laugh—she looked like a little general—but I was probably already testing her enough. She reached for my boots first, nearly tearing my foot off with them, her lips snarling with the effort. One thunked heavily to the floor, and then the other, and Bryony's eyes fixed to the crotch of my trousers where I was already half-hard and twitching under her examination.

She was less rough there, but I knew her plan. She untied the laces and then reached gently inside, wrapping her warm hand around my length and stroking perfectly. The grunt caught in my throat, and Bryony's smile was wicked.

"I said to undress me," I growled.

"I said to give me your cock," she answered, glancing up at me through her lashes.

I wrapped my hand around her wrist, stilling her movement, but it didn't stop her from taking a firmer grip that made me buck in response.

"Do you really want to finish me off in your hand, Bryony?" I asked, watching her brow furrow. "I'm two-natured, remember?"

Her lips pouted, and her grip eased. "You're only resistant in your second form, we think. But fine," she added huffing. "Lift your hips."

She pulled my pants down as I obliged, watching her as she crossed her arms stubbornly. "Now what?" she asked, arching an eyebrow.

Brat, I thought fondly. I stood and wrapped my arms around her waist, lifting her up to meet me for a kiss, lips and tongue stroking against hers until she was soft in my arms again.

"Now it's my turn," I said, brushing one last kiss to her mouth before setting her on her toes again and moving to her back.

Her hair had started to fall loose during the attack and while she was healing me, and I pulled the pins free now, twisting her curls around my hand and tugging on the strands to tilt her head. My free hand went to the laces of her dress as I bent my head to kiss her neck, glancing to our reflection in the mirror. She was watching me, her eyelids heavy, a soft smile on her lips.

"I can't help being impatient," she whispered.

I bit gently on her shoulder, looking down as the dress gaped, revealing the shadow of her breasts. "If I was going to rush, I would've fucked you up against a wall ages ago."

Bryony giggled. "Please tell me that isn't entirely off the table."

"No, we can do it on a table too," I said, grinning as she laughed.

"My laces are undone, Cress," she murmured.

They were. I tugged one shoulder down, a breast appearing from the loose collar, ready and waiting for my touch. Bryony arched between the grip on her hair and my hand on her breast, rising up to her toes. A long moan echoed up to the ceiling, and I moved my hand to the other breast, pinching the peaked nipple before tugging down the dress.

Bryony's hands pulled free of her sleeves, and she pushed the skirt down over her hips before I could stop her. I enjoyed one brief view of her in the mirror, small pert breasts and full hips, my large hand resting over her belly, and then Bryony was pulling free. Her hands pressed into the bed, knees climbing up and parting, ass lifted in invitation. My mouth went dry at the sight of her, the lips of her sex glossy with arousal, ass trembling slightly, clenching as if she was just waiting for the first thrust. I wanted to laugh, and I wanted to cover her back with my stomach and slam myself inside her and fuck her until she was sweaty and shaking and flat on the bed.

"Cress," she urged, back curving low in an arch to expose herself further.

I pressed my hand over her sex, stroking my fingers through her wetness, pressing the tip of one inside of her a little just to feel the way she tried to suck me in further. Bryony trembled and held her breath, watching me in the mirror. My cock was hard, brushing against the inside of her thigh as I pressed closer, running my other hand up and down her spine.

"No," I said, and then I kissed the center of her back.

Bryony's groan was strangled behind clenched teeth, but she just remained still, breathing unevenly as I kissed her shoulder blades, her ass, the nape of her neck. Up and down, back and forth, tasting every inch of her but the ones she and I were most interested in.

"Please, please," she began to chant.

I framed her clit with two fingers, stroking steadily, pinching her nipples with my other hand and tugging them one at a time, back and forth, as I kissed the backs of her trembling thighs.

"I can't—please, Cress."

Her hands were fisting on the mattress, threatening to tear the velvet, and there was a weak crying note in her voice, growing steadily higher. I pulled my hand away from her sex, and she sobbed as I tipped her over onto her back.

I took her ankles in both hands, spreading her legs as wide as I could, her knees bent. Her center was red and weeping, breasts tipped with darkened nipples begging to be kissed. She looked near to tears, cheeks flushed and lips swollen from my kisses and her own biting.

Bryony shook her head as I knelt between her thighs, and I knew it wasn't a refusal but only an objection to more teasing. She could take it, I was sure. There was more of her to taste, and I wanted every lick of her before either of us were satisfied. I sucked kisses on her stomach, holding her legs in place even as she tried to weakly tug away. I mouthed along her ribs up to her breasts, jumping away and grinning at her frustrated cry as I licked the inside of her elbows briefly.

"Oh fuck, yes!" she shouted as I jumped back to her breast, sucking one sharp peak into my mouth, laving it with my tongue.

The bed was shaking beneath us, Bryony rocking up into the air. She was too close and I couldn't blame her. I was iron hard, my cock weeping and pleading with me as fervently as she was to just bury myself inside of her. I made a private promise to never deny us as long as this again and then moved to her other breast.

"I'll never forgive you for this," Bryony moaned.

"Yes, you will," I mumbled into her skin. She laughed a little, an anxious broken sound, and then whimpered as I pulled away.

"Please, Cress, just let me—"

Her voice stuttered as I released her ankles, cupping her ass with my hands and lifting her to my mouth. Her heels pressed into my back, and I wiggled one finger inside of her so I could know the moment she fell apart.

It only took one lick, right up her center and around her clit, and she was clamping down. She screamed behind pressed lips, head tossing, and I looked up long enough to watch her stomach shake in the mirror, her thighs trying to shut around my face, hold me to her. I lapped up her arousal, an earthy and vivid flavor on my tongue, and pumped my finger through the aftershocks.

"Forgive me yet?" I asked, taking one of her thighs down from my shoulder, leaving her stretched for me.

Bryony shivered, chest heaving as she caught her breath, eyes blinking slowly up at me. She smiled and stretched on the bed and then shook her head.

"Not quite."

I laughed and looked down. Her pussy was red, still wet, and gaping a little, waiting. I rose up my knees, lining myself up at her entrance, and then found her gaze again, watching her eyes grow wide, ignoring the urge to close my own as her cunt sucked me in inch by inch. She was as scorching as her magic, tight and grasping, silky wet and fluttering anew at my intrusion.

Her other leg shifted down, and I caught it in my arm as I leaned down, watching her moan at the stretch and pressure, my growl escaping as I sank in deeper.

"How about now?"

"Nearly," Bryony gasped, rocking up to meet me.

Her hands reached for me, nails digging into my ass and making me thrust, the other cupping the back of my neck and dragging me down for a kiss. Our tongues slid against one another, matching the rhythm we set with our rocking, bodies colliding with a gentle slap. Bryony's moans were musical, the sound vibrating in my mouth as she swallowed my own groans. She was soft beneath me, stretching to wrap herself around me tighter, hands squeezing and stroking, breasts sticking to my chest.

The room had been cool when we entered, but the fire was a hot glow against my side now and Bryony's magic was a bright buzz skimming over my skin after her release.

"Cress, I love you, please, please don't stop," Bryony whispered, pulling away and pressing her cheek to mine.

I released her leg, wrapped my arms around her back, holding her hips up for me to fall into, Bryony's gasp high in my ear, her fingers digging into me. I hadn't had a woman in months, but I'd never had anything like this in my entire life. It was as if I were falling apart, every thrust seaming me together with my princess. I found her mouth again, a pressure building in my skull, my chest, and at the base of my spine, barely soothed by the messy biting kiss.

She seemed to grow both softer and more desperate beneath me, legs wrapping tighter around me until our movements were pressed into a deep rock and grind. Bryony's mouth tore away from my mine with a high cry, and her cunt squeezed me like a vise, demanding my pleasure. Lightning raced up my spine, and I bit hard on Bryony's throat to muffle my shout.

I lost my edges as the room, the world, narrowed to the sensation of Bryony's body dragging me under the thick blanket of her magic and pleasure until the heat and trembles and teasing prickles were as much my own as they were hers.

9.
BRYONY

Cresswell's heartbeat was thumping steadily under my cheek, sweat cooling on my spine beneath the blanket he'd wrapped us in without bothering to slide under the covers. We were still sideways on the bed too, a realization that made my lips twitch, breath puffing and teasing the dark curls of hair on his chest.

He had a hand tangled in my hair, and his grip tightened, making me shiver. I wanted more, but something about Cresswell's never-ending teasing before he'd fucked me had left me especially limp and loose after my release. There was still craving, but it was worth ignoring to simply savor what I'd already indulged in.

I slid one hand beneath him, fingering over the scars I'd noticed there earlier, searching for the freshest ones from the attack.

"Let me see," I said, wiggling to sit up.

Cresswell's eyes were closed, but his lips were curled up, cheeks rosy, and he shook his head. "Doesn't hurt. It's just a scar. You have one too."

His hand slid up the arm I'd thrown over his chest, and he opened his eyes at last, the glassy green a little darker than usual. He ran his touch over the mark Emory had left on my shoulder and I shivered, less pleasantly this time.

"It pains you?" he asked.

"Not the scar."

"No," he agreed.

I pressed my lips flat, but Cresswell had already proved his patience. His fingers combed through my tangled strands, eyes tracing the features of my face.

"You told me not to do it myself," I whispered.

"It stays with you. *They* stay with you."

Emory. Emory would stay with me, the expression on his face as I'd stolen his life. The question of whether or not I could've made a better choice than to kill him. I tried to not to weigh it out in my head, afraid that one day I'd realize I did the wrong thing.

"I can't fix that for you now," Cresswell said, distracting me with a long touch from my forehead down to the tip of my nose. "And you can't either. You just have to walk alongside it."

I blinked and frowned. "You mean I can't leave it behind me in the past?"

He shrugged. "Maybe. Maybe not. I'm not saying that because you killed a man once, you will make the choice the same way every time. But it's there now. And maybe it will help you make a different choice someday."

I sighed and sank back down onto Cresswell's chest, listening to that steady drum beneath my ear, enjoying the careful tug of his fingers through my hair.

"You need to speak with the others," Cresswell said.

I nodded and added, "And then the maid."

"Do you think she was from your sister?"

"Actually, I... Not directly, no. I didn't recognize the woman and—"

Cress finished the thought for me. "Her uniform wasn't right. Are you sure you really want to be taking on ladies-in-waiting?"

"I wouldn't have agreed if I didn't think they'd be good choic-es," I said, thinking of Nora and Morgan. "They'll make communi-cating with allies easier, and choosing any reassures my mother that I'm being...normal, I suppose."

I *did* want to see the others, and I *was* eager to find out what Aric and Daniel and the guards had learned from the maid. And yet, I remained against Cresswell, soothed by the beat of his heart, by the warm color he had on his cheeks again, by this soft and paused moment in the midst of so much chaos.

"The others will be worried. We shouldn't fall asleep," Cress-well murmured.

He was right, and I hated to think of Cosmo pacing or Thao picking irritably at the others as he waited. I sighed, and Cresswell rolled us, pausing above me as he helped himself to a long and thorough look at me.

"What are you thinking of?" I asked, fairly certain I already knew the answer.

"Having you again." His voice was low, head bowing to brush a kiss over my forehead. "And again. And again. Hoarding you to myself in that massive bed as the others have to sit and watch."

I was about to laugh at the idea of any of my Chosen being able to stay out of the bed, but Cress's head dipped, full lips stealing my breath again. He kissed me in his perfectly thorough and patient way until the Hunger was simmering again, my arms circling to hold him closer, pull him back into me.

"But not now," Cresswell said, pulling away too easily. He laughed at my growl and skirted out of my reach as I sat up, kicking his pants up from the floor and dressing quickly.

My thighs were messy, and our release slipped out of me as I stood. There was nowhere to wash in the small bedroom, and I frowned at my dress on the floor. It was more formal than I really liked to wear, and Cress had thoroughly torn the laces free.

"Here," he said, tugging the blue velvet from the bed and holding it up in front of me.

"A blanket?" I laughed. "And a dirty one?"

"You're magical aren't you?" Cresswell asked, arching an eyebrow.

I hadn't ever *intentionally* made myself clothing, although new things did seem to appear and old ones vanished, so we'd suspected the Hunger made a game of my wardrobe. I sighed and closed my eyes, reaching for the velvet. I'd kept the magic I'd made with Cress more easily than I did with Owen or Cosmo or Daniel, as if he'd had a slightly resistant shell around him. It flooded my hands quickly now, rushing into the velvet, a stirring and weighty sensation. When it grew heavier in my grip, I opened my eyes and found a gown, dressed with delicate gold threads of embroidery.

Cresswell took it from me, lifting it over my head, and I sighed as it sank over my shoulders like warm water. The sleeves were loose, the skirt vast and covered in strange scenes of bears with antlers chasing tigers on their hind legs holding bows and arrows, everything dressed with stars and flowers. It was eerie and beautiful, and the longer I looked down at the images, the more it felt as though they were just about to leap to life.

My back was mainly exposed, and much of my chest, but Cresswell buttoned me up around my waist and then bent, kissing the center of my back.

"Sometimes, I feel as though the Hunger knows more about me than I do about it," I said, running my fingers over a depiction of a snake and a rabbit in an embrace that was either threatening or erotic.

"I'm not sure magic is meant to be understood, although don't tell Aric I said so," Cresswell said, moving for the door.

"Wait, you can't open it, remember?" I hurried to join him, and Cresswell placed himself at the entrance as I turned the knob.

I peeked around the edge and found Humphries standing guard. He was an older man, probably about Aric's age, with a perfectly impassive expression and eyes that remained respectfully above my head, even as Cresswell had carried me about.

"One of the Chosen came looking for you both not long ago," he said.

"We'll go now and reassure them you're safe," Cresswell said, wrapping his arm around my shoulder and pulling me to his side.

"*I* was never really in any danger," I said softly, glaring up at Cresswell.

"And you won't be," Cresswell answered, glaring back, but his lips were slightly curled, and even the hint of a smile on him left me giddy.

We found the others in the grandest of the sitting rooms in our suite, and Cresswell barely had the door open before Wendell was rushing over. His hair was sticking out in every direction, eyes red, and I stopped still at the sight of him, strangely surprised by the obvious torment and worry he'd suffered.

He loves me, I realized. We'd said as much, but Wendell was always so calm, so patient, even willing to remain at the fringes as my other Chosen demanded more attention or time.

I ran forward, crashing into his chest, his arms snapping around me and lifting me from the floor.

"Stars, there you are finally," he sighed into the top of my head.

My face was buried against his throat, but I heard the quick rushing of the others' approach, shadows surrounding me, hands on my bare back and wrapping around my waist.

Thao pulled me away first, slanting a quick rough kiss over my mouth, brow furrowed with that same tension as Wendell, and then he released me to Cosmo and Owen, who folded me between them.

"I was never even scratched," I said, my words muffled against Owen's chest, Cosmo's fingers digging into my waist and up into the hair at the back of my head.

"You're all right, Cress?" Wendell asked.

"I'm fine. She healed me up quick."

"Thank you," Thao said softly.

"You could've been worse than scratched," Cosmo whispered.

I wanted to argue. I would've been ready to defend myself, even if I'd been alone. Emory had done much worse, the maid had been a comparatively clumsy attack. But arguing was only going to raise everyone's stress, and being cradled in the arms of my men was always welcome.

"I'm sorry I didn't come right away," I said, turning my cheek to listen to the thump of Owen's heart.

"Aric told us you were safe," Owen said, reaching between us to tilt my chin up, kissing me briefly. He smiled and glanced at Cresswell before looking back at me. "We understood the delay."

"And you have your magic?" Wendell asked.

I nodded. I didn't have as much now as I had before healing Cresswell, but I was prepared for another emergency if I needed to be.

"Good, then come and sit down because we've already received word—"

"From Aric?" I asked, pulling away and hurrying back to Wendell.

"No, but from Head Guard Amos." Wendell took my hands and urged me down onto the couch, sitting down to face me. "Your mother's lady Amelia fled the palace with a carriage and her niece shortly after your luncheon ended."

The room stilled around me with a sudden hush, my own mind going blank for a beat as the news sank in.

"No." I don't know why I said it, what Wendell said made a

kind of sense. Amelia had been insistent on placing her niece in my court. I didn't know of any direct connection she had with the council, I'd only refused out of the Hunger's jealousy, but it was certainly possible.

"My mother?"

"I'm not sure. I assume she's been informed, but I know they're questioning the maid to see if there's a connection," Wendell said, frowning. "Bryony, are you *sure* you want to take on ladies-in-waiting for yourself?"

I gaped around the room, the others drifting closer. Thao wedged himself in at my back, one hand cupped around my side possessively, his chin resting over my shoulder.

"I'm not sure of *anything* at this point," I said softly.

"Even if they have the right political ties, you may be putting them in danger by adding them to your court," Cosmo said carefully.

Ice trickled through my veins, my heart squeezing at the thought of tangling young Nora into the mess of my path to securing the throne.

"There will be no keeping a secret about what took place today," Thao said. "You can be honest regarding the danger and allow them to make their own choice."

My fingers were picking absently at the embroidery on my new dress, and Wendell's hands tangled with mine, squeezing gently. "Speak with your grandmother on it," he said.

I released a breath I hadn't even realized I'd trapped in my chest and nodded. Grandmother would be both honest and cunning. Growing up, I'd been forced to sit through her lectures or to perform perfectly at a tea for her to interrogate me. Now I went to her every day to speak. She'd been as unprepared for the revelations regarding Kimmery as I was, but she had the lifetime of *interest* in our Kingdom that my mother seemed to lack.

"I want to go down and listen to them question the maid," I said, twisting and finding Cresswell back against the wall. He was awkwardly dressed in his pants with only his uniform jacket on, half-buttoned to reveal appealing planes of his chest, but he stood as if he were stationed, and I frowned, reaching out for him.

He stepped forward slowly, glancing at the others as if they might object. No one so much as blinked.

"I can take you down myself. Leave Humphries and Brummer here to watch the suite," Cress said.

"I'll come too," Thao said. "I sat in as our palace guards questioned an assassination attempt on my father. Has it never happened here before?"

"Not that I've known of," I admitted. "But I think we all know that plenty has been hidden from the queen's line in the past."

❦

THE HUNGER PRICKLED and snapped as we traveled down to the dungeons. This was a part of the castle I had never had cause to visit before. I'd been fooled as I'd grown up, believing my family was beloved by our kingdom, that we were actually serving our people. I'd known there was a dungeon, but I'd never given thought to who might be found within.

The space was vast, an entire structure of its own beneath the shining surface of the castle, a dark root system with staircases that seemed to sink indefinitely. We circled down, and out of the corner of my eye I saw a long hall of cells.

"Who is kept in those?" I whispered to Cresswell, seeing a glimpse of figures pacing behind bars, arms drooping out of the cage.

He shook his head. "I've spent my time at your side. Brummer or Piper might know."

"I want a full record of who is kept here and their crimes," I said, an uneasy feeling swirling in the pit of my stomach. How could there be so many people kept in the dungeon when I'd never heard of any crime against the crown?

Aric, Daniel, and the guards were another floor down. There were no windows this low, and the air was tangy and metallic. The maid sobbed loudly in the room, words unintelligible, and I paused at the threshold, suddenly wishing I'd waited to hear from my Chosen about the answers they gathered. The room was long and dark, candles flickering in sconces along the wall cast threatening shadows from the strange instruments littered about.

This was a torture chamber.

Daniel was away from the others, head down and feet pacing back and forth, arms crossed over his chest. He paused suddenly and looked up, finding me immediately, a deep frown creasing the corners of his lips.

"Go back," he mouthed to me.

I swallowed hard at the sudden scream of the woman until it shattered into breathless sobs, my steps stumbling back, running into Thao and Cresswell's shoulders.

"Stop!" I shouted, still unaware of what was happening.

The circle of guards stumbled back, Aric amongst them, his eyes unseeing for a moment before finally landing on me.

"Come here, princess," he said gently.

I wanted to take Daniel's advice and run. Cress and Thao would certainly let me, but then Aric tilted his chin up, confidence and a challenge in his steady gaze on me. I took a deep breath and walked forward, Aric meeting me halfway.

Over his shoulder, I saw the woman who'd charged at me, sagged sideways in a chair. She was sweat-stained, face red with crying, but I didn't see any visible injury.

"It's magic," Aric whispered in my ear, his hands covering my shoulders with a gentle touch. "It isn't kind, but it's not causing permanent harm. They wanted to use rocks to crush her. I know," he said as I shuddered. "We're almost done, but there's something I'd like to try with you now."

"To hurt her?" I asked, closing my eyes as if it could block out the moaning sobs of the woman.

I had been so eager to destroy Emory when he'd come for me, had nearly sent Owen to his death in that fire. Perhaps Cresswell was right and the memory of Emory made me more reluctant to do that same harm again, or perhaps the knowledge that Amelia was in some way entangled in the scheme made the question of who was to blame less clear. Emory had been largely his own agent, and his attack on me at the Winter Palace had been self-motivated. He'd earned his punishment. I wasn't sure this woman had.

"I don't think it will hurt her. Not the way I've been," he said darkly.

I reached up between us, my fingertips finding Aric's throat as he swallowed. I leaned back and rose to my toes, pressing my face to his without a kiss. He took a deep breath of me and released it slowly, tension bleeding away.

"Show me," I said.

"You have magic?" he asked, and I nodded. "I want you to use something like what you would if you wanted us to perform for you."

"What?!" I asked, choking slightly, my eyes going wide.

Aric huffed. "Make her pliable, wanting to please you."

My lips formed an O, and I glanced over Aric's shoulder again. Whatever he'd done to plague her was subsiding, and she was taking great gulps of air. Her features were soft and smudged, and she looked a little younger than me, heavier set, and yet she had deeper lines and darker circles under her eyes. Her eyes were bloodshot now, but they found me and she whimpered, her whole body trembling.

Could my magic do as Aric asked? I didn't see how the Hunger's lust would help now, but I remembered the empty look I'd given Owen the first time I used it on him accidentally.

"All right," I said.

Aric nodded and stepped back, his voice rising out of the whisper we'd used. "We know she came here with the young Lady Ophelia. That she was charged to attack if you didn't take Ophelia on as one of your ladies."

"What more do you need to know?" I asked.

"Nothing to charge her with the crime, Your Highness," one of the guards said. He was tall and broad, not handsome but certainly impressive. "Head Guard Amos."

He bowed to me and so did the other guards. I glanced at Aric, who was grinding his jaw.

"We ought to know *why* she agreed," Aric said firmly.

"Please, Your Highness. Please, pardon me. I was only following orders. I wasn't even trying, was I?" the woman sobbed. Her wrists were pinned to the arms of the seat she was trapped in, but her hands flexed as if she were trying to reach for me.

"Not trying? You stabbed my Chosen twice," I said frowning, and she gasped and then began to cry again.

With a little less sympathy at the reminder of Cresswell's

bloody back, my hands filled with magic. Aric nodded to me, and I reached out, pressing my hands over her rigid strapped arms. The woman stiffened, eyes going wide with shock, chest filling with one great gasp, and then she sagged and moaned.

One of the guards behind me snorted, and there was a resulting punch of flesh on flesh and a stifled grunt.

"Focus," Aric said to me softly.

Meaning make the woman agreeable, not aroused. *Friendly thoughts. Sleepy thoughts. Honesty and sweetness.*

The woman hummed, the tight rigid strain in her arms melting as she sighed. Her eyelids grew heavy, blinks slow, the pale blue of her gaze stark against the red of all her crying.

"What's your name?"

"Lily, love," she said, and then repeated the words in a sing-song until they blurred together.

"Lily," I began, stepping a little closer, hearing the echo of men shifting closer behind me. "Lily, why would you agree to kill me?"

"Oh noo, no. No, I didn't think I would. I didn't think I would have to. They said you'd take Miss Ophelia on like you took the steward."

Daniel. Which meant this did lead back to the council. Of course it did.

"But you must've known. They gave you instructions."

Lily's lip wobbled, her smile failing, shoulders thrusting forward to me. Cresswell appeared at my side, vibrating with tension, ready to throw himself between us again.

"I didn't want to, of course, but I had to," Lily said, eyes growing wide. "I'm so sorry, Your Highness, but you know I had to. And they said I wouldn't even get in trouble. Or only for a little bit. They really did promise."

"Why agree? Why agree at all?" Head Guard Amos snapped.

Lily whined and shrank away, starting to cry again, but the sound hiccuped into a sigh as I pushed more magic into her.

"Not too much," Aric whispered.

I ignored him and knelt down before Lily, resting at her feet, staring up at her. Her head lolled on her shoulder, thin curls sticking to her damp brow, and she smiled at me through the tears still clinging to her lashes.

"You are so pretty, princess."

"Why did you have to agree to such a terrible plan, Lily love?" I asked.

Her breath hitched, eyes fully glazed now. "You know I didn't want to do that either," she said nonsensically. "I begged him not to. He promised it would feel good, but it didn't. It didn't at all! It really hurt you know! I knew I would get in trouble. Mother always *said* I would get in trouble, but it wasn't my fault, I didn't even want to. Oh it *hurt*!"

My hands were on fire, too tight around Lily's arms, but she didn't seem to notice. I didn't think she was really with us at all.

"He always said what a nice man he was, but I really hate him, I think. If it weren't for the baby, I wouldn't've agreed, but they said they would make him marry me if I said yes, and they really said I wouldn't have to do it you know, and—"

Aric pulled me away, drawing me into his chest, my heart hammering roughly as Lily continued.

"They promised I wouldn't get into very much trouble. Not for long. And I just thought, wouldn't it be better if the baby was a little lord or lady instead of turning out like me? Always getting pushed and forced to do the things I don't want to do. They don't do that to their own kind, do they?"

My hands were clenched in Aric's shirt, tears falling silently.

"Who's that man you're going to marry, Lily?" Head Guard Amos asked, voice gentler now.

"Young Mr. Clemont Goddard, of course."

The room was quiet at her answer, as if we were all too disgusted or horrified to move, like the moment might be erased if we just held still and waited. Lily was sniffling and hiccuping softly, still dazed from my magic, and the guilt of pulling these secrets from her left a bitter flavor on my tongue.

"We assumed the family might be involved after the two women fled earlier," Amos said in my direction. "We sent word for their estate to be searched, but there was a report of a sighting by the docks. We think they might've fled Kimmery."

"Speak to their staff then, to any extended family that might be tracked down. Anyone with a chance of confirming Lily's claim," I said.

"Yes, Your Highness," Amos answered.

I straightened in Aric's embrace, and he wiped my tears away, careful not to allow anyone else to see. Daniel and Cresswell had moved in to surround me, a reassuring blockade against the rest of the room.

"Frances Goddard is now Lady Roderick," Daniel said to Amos, adding to me, "although the Goddard family has no members on the council themselves."

I nodded and squared my shoulders, turning as Cresswell and Daniel stepped back to my side. Head Guard Amos stared back at me with naturally narrowed dark eyes, awaiting any verdict I might give on the girl's fate.

"I would like Lily to be taken somewhere more comfortable. Please... Not with the others," I said, frowning as I thought of the dark cells I'd passed on our way down.

"Yes, Your Highness."

"She should be guarded, protected," I said, and his eyes widened slightly. "We suspect that those responsible for her orders have fled, but I would rather not assume that means there is not someone else who will object to Lily's honesty."

Forced honesty. Dragged out from a magically drugged tongue.

But at least I know now that her violence was born of desperation rather than a genuine interest in seeing me dead, I thought.

"And...perhaps a doctor?" Head Guard Amos asked very carefully.

I frowned, wanting badly to turn to Aric or Cress or Daniel for advice. Could we trust a doctor?

"Not a castle doctor. Someone from the capital," I said, weighing the idea in my head. A castle doctor might be aligned with the council. At least a hired doctor from the city would be an unknown. "And either I or Aric should be present." We would have the magic to intervene if anything went awry.

"I'll go," Aric said quietly behind me, and I nodded, reaching back gratefully and pushing him more magic. We were both low now, and I'd probably never been in *less* of a mood to be made love to.

"Of course, Your Highness," Head Guard Amos answered with a bow. He rose again and looked over the four of us before back to the wearily weeping Lily. "An attempt on the crown is a serious offense. If Your Highness has the time, we should sit and speak soon on the matter."

He spoke cautiously with no direct glance at the other guards around us, but I appreciated what was unspoken. Head Guard Amos understood our suspicion against the residents of the palace, even against his own men.

I nodded curtly. "It would be greatly appreciated."

10.
BRYONY

The conversation did indeed take place soon. The very next morning in fact.

"And you only have the former Chosen's word in regards to your sister?" Head Amos asked. He'd worn the same grim expression for the entire meeting in the small meeting room of my suite, sitting stiffly at the edge of an armchair.

"Why shouldn't that be enough?" Cosmo snapped, and I slid my hand into his, drawing it to my lap and soothing the fingers of my free hand along the inside of his arm.

"Yes, and he never made any attempt," I said simply, Cosmo huffing but leaning his shoulder against mine.

We sat on the couch facing Amos, Thao and Wendell pressed closely on my other side, Daniel and Owen perched on the back of the couch. Aric was with Cresswell, guarding Lily through the hired doctor's visit.

"We are speaking frankly, Your Highne—"

"Bryony, please," I said for the third time.

Head Guard Amos pressed flat lips into an even thinner line. I couldn't tell if he disapproved of my informality, or if it simply made him uncomfortable, but he nodded briefly.

"Princess Camellia has had four attempts on her own life from her Chosen," Head Guard Amos said, and I stiffened. "One of those men remains locked up in the dungeon, awaiting execution."

"And the other three?" I cried out, eyes growing wide.

"Their executions took place, Your Highness."

"When?"

"One was a year ago, the other two shortly before your choosing ceremony."

"But I never heard of such a thing!" I glanced at Cosmo and Wendell, who both shook their heads, faces pale.

"Conflicts between a woman of the queen's line and her Chosen are mandated to be privately handled," Head Guard Amos said.

I leapt up from the chair, shielding my face with my hand as I started to pace. "Stars. Who else knows of this? How often has this happened?"

The older man shook his head. "There's no record kept. I only know of those four. But it's not a new duty for my role, so there must be a precedent."

"And my mother?" The room was too small, and I hurried to the window, ignoring the grunt of the guard's objection as I pushed it open, closing my eyes against the sharp breeze that rushed in, cooling the hot anger on my cheeks.

"She ordered the current execution postponed indefinitely."

I spun, mind racing. "At my grandmother's urging?"

"Not to my knowledge, Your Highness."

I glanced at my Chosen, pain striking my heart at the thought of any of them being left to waste away in a dungeon. I was nothing like Camellia. I chanted the fact as a refrain in my thoughts, but it didn't eliminate the fact that she existed, a persistent, growing thorn in my side.

"There are a couple of others there, imprisoned for attempting to kill others of her Chosen. One is very ill. I don't expect him to make it through winter. Another is...ill in a different way, I suppose."

My knees crumpled, but Owen had hurried over before I could sink to the floor, shielding me from the room and holding me up with his large hands around my waist.

"Send the doctor to him as well," Thao snapped.

I nodded but couldn't find my tongue to voice my agreement. There was a grumble of assent from beyond Owen's chest, and I only leaned forward to press myself into his warmth. Everything was wrong. Everything was crooked and ugly here in the castle, smothered under a glistening facade, and I wanted desperately to find my way back to the north as if it might rewind or erase the problems we'd tangled ourselves into.

"Your Highness," Head Guard Amos said, standing from his chair.

I pushed against Owen, and he turned us slightly, refusing to pull away from me.

"My vows are to the crown and to Kimmery."

"To the queen," I said, nodding.

He nodded slowly, eyes drifting aimlessly around the room. "I cannot... I would not..."

"I want no secrecy, Head Guard Amos. I don't trust my sister, I don't want her to take the crown from my mother, and I will act openly in that regard," I said, adding after a moment, "Lawfully."

Wendell sat forward at that. "If it is possible, I would like to examine any record or written word of this measure that allows for secret executions. If there's any way to allow for their testimony to be used against Princess Camellia, it could be very valuable."

Amos blinked at that. "A criminal trial against a member of the queen's line?" I held my breath as he seemed to consider the idea. That broad flat face was almost unreadable, just the faintest flickering of thought. "I won't deny you any information that would help build a case."

I let out a whoosh of air, and Owen hauled me back to the couch, fitting himself between the others with me on his lap.

"My mother will have to know," I said softly.

"Is that wise?" Thao asked.

"I requested she join us, but was informed that she found Lady Amelia's departure too distressing," Head Guard Amos said quietly.

My hands clenched to fists in my lap, and I twisted to face Thao, shaking my head. "I don't know."

❧

IT TOOK two days and my grandmother's demand before the queen would leave her chambers.

She arrived to my grandmother's bedchamber nearly an hour late and with three of her Chosen surrounding her.

"Peony," my grandmother snapped, but her voice was growing wearier by the day. "We said this would be private."

My mother blinked and cocked her head, and it took her several moments before she turned and glanced at the men at her side. "Oh. But surely you didn't mean—"

"Surely I did," Grandmother said, eyeing her daughter impatiently.

"Her Majesty has been greatly aggrieved since her lady-in-waiting left her service," one of the men said.

Grandmother growled but fell into coughing, and I frowned at my mother, waiting for her to meet my gaze. "You mean since the Goddards ordered their maid to try and stab me to death?"

It had been days, and there'd been not one word of concern from my mother after the attack. I knew she'd been assured of my safety, but I'd expected...anything, any tiny show of her worry.

"Oh, we don't know that, Bryony," my mother gasped, striding forward. "That girl might say anything to place the blame elsewhere."

I opened my mouth to say I'd forced the truth out of the girl, Lily, and then snapped it shut again with a glance at my mother's Chosen. I wasn't sure I wanted them to know how I'd used the Hunger. Camellia seemed to misunderstand her power, my grandmother had and so surely my mother did too, which meant so might anyone else.

"Wait outside," my grandmother said to the men after clearing her creaking throat. "Vincent will entertain you, I'm sure."

My mother gasped in dismay, turning to watch her Chosen leave the room, clearly bereft. "You know I trust them implicitly," my mother said, frowning at us.

"I don't. I find myself less and less trusting by the hour," Grandmother muttered.

My mother huffed and rolled her eyes, glancing at me with something in her expression that said 'isn't she ridiculous?' I only turned away. I'd never expected to be aligned with my grandmother's strict and demanding personality. I'd always considered myself like my mother. Kindly and sweet. I was learning that my mother was sympathetic but not empathetic. She pitied those who were unhappy, but she didn't *feel* with them.

She crossed to us, sitting on the bed at my grandmother's side, her knees bumping against mine. She reached for my hands, and I had a fleeting impulse to pull away, but then her soft touch was on me, squeezing gently.

"You poor thing, how stressful. And it just breaks my heart to see you this way, Mother. Everything has just been terrible for us lately, hasn't it? Bryony I am so *glad* you have Chosen now to comfort you."

I wasn't sure what to say to the messy, weak sentiments of my mother, but there was one simple answer I could give. "I am very grateful to have found men who are so supportive to share my thoughts and troubles with."

"Oh yes! That's just what I hoped for you. But with a great deal less trouble of course. How *could* someone ever wish to harm you, I can't imagine it!"

I glanced at my grandmother, her lips pursed and her eyes narrowed on my mother. Emory had been my only solid proof against the council wanting me dead until now, and he was useless to the argument now that I'd killed him. And Head Guard Amos was right to doubt my sister's attempt on my life according only to Sam. But I knew before I'd left for the north that my mother had wanted me to be the one to take the crown. There had to be a reason for that.

"And Camellia? Can you imagine why any of her Chosen might wish to harm her?" I asked.

My mother went pale, her eyes flicking back and forth between me and Grandmother. "You know," she said, a soft and sorrowful sigh.

"I'm afraid I've learned a great deal about Camellia and her Chosen," I said.

My mother fixed her stare on Grandmother then. "I was mistaken on many matters. Hoping that Camellia would grow out of her spoiled nature was one of those," my grandmother admitted slowly.

"We did think...for a time, that she was only learning her control," my mother said, frowning with a hint of a pout.

"She was, *is*, abusing it," I said.

"Yes," my mother said, nodding, and I sighed with relief. "Oh, Bryony. You know, you must of course, that I am so relieved you've found your Hunger and your Chosen. There should be no obstacle for you now."

"Aside from attempts on her life, you mean," Grandmother grumbled.

"Well, yes, but I simply can't *imagine*—"

"Don't imagine it, Mother, it happened! My Chosen was stabbed twice—" my mother gasped, clapping her hand over her mouth at this news, "—protecting me. I believe the maid. She was threatened and bullied and forced to this action. I drew the words from her myself, and she was not happy to give them. Powerful people *preyed* on her in an attempt to fashion a weapon against me and—"

"Oh!" My mother began to weep, and I wasn't sure if the sound my grandmother made was a cough or a huff of annoyance.

"They were very nearly successful in doing serious harm to me, my heart if not my actual life," I snapped and exhaled roughly.

"Peony, you and I have discussed, at length, the great amount of misinformation being slipped in our ears," my grandmother began.

"I really do think it might all be a misunderstanding," my mother objected, sniffling.

"Why? Because Thomlinson said so?" Grandmother asked, and my mother sighed and fell silent. "We've given the council too much power. Over Kimmery and possibly over the queen's line."

My mother's face scrunched in thought, turning to the light falling through the slightly shuttered window. "I wish you hadn't passed the crown to me so young."

"You were with child, continuing our line. It was natural," my grandmother said, and they reached for each other, the first moment of quiet and apparently genuine affection. "And look at what you created. Bryony will make a fine queen. She is sharp, she loves Kimmery, and she sees it clearly."

I blushed as they both turned faint smiles to me. Had I ever been offered this kind of praise before? Certainly not from them both. Not when it weighed so heavily on the future.

"What shall I do then, daughter?" my mother asked me softly.

"I have one small request at the moment. I would like my Chosen, Wendell Pope, to be appointed to the council. The crown has no real influence on their number, and I think the link may be a valuable and small change."

"Your Chosen?" Mother frowned and tilted her head at me. "But...wouldn't you rather it was his brother? What if he is busy when you desire him, or his thoughts are occupied with...whatever it is the council manages, rather than with you?"

I laughed, surprised and sudden, and then fell quiet as I realized this was an *actual* concern to my mother. "Wendell is every bit as occupied with what the council is doing as I am, and much better prepared to defend my interests there. I love him dearly, as I do all my Chosen, but I also trust him absolutely. There is no one else I would prefer to take his place."

My mother looked between us, brow furrowing. "But what if you should *need* him while he is in a meeting?" she asked.

I blinked at her, puzzled at the idea that I might be suddenly struck by an immediate urge to fuck Wendell while he was away, and then shrugged softly. "I shall wait."

My mother burst out in giggles, but they faded quickly as she realized I was serious. "What an odd notion, Bryony."

I choked on my scoff, and Grandmother sighed, patting her daughter's hand. "It seems so to me as well, but I am quite convinced of the strength of Bryony's Hunger. And there will always be her other men to occupy her if she grows impatient."

My mother hummed and smiled at that, satisfied with the solution. I bit my tongue. As much as I loved and desired Wendell as easily as breathing, I didn't understand my mother's concern. He was more to me than a convenient body when he suited my mood. My desire for him came from his mind and warm heart first, and longing for him when I didn't have him at hand was a sweet feeling, not an irritating one.

"Very well, I will have Ame—one of my ladies draft a note to Thomlinson to let him know. He's been such a pest lately, so perhaps this will distract him."

"A pest? On what topic?" I asked.

"Oh, what doesn't he want lately," my mother said with a dismissive wave of his hand.

"Is it to do with me? Or with the shifters? Taxes in the north?" I pressed.

"Pft, I barely give it my attention," my mother scoffed.

I ground my jaw, and my grandmother heaved a sigh that quickly turned into a coughing fit that demanded our focus. I wrapped an arm around Grandmother's seizing shoulders, Mother helping to sit her up as she struggled through wheezes and hacks, the sounds growing thinner as she failed to catch a breath.

The door to the bedroom burst open, Vincent rushing for my grandmother. *Magic*, I thought in reflex, as I had with Cresswell when he'd been stabbed. I forgot what Aric had already told me and splayed my fingers against my grandmother's knobby spine. My grandmother needed air, room in her lungs to breathe, and I pushed my power into her skin, through her ribs. I was met with painful, sharp friction. My hand spasmed and cramped, and I yanked it away the moment my grandmother whined.

Aric and Wendell, who had been waiting with the men in the other room, rushed toward me, and I stepped away from the bed, pushing into Aric's chest.

"I forgot! Oh, I forgot the magic," I whispered, staring as Vincent helped my grandmother stretch upright, tipping her chin back. She calmed slowly, tiny gasps catching in her throat, one by one until she could take a full breath.

"It's all right. See, she's recovering," Aric answered against my ear, pressing a kiss to the spot.

My mother clutched Grandmother's hands, eyes fixed desperately on her face, waiting for the fit to pass.

"I'm sorry, Peony," Vincent said gently, pulling my grandmother into his chest as she trembled. "I think that better be all for this morning."

My mother's chin wobbled, and she nodded back at him.

I saw it in a moment—the gentle roundness of Vincent's face a mirror of my mother's, so close to my own too. *Oh*.

There'd never been any real mention of male parentage in the queen's line. A daughter might come from any of a woman's Chosen, but I'd spent no real time with my mother growing up, let alone any of the men at her side. Sometimes, it was almost easy to forget we came from anyone but our mothers. And yet...

There was an earnest affection between Vincent and my grandmother, and it seemed to belong to my mother as well. Was he my grandfather? Who was he, where did he come from? Was he from a noble family like Wendell or the northern country like Owen and Cosmo and Aric?

I whipped around in Aric's arms, finding my mother's three Chosen hovering nearby. I searched their faces now, suddenly curious about my own origins. And Camellia's for that matter.

My mother had mentioned a man's name once. Matthew...or, or...

My search stopped as I found a pair of eyes on mine. I couldn't tell their color from this far away, but I knew their narrow, angled shape, lids heavy and lashes thick.

Michael, I remembered suddenly. I recognized him, although not as well as some of my mother's other Chosen. He wasn't one she had constantly at her side. I wracked my brain, trying to remember if we'd ever spoken, ever even looked at one another this way. Aside from his eyes, a near-exact match to mine with deep crows feet at the corners, I didn't really see any other similarities. I had my mother's face and mouth and dark golden hair, Vincent's features really.

"Come," Wendell whispered, he and Aric ready to shepherd me out of the room.

I pulled myself out of my thoughts and away from my men, rushing back to my grandmother and pressing a long kiss to her clammy cheek. She nodded and waved me away with a roll of her eyes, but she was still struggling to breathe, so I didn't wait for her goodbye.

"Bryony love," my mother murmured, taking my hand as we left my grandmother's chamber together. Her skin was pale, smile not quite as easily full and beatific as usual, but she was recovering from my grandmother's fit quickly. "There is someone I thought I ought to introduce you to."

It was obvious immediately. The man I'd been studying smiled tightly and waited for us as the other Chosen pulled away, and my mother began to bounce on the balls of her feet.

"Your Highness," the man said with a respectful bow of his head. As my mother's Chosen, he wasn't quite my rank as princess, but he also didn't owe me the deference anyone else would.

"Bryony, this is my Chosen Michael. I know it's very silly and I really couldn't say one way or another, but I think there is a likeness, don't you?" she asked, but she was turned to him and not to me.

Michael's smile to my mother was fuller than the one he'd granted me, but I knew those eyes and I didn't think the warmth was reaching there.

"We really aren't supposed to make a fuss about this kind of thing, but I am so proud of you, Bryony. And I thought it might be nice for the two of you to speak," my mother said, teasingly bumping her hip against Michael's.

His eyes glanced in the direction of her other Chosen, and then he stepped and turned, so they could only see his back. His smile brightened then, one hand lifting my mother's knuckles to his lips as he mouthed 'thank you' and winked.

My mother blushed, and I recognized immediately that hazy happiness and tip of her chin right before she called a Chosen to her service. But this time, she shook herself and blinked, glancing at me.

"See Bryony back to her suite, Michael. And then come back to me immediately, won't you? I shall practice *waiting*," she said with a little conspiratorial laugh for me.

I grit my teeth and ignored the urge to wrinkle my nose as my mother bustled to her Chosen. Aric and Wendell stood at either side of me, Wendell's hand resting on my waist and Aric's cupped possessively around the back of my neck.

Michael's smile was benign, and he gestured for me to lead the way. I followed my mother out of my grandmother's suite at a slower pace, letting her hurry her Chosen back to their rooms until they were far enough ahead of us not to overhear. I turned to ask Michael some innocent question, what part of Kimmery he was from, or if he had any interests—outside of making love to my mother, of course—but he beat me to speaking.

"I've always wondered if you might've been mine," he said, still smiling, but I thought I knew the grimace of discomfort wrinkling the corners of his eyes. "We aren't supposed to... Well, a Chosen's duty is to his lady's pleasure."

Aric was practically simmering at my side as we walked, his finger's a comforting kind of pressure on my skin.

"But I...I've been hinting to your mother about you for a number of years," Michael said, his tone light, but his eyes making a constant study of our surroundings. "I'm not one of her favorites. I think Lady Amelia was more indispensable than I am. Of course, that was Lady Amelia's aim."

My lips parted as awareness sank in, cold and heavy. This was not an affectionate first meeting between father and daughter. Of course it wasn't.

"Are there others in my mother's circle who seek to be so indispensable?" I asked softly. There were guards posted, but they were still far away enough not to overhear, and Cresswell had sent Piper with us so he could work with Head Guard Amos for the day.

"Oh, absolutely," Michael said. "Much closer to her ear than I. And all the ladies do their best."

My steps stumbled. No wonder my grandmother and I had such trouble convincing my mother of the council's aims. She had Chosen and ladies-in-waiting feeding her the opposite cause.

I glanced at Wendell and Aric, who both seemed equally as tuned in to the nature of the conversation as I was.

I looked back at Michael. He had a great deal of gray in his hair and a square face, a little full and flushed. He was handsome but maybe plain. If things had been simpler, I might've sat with him over tea and asked him about his family, perhaps my family too. But things weren't simple here in the capital.

"You're not Camellia's father."

"No," he said, certain. "I think that man was excused from your mother's service long ago. He brewed too much friction amongst the others."

I huffed. Sounded about right then for Camellia.

"Your mother wants to see you wear that crown, Bryony. I don't think it will be long before she's ready to pass it to you," Michael said. Wendell sighed next to me, but I kept my gaze fixed on the other man. "And when she does, they will be ready."

Aric's grip tightened, not painfully so, and both he and Wendell stepped in protectively.

Michael stopped in the center of the hall, and so did we. "Keep your head down," he whispered, eyes widening. "Let the council have their way long enough to birth a child and secure your position with an heir. They won't give up their hold on Kimmery."

Aric was ready to snap, and Wendell was his wonderfully stoic and patient self, but neither of their opinions mattered to me at the moment. I had my own.

"They will," I said, lifting my chin and narrowing my own gaze back at this man. Perhaps he was my father by blood, but he was next to nothing to me in reality. "I will pry their fingers away myself."

Michael sighed and shook his head, and his worry seemed sincere. "You don't have the power. You don't have enough hands to manage to hold back all their efforts at the same time. Not with them in your mother's ear. In her bed and constant company. The grip is too strong."

"Then I will cut them away at the knuckle," I snapped.

Michael blanched and stepped back. Aric's throat cleared, and I suspected he was stifling a laugh.

I turned my chin to Wendell and offered him a tight smile. "You are appointed to the council, by the way. By the queen."

Wendell nodded, eyes smiling. It wasn't a surprise to him, we'd already discussed the subject.

"Perhaps I shall appoint Aric to Head Mage next," I mused.

"Don't you dare," Aric growled, laughter in his tone.

I turned back to face Michael, and he had the same kind of confusion in his expression that my mother had worn when I asked for Wendell's place on the council.

"I'll do what I can for you," Michael said, so obviously doubtful that it wasn't really any kind of support.

I shrugged, swallowing all the newly bubbling hopes I might've invented when it came to this man in my life. "Your duty is to your mistress."

He looked thoughtful but nodded, and we walked the rest of the way to my suite in near silence, only exchanging a polite goodbye at the door. I didn't know if Michael felt a fatherly duty to me, if he was lying and trying to get me to ease my battle against the council for their sake, or if his temperament was so similar to my mother's—just wanting to keep the peace for the sake of it.

Wendell shut the door on the hall, and I paced away from them both quickly, scrubbing my face with my hands.

"This place is absurd," Aric snarled, following me closely.

"You really never knew who your father was?" Wendell asked more tenuously.

I could hear footsteps approach, my other Chosen drawing closer at our return. I shook my head, stopping my feet in the center of the room, biting down the urge to scream.

"Truth be told, I never gave it much thought. It wasn't discussed," I muttered.

"Who *raised* you?" Aric bit out, snatching my waist in a firm grip before I could start pacing again.

"Nurses, maids, tutors. My grandmother, when I'd reached an age to be reasoned with."

"Look at me," Aric said, reaching up briefly to snatch my hands from my eyes.

Thao and Cosmo had entered from one end of the room, and Wendell filled them in with a low murmur as Daniel and Owen came in from the other door.

I turned my face up to Aric's, trying to keep my expression steady so he wouldn't have to see the turmoil churning through me. It was a useless effort. Aric could probably feel the magic biting at me, snapping with my temper.

"You know I will obey you," he said. I snorted, and Aric's lips twitched. "Well, within reason. But I swear to you, if you have a child by *any* one of us, I will act as a father to them. And I will positively turn you over my knee and spank you raw if you do not act as a mother."

My eyes filled immediately, stinging and burning, and Aric growled at the sight, tugging me roughly against his chest. His arms wrapped around my back as sobs clawed their way up my chest and into my throat where I bound them behind clamped jaws. The only sound that escaped was a faint and strangled whine.

"Darling girl," Aric whispered in my ear, pressing firm kisses to the side of my face. "For all their carelessness, you really turned out spectacularly."

I could hold in my screams and sobs, but not my sudden and surprised laughter, so they all rushed out in a tangled mess. My arms whipped around Aric's shoulders as he lifted me into a tight squeeze. The others were moving closer, and the door to the suite squeaked.

"Shit, what's happened?" Cresswell growled with one glance at us upon his arrival.

"I'm not sure, but it doesn't matter. Bryony just needs us," Cosmo answered.

"I won't even know where to begin," I moaned to Aric.

"Well I certainly wouldn't either, but I imagine we'll sort our methods out as it goes. We can't do worse than they did." I made a strange noise, a squawk and a sob, and one of Aric's hands reached up to cup the back of my head. "I could've strangled him, but I object to hurting the elderly."

I choked a little and leaned back, Owen's temple touching my cheek as his head bent to kiss my shoulder. Aric was smirking at me, mad humor in his eyes. Strange as it was to admit, Michael probably wasn't a great deal older than Aric.

"I love you," I said.

Aric smiled and leaned in, pressing a kiss to my nose. "We love you too, princess."

11.
COSMO

"**O**h, stars! Daniel!"

I glanced up from my sketch, smiling and flipping the page. Bryony's hands were clutching at Daniel's thick strands, her knees high and bent. Her heels rose off the bed and toes curled in the air as her back arched, breasts tipped sharply and begging the air to be sucked. Daniel wasn't faring much better, hips bucking into nothing as he sucked and licked and feasted on Bryony's sex.

I waited before setting my pencil down on the page again, eyeing the others. Thao and Wendell were kissing and groping one another on a couch by the fire, waiting patiently for their turn with our princess, torturing themselves for fun. Owen was in the bath, washing up from the stables before joining us, and Cresswell stood to the side, eyes too focused on the couple on the bed to really be guarding us.

"How can you stand to be sketching and not touching?" Aric muttered, sitting at my side, his heel jiggling on the floor.

Bryony came again with a bright cry, eyes going wide and hands fisting in the sheets.

"The sounds she makes for him while he does that make me feel as though I should grow a beard," I said, laughing at Aric's almost feral focus on Bryony. "How can you stand to be reading? Sketching *is* like touching."

Vaguely, but it was a tangible experience in my mind, and I knew what I wanted from Bryony this evening. Sketching passed the time until she was ready for me.

"I'm *not* reading," Aric bit out, snapping his book shut.

Bryony scrambled out from under Daniel, yanking him up onto

the bed and pushing him down onto his back. She straddled him quickly, an intense focus fixed to his face as she settled herself onto his cock.

"We ought to make her a saddle for that thing," Aric said.

"I am her saddle," Daniel said with a note of strain in his voice, a faint quirk on his lips. His eyes never left Bryony's.

I snorted and waited till Bryony was fully seated on Daniel's ample length—and girth—before putting my pencil to the page again. This time it was Daniel's face I sketched, the utter rapt attention he gave to our princess, the sudden open devotion he wore.

Daniel was still fairly reticent, hovering at the edges of our numbers, and if it weren't for moments like this when he came suddenly alive under Bryony's attention, I might still resent the man's presence. But the second Bryony turned to Daniel for any reason, he lit up, and it became so obvious that our princess was his entire world.

Aric and Cresswell both moved for the bed, and I watched with interest as Aric deferred to Cresswell's determined pace. Bryony gasped as Cress took the back of her neck in a firm grip, pushing her down chest-to-chest with Daniel.

My pencil froze as Cresswell spread Bryony's ass open to his gaze first, and then his fingers. She squealed, riding Daniel's cock roughly as Cresswell stretched her.

Footsteps slapped against carpet as Thao and Wendell abandoned their post to hurry onto the bed and watch Bryony. I turned the page again, quickly outlining the figures on and around the bed.

Pages and pages of erotic unions, tender embraces, every single feature of Bryony outlined and shaded. Not for the sake of art, not really. I was trying to capture the power of the moments, as if one flat image by my hand might preserve a perfect memory. Except every one of those memories was me on the wrong side of a page. I hadn't learned how to sculpt my favorite flavor—Bryony's sweat and violets. Or the sound of her voice breaking, breathless pleads for mercy and for *more*.

I closed my sketchbook on the attempt, setting it to the side and watching as Cresswell sank himself into Bryony, sandwiching her between his and Daniel's chest, their bodies taking over the rhythm she'd wanted, slowing and extending it to make her tremble.

What kind of artist am I if I'm only interested in one subject? I thought, and I was only really surprised to find there was no note of bitterness. I would never say as much to Bryony. She wouldn't accept it. She still visited me in the studio I'd fashioned in our suite, poking about and quizzing me on projects I had less interest in than she did.

She would balk if I told her the truth. I was hers, her Chosen. I would sketch and sculpt to pass the hours where she was busy wrestling for the reins of Kimmery, just as Owen would tend horses and sneak down to the beach. Wendell had a purpose now that Bryony had positioned him onto the council. Aric spent his time sneaking around the castle for one reason or another. Even Thao was helping navigate Bryony through the public role of being princess and eventually queen. But Owen, Daniel, and I, and probably Cress too, now that he'd surrendered the grip he'd had on his role as her guard, we were Bryony's Chosen in the more traditional sense, waiting for her to call on us for comfort or sex or just company.

I watched them take their turns with her, Thao and Wendell hurrying to take Daniel and Cresswell's place when their will to resist joining Bryony as she came apart failed. Owen returned from the bath, kissing Bryony so senseless, she barely noticed as Aric helped himself to her magic and fashioned vines around her wrists and ankles, suspending her in Thao and Wendell's embrace. The vines bloomed with Bryony's ecstasy, breathed at half-time from her gasps.

I still waited, undressing slowly, kneeling at the edge of the bed, barely able to feel the movement as Thao and Wendell collapsed in heaps and Aric claimed Bryony for himself, urgent and consuming, fucking her to the precipice and then pulling away for Owen to chase her there again, the pair of them taking turns back and forth.

"Please! Please, both of you," Bryony begged, tears glistening at the corners of her eyes.

It was the first sensible words she'd managed since she had

mounted Daniel, and Aric and Owen both raced to obey her, thrusting into her cunt together. Daniel gasped at my side, but Bryony's own shout was obviously one of satisfaction, and Aric and Owen were too close to their own finish to stop once they knew she was fine.

"Why are you abstaining?" Thao whispered in my ear, his arms circling my chest. One teased down to where I was half-hard, and I sighed as his fingers circled my length, stroking me. Aric and Owen were both moving wildly, near their finish.

"I'm not abstaining. I'm just patient," I answered Thao, turning my head and stealing a kiss from his swollen lips.

"He's smart," Wendell added, stretching on the bed and grinning at me. "He's done the math and realized if he's the odd man out, he'll have her to himself."

Thao scowled, and we laughed as Aric let out a great bellow, Owen's own voice swallowed in Bryony's kiss. They lowered Bryony down to the bed with kisses on her skin, limbs still tensing and quavering with aftershocks.

"Wa-wait, where's—" Her voice was slurred, but it pulled my smile higher.

"Here, little muse," I answered.

Bryony sighed and shivered, tried to lift her head, and then immediately gave up. Her body was splayed out, release leaking out of her and painting her inner thighs glossy. I stroked her legs gently as I knelt between them, balancing on my palms to hover over, finally feeling the shine of her smile beaming up at me.

"Where have you been?" she asked.

"Watching."

Bryony pouted, and I leaned down, kissing her swollen bottom lip gently. She was almost never sore, even after demanding more from all of us, but I wanted to bring her down from the high she was drifting on until she was grounded back in the moment with me.

"Was it inspiring?" she teased.

I laughed and sank against her, stroking my cock against her soaked sex and watching her arch and moan. "Very."

Bryony was always inspiring, in any number of ways.

"You look tired," I said, watching the slow blink of her eyes.

She was either sinking under pleasure or exhaustion, but she tried to widen her gaze and look alert at my words, struggling to raise her hand to reach me.

"I've been told I sleep poorly without you," she murmured, and it was stated in a dazed honesty that gutted me, an exquisitely sweet blade.

I'd wanted to draw this out, tease Bryony to begging, but the compliment of her confession left me pressing myself into her swollen and sensitive cunt, my arms circling her back to hold her to me.

Bryony gasped, her sex clenching and sucking me in as she came immediately. I buried my groan against her throat, wrapping my lips over her pounding pulse and sucking on the spot as she rocked weakly into me from below. The bed shifted slightly around us as the others moved, but I was absorbed in Bryony's cries as I pulled nearly out of her and then let gravity and her fluttering walls do the work of drawing me back in again.

"Oh, Cosmo, I love you," Bryony breathed out, voice hitching, and one hand clutching at my back.

You possess me, I thought, but I knew Bryony well enough to know the words would unsettle her. I kissed her instead, tenderly probing, swallowing her sighs. The others had worked her body into an unending loop at the edge, every stroke of my cock making her spasm and gasp. I wouldn't last long with her body demanding I join her this way, but I moved as slowly and steadily as I could, drawing the minutes out. I'd wrap myself around her as she slept and claim those hours, but I wanted this too—this moment of being Bryony's entire world, as she was now and forever mine.

"Mine, little muse," I gasped, a strangled half-version of the thought.

"Yes!" Bryony whimpered.

Her legs wrapped around my hips, heels hooking together to hold herself in place, and the fire of the Hunger licked between us until the heat was burrowing at the base of my spine, shooting warning shots of lightning into my sac.

Bryony's nails dug into my skin as she came again, and I followed her, my teeth claiming her lip as I buried my groan in her kiss, hips finally bucking out of the rhythm I'd set.

If I could've, I would've sculpted this—the mindless moment where I didn't know my own edges, so wholly joined with the woman I loved. I'd seen her tangled up with the others, but I'd always seen the lines of shadow between their limbs, and at that moment I couldn't imagine them between us.

The feeling faded, replaced with Bryony's thighs shaking weakly against my hips, her breasts swelling with her catching breaths, nose nudging against mine. I sighed, and the bed dipped near our hips. I rolled to the side, turning Bryony with me, and Wendell was there with a cloth, Cresswell approaching the bed with a tray of glasses. The world was closing in around us again, and even in the peace of the moment, it drew out a slightly sour note.

And then Bryony's fingers stroked my cheek, drawing my eyes to hers, a king's wealth of love in her stare.

"I love you, muse," I whispered. She nodded, our eyes closing as our foreheads pressed together.

12.
BRYONY

The room was stirring around me, my Chosen taking care to try not to wake me, or at least to let me continue the illusion of sleeping.

"Her ladies-in-waiting arrive today," Daniel whispered on the other side of the room.

"Doesn't matter. Waiting is in their title," Aric answered.

Someone snorted, probably Thao or Wendell, and a faint kiss brushed over my eye. There was a soft scratch of stubble, and I pressed my face into warm skin, finding a sweet and potent scent. Cosmo. My hand clutched a little against his chest, and his fingers covered mine. There was an especially hot and long body at my back, and since there weren't thunderous snores ruffling my hair, I guessed it was Cresswell rather than Owen.

"If you keep pretending to sleep, I will wake you up with my mouth between your thighs," Cosmo whispered warmly. "But you will probably miss the pies I heard Owen mention were waiting for us."

I sat up immediately, my stomach growling, and Cosmo let out that wonderful belly laugh that was so rare.

"They might already be gone by now!" I cried out at Cosmo, wrestling back Cresswell's arm that tried to wrap itself around my waist.

"I think there are a great many," Cosmo said, grinning as the others gaped at me. I was scrambling out from under male limbs and the thin blanket, stark naked, and I gasped as I looked down. There were faint little bruise marks all along my limbs.

And then I blushed and swallowed hard as I remembered the vines Aric had fashioned to hold me up for their taking and the little tendrils that had teased my skin like mouths while I'd been fucked and caressed by my lovers. I looked up, found Aric admiring his work from across the room, and huffed.

"I never underestimate Owen's appetite," I muttered.

And it must've been Wendell who'd laughed at Aric's assessment of ladies-in-waiting because there was no sign of Thao. My lovely prince would absolutely *not* defend my right to breakfast pies.

Daniel picked up a velvet robe from a chair and brought it to me, holding it behind his back and grinning up as I balanced at the edge of our massive bed. He was face height with my breasts, and as I reached out for the robe, his free arm wrapped around my hips, lips helping themselves to my nipples. My Hunger applauded him. My stomach growled in warning.

Daniel laughed and brought me down to my toes on the floor, swinging the robe around my shoulders and leaving me to tie it shut. I marched for the door, and Aric jogged to join me.

"If I'd known what appetite really ruled you, I might not have balked when I discovered you had the Hunger," he said, biting down on his lip to hide his grin as I shot him a glare.

"She ought to be hungry after last night," Cresswell muttered from the bed.

"What do I need to know before Nora and Morgan arrive today?" I asked Wendell, catching his arm so he could escort me to breakfast.

"We've already sorted out their rooms. I suppose you only need to give them some idea of what their duties will be. Dressing is common—"

"Don't you dare," Aric growled at my back.

I laughed at the idea of anyone but one of my Chosen getting the opportunity to undress me, and even Aric had become adept at helping me lace a gown.

"Correspondence, as well, and given who you are likely to be writing to, well..." Wendell shrugged. I was most likely to be writing to Nora and Morgan's family since their male relatives were the men on the council I trusted.

"Grandmother always said I should be hosting soirees and

concerts once I had Chosen," I mused, frowning. "Camellia doesn't, but she's—"

"Feral," Aric supplied.

We reached the small breakfast room in the suite, with its wide windows overlooking the Coraletti Sea, and I nearly growled at the sight of Owen sitting with a plate stacked high with small pies. Perhaps Camellia wasn't the only feral one. Then he smiled at me.

"I saved you breakfast."

"Oh, you are my favorite," I gasped, releasing Wendell and running over to Owen to perch on his lap.

"It was my idea!" Thao gasped, still filling his own plate from the buffet at the side of the room.

"Then I love you both," I said, not bothering with the knife and fork resting on either side of the plate, simply picking the flaky pastry up with my fingers and taking a bite.

"You already did," Thao muttered with great disappointment.

Owen kissed my cheek, leaving a buttery smear, and I grinned around my breakfast, aware that I was not at all the picture of an appropriate princess with food in my fingers, my robe slipping from one bruise spotted shoulder, and my hair a tangled mess. Aric brought me a cup of chocolate and, thief that he was, stole a pie from my plate. Since there were still six remaining and I now had a cup of chocolate, I was inclined to forgive him.

The morning was shining, the sea glittering with heavy waves crashing and sparkling against the shore. My Chosen trickled in, chatting with each other, barely dressed, and I was inclined to play the part of the queen's line princess and ignore my duties for the day in exchange for dragging them all back to bed and repeating our night.

I was, I realized with a note of surprise, genuinely happy in that moment.

And then Cresswell entered the room, still drawing his shirt over his head, with a grave faced Guard Piper at his side. My heart sank as the young man's eyes met mine.

"The dowager queen is asking for you, Your Highness. They say, well—" Piper cleared his throat, and shot a panicked glance at Cresswell.

Clear green eyes, the same shade as the churning sea out the window, met mine. "It's time, Bryony," Cresswell said gently.

The moment fractured, buttery pastry turning to dust on my tongue, dread weighing heavily in my belly.

⚜

THE MORNING DID NOT SHINE in my grandmother's bedchamber, heavy curtains pulled tight, candles resting on the mantle, and still there was a veil placed over my grandmother's eyes to shield her. I didn't know if she was sleeping, I only knelt at her side, my knees numb against the hard floor, counting her breaths and the seconds between.

"What shall I do?" my mother moaned, her fingers twined around my grandmother's, head bent to touch their tangled grip.

Grandmother's breath wheezed.

And at the foot of the bed, standing in the shadows, my sister watched, trembling slightly. I hadn't forgotten I was residing in the castle with Camellia, but ever since Aric had declared we would not be joining the queen for dinner, I'd managed to avoid Camellia and her Chosen. I glanced at her now and found her eyes flicking around the room, hands fisted at her side as if she were searching for an escape.

"Bry-"

It took me a moment to hear the cracking note from my grandmother's lips for what it was—an effort to speak my name. My spine went rigid, and I reached across the blanket, my fingers resting over her sleeve, chilled by how thin the arm inside really was.

"Bryony—" Grandmother's breath strangled.

I shook as I rose. We'd been here together in this room for hours, and I'd barely moved an inch. I sat carefully on the mattress, afraid to jostle her.

"I'm here," I said, surprised by the clarity of my own voice.

Grandmother only breathed for a few minutes, each intake labored, each exhale rattling as if it would be her last. My mother's eyes were fixed to my face, a strangely frozen expression on her face I'd never seen before.

"You..." Grandmother's hand trembled, trying to rise off the bed, landing heavily on her own chest, fingers twitching up to her face.

Carefully and slowly, I reached for the veil over her eyes, drawing it away, waiting for a note of objection. My grandmother's eyes were red, the cold color drowned in burst blood vessels, pupils full and black. I shivered at the sight, shaken and wishing to run from the room.

"You are strong, Bryony," my grandmother said, barely above a whisper, with a sudden, fragile ease. "You won't fail. Kimmery will thrive. I am...so..." Her mouth remained open, eyes blinking. My heart pounded in my chest, my own eyes beginning to blink rapidly, trying to keep my vision clear so that she would know I was listening. "So glad," she said, on an exhale.

My mother let out a garbled little cry, but I was entirely still, staring back at my grandmother, trying to decide if I was imagining the slight tilt of a smile on her lips. Her eyes closed, and my hand clutched at her arm. She couldn't go! I needed her, needed her influence on my mother and her force against the council and...

Oh, wasn't that awful.

I hated myself in that moment, watching my grandmother wither quietly in front of me, dreading the loss of my ally in the battle for Kimmery, but not...

I stood from the bed, stepping back and searching the shadows, ignoring the glint of Camellia's stare.

"Hector, Vincent?" I called.

They moved slowly closer, tears rolling down Hector's face, Vincent's shoulders slumped lowly.

"Please," I whispered, gesturing to the bed for them to take my place. I would want my Chosen at my side if it were me. Stars, I wanted them *now*.

My mother wept into the bedding as Hector and Vincent settled at my grandmother's side, Hector kissing her hand, Vincent her forehead. We waited in the quiet, the seconds piling up between each breath, my head counting them, my own breath trying to match my grandmother's.

It wasn't until my chest burned and my vision went blurry, my head losing track of the count, that I realized another breath wasn't coming. I gasped, swaying in place, and turned away from the bed.

Camellia had backed away too, close enough to the mantle that the tensing of her muscles, the anxious shifting of her feet was clear in the dark room. She looked as though she was about to shatter, but it wasn't sorrow for our loss in her eyes. It was Hunger, and she was going mad with it. Her eyes flicked up to mine, and she bared her teeth at me. My heart stopped in some kinship with my grandmother, and Camellia turned on her heel.

My sister left the room, my mother's cries fading to sniffles, and I sank to my knees, my back leaning against the shuttered curtains, my head empty and echoing with the sound of the ticking clock.

❧

I DIDN'T KNOW if it was my mother or my grandmother's Chosen who informed them, but Aric and Daniel came to find me eventually.

"Come on, princess. They're about to let the vultures in for viewing," Aric murmured.

Daniel scooped me up from the floor with ease, cradling me to his chest, carrying me into the too-bright sitting room where the others waited. I pressed my face into Daniel's shirt to hide my dry cheeks.

"There's a back hall and stairs we can use," Cress said. "I'll show the way."

In the shelter of the dark hall, with no one but my Chosen around to hear me, I lifted my head and searched the shadows for Aric.

"Here, princess," he said, a soft shredded note in his voice.

"Aric, did I hurt her when I tried to use magic to help her?" I asked.

"Of course you didn't!" Cosmo answered immediately, but I waited for us to reach the light of a lamp on the wall, and then pushed against Daniel's shoulder until he set me on my feet again.

Aric's expression was grim, gaze hovering above my head as he remained silent. I thought he might lie to save my feelings, although that wouldn't be like him, but when he finally looked me in the eye, I straightened my shoulders and prepared for the worst.

"No, princess," he said. "I think her own magic reacted defensively, but I don't think your attempt did her any harm."

There was no exact reason to believe Aric, except maybe that I wanted to and that something in his face promised he would've told me an ugly truth, if only because he knew I trusted him.

His hand reached out, fingertips lifting my chin a little higher. "Whatever struck your grandmother ill did harm that couldn't be undone so far along. There are things magic just can't repair."

I let out a shuddering sigh and nodded, and Aric bent a little to kiss my brow.

"Let's go to the suite. Now isn't the time to analyze what happened," Thao said, stepping up and wrapping an arm around my waist, leading me forward and nodding to Cresswell.

I opened my mouth, the question of what it *was* time for on my tongue, and then closed my lips again. The back halls through the castle were long and narrow, but Cresswell appeared to have taken the time to memorize the routes, leading us down a side hall and to a winding staircase until I recognized the wallpaper as a match for what we'd passed after the assassination attempt.

There was a hollow feeling in my stomach, and I realized I had no idea what time it was, how many hours had passed in my grandmother's suite since I'd been called there that morning. It wasn't until Cresswell opened the door into a private resting room in my suite and I caught the notes of feminine voices through another door, that I remembered what today had been.

My back bristled, that feral feeling of the Hunger rising, and I turned and pressed myself against Thao's chest, halting our movement. His arms wrapped around me, patient as I settled myself.

"What's wrong?" he asked.

"I forgot they'd be here." There was a nervous, soft laugh from the next room. Nora, I thought.

"We'll dismiss them," Thao said with a shrug.

I shook my head, pulling away slowly, my eyes drawn down to the floor, strangely shy of the men around me as I headed for the door. I wanted to tell them to wait there so I could deal with my new ladies-in-waiting alone. I was all frayed at the edges, my control unraveled in the wake of my grandmother's death, but I couldn't really leave all my Chosen sitting in a room that was meant for me to retreat in.

The voices died immediately as I stepped into the doorway of my dressing room, and I lifted my eyes to see Nora and Morgan straightening and stepping together, falling into low curtsies. They were already dressed in black, and it struck me that noble families must already have had their mourning garments ready once the news was released of my grandmother's illness.

At the heart of my dressing room was a long wide bench, Nora and Morgan standing on the far side of it, with a great black gown draped across its surface. For me.

"I'm sorry I wasn't here to receive you upon your arrival," I said, my voice sounding far away and echoey.

Nora and Morgan glanced at one another with wide eyes, Nora's pale hands wringing over her dark skirt.

"You don't need to worry about us, Your Highness," Morgan said, obviously taking pains to make her voice sound soft and demure. "We...we laid out a dress for you, but only if you—you don't have to, um...wear it."

I gaped blankly at the dress, none of my thoughts seeming to fire in the right direction. I'd been nervous for these two women to join my service, but now I was barely able to focus on them. On anything for that matter.

"Thank you, that was very thoughtful," Wendell said, joining me at my side, his long fingers sliding against mine and clasping. "You were shown your rooms?"

Morgan and Nora both murmured yes.

"Very good. I think that will be all for today," Wendell said.

My cheeks flushed, the heat of shame burning there, but I couldn't argue, my eyes fixed to the gown on the bench. It was so... ornate, which seemed wrong somehow, as if elegance should matter at the moment.

Fabric rustled as my ladies-in-waiting made a quiet escape, and Wendell's free hand not tangled with mine turned me around so I was facing my Chosen and not the black gown.

"What do I do?" I whispered, frowning.

"You've barely eaten today. You'll take a little supper and a long soak in the bath, and you'll let us read to you," Wendell said, soft and matter of fact.

"There's too much to—"

"Not today," he said more quickly.

My head turned, and Wendell caught my chin. "I don't want to wear that thing."

"It's hideous, where did they find it?" Thao asked and then went silent with a stern glance from Cosmo.

"Six weeks of mourning start tomorrow," Wendell said. "But tonight, you rest."

"Who am I mourning?" My Chosen all looked suddenly stricken, and I shook my head, my voice rising, growing tight. "I don't mean—I *know*, but I... When she...when she died, I thought to myself, 'But who will support me to the crown?' And stars, what kind of thing is that to think when—"

"Oh, Bryony," Cosmo gasped out, rushing forward and wrapping me up in tight arms. "Stop. It's all right."

"She's my grandmother, and all I could think was that I'd lost my best ally!" I cried out. My body was shaking in Cosmo's arms, but everything was so disconnected and I couldn't sort out how the pieces of myself fit together.

"She *was* your best ally," Cosmo said.

"I was political when I should've been—"

"Bryony, when the dowager queen arrived at the Winter Palace, it was obvious the two of you weren't...close," Cosmo said, leaning back and wincing.

The last time I'd seen her, she called me a mutation, I thought vaguely.

"I can honestly say that I am so glad that your relationship improved. Not just for the sake of a crown, but for *you*." Cosmo kissed my cheek for a long pause. "You're not unfeeling, little muse. Any one of us could tell you that. *She* would've told you that."

"You can grieve your ally and your grandmother, darling girl," Aric said, brow furrowed. "There's no organizing these kinds of feelings into the right order. Wendell is right. You need to eat and rest tonight."

"But—"

Aric's lips pressed flat, and as he moved forward, so did the others until I was surrounded by them. "Grief is chaos, princess. One day, not long after Charlotte died, I was so *angry* with her, I couldn't shake it. She should've known better than to let herself get so sick. She was half of what made me the king I was, more than half of what made me the man I was at that time. I was furious and ashamed of myself, but the more I fought my anger, the stronger it grew. Half of mourning is sitting with your own ugly feelings and letting them pass."

"He's right, I went through the same with my mother when she passed," Daniel said, catching my eye. "And you should always remember that none of us here would ever judge you."

Aric's lips twitched, and I glanced at Cosmo, his answering smile tight. "Not for this, certainly," he said.

I closed my eyes and tried to let go of the eerie floating feeling I couldn't shake, of the echo in my head and odd numb turning of my thoughts. And when that didn't work, I simply opened my eyes and accepted that I would have to carry on with them.

"Someone get me out of this dress," I said, and I leaned into my men as they closed in closer, holding me up.

13.
WENDELL

"I am sick to death of this," Thao groaned, glaring at himself in the mirror.

I huffed and glanced around the room to make sure Bryony wasn't here to hear him.

"It's been two weeks, and there hasn't even been a funeral yet," Thao hissed, buttoning up the black vest over his black shirt and trousers.

"There has to be time to allow dignitaries' arrivals," I said, pausing at the sound of girlish laughter from the next room. I caught Thao's smile in the mirror. "Thank stars for them."

Thao nodded, moving to the side as Cosmo joined us in dressing. "I didn't see the need for Bryony to take ladies, but now..."

"It's good for her to have friends," Cosmo finished for him, smiling at me. "Where are the others?"

"Owen and Cress are with Bryony," I answered. "Daniel's gone to check on Lily on Bry's request. Aric's snooping, I think."

"You're looking very formal," Cosmo said, eyeing me up and down, leaning into Thao's side.

I pulled the note from my pocket. "The council is meeting today. Weston wrote me."

"In the mourning period?" Cosmo asked, eyes widening.

I nodded. "I haven't told Bryony yet, I only got the note at breakfast and I..."

"Don't. She's...peaceful this week," Thao said, and I nodded.

Aric had told Bryony that grief was chaos, and she'd seemed to take that to heart for the first days after her grandmother had died, vacillating wildly between a quiet depression and an almost manic energy to *act* or do something. It didn't help that the early half of the mourning period dictated a certain stagnancy that Bryony was disinclined to.

Aric and Thao had accepted the brunt of Bryony's impatience and ire, but sometimes the shots bounced too easily off of them. After one snappish remark had left a stunned Owen pale and silent, Bryony had burst into a fit of weeping and locked herself in her private sitting room until hours later and with no apparent prompting, Morgan Weston had appeared.

"We are playing chess," Morgan had said to our princess, just shy of an order, and then she'd snapped the door shut on our stares.

There was another burst of giggles from the sitting room, one of them distinctly Bryony's, and I checked my appearance in the mirror one last time.

I looked sallow in black, but at least appropriate, and it was unlikely anyone would dare wear any other color at the council meeting.

"Are you nervous?" Cosmo asked, and I knew by his smile that the question was only meant as an invitation.

"I am."

"Why should you be? You have a better sense of justice than any of those fools and more right to be there," Thao said.

I blushed, flattered by his pride, although Thao was unlikely to think anything else. He loved me, and therefore I *must* be the best. His taste would allow for no less.

"Whatever Thomlinson or any of the others think, your presence on the council is Bryony's best coup yet," Cosmo said.

"Not more than her quashing the vote against the shifters," I said.

"You don't think so? She was lucky to even know to arrive for that meeting. Now, with you on the council, she'll always be on top of their schemes."

"You'll make a much better spy than Farraque ever did," Thao whispered, leaning in to kiss below my ear. "Much more handsome too."

"Thank you, my love," I said, trying not to laugh. "I'll be a late spy if I don't leave now though."

"Are you working today or playing games with the others?" Thao asked Cosmo.

"Games, I think. I haven't seen nearly enough of Bryony's smiles since we left the north."

"Save some for me. Hopefully, I'll bring her good news," I said.

We left the room together, and I paused to watch Cosmo and Thao join Bryony. She was seated on a carpet, Owen and Nora on the floor with her, a pile of patterned paper between them. Cresswell sat at Bryony's back, leaning over her like a great wall against anything that might harm her, and Morgan Weston sat on a couch opposite them, her legs folded carelessly under her. She looked up, finding me, and nodded briefly, awareness in her eyes. She must've known from her uncle that there was a council meeting today.

Bryony was lucky to have the two girls as companions, luckier even that they suited her as well as friends as they did allies.

"Wen, aren't you joining us?" Bryony called.

I shook my head, debating on my answer. "I'll be back after lunch though, for whatever entertainment you have then."

She frowned at me, lips parting to no doubt ask where I was going, when Thao picked up one of the folded messes from the floor and waved in front of her nose. "What on earth is this meant to be?" he asked, distracting her as I snuck out of the suite.

I would bring her back good news one way or another, I decided. I wanted to be as good an ally to her as I was a lover, her Chosen.

⚜

"THERE WILL HAVE to be some kind of entertainment after the funeral. Something appropriate of course," Thomlinson said with a wave of his hand. "A feast, no doubt, to sate the nobles and our illustrious guests."

I resisted the urge to roll my eyes. Thomlinson, from what I could tell from the droning and ambling conversation of the meeting thus far, was the kind of man who only took entertainment from gambling, bedding women—specifically ones who had little to say by his own preference—and feasts. Of the three, certainly the latter was the only appropriate offering.

"Speaking of the queen's line," Thomlinson continued, "I have spoken with Her Majesty. Seeing as how she is now taking it upon herself to appoint members to our numbers—"

Eyes glared in my direction, and I stared back at Thomlinson, my hands clenching against my thighs at his slow-growing smile.

"—she felt it would be appropriate to offer us more agency in managing new legislation."

"Meaning?" Sir Weston asked, sitting up sharply.

"Only meaning we need not seek her approval before presenting a bill. We have her trust to do the work we see fit. Obviously, if a *Chosen* may have a seat, we are here to serve our queen and princesses."

Well, fuck.

Two weeks, that was all it had taken. Bryony had taken dinner with her mother just five days ago, and I suspected Thomlinson had wrestled this permission sometime after that, otherwise Bryony probably would've heard about it. I'd wanted to bring my princess good news, and now I was going to have to tell her that her mother had given the council more freedom to do as they pleased. My single vote was not going to turn the tables. I would have to argue in Bryony's stead, and I wasn't sure I'd hold the same influence over these men as she could.

⚘

"It isn't a victory for Thomlinson and his ilk, not really," Jack McCallum reassured me as we walked through the castle halls toward Bryony's suite. "The vote Bryony roused is proof of that alone. The princess must have chosen you to be her mouthpiece."

"She did, but Thomlinson's move is just proof of how much influence the council still has over our queen," I said.

"Most of the men choose to side with whichever party of us is most likely to win the argument," Jack said wryly. "I find it surprising how many of them really have no opinion of their own."

"I find it disheartening," I answered, glancing at him out of the corner of my eye. The viscount was probably only a few years older than I, and there was a constantly shifting quality about him that I thought must've bared some resemblance to his second nature.

"You know you are the first openly two-natured member of the council?" Jack asked.

"It's not quite the same. My tiger is a gift from the prince," I said, shrugging.

"It doesn't make a difference to them," Jack said with a wave of his hand. "They're not likely to forget the size of your teeth the next time a vote comes up."

My laugh was nervous. I didn't want to *intimidate* the council into cooperation, but perhaps Jack was right. I needed to use every available weapon in my arsenal for Bryony.

"I don't think you'll be the last, either," Jack said, more quietly, wearing a half-smile on his lips.

I wanted to ask him more, but we'd just arrived at the suite doors, and there was an unfamiliar guard posted there—one of Cresswell's picks that we were hoping would prove loyal but hadn't really been tested yet. The doors opened, and I gestured for the viscount to enter ahead of me.

"Jack!" Nora McCallum leapt up from her seat by the window and ran for her brother, a beaming smile on her lips.

I spared them a brief glance, but my eyes were immediately caught by Bryony. She stood by the fire, eyes glinting with irritation, spine perfectly straight.

"How was your meeting, my love?" she asked tartly.

Thao was slouching in an armchair, fighting laughter and avoiding my gaze, and the others aside from Aric were all gathered in the room, their eyes flicking between us.

"I didn't want you to worry," I said lamely, crossing to Bryony.

She arched an eyebrow. "Why should I worry?"

I gave the rest of the room my back, shielding Bryony from their view and bowing my head so I could lower my voice. "I only heard this morning, and I didn't want to disrupt the peace you were enjoying. You've had so little of it lately."

Bryony's expression softened, humor bleeding through her annoyance. "Well, thank you, I suppose, although it didn't help when I *did* find out where you were."

I ducked a little lower, and Bryony sighed, lifting her face so I could kiss her. "Apologies."

Bryony leaned into the kiss for another moment, voices

moving on with their conversations behind me as Nora caught her brother up on her entire week. Bryony's lids were heavy as she pulled away, and she softened into the circle of my arms around her, but her eyes widened expectantly.

"Well? You'd better tell me how it went."

I took a deep breath and drew back, tugging Bryony along by the hands and setting her down on the couch between Cosmo and Owen. I sat on the stool across from her, and she sat up straighter, bracing herself.

"Most of the meeting was spent discussing formalities for your grandmother's funeral," I said.

"The council isn't arranging it, are they?" Bryony's nose wrinkled, and she glanced between me and Jack.

I laughed and shook my head. "No, but we're expected to do our best to represent interest to visiting dignitaries on your mother's behalf."

Bryony's lips pursed, and her gaze drifted up with thought. "I'd like to know what interests they're representing and with whom."

I nodded and stroked my thumb over the back of her hand. "I'll go over it all with you. You'll make a stronger impression on other royals than any council member. There's to be a dinner too."

"It's almost certainly better handled in your hands than whomever Thomlinson would've passed the task to," Jack added.

Bryony nodded slowly. "I think a little planning might be a good distraction for me," she said softly.

"Morgan and I can manage the planning if you'd rather not," Nora said brightly, glancing at the other young woman.

Morgan's face twisted uncomfortably—from what I'd seen of her so far, she was more interested in the magical texts Aric set aside, or Owen and Daniel's opinions on horse racing. While Nora was shy around most of us and so obviously eager to please and emulate Bryony, Morgan was unabashedly opinionated, noisy, boisterous, and thoroughly disinterested in every single one of us as any kind of sexual creature. I'd caught her eyeing Bryony and Nora with more interest than she had when Owen had jogged to breakfast shirtless, and aside from her connection to Sir Weston, it was obvious why Bryony was comfortable taking Morgan on as a lady-in-waiting.

"No, I'd like to be involved," Bryony said slowly. "It's something to do now, at least."

I reached forward and took her hands in mine, brushing my thumbs over the smooth backs and raising one to my lips until I had her focus on me again. "You'll make it a beautiful and appropriate occasion. And if you find a moment to speak..."

Bryony laughed and grimaced, but she nodded.

"You do give a compelling speech, Your Highness," Jack said.

I was perversely pleased that Bryony didn't grant him more than a glance. I knew seven was a low number of Chosen for even a princess, let alone one of our queens, but I was oddly jealous at the idea of Bryony taking more of us.

"I hope there was some good news to the meeting," Bryony said, sighing.

Jack's laugh cracked through the quiet, and Bryony's eyes widened on mine as I winced. "That was the good news, love."

"I'll deliver the bad, Pope," Jack offered, joining his sister on a bench facing Bryony. "Thomlinson wheedled permission from your mother for the council to legislate without seeking the crown's approval first."

"What?!" Bryony cried out, trying to stand up. Owen and Cosmo restrained her gently, soothing their hands down her arms.

"Thomlinson said it was only fair if the crown was going to choose who sat on the council," I added, grimacing.

Bryony huffed and rolled her eyes. "One man. My mother put *one* man on the council. And you should've been granted a seat if you wanted one anyway! Oh, how could she?!" Owen's arm covered Bryony's shoulder as she pressed her face into her palms, hunched over with her elbows propped on her skirt. "Of course she did."

"I'm sorry, love," I said softly, for all it could change anything.

"For what it's worth, I do think Wendell's influence with us will carry more than just one vote," Jack said.

"Can't you just convince your mother to abolish the council? It's just a dusty old pack of perverts drinking their livers away," Morgan muttered, and then she shrugged as Jack shot her a look of offended amusement. "Aside from the two of you and my uncle, of course," she added half-heartedly.

"I'd turn every noble family in Kimmery against the crown if I did," Bryony murmured, lifting her face. "I have to... Stars, I don't know what. Get rid of Thomlinson and Roderick? Someone like them will just pop up in their place."

"They have enough support still that uprooting them will create waves," Jack said. "There's no one you could give their position to yet who would hold confidence."

I knew what Bryony needed to do. So did she for that matter. She needed to convince her mother to give the crown up to her so that Queen Peony couldn't grant permissions to the council that would carry serious consequences. So that the magic that was bound up in the castle's conduit might be resolved and allowed to soak back into Kimmery. So that her sister could face her crimes and be appropriately punished for them.

Bryony's eyes met mine, fear thick in her gaze, revealing the whites of her eyes. Her thoughts were in the same place as mine, and I knew perfectly by the slow paling of her cheeks that nothing any one of us might say would convince her she was really ready for that step. Truthfully, I wasn't sure Bryony *was* ready to carry Kimmery entirely on her own shoulders, even if they were the best pair for the kingdom. But she would be soon. She just needed us to push her those few inches further.

"Let me handle the council for you. I won't rest on an argument until I know Kimmery's best interests are safe," I said.

Thao squeezed himself on the stool with me. "If anyone can do it, you know it's our Wen."

Bryony nodded immediately, and I thought there was more gratitude than confidence in her smile, but I would prove myself to her. "Thomlinson will try and bar you as much as he can. And he can't be blind to the fact that we're gaining allies," Bryony said, turning to Jack. "Is there anyone who can be trusted to keep us apprised of conversations taking place outside of meetings?"

"Yes, there's a man I've been using for as much when it comes to two-natured issues," Jack said. "And as it stands, the council can't vote on new measures without every member given the opportunity to vote."

Bryony's smile was tight. "I'm beginning to see my mother's point about why I should rather have my Chosen at my side than chasing the council all around the kingdom."

As poorly timed as it was, Bryony's regret created warmth in my chest, and I tugged her out from between Cosmo and Owen and onto my lap. I rested my chin on her shoulder and let my lips brush against the corner of her jaw, my arms wrapping tight around her waist.

"I promise to serve you perfectly at every opportunity, including this one," I murmured, savoring the shiver of her in my arms.

14.
BRYONY

I paced the floor of my mother's sitting room, Daniel's eyes tracking the line my feet carved through the dense carpet on the floor.

"I don't think that woman even told her I was waiting," I muttered, glancing at the door again.

"We could come back," Daniel offered softly.

I shook my head. "She's just as likely to be *occupied* later as she is now. Or simply not in the mood to see me."

"I think you're making yourself more anxious, pacing like that," Daniel said. His voice was mild, and it occurred to me, a little late, that Daniel usually grew quiet when he was uncomfortable.

It was barely perceptible just by looking at him. If I hadn't grown to know the man from the past few months—his laughter and smiles and the easy drape of him in a chair when he was relaxed and not constantly judging himself and his place in our company—I would've said he was fine. I was learning that stillness and measured volume and tone were Daniel's way of hiding.

I slowed to a stop and then crossed to the armchair where he was seated, perfectly frozen in a tableau of patience. He stiffened as I helped myself to his lap, eyes on my face as I wrapped one arm around his shoulders and gripped at his collar with my free hand, flicking a button open and watching his throat bob with a swallow. He released a soft sigh as my forehead touched his, and together we melted into the cushions of the chair.

"What's wrong?"

"Nothing," he answered immediately.

"Tell me. Or I'll start pacing again," I teased.

"What are you going to say to your mother?" Daniel asked, arms circling me in return, one hand sliding to cup my bottom.

I frowned and lifted my face to look more closely at him. "I... I'm not sure really. I just want her to know what a terrible idea it was to give Thomlinson that permission."

"Is it wise to question the queen like that?"

I blinked at the question, lips parting without an answer ready. It struck me finally that Daniel was tense on my behalf, afraid of what might come from this conversation I was waiting to have with my mother.

"I think...if anything, it might be a waste of time," I said slowly, frowning. I hadn't meant to say as much, but it wasn't untrue. "My mother is too agreeable. She'll agree with me just as she did with Thomlinson."

"Then why come here?"

I hesitated, one finger absently tracing a swirling pattern over the muscle of Daniel's throat. "My grandmother and I agreed that Kimmery's power was moving out of the crown's hands and into the council's. But I don't think she disagreed with the treatment of the two-natured. And I know we had different opinions in regards to Chosen."

Daniel sat up a little at that. "Did you?"

I nodded. "She thought of it as a duty that men should answer, and I think it ought to be something that a woman and her Chosen want equally to share. She believes—believed in the right of the nobility, and to be honest, I'm not sure I do."

"And your mother?"

I took a deep breath and lifted my head to gaze out the window. "I want to believe that my mother's gentle heart would mean that it was impossible for her to approve of the rights of the two-natured being impeded."

Daniel leaned in, kissing my throat, and it was that exact moment that the door to the sitting room opened. Michael—my father, although I wasn't quite ready to think of him as such— entered first, my mother flushed and smiling behind him with two more of her Chosen. They were the same men whom I'd seen with her most often recently, and I remembered Michael's warning about all the voices in my mother's ear. Were these two of them?

"Look at how lovely the pair of you look together. No, don't get up, please!" my mother said as Daniel nearly knocked me off his lap. I pushed him back into place, kissing his frozen mouth before turning on his lap to face my mother. "You weren't waiting too long, were you?"

If she had looked at a clock, she would've known it was over an hour, but I didn't point that out.

"I didn't mean to interrupt your morning—" I absolutely did, "—but I'm afraid..." I hesitated, glancing back at Daniel, mulling over the conversation we'd barely finished. When I turned back to my mother, she was seated prettily between her two Chosen, Michael watching me as one of the other men toyed with Mother's fingers, teasing her and holding her attention.

I'd meant to come and rail at my mother, to try and shake some sense into her. It was never going to work. One of the men at her side would soothe her as soon as I left, reassure her that all her choices had been right in the first place. And because that would certainly be easier to hear than a tirade from me, she would believe them. Force suited me for the council, but it wouldn't serve here.

I took a deep breath, let my shoulders sag, and released the most pathetically pitiful sigh. My mother's head turned at the near whimpering sound, her eyes widening with sympathy.

"Mother, there is something I've learned since I left for the north, and I wonder if you might be able to help me think of a way of fixing it all," I said meekly, dropping my eyes to my lap and wringing my hands. Daniel wrapped supportive arms around me and leaned his head against mine, adding to the act.

"Oh, my darling. You know I will do anything I can," my mother rushed to say.

I wasn't sure I was much of an actress, but I managed to fight the smile that wanted to appear in that moment.

☙❧

DANIEL'S HAND was in mine as we left my mother's suite. "That was neatly handled," he whispered.

"It was manipulative," I said, frowning, unable to shake the greasy feeling in my head after I spent the better part of an hour whining and blinking back tears as I illustrated the two-natured's plight to my mother.

I was more certain than ever that her two nameless Chosen reported to the council because they'd barely restrained their glares. One had even tried to refer to the two-natured as violent beasts.

"Nonsense, I love three and they are the gentlest of men." It was for the best that Cresswell had been waiting for us outside of the suite and not in the room when I'd said that.

Daniel drew us to a stop, and Cresswell framed my back as I faced him. "You know that you captured me with your honesty and integrity," Daniel said, and I brightened. Maybe I had known, but I liked when he told me so. "But manipulation has its place in a kingdom, and your cause wasn't ignoble."

"We don't know for certain she hasn't already changed her mind," I said.

"Thomlinson will wheedle her down," Daniel allowed. "But there was fire in her eyes by the time you were done. And I know exactly where I've seen that look before. Even if she can't bully Thomlinson into undoing every restriction against the two-natured, I am sure she will never allow them to be tagged and corralled as they planned to attempt."

I blushed as Daniel leaned in, kissing my cheekbones on either side.

"I thought you were going to try and get her to change her mind about letting the council raise legislation without her approval?" Cresswell asked. I spun to face him and found him startled and wide-eyed.

"I thought I would, but Daniel reminded me that appeals of kindness and generosity are always more successful with my mother. Since we know the two-natured were the council's most likely target, I decided giving them a defense was better than trying to bully my mother."

"Queen Peony has just vividly expressed her disapproval of the shifters being forced into labor work, and their disproportionate taxation," Daniel said, proud and bright.

Cresswell looked as though I could've knocked him over with a little touch. "Only to us," I said, looking between them. "But I am relieved to know that she seemed unaware of the state of things."

"Bryony this is...this could *change* things," Cresswell said, a slow smile growing.

"We are still relying on her," I whispered, looping an arm into each of theirs and pulling them along with me before anyone in the castle might find an opportunity to eavesdrop on us. "There's a great deal between what my mother just said and her actually doing something about it. Let's just see where her head is at when the funeral comes."

Cresswell was about to say more, when Head Guard Amos appeared ahead of us in the hall.

"Your Highness," he said with a quick bow. "I was wondering if you had a moment."

"Of course."

"It's Miss Johns. Lily," he added at my blank stare.

Cresswell and Daniel both stiffened on either side of me. "Oh!"

"Did she escape?" Cresswell barked.

I wanted to laugh at the obvious offense Amos took at the question, but I didn't think it would make him any less annoyed if I started giggling.

"Of course not," the older man said. "It's just...I wonder if Your Highness has considered the matter of what to do with the girl. She is with child, and there's been no mention of a trial or..."

Or execution. My heart sank at the very idea.

"Your mother was made aware of her questioning and imprisonment, but I haven't had any questions from Her Majesty, and as it stands, you are... Well, at the moment, we are the ones who know where she is held. It's not how things are generally done, but I thought I ought to inquire if you had any opinions regarding her fate."

"I have several, as a matter of fact," I said, mind racing. Cresswell was going to kill me for quite a few of them, I suspected. "Could you take me to see her?"

"Us," Cresswell corrected, not relaxing as I soothed a hand over his arm.

"Of course, Your Highness," Amos said, bowing and then gesturing for us to follow.

"You don't have to come, if you don't want to," I said to Daniel. He'd checked on Lily a couple of times for me already, and I knew he held a kind of sympathy for the girl. He'd been manipulated by nobility himself, and I suspected Lily's plight reminded him of his mother as well.

"No, I want to," Daniel said, gravity and worry softening his tone again.

I nodded, and together we followed Head Guard Amos through the castle.

Lily Johns was kept in an entirely different part of the dungeons now. The light in the halls was brighter, there were no echoes of men's voices moaning from within dank cells, and the guard in the hall was seated until we reached him, a book open on a small table with a small plate of food. Still, her door was locked and the window of her small but comfortable room was high and narrow. She startled as the key turned, and I watched her through the small slitted window on the door, her hands trembling as she smoothed her skirt and stood.

"Oh! Your—Your Highness!" Lily sank into a low curtsey, her face paling at my arrival. "I was not—I did not expect..."

She wobbled in place, head shaking a little. They had found her a new dress, taking away the maid's uniform, and the waist was tight around her middle, the start of her swelling belly now apparent. Her hair was braided down her back, a pretty shade of auburn.

"I'm sorry to surprise you, Lily. Please, sit."

She stood straight, arms covering her stomach, and looked between the four of us, eyes wide and terrified. "Have you... Is my fate decided then?" she whispered, looking to Head Guard Amos.

"Not quite," I answered. "And some of it depends on you."

Lily swallowed hard, eyes welling with tears and blinking quickly. "Please, Your Highness. Please, just let the babe be born— Please, don't—"

"You're not going to be executed," I said quickly, my own voice catching as I hurried for the young woman.

She flinched at my approach, but she didn't pull away as I reached for her arms. I let her go immediately, realizing that the last time I'd touched her, I had forced her to confess truths she almost certainly would've preferred to remain secret, regardless of what it might mean for her life.

"I won't make you speak as I did before, just please, come sit with me," I said more gently, guiding her to the bed.

Cresswell was close behind me, taking the small chair from the little table in the corner and drawing it closer to where Lily was fidgeting and watching me. I sat across from her and met her eyes, waiting for the Hunger's warning. It didn't come. This girl had stabbed Cresswell right in front of me, but my magic didn't see her as a threat now. If anything, I suspected I was the predator between the two of us.

"The Goddards have fled Kimmery, Lily," I said. "There won't be a place for you there, and I'm afraid what they promised you is impossible now."

"Of course, Your Highness. I can't go back to service at all now, I shouldn't think," she said, those tears rising again and choking her voice.

"Well...you could. If you were serving someone who understood your situation." I hadn't really known what I would do until I found myself sitting across from Lily, meeting her eyes. Cresswell was almost certainly going to strangle me. "I would like for you to stay here in the palace as my personal maid."

"What?!" It came from three directions, and when I glanced over my shoulder it was clear that Daniel, who was leaning against the wall and smiling patiently back at me, was the only one who wasn't horrified by the suggestion.

"Bryony," Cresswell growled, and I ignored him.

"Obviously, arrangements will need to be made for when your child comes," I began.

"Your Highness, I could never," Lily said, quite breathless and pale, so much so, I was afraid she might faint. "I tried to kill you!"

"Not very *well*," I said in a small voice.

Cresswell yanked me up from the seat, spinning me to face him and glowering down at me.

"I can attest to her determination, Bryony," Cresswell snarled, arching an eyebrow.

I winced and nodded. "I know, of course. And believe me, if I thought she was a threat, you *know* I wouldn't be offering this," I answered, willing him to understand me. "You know I'm not that forgiving, Cress."

He frowned, eyes narrowing, remembering the morning he'd tried to persuade me not to kill Emory myself.

"This is...not quite the leniency I imagined, Your Highness," Amos said slowly, watching us all.

"It's not really what I would imagine either, but I do think it is the safest option both for Lily and myself. No one will be able to punish her or influence her, especially not if she is being guarded and in my company. You will have to work within my suite, I think," I said to Lily as I reached out and placed my hand over Cresswell's chest. His heartbeat drummed under my palm.

"Think of what will happen to her," I whispered to him.

"It's not my duty to think of her," Cresswell answered, but I could see his frown turning thoughtful.

"Your duty, my *Chosen*, is your love for me." I rose to my toes, smiling against Cresswell's glaring stare, and pressed my lips to his.

"My love for you drives my need to keep you alive," Cresswell muttered into the kiss, but he sighed as I pulled away and turned to face Amos. "What do you think?"

"I think we might assure both Your Highness' and Miss Johns' safety outside of this arrangement," Amos said, glancing between us. "But if you're determined—"

"I am." I was close to determined, if not absolutely.

"Then I will ensure you have no cause to regret it," Amos said. He stepped forward to Lily, not really intimidating but undeniably threatening by his stature alone. "If you ever try to harm so much as a hair on anyone in the princess's court and company—"

"I won't, I swear it! I don't ever want to see a knife again!"

"I will have the entire guard escort you to the gallows myself," Amos finished, glowering down at the girl who began to cry with some mix of relief and terror.

"I swear to be good, I really do."

"This is a risk, Your Highness. And not one I'm sure you'll find especially fruitful," Amos said.

He was right. Even if Lily was obedient and loyal and trustworthy, what was I gaining but a maid with a child? One who would certainly need more care and attention from her than I did. But as

I looked at Lily, who was trying to contain her sniffles, a hand pressed flat and protectively over her rounded stomach, it was relief and not worry rushing through me. I was doing this because I didn't want this girl to fall prey to any more men or women who would use her for ill, because I was stronger than she, and I could use my own strength to offer protection, even without gain.

"I understand," I said, nodding.

"You're giving me gray hairs," Cresswell whispered in my ear as Amos told Lily that she would be attended by a guard—for my sake more than hers, I suspected.

"I think you'll look very handsome with gray hairs," I whispered back, trying not to smirk at his answering snarl.

15.
THAO

On the morning of the funeral, I found Bryony seated at the long vanity in her dressing room, her new maid twisting her curls up in an intricate style. There was a guard stationed closely, watching every shifting of the maid's hands, but Bryony was staring blankly into the mirror.

Even her robe is black now, I noted with a frown. We'd reached the tail end of full mourning, and I was sick to death of seeing Bryony in black. It made her look eerily pale, and I'd caught her more than once glancing down at her own skirt during dinner or a game, her face falling as she remembered that her grandmother was dead.

It was earlier than she usually rose from bed, and one of the rare times she'd snuck away without waking one of us.

I waited for the skittish maid to finish pinning a curl before knocking on the frame of the doorway. Bryony could've had the door closed to us, but she never did, just as Aric never shut the door on his study, where an unfortunate number of sounds and smells always seemed to be created. We were all open to one another now, a bond forged quickly and powerfully between the eight of us.

The maid jumped and the guard spared me a glance, but Bryony remained lost in her own head until I crossed the room, pushing a spare pouf closer to her seat and nudging her hip with my knee.

"Should I leave, Your Highness?" the maid asked, and I wasn't sure if she was speaking to me or Bryony, but we both shook our heads.

"Did you eat?" I asked.

Bryony blinked slowly at me. "I don't think I can this morning."

I opened my mouth to chide her and then fell silent as her hand lifted from her lap and fell into mine, fingers turned up and waiting. It took me longer than it should have to clasp her hand in mine, startled by the gesture.

"Be at my side today. I don't...I don't know how to behave. And there will be crowds," she said, wincing.

"Of course."

I hadn't given it much thought, but I'd assumed she would want Aric, Cresswell, Owen...actually, I'd assumed Bryony would want anyone but me at her side today. Bryony and I teased one another, played with and flirted and fucked one another. We *enjoyed* one another, but I'd never really felt that she *needed* me. I opened my mouth, wanting to address the idea, and then closed it again. She had enough on her mind without having to reassure me of my place with her.

"In my experience, your people will want to offer you sympathy. You don't need to perform for them or console them," I said, trying to remember my mother and father's behavior when my grandmother had died when I was younger. "Be genuine, as you always are. Emotion is not undignified, and I don't think stoicism is unsympathetic either, under the circumstances."

Bryony's gaze was fixed to my face, her fingers close around mine.

"It's good that we have our own carriage," I said.

"Camellia's will be behind ours in the parade," Bryony said. "And since there are only seven of you, I won't have to leave anyone here at the castle like she will."

"Have you considered leaving Aric here?" I asked, lips twitching.

Bryony's eyes narrowed at me, but there was a glint of amusement in them. "I have not."

"He might prove useful in an empty castle," I continued, shrugging and rolling my eyes. "And the crowd may mistake him for your grandmother's Chosen."

Bryony's laugh was sudden and awkward. "Stop! That's not

true. Well, maybe the bit about letting him snoop while everyone's away. But no, I want you all with me, please."

I nodded and hid my smile as I ducked my head, kissing the back of her hand. "The funeral and the parade will be simple. You *are* prepared for this, Bryony. You don't need to worry."

"I spent all my life learning from tutors and my grandmother how I should behave. Now that she's gone, it feels as though it's all been erased," Bryony breathed out.

I leaned in as the maid finished Bryony's hair, and she and the guard slipped out of the room, leaving me alone with my princess. "Nobility and grace can be taught, but you have those traits naturally. I think you would give your grandmother a great deal of pride today no matter what."

Bryony's eyes blinked rapidly, a soft shudder running through her shoulders until I drew her out of her seat and into my arms. "I never imagined that I would feel so...unmoored without her. I can't imagine..." Bryony cursed and tucked her face against my throat. "I am still thinking of how to become queen, today of all days."

"You're ambitious," I said shrugging. "If you were a Mennarian prince, you'd be applauded for it, regardless of the occasion."

Bryony sighed and went quiet.

I tugged on her hand as I stood from the pouf. "Come. I'll dress you, and we'll walk through the gardens until it's time to leave."

"It's still winter," she said, lips quirking a little.

"You like winter. I'll manage."

Bryony nodded, but instead of moving away, she only wrapped her arms around me, sinking against my chest. A soft shuffling sound came from the doorway, and I looked over Bryony's head to see Cosmo peeking in, dark curls rumpled with sleep. I nodded toward Bryony's black gown, and Cosmo crossed to the dress, lifting it up to cradle in his arms as he joined us.

"I just want this week to pass," Bryony murmured, glancing back at Cosmo.

"It will, little muse."

It might feel like an eternity in the meantime, but yes, it would pass.

Together, Cosmo and I dressed Bryony between us, moving her gently into her sleeves, tightening the laces on the corset she hated so much. Cosmo's quick fingers navigated the buttons up her spine as Bryony's cheek rested on my chest. I wanted my warrior queen back.

❧

THE ROYAL TOMB was full of bodies, and every scuff of a shoe and soft clearing of a throat seemed amplified as it floated up to bounce back and forth against the high marble arches. The volume was high, even with the funeral's audience all speaking at whispers. Bryony and I had separated briefly to do our part bending the ear of nobles, and I was on my way through the crowd to her when a vaguely familiar face snagged my gaze.

Victor—no, Vincent. One of the remaining Chosen of the now deceased dowager queen. He looked a little lost in the crowd, eyes searching, and my chest squeezed dully. He was probably only looking for the other, Hector, but there was a distance in the look that made me wonder if he knew what to do with himself without his mistress. Would I know what to do without Wendell or Bryony?

I drifted to him unconsciously, and his face smoothed, a faint smile rising at my approach.

"Your Highness," he said with a soft bow.

"My condolences," I answered with one of my own.

He released half a sigh, nodding, and then held the rest of the breath, eyes scanning the room again. "I had enough time to prepare myself, and yet..." He trailed off, swallowing hard.

"What...what will you do now?" I asked, my own eyes traveling to Bryony. What if something were to happen to her? We knew now that the Chosen didn't take part in their daughter's life and that most of the queen's line used them as a tool for relief in some fashion. Would we all be discarded from Kimmery?

"Her Majesty has offered me a seat on the council," Vincent said with a slight wrinkle of his nose. "Not to my taste, but it was a request from Violet and I do want to be of some help to the princess."

"And Hector?"

Vincent smiled at me, head tipping. "They don't kick us out, Your Highness."

I wasn't too proud to breathe a sigh of relief. Wendell and I would've managed, I supposed, but to be ripped away from the others too after losing Bryony? I was surprised by how distasteful it sounded. I didn't want to return to Mennary, even in my occasional homesickness.

"I am all the family Heck has left. He'll remain in the castle with me," Vincent said with a nod.

"Bryony will be glad to hear it," I said. Perhaps a little more to hear that Vincent would be representing some of her grandmother's voice on the council, but she was more tenderhearted than she gave herself credit for too. And then, as if it was her voice speaking through me, I offered, "The two of you should take dinner with us when it suits you."

Vincent brightened a little. "We'd be very happy to do so, I'm sure. Ah! I see Hector."

I saw Bryony too, searching the room for me, and I made my goodbyes to the older Chosen, heading for my princess.

"Incoming," I murmured, dipping my head down to Bryony's ear, my eyes narrowed on the tall man approaching us from the opposite direction.

Bryony's vague gaze turned to follow my stare, and I glanced down to watch her shift between confusion and then a sudden and surprising embarrassment. Color rushed into her cheeks, and her eyes flicked away from the man and back again. He was tall, handsome, and fairer than Wendell. He was also irritatingly familiar looking, although I couldn't place why.

"Your Highness," the man said, and I studied the many medals on his dark jacket as he bowed shallowly.

"Prince Holden," Bryony said with an equally shallow curtsey, her lips twisting nervously as they both rose. "How...how very kind of you to travel so far. And so soon after..."

It clicked at last, and I let out an inappropriate choking sound as I struggled not to laugh. Here was one of the fools Bryony had dismissed so abruptly after her choosing ceremony. I searched the crowd around me and jerked my head as I found Wendell, urging him to us.

"Holden, did you ever even leave Kimmery?" I asked, and I smiled through Bryony's elbow jamming lightly into my ribs.

The prince glared back at me. "I did, although I feel I've spent more time on that road this year than at home."

Bryony's blush deepened as Wendell joined us, wrapping an arm around her waist and gaining Holden's glare. "I really do apologize for my confusion at the choosing, Your Highness. I was quite overwhelmed and—"

If it had been me, I would've been wholly disarmed by Bryony's delicate sweetness—or at least I liked to think so—but Holden only puffed his chest and raised his stare above her head.

"My family still desires a friendly alliance with Kimmery, and so I'm back to try my luck with the younger princess. They say *she* is amenable," Prince Holden declared. "And that she has much appetite."

"Camellia?" Bryony said in a barely restrained squawk.

"Unless it is your intention to take on more Chosen of royal blood?" Holden finally stared down at Bryony.

For half a second, I tried to imagine how we would fit this man into our number. Bryony would tame him, no doubt, just as she had with Aric, Daniel, and I. He was proud like I had been, and prejudiced against her just as Aric was. He was also apparently desperate to have a better position than a lesser prince of a small and unprosperous kingdom.

"It is not," Bryony answered crisply, chin high, and Wendell and I shared a brief glance of relief.

Holden's jaw gritted, and he nodded once. "Ah, I see her now, excuse me."

Bryony's eyes widened as he marched away. "Oh dear, do you think we should warn him?"

"I think he deserves what he gets," I said in a low mutter.

"This may become a bit of a scene," Wendell whispered. "Your sister is..."

We turned and watched Prince Holden approach Camellia, who was, quite publicly, holding one of her Chosen and forcing him to rut her up against a marble pillar.

"She looks...ill almost," Wendell added as we watched Holden weaving his way through the crowd.

"Not ill," Bryony said darkly. "Holden is right. Camellia has a great deal of *appetite*. Less and less of anything else it seems."

I'd taken as little notice of Camellia as I could, but the girl did seem to be changing. She was paler than I remembered, and she'd been visibly tense all through the public parade and funeral as if she'd made her best effort to restrain herself up until now.

"Should we do something? Urge them somewhere more private?" Wendell asked, frowning. "People are taking notice."

"No, let her make a fool of herself," I answered.

"She had some princes in her first batch of Chosen, but they left within a few months," Bryony murmured, frowning and watching. Camellia's head tossed in something between pleasure and frustration. It was obvious the moment she caught sight of Holden's approach. "Look at them, he doesn't even realize he's the prey rather than the predator."

"If she kills him, there will be war," I said in a low warning.

Bryony's expression hardened and grew thoughtful. "Well...she can't do it in one night can she?"

Wendell twitched, gaping at her. "You want to let her take him in the hopes that she will harm him?"

"We need more witnesses to Camellia's cruelty," Bryony whispered.

Camellia's arm reached out, sudden and making anyone close by skitter away, wives dragging back their husbands. Anyone but Holden. Holden approached her, entirely fearless. Ignorant. A moment later, Camellia had him in her clutches as he pushed her and her Chosen into a further off shadowy corner.

"He may be too proud," I warned Bryony, turning her away from the scene.

She hummed and nodded. "We need some way to keep an eye on things in her suite. Bribery maybe? A maid? Or a guard?"

"Cunning woman," Wendell said with a grin, wrapping Bryony's arm around his. "Look to your mother."

I looked too, found Bryony's mother still staring in Camellia's direction, a knot of tension marring the queen's normally smooth forehead.

"Look to Thomlinson," Bryony said with a snort.

The man was near the queen, which was probably to be expected, and he appeared equally as perturbed by Camellia as Bryony's mother. Good. His choice of princess made him look like a fool.

"We're nearly done for the day," I said, smoothing my hand over Bryony's shoulders. "Accept a few more condolences with dignity, and you'll do your grandmother proud."

Bryony straightened under my touch, and she nodded, Wendell guiding us to where a few councilmen—ones whose support was still up in the air, I noted—stood with two foreign ambassadors.

⚜

"THE DINNER WAS GOOD," Bryony murmured, eyelids heavy as Owen rubbed the soles of her feet.

We were gathered together in the suite's lounge, the moon high in the sky and only a fire in the fireplace to light the room. Morgan and Nora had already been dismissed, so it was only us Chosen with our exhausted princess.

"You mean aside from the interruptions of your sister?" Aric asked, his head tipped to rest on the back of the couch, fingers working tension out of his temples.

Bryony's head rested on my chest. The laces of her dress were undone, corset slipped out from beneath the dress in some kind of feminine magic trick.

"Camellia's appetite for cock didn't seem to impress some of the council," Cosmo said with a shrug, sipping on a glass of brandy, his bare feet propped up on a decorative table.

"Or the queen," Daniel added, nodding.

"I don't want to think of her," Bryony whispered, and we all fell silent. Her fingertips picked at the weave of my shirt, and I placed a hand over hers, stilling the movement. A minute of quiet later, and her trembles started, little sniffles soon following.

"Your grandmother would be proud of you today, Mistress," Owen said, bending down and pushing Bryony's skirt up enough for him to kiss her shin.

Bryony shuddered and nodded against me. "I know," she said, words choked with tears.

"It's late. There'll be more visiting and opportunities for politics tomorrow," Wendell said, rising from his chair.

"You should get some rest," Cresswell said, moving for the door to the bedroom.

Bryony nodded again, but her hand pressed to my chest. "I'll come in. In a few minutes."

One by one, the others took the gentle cue, heading for the bedroom to wait for Bryony to come in and be bundled up in the arms of whomever could claim her first. I watched them go, my heart drumming slowly beneath Bryony's firm hand that held me in place. Had I angered her? Or aroused her? Or was she merely comfortable here and wanting privacy and a good lap to mourn on?

"I'll be in soon," Bryony said to Owen, who hesitated longest. He smiled at me, a secretive look I wasn't sure I could really read, and then stood and left us.

Even after we were alone, Bryony remained in place, her sniffling slowing and growing quiet, her hand still holding me in place. I relaxed, my arms already looped around her waist, and I lowered my cheek to the top of her head.

"Will you take the pins out?" Bryony asked.

I smiled. This was usually Cosmo's job, and it was one I coveted. I reached one hand up, searching blindly for the thin pins, working them gently out of Bryony's hair as she sighed and softened fully against me.

"Thank you."

"Any time," I said, shrugging a little beneath her.

"No. I meant...for today."

Oh. My fingers paused in their work, spinning one soft curl around my thumb as I resisted the urge to preen under her thanks. "I did very little."

Bryony chuckled and pushed herself up, half her hair loose over her shoulder, eyes crinkled with her smile and a little red from crying. "It's not like you to resist praise," she said.

That was true, and I was about as clueless as Bryony as to the cause, so I went back to searching for pins as I thought. "I promised you my loyalty as an ally when you first took me and

Wendell on as Chosen," I said, ignoring the pinch of discomfort in my chest as Bryony frowned in response. "And I promised you my deference and obedience—"

"Thao," Bryony said, a little ache in her voice.

I pressed my thumb over her lips to quiet her and then pulled the last pin free, accidentally snagging a strand and soothing the spot. I sat up, Bryony still perched on my legs which had gone somewhat numb, not that I cared. We were nose to nose, our eyes shifting back and forth to meet one another.

"I promised you that when you reminded me of my place in your court. But I will stand by you whenever you need me to, not out of loyalty or obedience, but out of love."

Bryony's smile bloomed, even as she glared at me. "You drew that out on purpose."

"I did," I said, grinning back before leaning in to nip at her lip, combing my fingers through her hair until it draped over her back. Her dress was loose, one shoulder slipping off to expose smooth skin, and I tugged on the sleeve to reveal a little more.

"Anytime I felt lost today, I just looked to you and tried to model myself after you," Bryony said.

"You're joking."

"I'm not! You said I have grace and dignity, but so do you, and I think it comes more innately to you. So thank you," she repeated slowly, leaning in and kissing a path down from my brow to the end of my nose, "for standing at my side today."

"You're very welcome."

She pulled her arm free from the fallen sleeve and wrapped it around the back of my neck, twisting on her seat to face me, gaze warm and catching a little of the warm glitter of the fire. "I have another confession to make," she said, arching her neck for me as I hunted for the spot on her throat that made her shiver as I dragged my bite across the spot.

"Mmm, what is that?" I asked.

"Camellia is not the only one who struggled to contain the Hunger today." Bryony circled her hips over mine in emphasis, and we both groaned. "I know it sounds strange, it was Grandmother's funeral but—"

"It's part of you," I said, the old refrain we always seemed to be reminding her of.

I pushed down the other sleeve until she dragged her arm free, the bodice of the dress falling away to reveal Bryony's pert breasts. I pressed my hands to her shoulder blades, her back arching in offering. My lips landed delicately over the pillowy flesh, Bryony's sigh musical and her body growing heavier in my grip.

"I can take you in to the others," I offered weakly before sucking one nipple between my lips, swirling my tongue over the puckered flesh.

"Not yet," Bryony gasped, rocking on my lap, my cock rising to her call, the throb sweet and painful all at once, begging for the same relief my princess wanted. Bryony's hands braced against the back of the chair, and she sat up straighter, lifting off me slightly. She smiled as I gazed up at her, a great tangle of skirts and fabric dividing us.

She slid off my lap and held my gaze as she pushed the heavy black fabric of her dress off her hips first, and then ruffling black underskirts, and finally the slip until she stood only in black silk stockings.

"Those too," I said, unbuttoning my own shirt as Bryony arched an eyebrow at me.

She shimmied out of the stockings, her eyes on my shoulders. She liked my tattoos and made a game of tracing the lines with her tongue when we were in the mood for slow seductions. I suspected tonight was not one of those moments.

"That's enough," she gasped as I pushed my trousers down to my thighs.

I opened my mouth to argue, but Bryony was already kicking away her skirts and climbing back onto the chair, straddling my lap and pressing herself against my chest, forcing me to lean back and crane my neck to stare up at her.

"I love you too," she said, girlish, sweet, and utterly disarming.

Then she took me in hand and sank directly down onto my cock, dense slick heat seeming to swallow me whole. I groaned, my eyes falling shut and all the breath rushing out of me as Bryony seated herself to the hilt, her own soft moan pressed open-mouthed to my cheek.

"Wicked, wanton girl," I rasped, nuzzling against her throat.

"Yes," she agreed, hands on the back of the chair, her body already beginning the eager work of riding me.

"You're going to rule all of Kimmery the way you do your Chosen," I said, grasping her hips and making the rhythm rougher, more urgent, our skin slapping together as I bucked up to meet her, the grasp of her dizzying.

"With a great deal of sex?" Bryony giggled.

"With absolute devotion," I growled, and then I took her mouth with my own, fucking it as roughly as she did me.

Bryony's hands moved from the chair to my back, nails digging in as I wrapped her up tighter, took control of our union, grinding my hips into her pelvis. The chair rocked and thumped beneath us, and I buried my snarls into the kiss until Bryony pulled away with a gasp. Her head fell back, eyes shut and mouth parted, releasing soft cries and whimpers to the air.

I didn't have the others' patience or their interest in Bryony's pleasured agony. I wanted her relief as much as my own, wanted to throw her over the edge and have her drag me there with her.

Bryony's nails coursed my back, the anxiety and tension of the day released with the fight and play of our fucking. I bit her throat, her shoulder, down to her breast, until Bryony grew louder, my name high on her voice, declaring me as the man who was occupying her every thought in the moment. Pride was always my weak spot.

I shoved one hand between us, my bucking turning into a determined rocking, my fingers searching for Bryony's clit. She let out a garbled yell and squeezed tight around me, and I teased and tortured the spot until she was shaking, trying to escape bliss.

Her hands slipped into my hair, tightening and tugging as she came, our chests sticking together as her breaths stuttered. And like the animal I sometimes was, I took my princess down to the carpet, covering her softening form with my still rigid one.

"Yes, Thao, come for me," Bryony sighed.

I fucked her roughly, chasing my own end, and Bryony arched her hips into mine until we were fused and I was crumbling, fire in my blood, and a roar buried against her throat.

Her scratches were hot on my back, her breath damp on my

cheek, thighs still trembling against my weary hips. One hand loosened from my hair, and Bryony's touch was sharp with magic as she reached for my back.

"Leave them," I said, nipping at her jaw.

"I didn't mean to," Bryony said, running a finger over the raised marks she'd left on my skin.

"Mmm, I don't mind." I blinked heavily, wondering if Bryony minded my weight pinning her in place, but she seemed content in the spot, and I didn't want to separate yet. "You would make a good tiger," I said absently.

Bryony laughed and then stiffened beneath me.

I pressed my elbows in the carpet, lifting enough to see her face. It was shadowy and warm from the fire, but her eyes were wide, cheeks still flushed.

"Did you—"

"Would you—"

We spoke over one another, and both stopped abruptly.

"It's something I've been thinking of," I admitted, smiling as her lips rounded in surprise. "Would you like my bite? To be a tiger, that is?"

"I—but...Wendell?"

I shifted, and Bryony's hands tightened on me until she realized I was moving her with me, shifting up on my knees and pulling her up to my lap. "It won't change anything between Wendell and myself. And I did mention it to him."

I thought I caught a glimpse of excitement in Bryony's face, but she stamped it down quickly. "We don't know how it would work with my magic, so I imagine Aric will have a lot to say about the idea."

I nodded and shrugged. "It isn't his decision. It's yours. But it is a large one."

"Princess, King of Thieves, and tiger seems like a lot of roles to play," Bryony said softly, gaze going distant.

I was surprised to find I wasn't injured by her hesitation. It was a great honor to be offered the gift of my family's bite, and not one that anyone usually refused. But Bryony was right. The combination of the tiger's magic and her own might have unknown results.

"Think on it. The choice won't go anywhere. You, on the other hand, are going somewhere."

"Am I?" Bryony laughed as I grunted, lifting her up from the floor with me, still wrapped around my body.

"Indeed. To bed. To sleep here in my arms, until someone wrestles you away, I suppose."

Bryony's arms tightened around my shoulders, and I secured my arms more firmly around her waist. They could try.

16.
BRYONY

While I have some support here—Scrapper's behaving while others are around, although he takes every private opportunity to tell me how shit it's all going—the simple matter is the court's king is away and some men have their heads too far up their own asses to fall in line. We're losing more members of our court than we're gaining.

I sighed and set Griffin's latest letter aside, pushing back from my writing desk and raking my fingers through my hair. Wind beat at the tall windows of the room, rattling the glass. The day was gray, dark tangled clouds gathering, and waves growing tall and frothy white before slamming against the shore.

"What's wrong, princess?" Aric asked.

I looked around the room, making sure Morgan and Nora weren't nearby, before crossing to curl up in Aric's lap where he was sitting in an armchair by the fire. "I've been feeling like a useless princess since my grandmother died, and now I appear to be an equally useless king."

Aric grunted and set aside his book, taking Griffin's letter from my hand and reading it himself. "I lost a quarter of the court when I first took it. Emory would've lost a great deal more. This isn't unexpected."

"The difference is that you were *there*."

"Did you want to be King of Thieves, princess?" Aric asked, looking up at me.

I paused, my mind going blank for a moment. "Well, no. I was just trying to keep your head on your neck. But now that I am..."

"You want to give up the life of the crown princess, move back north, and live as a rogue with seven men crowded together in a room above a tavern?"

I smirked at Aric. "I know you think it sounds like a nightmare to have us all in your den, but actually, that's not an unappealing picture you're painting for me."

Aric laughed and tossed the letter aside. "I'll write to Griffin if you like, give her a little advice. And I think you should reconcile yourself to the idea of giving up one crown for the other."

"Mmm, I suppose you're right," I said, wiggling down to nestle into Aric's chest.

"Are you getting comfortable?"

"Are you complaining?"

"Weren't you just saying you felt like a useless princess?"

"Ah, thank you, my love, for reminding me."

Aric laughed again and sat up, jostling me. "While you've been moping, I've been sitting and having a think."

"You really are too sweet," I snapped, sitting up, annoyed by how Aric's humor seemed to infect me even when it was at my own expense.

"Are you feeling well-stocked on magic?" Aric asked, and I nodded. "Good. I'd like to take you to speak with the mages."

"The royal mages?!"

Aric gave me a wry look. "I could take you out into the street to find some local ones, but I doubt it'll do us much good."

"You're in a rare mood, you know that?"

Aric grinned. "Maybe the rich food agrees with me. Come on. We'll grab Cress so he doesn't feel left out."

Meaning we'd have to take Cresswell anyway or he'd panic when he realized I wasn't in the suite. "Is it safe for me to go near the conduit you found?"

"I think so. I resisted its pull. I'm assuming you can too. But if you feel the slightest bit uncertain, we'll leave."

I stopped my feet as Aric tugged me toward the door. "Wait, I'm not dressed to see royal mages."

"How on earth should you be dressed? You're not indecent," Aric said, frowning as he looked me up and down.

I laughed. With high mourning at an end, I had a little leniency in what I wore, and I'd given up the heavy black gowns and underskirts in favor of the simpler clothing I'd worn in the north, still in black. To Aric, there was probably only a distinction between my being dressed for public and being dressed—or undressed—for my Chosen. He might've been right too, more formal garb would be a reminder to the mages that I was their princess, rather than someone they might safely discuss magical theory with.

"Fine, you're right. Let's go."

We'd moved bedroom furniture out of one of the spare rooms, creating a sort of office for Cresswell and a bit of a break room for the guards assigned to me. We found my bear there, playing cards.

"Aye, of course you leave now while you're winning," an older man griped, but he stood and bowed to me and shook Cresswell's hand before we left.

"The mages might not let you in," Aric warned him. "They'll have enough complaints about Bryony and I barging in."

"They will if I tell them to," I said, lifting my chin high as we marched to the far wing of the castle near my mother's suites.

"You trust these men?" Cresswell asked Aric.

"Stars, no! Well, with Bryony's safety, yes," Aric rushed as Cress bristled. "With Kimmery's magic...no. Two of them don't even trust themselves with it. But Simon will be there today. He's a halfway decent magician and curious enough that he'd be willing to listen."

I couldn't remember ever coming to the mage's hall before, at least not intentionally, and before my own Hunger had grown, I never would've noticed the slow pulse of magic that echoed from the large double doors.

"You feel it?" Aric asked me as my steps slowed.

I nodded. "I don't get much tug, though. I'm just very aware. It's funny to me that I never felt these things before."

"Most Kimmerians wouldn't. The first step of learning to use magic is learning to sense it, and your Hunger creates your advantage," Aric said. "Now, let me see what they've tried this time to keep me out. Feels like Nathan's work...ahh, and a bit of knot this time?"

I turned and shared a private smile with Cresswell as Aric brightened over his puzzle.

"This might take a bit of time," Aric warned.

"May I try something?" I asked, smiling and trying to appear innocent.

Aric frowned and glanced at me over his shoulder. "Try...? I suppose you might."

I nodded and waited for him to step aside. I didn't know even a quarter of the charms and spells and structures as Aric, but I didn't really need to. *I am the source*, I thought, pressing one hand over the lock and taking the knob with the other. There was magic in the door, yes, but it wasn't as fresh and eager as my own. Aric wanted me to show these mages a demonstration so I needed to save most of my power, but I spared a little then, letting it leak into the door and the seam where the mage's charm held.

"Well that's just not fair," Aric muttered, but he grinned at me with pride as the spell grew muddled with the touch of my magic, like hot water dissolving thick honey until the two blended together.

The knob turned, and I bounced into the room on light feet, delighted with my own victory.

"Oh, now what do you wa—Ahh!"

The young man who'd come storming in to find me nearly toppled over in surprise, but I didn't pay him any attention, transfixed by the sight in front of me. My Hunger rose, not in arousal, but in something like jealousy or anger. Here was power, glowing and gilding and *dense*. Not just my mother's, but generations of the queen's line's magic all mixed together and trapped in glittering facets of this conduit.

"Bryony," Aric said.

"Who made this?" I snapped out, looking directly to the young man, who'd gone pale and frozen at my arrival. "Who created this? Whose idea was it to take *our* power and let you men hoard it like some greedy wasteful creatures?"

"N-N-Nathan!" the young man howled.

I stiffened as a gentle palm rested on my shoulder and then sighed as Aric drew me back from the prism in its cage at the heart of the room.

"I'm fine," I said, a little breathless, but I turned to face him so he would know I was still here with him, and not overtaken.

"Ah, Chosen. Now you've done it."

I spun and found two more men in the opposite doorway, one elderly and annoyed, the other middle-aged and smirking at Aric.

"He's-he's brought *one of them* here, Nathan!" the young stammering man cried.

"I see that, Kenneth," Nathan, the eldest mage snapped.

Aric was right, these men didn't look at all as I imagined mages to look. And not one of them had so much as bowed since my arrival.

"Martin," said the third man. That must've been—

"Simon," Aric greeted with a nod of his head.

"And Your Highness, welcome," Simon added to me, tipping forward in a jaunty maneuver. He was a stocky man, with unruly hair in shades of blond and red and gray, and a beard that actually looked as though he'd burnt the end and not bothered trimming it since.

"Sir!" Kenneth cried.

"Oh, go and get back to counting stores, Ken. She's not going to make the palace explode just by seeing the conduit," Simon barked at the younger man.

"She *broke* the ward," Kenneth snapped back.

"Seeing as how that was my little test, I don't see why you're so offended," Simon answered back.

"Enough! The both of you. Your Highness, how may we assist you and see you on your way again?"

Aric was shaking with barely repressed laughter, and Nathan's cheeks darkened as his own impertinence caught up with his good sense.

"That is to say—"

Aric cleared his throat before I could think of the right way of cutting this mage down to size. "I am, as usual, to blame for the disruption. I thought the princess and I might speak to you on the nature of the source."

"Absolutely not," Nathan said as Kenneth gasped.

"Sounds like a better use of my time than recording this week's temperature," Simon said with a shrug, earning a glare from the others.

Angered by Nathan's words and Kenneth's expectation that at any moment I might set the roof caving in on them, I acted impulsively. Aric would have his revenge on me later, but that was half the fun.

I reached for the prism conduit, the magic thrumming in response, a brief tug of war between my Hunger and the prism's.

"Your Highness, no!" Nathan cried, eyes widening and feet stumbling forward.

I reached into my pocket with my other hand, pulling out a pocket watch I'd tucked away there.

"Bryony!" Aric and Cress both snapped.

But I was already a current of magic, greedily stealing a great mass from the conduit and letting it rush through me. It wasn't as comfortable as my own, more electric, like when Aric had placed glamours to disguise me, but it didn't hurt, and there was a kind of harmony to my magic and what I'd taken from the prism. We were related after all, this magic and I.

The pocket watch in my palm whirred and clinked and disassembled in my palm, the men's eyes going wide. Kenneth overcame his fear and rushed closer, held back from me by Aric's arm. The pieces of cogs and metal multiplied until there were too many to hold in one hand. I cupped my palms together as the collection grew and pieced itself together in new ways, aimlessly guided by my own petty spite for the mages and their rudeness.

I knelt and at last, the men bowed, their eyes tracking the creations in my hand. Three little miniature men. One tall and thin and gawkish. One stooped and toddling with a cane. One rounded and leaning back with his belly displayed proudly. Three golden mechanical mages marching about in useless circles on the tiled floor as their inspiration watched from above.

"Clever," Aric said, a soft, relieved whoosh of air accompanying his praise. A hand dangled in offering out of the corner of my eye, and I reached for it, letting him pull me up and into his side.

"I'm fine," I said softly. "I took more than I really needed so those little buggers aren't likely to stop anytime soon."

Simon was the first to recover after the miniature clockwork Kenneth marched determinedly into the toe of his boot over and over. He did so with a roar of laughter, standing up straight and slapping his thigh as Kenneth and Nathan continued to gape.

"You—you can't just..." Nathan trailed off, undecided on what I could not do.

Simon grinned, bending over to send little Kenneth in the real Kenneth's direction before picking up his own replica. "How much intention did you have?"

I startled, realizing he was speaking to me even, as he set the Simon toy into his palm. The little golden man sat down with thick legs hanging over Simon's fingers, kicking aimlessly.

"None to start, and then only a little," I admitted, embarrassment starting to outweigh indignation. "I was showing off."

"I should say so," Nathan hissed, but he was fixated on the toys and not me.

Simon plucked the toy in his hand by its arm and then raised it to the air, shaking it roughly. It clinked and rattled a little, but when he returned it to his palm, it was every bit as calm as before. "At least you didn't breathe real life into it, although I think it's safe to say, Your Highness, this is work no mage could manage."

I glanced at Aric, and he nodded to me, clearing his throat and drawing their attention. "I...I could. Not as Bryony did, with a whim, but with a great deal of intention and magic moving from her to me directly."

For some reason, unknown to me, this made Kenneth stare at me in absolute horror, before wailing and taking off to the door from which he'd appeared. It slammed shut behind him, and Simon sighed, looking to Nathan.

"I see. I *see*," Nathan said. "Very dangerous, I should think."

Simon hummed and shrugged. "With a dangerous intention. Not everyone has one, Nathan. And in the right situation, dangerous can be a positive."

"What would be created *without* intention, though?" Nathan continued.

"I could show you."

The men both turned to me again, and I had a feeling they'd forgotten me in the brief conversation.

"While I was at the Winter Palace, much of the magic did its own work until Aric taught me how to contain and control it."

"She transformed the palace and the grounds. Brought an abandoned orchard back to life," Cresswell said, taking my hand in his.

"The Winter Palace...the north!" Simon barked, staring at Aric, who nodded.

"You could send Kenneth to get a soil sample. Everywhere north of Indiva is fairly rich with a healthy stock of magic."

Simon wheeled around to Nathan again. "I told you! I told you those kinds of harvests don't come by chance."

"We have a theory about the harvests," I said.

Simon threw a grin in my direction. "Oh, Your Highness. I love a good theory."

⁂

I'D REFRESHED DRIED flowers to fresh and gilded their glass vases. Cleared the foggy windows with a careful sprinkle of power and soaked a cryptic project of Simon's, which Aric had referred to as 'mostly safe,' with a good supply of magic. I'd cluttered the mage's office with magic and only gone back to the conduit to take a more careful supply once more.

"The conduit was fashioned by one of Kimmery's best mages, Ambald Ymfrey," Nathan said slowly, rolling a glittering marble around the surface of his work table. It held a scene of the palace tucked delicately inside that I'd made upon his request.

"That name sounds more Dunsany than Kimmerian, doesn't it?" I asked.

"She's very clever," Simon said to Aric, and he grinned back as I shot him a glare.

"There were rumors he was foreign," Nathan said, nodding. "Very ambitious man, very experimental. Great favorite of the queen and council's."

I sat up sharply. "The council?"

"Indeed. They had just started managing appointments of mages on the queen's behalf," Nathan said. "And they took a great interest in Ambald's work with the conduit."

"I'll just bet they did," Aric muttered, leaning forward at my side. "You have his notes?"

"Of course," Nathan said stiffly.

"Head Mage Hawes, in all your theory and research, haven't you ever wondered if the magic, the *source*, is meant to be rich in

Kimmery?" I asked, my hands clasped in my lap as I leaned forward to catch Nathan's eye. "We've found texts and records that show that the queens of Kimmery took great care to visit the north, to participate in the harvest festivals, just as I did. The north has only suffered so greatly since that tradition ended. Since the council has taken such responsibilities!"

"Even the samples of the past fifty years here in the south have changed, Nathan," Simon said, and I was glad he was taking care to speak more gently. It seemed like the two men had a companionably antagonistic relationship usually, but at least Nathan was willing to listen.

"Mages aren't learning nearly the work they were when I was younger," Nathan murmured.

"And it's the council appointing the teachers at the royal academy," Simon said, guiding the other man.

"In every breath of magic, and every intentional act, I have never seen Bryony's power do harm," Aric said.

I flashed him a look, thinking of the crown of blades I'd fashioned. But Aric was right, the magic had only done what I'd needed to protect myself. I'd been the one to commit the violence, and I was wholly conscious during the act.

"The conduit has generations of queen's magic in its facets. How much was it *really* meant to hold?" I asked.

Nathan and Simon shared a significant look and I wanted to scramble between them and demand an explanation, but Aric's hand on my shoulder held me in place until they were ready to speak.

"We've had concerns about how long it would remain stable," Simon said.

Nathan rushed to speak over him. "We can't simply release that excess of power into the capital all at once! It needs to be contained in some fashion!"

"Of course not," I said, more to assuage Nathan's temper than whether or not I really agreed. "But I can take power out of that conduit. Store it in another. What access to the source does the royal academy have?"

Nathan perked up at that, and Simon winked in approval at me.

"Ley stones could be fashioned and buried, a slower way of putting some of the magic back into the ground. Place them in the most fallow areas," Aric said, helping himself to a piece of parchment and a convenient inkwell.

"We will send Kenneth to the north for your samples," Nathan said, sitting up in his chair, a kind of fierce brightness in his gaze behind the smudged spectacles. "Better to have him out of our hair while we make decisions anyway."

"I'll set my experiments aside. This sounds like more fun," Simon agreed.

"Gentleman, may I recommend you not mention your new efforts to the council?" I asked.

Nathan made a soft sound of dismissal. "Thomlinson doesn't bother with us. And he knows next to nothing of what we do."

"We'll send him in the wrong direction if anything comes up," Simon said with a nod. "We'll likely need your help when it comes time to unload the conduit, princess."

"*If,*" Nathan muttered.

"Aric and I will assist in any way you require," I said brightly, trying to subdue the glee of triumph rushing through me.

Nathan, for all his shift in temperament, was eager to shoo me and my Chosen out of his office after that, as he tugged down one old hand-bound notebook after another and Simon made goodbyes to us on behalf of both of them. In the main room, the three golden toys wandered aimlessly about, although I got the sense that the Simon toy was antagonizing the Kenneth.

"Do you think they'll stay true?" I asked Aric as we hurried back to the suite.

"Simon will keep at Nathan. I will too, for that matter. They train royal mages how *not* to use magic, but the man's a scholar and a new route of thinking will be good for him," Aric said. "What's important in my mind is that you can take back from the conduit. Even if we have to play thieves in the night, I'm determined to take that thing apart. And look, I snagged Ambauld's notebook."

I laughed and bounced on my toes as Aric pulled a black leather notebook from the inside of his coat.

"He'll notice that won't he?" Cresswell asked, frowning.

"I'll make my own notes tonight and take it back tomorrow.

Don't mind me, royal guard," Aric answered, smirking at Cress, who huffed and rolled his eyes. "You *were* very successful with them, Bryony. You should go and celebrate."

"You mean I should avoid distracting you now that you have a new toy?" I asked, nodding at the notebook. "Very well. Cress, let's find Morgan. It's been ages since I've done any fencing, and I heard her boasting the other day."

17.
OWEN

The morning seemed brighter just for seeing Bryony in a shade other than black. She twisted in front of the mirror, examining herself in a deep shade of blue-gray, brow furrowed in concentration.

"Don't know how you can make that face. Seeing you always makes me smile," I said, sitting at the edge of the bed, and watching her.

Bryony spun, that smile I loved so well finally blooming, and she bounded over to me, climbing onto my bare lap, all the folds and flounces of silk draping across my legs.

"It might be a bit of a feminine tradition to frown at oneself in a mirror," Bryony said shrugging. "I was thinking I might like to change some of the fashions, and wondering if that wasn't very vapid, considering the state of the kingdom."

"If you can change fashions and restore Kimmery's prosperity all in one year, I don't see why it should matter," I said with a shrug.

Bryony's smile softened, and she melted into me, her arms wrapping around my neck. "Very well spoken, my love."

Her mouth landed on my jaw, and I stretched for her kisses and nibbles, groaning as the presses grew longer, wetter. I was ready to fall back onto the bed and drag her down with me when the door squeaked.

Another squeak followed, girlish and startled. "Oh! My apologies—"

The door snapped shut again, and Bryony pulled away with a giggle. "Poor Nora, I've scandalized her three times this week. No room is safe."

"Certainly not our bedroom," I reasoned.

"It was probably the only room she hadn't caught me in yet, I can't blame her. But it means she has my tea ready."

I nodded as Bryony slid away, the chill of the room helping cool the fever of arousal that had risen up. "Have you spoken to her yet about...you know?"

Her second nature, just like her brother's.

"Not yet," Bryony said, stroking a fingertip over her bottom lip. "I can't decide if we're both dancing around it. Or if I might accidentally surprise her and leave her feeling caught."

"She knows she's safe with you," I said. "Jack would've told her."

We'd seen a little of Nora's brother, the viscount, coming and going with council business. I was surprised by how well I liked the man, considering he had such a fancy title. I wondered if a second nature kept a high man down to earth. Wendell was like that too, although Thao really wasn't.

Bryony nodded absently, moving for the door and then glancing back at me. Sweet warmth took over her features. "Speaking of the two-natured, I have a task for you and Cresswell if you're willing."

"Of course," I said.

Bryony arched an eyebrow at me, her smile going mischievous. "You'll have to be dressed for it, Owen."

I glanced down and grinned at my own nudity. "Just making sure you didn't need me first."

Bryony giggled and ran for the sitting room door. She shut it behind her, and a murmur of conversation filtered through. Good, maybe she'd talk to Nora while she waited for me. I had a feeling Jack was a fox shifter, but I wasn't certain about Nora yet, although I thought she might've been some kind of bird.

When I was younger, unaware of my own extra senses, I hadn't been able to tell the second natures apart, but I was learning with time. Nora's was faint, delicate, and a bit nervous. Jack's had more strength and a predator's hunger, but it was still nothing compared to the great boom of Cresswell as he took a step or the hollow belly hunger he had when he looked at Bryony.

I dressed quickly, forgoing some of the fine clothes that had started to appear in my small collection for a soft, warm pair of pants and a loose linen shirt. I hesitated in the wardrobe, and then went ahead and borrowed one of Thao's sweaters. It'd be worth it just to see the pinched expression on his face as I returned it to him.

Bryony was sipping her tea in the windowsill, chatting with Nora, who sat curled up in an armchair and who blushed deeply as I entered the room, her eyes refusing to land on me. I didn't know if Nora was naturally shy of men, or if she was just suitably aware of Bryony's possessive habits, but I was happy for my mistress that she'd found a friend she could be comfortable with.

"You look just right for what I need from you today," Bryony said smiling at me. "Cress has gone to change into plain clothes."

"Are we running an errand?" I asked.

"Not an errand exactly, but I am sending you into the city," Bryony said. "Word is thin from Griffin these days, and I feel out of touch with the two-natured. I was hoping..."

I picked up as she trailed off, not minding the thought of revealing my extra talent to Nora. "You want me to see if I can find some in the city?"

"Owen has an extra gift," Bryony said softly to Nora, whose eyes widened. "He can sense second natures."

"Oh! That's—well—"

"I mostly ignore it," I said to Nora. "Feels like prying."

She sighed and nodded, but her face turned down to her lap, where her hands were twisting together. Bryony would soothe her once they were alone.

"If you can find a community, Cresswell might be able to work his way into the conversation," Bryony said. "See how people are feeling, what their concerns are."

I smiled at Bryony. "Feeling like you've run out of things to do?" I asked.

"Stopping this from becoming worse is not the same as fixing what was wrong to begin with," Bryony said. "Destroying the council's attempt at a new bill doesn't make up for what the two-natured already suffer."

"They'll be in hiding." Nora looked up from her lap, glancing between us. "Any two-natured in the capital, they probably won't be registered. Most of the work moves the families north, and it's easier to hide farther from the council."

Bryony hummed, her focus glued to Nora as she nodded. "That's a good point. You think it's a fruitless mission to send Cresswell to speak to them?"

"Not fruitless but dangerous, perhaps," Nora said softly. "Any you might find on the street...well, they'd want to know how you discovered them, wouldn't they?"

Bryony looked to me, her eyes growing wide. "Of course. Of course, you're right. And two-natured in hiding won't like the idea of a man being able to spot them out from yards away."

Nora nodded again, more quickly, sitting up straighter. "They'll assume it's a trap of some kind. It won't help if anyone is able to recognize Cress or Owen as your Chosen."

"And we just rode at your side in a carriage during the funeral parade," I said to Bryony.

She groaned and slouched back in her chair with a huff. "Damn."

"Your Highness, if I might be...well, honest," Nora said with her own huff, "you have a great deal of support amongst the shifters. I-my—"

"Your brother," Bryony murmured gently.

Nora's lips pressed together, and she nodded. "You have his support and he's very involved. And it isn't just him."

"My friend Griffin," Bryony said.

"You know Griffin?" Nora asked, brightening and eyes glowing. "Oh! I haven't seen her in ages. No wonder Jack trusts you so, he is very—well, never mind that. It's enough to say that the two-natured know you have their interests. It's simply a matter of when you may act on them."

Bryony sighed and nodded. "Which just brings us back to the crown. As usual."

I studied Bryony. She was getting weary of the chase, and I think she only saw a brick wall ahead of her when I was sure she was really facing dozens of pathways to the throne. Enough to overwhelm her.

"Did Sam say there were other two-natured amongst Camellia's Chosen?" I asked.

Bryony nodded absently, picking at her bottom lip. "But Camellia is running through them. Who knows where those men ended—Oh! We do. Amos said there were some in the dungeons didn't he?" I shrugged as Bryony stood, expression growing sharp and predatory. "Then I think we should go and visit them. If Camellia threw them in there, I'm sure they must have *something* interesting to say."

❧

"I TOOK the liberty of moving them into...better accommodations, Your Highness," Head Guard Amos said, leading the way into the dungeons.

Bryony's hand was in mine, Cresswell on her other side, his eyes carefully scanning the hall, ever the guard.

"Have they seen doctors?" Bryony asked.

Amos nodded, "With great improvement, for the most part. Their bodies are healing, at least."

Bryony's fingers tightened around mine at what was unspoken. Not unlike Sam, I suspected that Camellia's former Chosen were a long way from healing their own minds.

"Is it safe for you to speak to them?" I asked Bryony, and Cresswell stood straighter at her side.

"You'll take every precaution," Cresswell said.

Bryony nodded. "I will. Owen will you...be able to tell from outside the door?"

"I think so."

"He can go in with Amos," Cresswell said, and Bryony's lips pursed with her own unspoken objection.

I raised her hand to my lips, kissing her knuckles to hide my smile. She wouldn't like me taking any risks she too wasn't allowed to take.

"As I am not a small, fierce, blonde princess, I think it will be safe for me," I said and grinned as she rolled her eyes.

Bryony leaned around me and Cress as we arrived in a brighter, more open hall. "This is where Lily was held."

"Yes, Your Highness. These were originally intended for nobility. I would've kept the Goddards here if they hadn't fled the country."

Our steps slowed as we approached a door, Bryony rising to her toes briefly to glance inside the grate. She grimaced and turned away quickly, looking at me.

"Igor. Do you get anything?"

I released her hand and stepped closer. The man inside—who was pleasuring himself in a way that seemed a bit bored and compulsive—was familiar. He'd been one of the ones Camellia had brought with her to the Winter Palace. His head turned, eyes skimming aimlessly over mine as his hips began to buck.

I leaned away, frowning and shaking my head. "Just a man as far as I can tell. Is he...okay?"

"He does that a lot," Amos said flatly, glancing at Bryony. "I wouldn't recommend we alert him to your presence."

She nodded and swallowed, staying intentionally quiet as we passed. "I always thought Igor suited Camellia. He was a bit aggressive. What crime did he commit?"

"Tried to kill another Chosen. It was the dowager who sentenced him here," Amos answered.

Bryony paled and glanced back at the door, where faint snarling sounds were filtering through. "Is it the Hunger doing this to them?" Bryony whispered, more to herself than us. Her brow furrowed with concern, and her shoulders drew up a little higher. "Amos, do you know if there is any...pattern of aggression rising amongst Chosen who have been serving for a long time?"

"Bryony, you don't think—" Cresswell started, reaching for her, even as she held herself tighter.

But I knew my mistress, and if there was a way for her to worry over others, she would find it.

"No pattern, Your Highness," Amos said. "Just individuals."

"Bryony," I murmured, reaching slowly for her chin, turning her gently toward me and bending down so I could whisper only to her. "You're not corrupting us."

"But—"

"If the Hunger is corrupting your sister or her Chosen, it is because there is something in them that feeds that," I said, holding her gaze, seeing the hope catch in the colors until they warmed a little.

"Like after...when I felt so angry and ready to snap," she whispered back.

"It makes sense. But you resisted that anger and you let us care for you the way you care for us." I leaned in and kissed Bryony's forehead, the warmth of her sigh caressing my jaw.

"And Camellia has never resisted a bad impulse when she could revel in it instead," Bryony muttered.

Amos had turned himself respectfully away from us, but Cresswell moved in to frame Bryony's back, his hands stroking her shoulders and body bowing so he could kiss the crown of her head.

"Igor may have to pay for his crimes. Or at least visit some kind of sanitorium where they can determine what are his own impulses and what Camellia might've driven him to," Cresswell said.

Bryony nodded and relaxed between us. "All right. Who is next?"

"Here, Your Highness."

I walked up to the door where Amos waited, and I was still a foot away when I got the first hint. The urge to run struck me, the frustration of being caged, restlessness, and depression. I frowned and looked through the small window to the cell. If I hadn't already been certain that the man inside was two-natured, I would've been simply by the expression on his face. There was a small, narrow window high on the wall, but the man was tall enough to see out of it, and he leaned there against the brick as if he'd been there for days already, eyes turned out to the yard with pure longing.

I glanced back at Bryony, chest aching for the animal inside the room, if not the man, and nodded.

"His crime?" Bryony whispered.

"Trying to kill the princess," Amos said with a wince.

"Oh dear," Bryony murmured.

"Why?" I whispered, moving back to her. "Why 'oh dear'?"

"It's just...that's not a light crime, Owen. I'm not likely to be able to get a pardon for him."

"But Camellia, she—"

"I know," Bryony said quickly, nodding. "I know. And his testimony will be valuable, but even then it might not be enough. Go on, we'd better hear his reasons first before anything else."

"He hasn't spoken much," Amos said to me. "You might be able to get him to open up."

"We'll stay out here," Cresswell said, which seemed more like a reminder to Bryony than to me and Amos.

For a moment, I wondered how much help I could really be where Amos had already struggled. I looked to Bryony and rather than her worry, I found her warm smile and confident nod. My princess had faith in me, and so I simply *wouldn't* fail her, even if I had to spend days sitting and talking with this man.

Amos opened the cell, and I followed him in, but the man at the window didn't so much as blink.

"Atticus Darby, this is Owen Dunne," Amos said.

"Have you picked a date?"

"You haven't been sentenced yet, Darby," Amos answered easily, and I realized the man, Atticus, was asking about his own execution.

He turned, and I got a better look at him. He was tall, bone-thin, and haggard as Sam had been, with a long face and hair the color of mud with an ample peppering of silver.

"Why not?" Atticus asked, ignoring me. "I confessed. I'd try again. Why not sentence me?"

"You never told me why—"

"Because I wanted to. I want to see that woman dead," Atticus said, without inflection.

"Do you really want to die without ever getting the chance to run again?" I asked.

That stirred life in the man. He didn't look much older than me. He might even have been younger, but there was a century of weariness in him, and every minute of it flinched at my question.

"What?"

I nodded to the window. "You miss it. More than that, you might as well already be dead without being back out there. Back in the fields, running, *breathing* again."

The fields were a guess, just a sense. He felt grounded, rather than flighty, and I'd never met a two-natured that belonged to the sea, although that might've been because I was in the north.

"Who are you?" Atticus asked, standing straighter, his hands fisting at his side.

"Owen Dunne. Princess Bryony's Chosen."

Atticus's head cocked, eyes narrowing as they flicked between me and Amos. "You're two-natured."

"No, but my friend Sam is," I said, and Atticus's eyes widened. "And I know how much it hurt him while he couldn't fly."

"Sam?" Atticus breathed. "Sam, you know—*couldn't* fly?"

I nodded and brightened. "My mistress healed him."

There was a scuffle at the doorway, and I wasn't the least bit surprised when Bryony entered the cell, Cress's arm around her waist as he half-heartedly tried to wrestle her back.

"Not without you and Aric I didn't," Bryony said, smiling at me.

Atticus stood straighter, movement sudden, and Amos was about to jump between us when the man bowed.

"Your Highness, I heard from your sister what you did for the two-natured. She raged over your defeat of the council. I didn't know about Sam too, but I am so..." Atticus stood again swallowing hard, losing the words of gratitude as his eyes dropped from Bryony to the floor again.

"Mr. Darby, did Camellia hurt you the way she hurt Sam?" Bryony asked softly.

"Your sister never knew about..." He glanced between the four of us and then back to Amos.

"I am here only in my capacity to protect Princess Bryony," Amos said. "Anything else that is said will be disregarded."

"Even my motivation?" Atticus asked, frowning.

"If that's what you wish."

Atticus stared a second longer at Amos and then let out a slow breath. He wasn't like Sam, I realized. His spirit hadn't been so broken. He held obvious respect for Bryony, which I felt was only natural, but it was clear he had some for the head guard as well.

"Your sister never knew about my second nature," he said to Bryony. "Sam was her favorite when he showed her, but I saw the way she looked at him. Like he was a toy to entertain her. And her appetites have always been perverse. I didn't want her to know that I was..."

"A horse," I said blinking at him, seeing that same shy nobility in him that I knew from my friends at the stables.

Bryony let out a small disgusted sound and shook her head. "I understand."

"So you've been stuck as a man for years," I said, studying Atticus for that look of mourning he'd had as he gazed out of the window.

"I'm used to hiding," he said, raising his chin slightly. "Your Highness, the honest truth was, I was safer than most in your sister's collection. She found me boring and often left me alone. When I attempted to kill her, I did so because I thought I would get away with it. Camellia mistreated the men of her Chosen, made us mistreat one another for her entertainment. She made no secret of the fact that she wanted the throne and would need you dead to get it. I didn't want Kimmery in her hands."

"Is it treason?" Cresswell asked Amos.

"It's not his fault!" I cried out.

"Not Atticus," Bryony said, slipping over to me and taking my arm. "He means is Camellia wanting me dead."

"It is, but not from a reliable witness, and it's not proof," Amos said, frowning.

"I've made peace with my decision, Your Highness. And my fate."

Bryony's lips pursed, and Atticus's head ducked as she stared back at him with all the authority and confidence of the queen I knew she would soon be. "Well I haven't. Please, if there's anything you can offer Head Guard Amos, any name of another Chosen who might be willing to speak with us, anywhere we might look for proof of Camellia's plans—"

"She doesn't make plans, Your Highness. She just acts when it suits her," Atticus said.

"There must be something. You shouldn't be sentenced to death for—Ugh!" Bryony bit her own tongue and shook her head. She was trying to tiptoe along the same line as Camellia, I realized, shy cautiously on the side of it that *wasn't* treason and wishing her own sister dead.

"I'll tell you what I know," Atticus said softly to Cresswell. "It's mostly... I don't know that there are laws that protect Chosen from the things Camellia put us through, but I'll share it all and every word I heard from her if it might help destroy any chance of her becoming queen."

"Owen, take Bryony back to the suite," Cresswell said. "Humphries is in the hall, take him too."

"I should stay," Bryony said as I took her hand, but even she sounded uncertain.

"I'll tell you anything you need to know," Cresswell said. And he would keep anything painful from her that she might manage without ever learning.

"Come, Mistress," I said, tugging gently, relieved when Bryony didn't fight me. I looked back to Atticus and gave him a nod. "I hope you get a chance to run again, Darby."

The man nodded, his eyes sliding away from mine. He'd resigned himself to death when he'd decided to try and kill Camellia, and the hope of his fate changing was probably too painful a temptation to grab onto the idea.

"Running may be his only chance at living," Bryony whispered in the hall.

18.
WENDELL

"**S**urely the reason we cannot come to an accord on taxation is because the majority of this council doesn't find *bleeding the people of Kimmery dry*—"

"Sit down, Pope!"

"—to be a suitable consequence for some members' greed. If the majority has already voted to keep taxes at a reasonable level, why, *sir*, should we now vote to allow regions to levy taxes without concrete benefits to—"

"Mister Pope!"

"—the people whose pockets some lords seek to drain entirely?!"

I sucked in a deep breath, fire rushing up my throat to my cheeks as Lord Thomlinson thundered my name to me once more. My applause was small from most of the others, and there were plenty of eyes glaring in my direction, but I knew I had the support.

"Take it to a vote, Thomlinson. You're wasting time," Sir Weston called up the table.

I waited a beat, just to be sure Thomlinson would move to vote. Beady eyes glared at me, but it was obvious. If he pursued trying to argue the vote in his favor, I would fight him with every breath. And only his would be wasted. I was determined. I wouldn't let the council undo all the good work Bryony had already accomplished. Especially since this vote for letting lords levy and lower taxes to their own taste was a clear attempt for the vampiric council members to attack their subjects again.

"All in favor..."

I sagged into my seat, relief tentative, even as I counted the hands that went up in favor of Thomlinson's latest wicked proposal. A month ago, the measure might've passed. Now with time and effort on my part and the added support of the former Chosen Vincent...

"Thank the stars for you, Pope," Jack whispered at my side. "For your lung capacity at least."

I choked on a laugh.

"I've never seen a man talk himself blue in the face for such great causes," Jack continued, grinning, but he was smiling at the small show of hands more than his enjoyment of teasing me.

The measure was failing.

"All against," Thomlinson muttered.

It was a small margin of victory, only three more hands against Thomlinson's cronies, but it was still success. I'd made very little headway in Bryony's favor, but at least I was a consistent thorn in a man like Thomlinson's side.

"Very well," Thomlinson bit out, shuffling the papers in front of him. "We'll table the matter."

Sir Weston scoffed and rolled his eyes at me, but I only granted him the briefest agreement. Thomlinson had plenty more notes in his stack, and I wasn't about to rest on my laurels.

"A new proposal, drafted together by myself and a few of our *esteemed* party," Thomlinson said.

"He's always very quick to make that distinction isn't he?" Jack muttered with a glare up the table. Which was easy for Jack to say, he was a viscount. There was really no denying him his seat here. I was a Mister, several generations away and in the wrong direction from any Pope family title. Not that my lack of peerage had anything to do with Thomlinson's disdain.

"We here on the council have the most gratifying and sacred duty of safeguarding the interests of the crown and championing progress in Kimmery. With the dowager queen now, most mournfully, deceased," Thomlinson droned with a hand over his heart, "we are a generation shorter on the queen's line. And as I'm sure you're all aware, there is some dispute as to the...succession of our next queen."

Fuck. I sat up straighter, hands gripping hard at the arms of my seat, my eyes tracking the slow passage of Thomlinson's notes from one pair of hands to the next.

"Is there, my lord?" Sir Weston growled.

"Well, naturally. There is no clear tradition, nothing written, that might *prevent* the younger princess from taking the throne."

"And certainly nothing that would warrant Princess Bryony from being overlooked," I barked, and Jack kicked my foot briefly beneath the table.

"Of course, but that does leave the situation...sticky," Thomlinson said with the kind of magnanimous smile that only meant a man was up to something truly despicable.

"Does it? There's absolutely no reason to suspect Queen Peony won't name her eldest successor," another man said slowly. Lord Garret was not always my ally, but he wasn't always Thomlinson's either and I respected him for that much.

"Gentleman, it is our *duty* to see to Kimmery's welfare. To its future prosperity. To its longevity," Thomlinson continued, a hand rolling through the air with every edition.

"Spit it out man," someone muttered.

"I'm only asking that we vote that no princess be named successor until she has provided an heir to the queen's line," Thomlinson said, grinning in his false and friendly manner.

My stomach dropped to the floor. No, to several stories down from this meeting room. Jack sat up a little straighter at my side, and I think he understood the same danger I did. This could pass. It was already on the men's faces, as they glanced at one another. Even the ones who supported Bryony might not find this too abhorrent a measure.

There were eyes on my face, I could feel their stare boring in and I glanced up. Sir Weston was staring back at me, yes, worry in his gaze, but it was Thomlinson and his ugly grin who was really watching me.

"What does Queen Peony say of this?" I asked, already knowing the answer but wanting the others to hear it too.

"She could *hardly* object," Thomlinson said.

I arched an eyebrow, trying to keep a lid on my panic. "So you haven't even mentioned this to her."

"She is mourning, my good fellow."

Half-mourning, I corrected mentally.

"It is not unreasonable," one man said, looking over the text Thomlinson had provided. "It is securing Kimmery's crown to the queen's line."

"It is meddling a little higher above our duties than I should think the queen appreciated," Sir Weston said, taking a look around the table, trying to win back men's minds.

Stars, was Camellia *already* pregnant? Was that why Thomlinson looked so smug, or—

Or did he only know that Bryony was intentionally preventing herself from becoming with child still? It wasn't a single one of these men's business whether she was or wasn't, but I was almost sure a majority of them wouldn't see it that way.

"For however reasonable this measure is, it isn't a *light* one, Lord Thomlinson," Jack said. "The council has never involved themselves with succession."

"A queen's greatest duty, and a Chosen's highest honor, is of course providing Kimmery with an heir," Thomlinson said delicately, and a few of the men turned in my direction.

Of course. Of course he would make that dig. Camellia, whatever she was really about, certainly made an appearance of trying to get with child. Bryony, on the other hand, let her Chosen run about the palace, dealing with guards and mages and taking a seat on the council. She was political, and whether these men would admit it or not, she intimidated them.

"I propose a vote to delay," I said, holding Thomlinson's gaze, feeling a slight measure of relief at his flinch. "I agree that this is not something to be voted on lightly, and I doubt our intentions on the matter if we aren't interested in our queen's opinion."

"I second the delay," Jack said quickly.

Sir Weston and another both offered their support, and Thomlinson scowled briefly.

❧

"You're mad, absolutely *mad*!" Aric growled.

"Aric, it isn't a decision I've made already," Bryony said gently.

I paused in the doorway, drinking in the sight of everyone,

surprised by relief to see not just Bryony and Thao again, but the whole mess of us. Every one of Bryony's men was, in some odd way now, also my family.

"It better not be, princess, because there's not a chance I'd let you go through with it," Aric snarled. "What do you need to be a tiger for anyway?"

"It is a *great* honor to receive the gift of my family's bite," Thao said, a slight edge of offense in his tone.

Aric whirled on him and then seemed to settle briefly. "That may be. Is it one that's ever been granted to anyone with their own kind of magic? Has the ceremony ever taken place off the island of Mennary? Magic isn't baking a cake, there's more than putting the right ingredients together; environment is a factor. And in this case," Aric continued, jaw tight as he forced the words out while glaring at Bryony, "there is certainly more at *stake*."

"It's only something I'm considering," Bryony said mildly, holding Aric's gaze. "I'm not coming to you with my mind made up, I'm bringing this to all of you as a discussion. And to you in particular as a...puzzle, I suppose. Hello, Wendell."

The room turned to me as a whole, and I waved, crossing to sit on the arm of Thao's chair. "Hello, carry on. I'll take your attention in a moment."

Bryony's lips pursed at that, but Aric was faster. "What if you get the bite and it doesn't work, and you try to heal yourself and the bite's magic resists yours, so you can't?"

"I'm not going to take her arm off, Aric," Thao muttered, but he sighed as I slipped fingers through his hair. He was taking Aric's criticism of his offer to Bryony fairly well, I thought.

Aric took in another great breath, and Bryony stepped forward, settling one hand on his chest and reaching up to cup his cheek. I hid my smile as the breath all puffed out of him, entirely caught in Bryony's gentle, disarming gaze.

"Let's table it for now. I won't act, I promise."

His eyes narrowed slightly, but his arm circled her waist as she rose to her toes and kissed him briefly.

"It would be a good defense for her," Cresswell said, standing at the bar in the corner and pouring himself a drink.

Bryony twisted in Aric's arms and hushed him with a gesture

before leaning into her mage again, smiling at me with her chin propped on Aric's shoulder.

"How was the meeting?" She sounded so easy and optimistic. I hadn't brought her bad news since we'd learned about her mother handing over more control to Thomlinson, and her faith in me was obvious. And a little daunting, if I was being honest with myself. I never wanted to bring Bryony the news that I'd *failed* her.

"The tax measures were voted down," I said.

"Oh good! Wendell, you've made such progress already," Bryony said, and Aric released her, joining Cresswell for a drink as Bryony moved to sit with Cosmo in the chair facing me.

My smile faltered at her praise, and Bryony's head tipped to the side in an unspoken question. "There was a new proposal. Regarding the succession of the crown."

Daniel and Owen had been engaging in a friendly conversation of their own by the windows, Aric and Cress chatting, but all of that fell silent at my announcement.

"The crown?" Bryony whispered, stiffening on Cosmo's lap. He was quick to soothe her, his hands moving over her shoulders and straight spine almost unconsciously, trying to soften her again.

I stood and paced a small track, just to the edge of the rug at the heart of the room. "Thomlinson proposed a law where no princess could be named successor without first providing an heir."

Aric cursed, and so did Thao in Mennarian, but Bryony remained perched on Cosmo's lap, staring blankly at me.

"An heir," she repeated.

"It doesn't guarantee that Camellia would be declared, but it... If she..."

"If she gets pregnant first, it would give Thomlinson leverage to push at my—my mother!"

"She doesn't know," I said quickly. Bryony leapt up, and I hurried forward, catching her hands in mine. "She hasn't heard of this; it was half the reason I was able to delay the vote, but Bryony..."

I didn't want to be the one to say it. This wasn't an ultimatum I would ever have wanted her to feel weighing on her shoulders, and for possibly the first time, I resented my position on the council forcing me to always give the woman I loved bad news.

"It will be hard to convince men to vote against this," Thao murmured.

My shoulders sagged at the same time Bryony's did, my head dropping with a mix of relief and shame that Thao had lifted that burden from me.

"And Camellia, she must be—she must...know of this?" Bryony whispered, her voice cracking.

"I can't say." But I was almost certain.

Bryony nodded, chin lifting, hands settling on her hips. "She must." It was her turn to pace as we all gathered closer. "Of course she must. That's why she hasn't been hounding me. Why she's been gathering so many Chosen. Kept herself locked up in her suite. *Damn*. Only Camellia would chase motherhood with such heartless determination."

One hand rose up to shield Bryony's eyes, but I saw her bottom lip trembling.

"Mistress, you'll make as fine a mother as you will a queen," Owen offered sweetly, but Bryony's lip only shook harder until she ground her teeth together.

"Bryony, there's more than one answer to this problem," I said softly.

Her hand whipped away, eyes glossy as she stared up at me. "Is there?"

"Do you...do you feel *ready* to be a mother?" I asked carefully.

Bryony blinked up at me and the answer seemed clear on her face, but she took a slow breath and released it before speaking. "I could be. But, stars, not for *them*! And I... This is not the Kimmery I want to bring a child into. Oh! And what if Camellia or someone connected to the council might try to harm them as they have me? No, I can't!"

I made soft hushing sounds, beating Daniel to gathering Bryony to my chest, wrapping my arms around her shoulders. "We should find out what your mother thinks of the proposal. At the very least impress upon her that it is *her* right to name succession, not the council's." Bryony nodded against me, breaths slowing again.

"I have to be careful with her, she'd probably be delighted at the idea of her daughters both trying to have children. She's delighted with everything," Bryony added in a dark mutter. "In the meantime though, I think I know what to do about Camellia."

"Do you?" Aric asked, he and I both frowning with surprise.

Bryony nodded and pulled away from me, smiling slightly at all of us. "Of course. Mourning ends in a week. I'll just have to keep her very busy. I've been thinking of this anyway. I'll host a ball."

My brow furrowed as I tried to chase the line of thought. "A ball?"

"A fencing tournament and then a ball, I think," Bryony said with a nod. She wiggled between Daniel and Owen, heading for Nora's writing desk. "A local hunt too, I think. We'll invite the noble families to the castle, they usually come this time of year anyway. A hunt, lots of feasts. Card games in the evening."

"Bryony...public events aren't known to prevent your sister from um...making a show of it with her Chosen. They won't necessarily keep her distracted," Cosmo said.

Finally I understood, a laugh breaking through the tight feeling in my chest since I'd left the council. "You *want* her to make a fool of herself," I said. "Like she did at the funeral."

Bryony was already busy scribbling her plans, but she spared me a wicked smile. "I will, of course, have to make a few *discrete* exhibitions myself. Mother loves this kind of thing, and she's taken to whining a bit about the length of mourning. Aric, I'm afraid you'll have to reconcile yourself to some extravagance."

Aric scoffed and stalked to Bryony, bending over her in her chair and pushing her hair to one side to kiss her throat as she continued to write. "I'll do you one better, princess. We'll fill every event, every evening, with magical displays to dazzle your fool nobles."

"Oh!" Bryony gasped and arched as Aric's hand disappeared down her collar. "Yes, yes, I like that."

Thao grinned. "Finally, we get to enjoy ourselves again." I followed him toward Bryony, the others close at our backs, all ready to descend upon our clever princess. Thao sank to his knees, and Aric turned Bryony's chair toward him. "You'll have tigers at your hunt, Your Highness. What other Kimmerian queen could boast of that?"

I picked up Bryony's notes from the desk as Thao lifted Bryony's skirt and Aric fought the bodice of her dress down. There was a great deal of planning to do, but even more magic to be made first.

19.
BRYONY

"For the woman who trounced her way through more than half of Kimmery's best fencers, you look very much the delicate princess now."

I scowled at the mirror, even as I added a little extra stain to my bottom lip. "Don't remind me. I'm still sore over the losses."

Morgan laughed. "I imagine that's how many of the men feel."

"I've been too out of practice since I returned south. If I wasn't so rusty—"

"Stars, you *are* a sore loser."

I whipped around to glare at Morgan, but her jaw dropped as I faced her, gaze taking a very flattering path over me and back again. I glanced back into the mirror. I did think I looked pretty. It was nice just to be out of mourning and able to wear colors again, and while pastels might've been more appropriate, they were also the most popular shades in fashion lately. My gown was a deep shade of turquoise in a sheer fabric, pale and gauzy around my breasts and at the full skirt, and the color of dense evergreens in the mountains at my waist. It was beaded with vivid blood-red flowers and golden vines that caged my hips and waist, blooming up to my breasts to hide the sheer quality of the fabric. There was something almost gruesome about it at first glance, striking and shocking, but undeniably beautiful.

"Are you trying to make Kimmerian dressmakers go mad? That cut is..."

"It's new. Do you like it?" I asked, twisting side to side.

Morgan scowled at me, flapping her arms that were swallowed by the enormous volume of sleeves. My sleeves were just beaded lace cupped below my bare shoulders. "I am very cross with you for not sharing it sooner. I feel like a cream puff, and you look... It's a bit risqué somehow, though I can't place why."

My collar was a *little* lower than hers, although since my breasts were smaller, it just revealed more skin than décolletage. My hips were wider too, so while the new cut of my dress followed my natural shape before flaring out into great yards upon yards of skirt, Morgan's flared very intentionally below the waist, supported by a bustle around her hips.

"Have your men seen it?" Morgan asked.

I waved my hand through the air. "I should think they're fairly tired of seeing me in new dresses."

Morgan snorted and muttered something under her breath along the lines of 'out of them,' before clearing her throat. "Well, I just came to tell you that it's time to get downstairs."

I nodded and turned back to my mirror, reaching up to the top where Aric's golden snake rested. It slithered into my palm and then coiled happily around my throat, it's head nestling down at the hollow of my collar bone.

"Any sign of Camellia?" I asked.

"I caught a maid saying she was having a bit of a tantrum as they dressed her," Morgan said.

I smirked and fought the expression away, but my friend just rolled her eyes. Camellia had made a scene earlier at the fencing tournament too when she hadn't been allowed to interrupt a match to claim one of the fencers. Mother had finally released her from the duty of hostessing in the afternoon after a public display with a few of her Chosen, but there was no getting out of the ball. Our queen was too excited for the evening.

In fact, my entire schedule for the month had been received by Mother with great success. "Oh yes! This is just what we need to brighten our spirits until spring. And then we might have garden events. Good sporting. Days at the beach, don't you think?"

We had another week before the council would vote on the succession law, and I wanted to be sure that Camellia had well and thoroughly hurt her favor with the nobles.

I followed Morgan to the front room of the suite, and just as she had paused at the sight of me, I did so at the vision before me. Seven men, in tailcoats and high collars, their boots polished and fine clothes shining in the candlelight. Wendell, Cosmo, Daniel, and Cresswell looked the part of *perfect* Kimmerian gentlemen, and Thao was fully glorious in his longer, embroidered, vivid red coat. I'd been lenient with Owen and Aric's dress, so their collars were open, coats darker and a little less tightly fitted, but it left them debonair and rakish in appearance.

And in spite of what I'd claimed to Morgan, their stares on me were gratifying.

"Muse, you look like a goddess," Cosmo breathed.

I blushed but held my head high as I joined them near the door.

"Do you feel ready?" Wendell asked.

I nodded, surprised by my own answer. "I do, actually. I think I might even be looking forward to the evening since I have you all with me."

Aric moved to stand behind me, his fingertips touching the snake briefly, a wicked gleam in his eye. "Then let the night begin."

❧

THE BALLROOM GLITTERED WITH CANDLELIGHT, marble floors polished to reflect the gold moulding of the arched ceilings and delicate glittering arms of the chandeliers above us. The room was warm with so many bodies, and I was flushed and warm with the wine I'd been drinking.

The royal table was long, and luckily, I had my mother and her Chosen separating me from Camellia, who'd been forced to only bring a select group down from her suite. One of whom, I noted, was Prince Holden, looking grim and uncomfortable at the far end of the table.

I was sipping wine, pretending not to feel the stares of the many nobles at their banquet tables around the perimeter of the room, when someone touched my shoulder.

Michael, looking handsome and polished in finery, smiled tightly down at me. "Your mother thinks you should be the one to lead the dancing tonight."

"Me? Oh—I..." I paused on the refusal on my tongue, glancing at Thao on my right. He nodded at me, eyebrows rising.

"I'd be happy to," I said at last, the words a little dry on my tongue.

"You *can* waltz?" Thao asked me as Michael moved away.

I laughed that he would wait till now to check. "Yes, well, with a good partner. You or Wendell?"

"Take Farraque," Thao answered, smiling as I sat up in surprise. "Just trust me."

I did trust Thao, especially on this kind of matter, I just hadn't expected him to suggest Daniel. Daniel had the education for this kind of thing, it was true, but Thao had always preferred to promote himself or Wen.

"All right," I said, smiling at the idea. Daniel would never expect it either, and it would be a lovely mark of my appreciation for him at the same time it was a smack in the face to the council.

I waited for the clink of cutlery to quiet, until the room was only full of conversation and drinking. It was already late into the night. Camellia was not so subtly making demands of her Chosen beneath the table, and I was pretending my palms weren't sweating against the napkin fisted into my lap.

We hadn't had many balls growing up, and I'd only danced a little. I was practiced as I ought to be, but I'd certainly never been the one to open a ball, to be alone on the floor with my partner and all the eyes of the room watching politely.

But if you want to be queen, you'll get used to people staring, I decided, and when the musicians were taking their seat and conversation was in one of those strange lulls that took a room, I stood from my seat. Voices hushed further, and for a moment, I wanted to sink right back down into my chair. Thao covered my hand on the table briefly, a reminder to hold onto my courage, and the musicians on their small stage in the corner were quick to pick up their instruments.

I lifted my glass into the air, ignoring Camellia's growl at the end of the table. "Thank you all for your support and trust during this trying winter. The loss of my grandmother is a great wound to Kimmery, but as all wounds must, we will heal and grow stronger, prosper more richly, live more fully. Let our transformation begin tonight. To Kimmery!"

I hid my shuddering gasp of relief as a hundred glasses rose to the air. "To Kimmery!" the room echoed.

I spared a glance at my mother, pretending for a moment that I'd really earned her glittering smile. I *had*, even if she would've given me the same one for less effort.

I drank to my kingdom, drank *with* my kingdom, and then lowered my glass, moving behind the table to Daniel.

"Open with me," I whispered, bending to his ear.

"Me?"

I smiled as he echoed my own surprise, stroking my fingers through his beard and then smoothing it as I bent for his kiss. He leaned into me for a moment, the room watching our simple affection, and his eyes were bright as I pulled away. Daniel stood and offered me his arm, our audience rising from their seats to stand at the edges of the floor and watch.

It was easier to focus on Daniel, who seemed to do the same, the pair of us blocking out the vast crowd that surrounded us as we walked together to the center of the room. I could see our reflections in the dark windows that overlooked the sea, Daniel tall and broad—just a little coarse, but in the way that snagged women's stares. They didn't realize how gentle he really was, although that might've been for me alone.

My gaze caught briefly on my sister at the banquet table as Daniel turned me to stand in the perfect hold of his arms. My hands framed his shoulders, my arms resting above his, and I stared at Camellia. She was so thin, so pale, with dark shadows beneath her eyes. Her hair looked thin, and I wondered if anyone else thought she seemed...ill. Was she so busy satiating the Hunger, she'd lost any ability to care for her actual body? But there was no shadow blocking the fire in her stare, the white-knuckled grip on the table as she glared at me. Camellia hated me. It hadn't always been like that, but once the rift began, whenever it began, closing that wound seemed impossible now.

The music struck, sudden and swooning, and Daniel swept me into a turn, my gaze falling back to him, soaking up the warm humor of his expression, his devoted focus.

He had a hand splayed on my back, and I leaned into the touch, sighing as he took easy control of the dance. "Tonight is already a success," he said, quiet enough for my ears only, the whisper in his voice lending itself to secrecy.

"It must be, because I hardly care," I said, grinning back at him. "It's usually a good sign when I stop worrying."

Daniel's bright smile grew with mine, and he tugged me closer until our hips were fastened to one another, my dancing high on my toes as he carried me easily through the movements. This was a little easier than dancing at the festival. I was relaxed with Daniel and familiar enough with the steps to move without thinking.

"Remember when you mentioned wanting discreet displays?" Daniel asked, a dark little light brewing in his gaze.

I opened my mouth to answer, when I felt the slow glide of my necklace. My eyes widened, and my breath stopped short in my chest.

"Let me lead you," Daniel said, arm around my waist wrapping tighter, hiding the slow slither of the snake down my bodice.

"Who—?"

"Aric, of course."

I turned my head and found Aric standing at the edge of the crowd, his focus sharp, his fingertip moving in a slow trace over his palm as the golden snake curled around my breast, surfacing from my collar briefly before sliding below again, the tail tweaking a nipple. My eyes fluttered shut at the jab of arousal that shot through me.

"That's it," Daniel purred to me.

My breath hitched as the snake teased at my belly button, circling around my waist over and over, gliding back up to tease at the other breast. My eyes opened again, and I glanced around. No one else was dancing yet, although a few brave pairs might join us soon.

"They'll know," I gasped, biting down a groan as the snake nipped at my breast.

"They will," Daniel murmured. "Some already do. And they should know, Bryony. They should see their princess for who she is —sensual, beautiful, *powerful*."

Daniel's voice was a kind of magic of its own in my ear, slow and private. Not explicit like Thao, but tempting.

"They'll see nothing this way, but they'll know. We'll show them."

My feet were stumbling a little, but Daniel had such a hold on me, I doubt anyone realized. I was arching in his embrace, the golden snake licking cooly over my flesh, spiraling low on my hips, teasing me with its slow path.

"And the magic?"

"Let it go," Daniel said.

Damn my wonderful men, they'd *planned* this. Without me. Perhaps not the opening dance, although who knew if they'd found some way of whispering it into my mother's ear.

The snake dipped, and I gasped, my head falling back, eyes wide and then quickly pressed shut. I wasn't sure I could do it with the whole room watching. At least, not with my eyes open.

"Let us lead," Daniel whispered.

I giggled and shivered as the snake teased its way around my sex, toying at my opening. My breaths panted and I swallowed hard, trying to lift my head. I wasn't used to trying to hide my pleasure, wasn't even sure if I should in this moment.

I peeked out of my eyes. The room was staring. Even the dancers on the floor were really only trying to get a closer look at me and Daniel.

The snake stroked my clit, and I grabbed onto Daniel, holding my breath and pressing my cheek to his, releasing the smallest, quietest moan I could manage into his ear. He was growing hard against my hip, even as he moved us step by step in circles across the floor. The music suited the moment, swooping and keening through the air, bouncing from the glass and the gold moulding.

Stars, my mother was watching.

Forget them. Forget them all.

I found Daniel's gaze as the snake picked up its pace, Aric determined to push me through any reservations. I'd chew his ear off for not warning me later. I'd kiss him and thank him too. I was allowed to do both.

"You're beautiful," Daniel said with a soft smile. "Any man would be mad to think he deserved you. Except maybe Owen."

My laugh turned into a soft cry, and Daniel kissed me sweetly, not minding the iron grip I had on his shoulders or the way I wasn't even trying to dance now, just allowing him to carry me along.

"Make something every bit as beautiful as you. Something they can't ignore. Can't explain."

I nodded, pleasure racing in my veins, my legs and hands going numb. I softened my grip on Daniel so I would be sure not to accidentally push it into him. The snake was wrapped around my legs, head working at my clit, tail teasing my opening.

"You take me somewhere dark and private as soon as we are done here," I hissed.

"Yes, Your Highness," Daniel said with a broad grin. "I'll still fuck you until you scream my name for them all to hear."

I was sure Thao had put him up to that, but it didn't matter, the thrill of the threat and Aric's determined playing pushed me off one side of the precipice and into a dizzying free fall. My arms fell from Daniel's as he spun and spun and spun us in place. Gasps joined mine, a groan and creak of metal, a chink and crack of glass, the abrupt snag of the music coming to a halt as I shuddered and bit my lip through my climax.

Above me, chandeliers twisted into tangled wreaths and vines, ruby blossoms dripping down with emerald leaves. And in the windows too, flowers grew right into the glass panes, made of precious jewels, distorting the reflection of Daniel holding me in the center of the ballroom, of my mother standing at the head of the table, her eyes wide and mouth parted in shock, of Camellia, snarling across the room from me.

⁂

QUICK THRUSTS within the circle of my thighs, skin slapping wetly, pleasure sizzling through me to my fingertips before being reined in again. Aric's kiss was rough and hungry, tongue licking in, barely giving me room to speak or make a sound. Which was fine, since Daniel had already kept to his word of making me scream his name as he fucked me in a barely private alcove of the hall.

Aric's hips snapped once more, and I moaned into the kiss, holding tight to this latest burst of magic, my hands fisted in his shirt beneath his open coat. He pulled away at last, breathing roughly against my ear.

Then he began to chuckle. My eyes narrowed at the smug sound, and I pinched his back.

"What's that for?" we both snapped.

I tried to shift away, but Aric's hands on my ass held me in place, keeping himself buried even as he started to soften.

"Excuse me for having a moment of amusement that I just fucked my princess in a castle hall," Aric said.

I sighed and kissed his jaw. "You fucked me in the Winter Palace hall once."

"Mmm, suppose it felt a bit more like home there. At least toward the end. Here is still...very much another world to me."

I couldn't argue that, so instead I kissed him, my legs trembling as he loosened his grip and let me unwrap them from around his waist.

"Someone is coming," Daniel whispered from where he'd been standing guard in the hall. "Shit, Bryony, it's your—"

"For fuck's sake, just get on the floor." Camellia's sharp tone echoed off the floor.

"No! Enough. I've had enough of you! Your behavior has been disgusting enough as it is, but I am a *prince,* not your *mount.*"

Aric's eyes widened on mine. *Holden.*

There was a masculine moan of 'no' and the sound of grappling, and Aric's arm trapped me to the wall as I tried to jump out into the hall.

"Aric! He said—"

"I know, princess," Aric said with a grimace painting his face. He bent and kissed my forehead. "Just wait a beat."

I could hear the struggle of them together, Camellia's harsh cries and the grunts from Holden, until my heartbeat drowned them out with its pounding in my ears.

"Now," Daniel whispered, and Aric released me.

I whipped into the hall, my eyes finding them on the other end, Holden smeared on the floor with Camellia seated astride him. His hands were wrapped tight around her arms, but her own were on his throat, the garbled sounds he made suddenly clear.

"Camellia! No!"

"Bry—" Aric began before thinking better of arguing with me, and instead only chasing after me as I ran down the hall to intervene.

Magic was already heavy in my palms, and Camellia only lifted her face and grinned, face transformed as she chased pleasure. I knew that look, I'd been that predator, but never against one of my own Chosen.

Camellia groaned as Holden twisted and jerked beneath her. I couldn't tell if she was pushing magic into him already, forcing him to crave her brutal treatment of him. His face was red, hands growing weak, and I thought he might've been trying to toss her off, but Camellia moaned as if he was thrusting to meet her urgency.

"Camellia, stop!" I snapped, finally reaching them, finally grabbing onto her shoulders to try and haul her away.

She roared out a snarling scream, releasing Holden's throat to grab at my wrists. Pain like a hot iron, like the blade Emory had thrust into my shoulder, burned its way up my arms. I gritted my teeth against the blaze, focusing on the sound of Holden's strangled breath, using Camellia's grip to tear her off of him. I twisted my hands from her shoulders to wrap around her wrists too, our magic clashing like cymbals, shattering its way up into my skull.

"Get Cress and Amos," Aric said, his voice distant as I pulled on Camellia's wrists and her vise grip squeezed brutally around my own.

Her legs kicked and she screeched and thrashed, but she didn't have the strength to do more than hold on. Stars, she was so brittle looking now, her silver gown hung from her like wilted petals.

"Let me go! Let me go!"

"You're—" Holden's voice was wretched, tangled and faint. "You're going to see—see war for this."

Camellia's entire body bucked as I pulled her to the side, tugging her onto her feet and wrapping her arms around her own chest, holding her to the wall with all my weight.

"You could've killed him, Camellia," I hissed in her ear. "What are you thinking?"

She cursed me, spitting as she jumped and twisted in place.

"Bryony?"

"I'm fine," I answered Aric, refusing to take my eyes off my sister. "Holden?"

"Your Highness, let me ease your throat a little."

"Fuck you," Camellia hissed to me with great emphasis.

"He is a *prince*, Camellia." I frowned at myself and shook my head. "He is your Chosen."

"Yes, *mine*. He's meant to serve me, not bitch and moan and demand what he likes."

I gritted my teeth. She was like a bird against me, I was half afraid I would break something if I was too firm with her. She seemed to tremble, and there was a painful scratch and buzz everywhere she touched me, the twisted magic of her Hunger clashing against mine. All at once, Camellia sagged and went limp.

"Let me go," she moaned. "Oh, let me go, it hurts."

It hurt me too, the whole thing. Seeing her this way, knowing what she was capable of, the friction of our magic meeting and biting and clawing at one another just as we did.

Commotion followed, boots echoing in the hall, and in a moment Amos, Cress, Owen, and Daniel arrived with three of my mother's ladies.

"I'll take her, Your Highness," one woman said, she was stocky and older than my mother, with a firm and familiar stare focused on my sister. "We'll get her back to her rooms with her Chosen and she'll settle. It's all the activity."

"It's entirely her own doing," I answered back, but I pushed Camellia into the woman's arms gratefully, eyeing them carefully. Camellia fought a little, but I was right about her strength. She was too weak to really fight us off, and she began to whimper and cry instead. Her hips were squirming, and I realized she was trying to relieve pressure, unsatisfied after being torn away from Holden.

Holden!

I spun and found that Aric had moved Holden safely away, all the men quick to join them and keep their distance from Camellia. Holden was propped up against the wall, deep bruises starting to form around his throat, pants barely closed again, his gaze blazing on my sister.

"Bryony," Cress said, voice tight but watching my sister as he reached out for me.

I glanced back, marginally relieved to see the three women managing Camellia away easily, and then crossed to Cress, sagging briefly against his side.

"How is he?" I asked Aric.

"Lucky we were out here," Aric said, glancing at me and then back to Holden.

It was true, and also a kind of lie. We could've intervened much sooner on Holden's behalf. He might still have been grateful to us if we had. But we wouldn't be able to say we saved his life. Aric hadn't finished healing Holden either, when I was sure he could have, fresh with magic from me. That too was a kind of lie. We needed proof of Camellia's abuse.

"You'll try to cover this up, but I won't let you," Holden rasped, glaring at me. "And if you kill me, my family will declare war anyway when they don't hear from me. Your kingdom is fucked regardless, and that—that *monster* will never see the throne."

"She certainly won't, Your Highness," I said with a nod to Holden. I turned to Amos, who watched the scene with his arms crossed. "Would you please see Prince Holden to one of our guest suites? Perhaps near my own, and with a good collection of guards in case my sister might seek him out again. Prince Holden, I will do my absolute best to rectify this. A doctor will see you immediately. And I'll come in the morning myself to speak with you."

"Rectify? Are you mad? Because your sister certainly is! She tried to kill me! She—she—she forces every one of those men your kingdom granted her!"

I ignored Holden for the moment, and Head Guard Amos bowed to me. "Of course, Your Highness."

"Cress?" I murmured as Holden spluttered.

Cresswell bent and kissed my cheek. "I'll go with them. Make sure he's safe."

"Let's get you back to the dancing, Your Highness," Daniel murmured, just loud enough for Holden to hear as he, Aric, and Owen bundled me between them and swept me away.

"Are you sure it's wise this way?" I whispered to Aric when I was sure we wouldn't be heard.

"He'll think you're waiting to assassinate him. By morning, he'll be grateful for the deal," Aric said, raising my hand to his lips and brushing kisses over the fingertips. "It's an ugly maneuver, but he made his own bed pursuing her. He *is* lucky we were out here."

I sighed and nodded as we reached the door to the ballroom, straightening my shoulders and lifting my chin. As Owen stepped forward to open the doors for us, I pasted a soft and satisfied smile over my lips, bracing myself for the knowing stares.

They knew a pretty fraction of me, this audience of nobles. I had an armored underbelly now, and they'd be better off if they never found cause to meet it too.

20.
BRYONY

"He raged as much as his throat would let him last night, but he's been quiet this morning, Your Highness," Amos said.

So maybe Aric was right. Still, I wasn't about to underestimate the prince in the conversation. He had every right to request serious retribution for the injuries Camellia had given him. I just needed to make sure that his goal in that regard ran seamlessly into my own.

"Can he be kept a secret for long enough?" I asked Amos.

"Perhaps not a secret, but we can make excuses for his situation, I think," Amos said with a shrug.

I glanced at Aric and Wendell on either side of me, and they both nodded.

Aric smiled and squeezed my hand. "Why do you look so nervous, princess?"

"I think I've just realized how rarely I negotiate. I usually just persuade people."

"So do that. Persuade him to your compromise. You know he wants war, to be released to return home. Presumably, there's something within that war he's hoping to gain," Wendell said. "We'll sort through it, giving him enough of what he wants and his best chance of actually succeeding, and he'll agree."

I nodded, more to convince myself that I was prepared for the conversation ahead than anything else, and then turned to Amos.

"All right, yes, I'm ready."

In truth, I'd been at the ball late into the night, and then up for the remainder of it trying to think over what I might say to Prince

Holden to convince him to join my cause when all he wanted was a thorough revenge. My head started to spin again as Amos opened the doors, and Aric interrupted my thoughts with a nudge against my back.

Prince Holden was pacing the small sitting room of the suite, still wearing his white dress shirt from the ball, now undone at the collar to reveal the gruesome bruises around his throat. He stopped short at our arrival, and there was a flicker of panic in his wide eyes as he glanced at me. I didn't know if he saw something of Camellia in me, or if he only thought I was here to announce that we'd be sweeping him under the rug to hide my sister's crimes, but it left me strangely relieved. Aric was correct. Right now, Prince Holden had more cause to fear us than threaten us, and I only needed to convince him that we would make suitable allies.

"Your Highness, how are you feeling?" I asked, making a polite, albeit unnecessary, curtsey for his benefit.

"Wretched," Holden croaked, glaring at me and standing in front of the window. There were guards in the room with us, familiar ones I knew Cress and Amos both trusted, and their eyes remained watchful on the prince.

"Any apology I might offer you for my sister's behavior is surely useless," I said. "I am not her, and Camellia is not of a nature to offer an apology."

Holden squeaked as he scoffed, turning away from me briefly before spinning nervously back again as if he were afraid to offer us his back.

"May I sit?" I asked, gesturing to the settee.

"If you must."

For a man who had cause to worry over his fate, Holden really was an ass.

I helped myself to the seat, Aric and Wendell joining me, and then noticed the untouched tea tray waiting on a low table and the now cold breakfast at its side. Holden thought we would poison him.

I poured myself a cup, aware of the ice blue eyes watching me, and drank before looking up again.

"What do you want?" Holden asked, confusion and anger marring his handsome face.

"I want to ensure that Camellia never wears the Kimmerian crown, that she has no access to men whom she might harm, and that she is punished for her crimes."

Holden's folded arms dropped lamely to his side, surprise wiping his face clean, a soft squawk escaping his open mouth. I set my teacup down on the saucer and folded my hands in my lap, staring up at him, waiting.

"There is no law that prevents a princess from making demands of her Chosen. She is...quick to remind men of this," Holden said, voice slow, struggling and swallowing often, each time making a pained face.

"The tea will soothe your throat, Your Highness. I promise you, I have no intention of allowing you to die. You see, I know that there is nothing that prevents Camellia from abusing her Chosen. However, what she did last night was more than a demand. And you are more than a typical Chosen," I said, turning back to the tea set and preparing a second cup, setting it down on the other side of the table and waiting for Holden to relax and sit with us.

"It's cause for war," Holden said.

"It is. Although I wouldn't recommend you crusade for a war between Noren and Kimmery. To be frank, it wouldn't end well for your kingdom. We have a much stronger army."

Holden scowled and stormed to the seat, sitting down and leaning across the table to glare at me. "If you think I'm just going to return home with my tail between my legs—"

"You won't be returning home. Not yet, at least," I said, watching him pale and then waving my hand airily between us. "Please, don't misunderstand. Simply put, you are the best evidence we—*I* have against my sister. I don't need you to stay to keep her secret safe, I need you here to reveal the real danger of Camellia and her use of the Hunger."

"Evidence?" Holden rasped.

"Witness? Victim?"

"I am not—"

"We'll use a term that suits you," I said quickly, drinking from my cup and eyeing the one I'd left for him significantly.

He reached his hand out for the cup and then pulled it away again as if he thought the porcelain might leap out and bite him.

"What do you require me to say?" he asked, jaw gritting.

"Only your honest experience," I said.

He frowned and grew thoughtful, eyes turning to the fire in the grate. "People may...misunderstand. Hear my story and find me to be...weak."

I'd thought this fairly ridiculous when my Chosen first told me Holden might say as much. Why should it make any difference to his strength when my sister could use magic to force men? This wasn't to do with physique but with Camellia abusing the strength of our line. I was more sympathetic after listening, and I leaned forward to catch Holden's eye.

"You won't be alone. You are not alone, and it is my intention to ensure that you aren't the only man to speak out."

Holden gave me no response, and I relaxed into my seat, Wendell's hand sliding against mine as I left the prince to his own thoughts.

"I came here for position," Holden said. "A fourth son has... next to nothing in Noren. I am underfoot. Here at least as Chosen, there is luxury." He scowled at me, and I remained patient. This was the point where we would need to bargain. "I don't want to be your Chosen when this is done."

I made an odd sound, biting off a laugh but not quite managing to disguise it either, and Holden's glare grew fiercer.

"I would...certainly not ask that of you, after what's happened," I said, hoping that wouldn't prick his pride too much, but he looked more relieved than offended. "I'm not in a position to give you a title here yet, but—"

"I want the Winter Palace and the mountain that abuts our border," Holden said. "It's what I would take with a war."

"It's what you would fail to gain with the war," I snapped back. "Out of the question."

The Winter Palace was...undeniably precious to me, not to mention how close it was to Rumsbrooke. The mountain between us protected that part of Kimmery. Giving it to Holden would risk an advantage in Noren's favor in the future.

"Magic then," Holden said easily, and I wondered if he was compiling the list of his demands in his head or if he'd already been prepared with one. "I want access to Kimmery's magic. And a royal mage."

I huffed a breath of annoyance. "Unless you wish to take Camellia home with you, that's also out of the question."

"Well," Aric said. Both Holden and I whipped our stares in his direction. Aric smiled at me. "We could give him...the conduit."

I blinked, and Holden sat forward. "What is the conduit?"

"It's a device that the mages use to hold the magic of generations of Kimmery's queens," Aric said to Holden.

What the fuck was my thief up to? "Aric, I don't think that's—"

"And he might take Kenneth," Aric continued, holding the prince's eager gaze. "He's traveling at the moment, but he's an admirable royal mage. Younger than the others."

Holden nodded eagerly, and I pressed my lips together and narrowed my eyes at Aric. Mostly to keep from laughing. Kenneth was, by Aric's own declaration, near to useless. And what had Aric really offered Holden? I tried to think like a rogue for a moment. He'd offered the conduit. Not the magic in it, which we knew I could remove, but the *device* which we wanted to rid ourselves of.

"This isn't something we can just *give away* Aric," I hissed. "The *queen* will have to agree."

Holden sat up. "You'll have to arrange it. Those are my terms. I want the conduit and your mage Kenneth."

I ground my teeth together as I faced the prince, it had the added benefit of hiding my smile. "I will have to be guaranteed that my sister has no chance at the crown for you to win this kind of boon. It's outrageous."

"What is outrageous, Your Highness, is all I have witnessed in the weeks with your sister," Holden answered, eyes triumphant. "I will *blacken* her name beyond any favor."

Oh dear, I had to leave before I started crowing victory. I stood abruptly, and Wendell and Aric scrambled to follow. "I'll consider these terms. In the meantime, I recommend you keep to this suite. You'll be protected from Camellia here."

Holden leaned back, taking the tea from the table and drinking it without a second thought as I marched for the door, holding my grin in, tension tight in my grip around my Chosen's hands.

"Aric, was that wi—" Wendell breathed as the door shut behind us, but he stopped as I leapt at Aric.

I pushed him into the wall, slamming my mouth to his in a rough kiss. "You're wicked." Another kiss, and Aric held me to him, laughing and taking handfuls of my ass. "You're mad and horrible." I moaned as he wrapped his arms around me, bending me back as he licked his way into my mouth to devour the sound. "You're a genius, and I love you," I gasped as his lips traveled to my jaw and then my throat.

"I love you too, princess. Your indignation was the perfect tool to sell the fool's gold to the man," Aric rasped, nipping over my pulse before hauling me upright again, pushing me and swatting me on my rear. "We have to convince Nathan to let us move the magic. And to give up Kenneth, I suppose."

I laughed and bounced on my toes, linking my arm with Wendell's and stretching up to kiss his jaw. He was bemused, eyes bouncing between us with obvious questions on the tip of his tongue.

"Come on, I'll explain on the way," I said to Wendell before turning to Aric. "Which will be the greater sacrifice to swallow do you think?"

"Oh, definitely moving the magic," Aric said with a laugh.

⋙⋘

I MOANED, head thrown back and my fingers digging into the soft wet clay on the table, the same way Cosmo's fingers dug into the flesh of my hips as he thrust inside of me.

"Oh, stars! Cosmo, yes!"

Cosmo grunted, his speed picking up, patience finally breaking. My hips knocked against the table, barely cushioned by the muslin draped over. The legs squeaked against the floor, hushed beneath our grunts and cries.

"Come for me, little muse, make magic in that clay," Cosmo hissed, leaning against my back.

There was clay drying along my spine and on my breasts, smudged from and smeared from my interruption of Cosmo's work. I'd only come to see if he would join me for the afternoon of cards I'd arranged for the visiting nobles. He'd been scowling at his work, and I'd wanted to kiss into smiling again.

Half an hour later, and my dress was hanging down my arms, skirt rucked up around my waist, and it would surely all be ruined —the fabric, the start of Cosmo's sculpture, crushed in my fingers. He'd insisted, in my defense.

Cosmo's bucking grew wild as he gave up on me, more determined for his own finish, and the rare selfishness thrilled me. I fell with him, crying out his name, rocking back to meet him roughly until he was collapsing on my back, nudging me gently through the quake of my finish.

In my hands, clay roughened and grew hard, spindling around my fingers like a cage. I moaned and shuddered, landing on my elbows before I could fall into whatever I'd wrought.

Cosmo's arms circled my waist, dragging me back a little as he nuzzled into my neck. "We'll put it in the royal gallery."

I hadn't even noticed my eyes squeezing shut, but I opened them now and snorted. "We certainly will not."

"I like it. Sensual and scandalous."

I untangled my fingers from the strange globe made of twining rose vine and bryony blossoms and orchids. Inside, equally tangled, were two figures, joined but holding themselves open for the viewer to see the explicit union clearly.

"Not quite us," Cosmo said, kissing my cheek, reaching out to gently turn the globe.

One of the woman's hands was gripped tight around a vine, the other on her own breast. Her head was back, eyes shut and mouth open in obvious bliss. The man had his feet braced against the base, face furrowed in effort and determination, eyes fixed to where he penetrated the woman, his fingers digging into the flesh of her thighs.

I shook my head as arousal spiked in me.

"It's very good," Cosmo insisted.

"It's just magic though," I said. "That's like cheating, I think. There's no art in it if there's no effort."

"No effort! I object to that claim. I put forth a great effort." Cosmo rocked his hips against mine in demonstration, and I laughed, twisting to face him. He stepped back, grinning, and then pulled me toward the chair at the corner of his bright studio room. "I see your point, little muse, and I appreciate the reminder."

I leaned back against Cosmo's chest and stared at the strange object I'd made from across the room. Light filtered through from the large windows, casting strange shadows on the table and floor. Cosmo brushed at the dried clay on my chest, chuckling and straightening the bodice a little.

"I've made a mess of you. Might be time to go for a swim. Geese free," he murmured in my ear.

I hummed my agreement, although I would just as happily have fallen into a nap on Cosmo's lap in that moment. He pulled me up, tidying me as much as was necessary to move through the suite, and we headed for the bedroom. Owen entered at the same moment as us through the door leading from the main room, and my steps stalled at the frown on his face.

"We were just going for a bath. Do you want to come? Owen... what's wrong?" I asked, stopping still and holding firm until Cosmo paused too.

"Jack McCallum is here, he wants to speak with you. He says something's happened in the north. I just feel...trouble."

I swallowed hard and nodded, scanning the empty bedroom, Cosmo already ahead of me, snatching up one of Thao's sweaters from a bench and pushing it over my head.

"You have clay on your cheek too," Cosmo muttered, reaching a dusty thumb up as if that might help.

"It's fine," I said to him, already heading for the door. "It's not a state meeting."

Nora and her brother were together by the window, heads bowed and voices lowered. The viscount's shoulders were high, and his boots were splattered with mud. Wherever he'd come from, he'd done so in a rush and not bothered with the formality of redressing to present himself to me.

"What is it? Is it Griffin? Sam?" I asked. I'd heard so little from my friends in the north recently, and I was swamped by a sudden panic that the conflicts I'd left in Griffin's hands had left her in danger. I'd killed Emory in show, certainly, but what of the men who'd supported him?

Jack's head whipped up, and he looked almost surprised to see me for a moment. "No, Your Highness. It is...it is to do with the two-natured in general. There was an accident at a mine in the north this week."

"Oh!" Relief for Griffin and a new worry for these unknown shifters warred in me at the same moment, and I gripped the back of a chair as Jack moved away from his sister slowly.

"A cave collapsed with workers inside. Shifters are asked to work under dangerous conditions for a wealthy man's profit too often, Your Highness," Jack said. It was not quite a condemnation in his tone, but I could tell Jack had run out of patience. Not with me, exactly, but with the entire circumstance that had brought the two-natured into such regular danger.

"They were killed?" I whispered.

"Not all of them. Not yet. But that isn't to say there's great hope for them. There's a small opening in the mountain face. Not enough for a man to fit through, but perhaps for a bird... Your Highness, the manager of the mine was an especially brutal man. He clipped wings, broke paws and legs, of any two-natured working to prevent escape." Jack's gaze bored into me, his hands clenched at his sides.

I pulled my own stare away with great effort, searching the room around me blankly until I found Cresswell.

"I'd heard of such places," Cress said with a reluctant nod. "It was the worst kind of assignment we could be given. As a bear, I was less likely to be placed there."

"Too valuable," Jack said, eyeing Cresswell. "And too hard to subdue."

"Their means of escape is now gone," I murmured, and Jack nodded. "What can I do? I could go to the north and...my magic perhaps might be of some help?"

Jack's intense anger seemed to falter at last, and he too fell into a seat, Nora moving quickly to his side. "No, Your Highness, I didn't mean for—Efforts are being made to save the men. That's not what I came to ask you. I'm here with a warning more than anything. The two-natured are angry. This feels like..."

"It's not enough to stop further injustice. What's already done must be undone," I said softly.

"Soon, Your Highness," Jack answered with a nod. "Or I fear there will be a war within our own borders."

21.
BRYONY

Aric was bent over his desk, scribbling in a notebook with his arm around it as if he were a schoolboy trying to guard his answers. A thief's habit perhaps, equally wary of being stolen from as he was willing to steal.

"Aric."

"No, Bryony."

I glanced at the book just an inch from my hand and considered tossing it at his head. It would be so easy. Almost definitely satisfying.

"You're worried about my safety—"

"As *usual*," he growled.

I rolled my eyes. "That's very rich. Remember the time I saved your head from being separated from the rest of your body?"

Aric snarled and spun in his chair, glaring at me. But the second he set eyes on me, one corner of his mouth curled up, and a moment later he was laughing. "Vividly, princess. Never seen anything so beautiful."

My own smile soon followed, and Aric groaned, sinking into his chair, legs and arms spreading. It wasn't a real invitation, but I took it as such, crossing to him and settling myself into his lap, ignoring his grunt of protest.

"Oh, certainly, help yourself."

"You love it. Aric, listen—"

"Bryony—"

"I know there are risks. I'm listening to you. Now I'm asking you to listen to me. What is, if I decide to do this—"

"You clearly *have*—"

"—the best chance of my being safe, of the magic cooperating, and all going well?" I finished. Aric's head was resting on the back of the chair, eyes up on the ceiling, so I took advantage of the position, rubbing my fingers along his jaw and throat, over the stubble of his beard in the way I knew soothed him.

"I've been doing research on your queen's line. The mages have interesting texts, you know?"

I wasn't sure if Aric was trying to change the subject, but fighting him at every step wouldn't do me any good in this task. "What have you learned?"

"I suppose I've been confirming a suspicion. You're...you're not like us, Bryony," Aric said, head rolling to the side to catch my eye. "There's something in your magic, in your family line. There's never been a single son, did you know?"

I nodded. "Men aren't talked much about. Male lineage especially."

"And you don't come from Kimmery. Not really. It's funny that Holden wants your magic so much, because the queen's line seems to have come from the other side of the mountain."

"But there aren't women like us there," I said.

"I suspect you, your ancestor that is, traveled through there too and preferred it here. Bryony, I don't think we have a name for what the queen's line really is. You're not invincible, but you *create* magic."

I traced my finger over the furrow of Aric's brow. "It disturbs you."

He heaved a sigh and reached up to catch my hand, moving it to his mouth to press a kiss to the heel of my palm. "*You* don't disturb me, please understand. I'm very comfortable with my princess and increasingly...at ease with how your magic works. But the concept does, I suppose."

I nodded, even though the admission stung a little for all Aric's soothing. "You still think the tiger bite won't be safe."

Aric groaned, and his head dropped back again. "I... No. I have concerns, but I suspect your magic will be the more dominant of the two. My guess is that the bite won't work at all. And I'm not sure that warrants you getting bit by a tiger at all."

"Thao," I corrected. "Like he said, he'll be gentle. I've seen Wendell's mark, and it's faint really. More of a nip."

"You've made up your mind, I see."

"I want to put my name down on that registry."

"Bryony, no one is going to put you in a labor camp. You're talking about a symbolic gesture that may not change anything. Some might even consider it a slap in the face."

I frowned at that. "Do you think so?"

"Jack McCallum knows that there are two-natured who resent his privilege in keeping his status secret. And a princess who can be a tiger openly with none of the consequences might look equally unjust." Aric studied me as I thought through his words. "But..."

I glanced at him, and he grimaced.

"But I know you. And I know you will not rest your mind until you use your privilege to the benefit of others. Any resentment this act might stir up will be washed away when you have changed lives for good," Aric said. I grinned almost tearfully at the grumble of irritation in his voice, as if I were wrestling the words out of him.

"I want you to be in the room," I said.

"I'd like to see you try and keep me out," Aric answered, arching an eyebrow.

⚜

"THE SUITE IS CLEARED, and most of the castle is at the hunt we organized," Wendell announced, walking into our lavish bathroom where I was floating in the water with Thao. "Your mother didn't mind?"

"She thinks I'm having an orgy," I said, grinning.

Thao hummed with approval. "And perhaps you will later."

Aric was leaning against the wall, watching us as Thao poured water and fragrant oils over my head and shoulders. There were flowers floating on the surface, fresh off a boat from Mennary, and candles lit along the ledge of the tub interspersed with great glimmering stones and burning incense. Thao had said that the ceremony could've been dressed down to a simpler form, but Aric insisted on replicating it to the Mennarian tradition as much as possible.

"You never know what tiny ingredient can make the world of difference in a magical working," he'd insisted.

"When she shifts—" Wendell began, pulling his shirt off over his head.

"If she shifts—" Aric corrected.

"—you should leave the room. She'll be a tiger first, and it will take a little time for the woman to return."

I watched Wendell undress, blinking as Thao dabbed an especially pungent oil at my temples that made my eyes start to run. "Why are we undressed?" I asked in a whisper.

"Ceremony," Thao and Aric said together, making Thao's eyes roll.

I'd seen both Wen and Thao shift in and out of their tiger forms without losing a stitch on their clothing. The two-natured compared it to stepping aside to let the animal move forth, and Aric explained that some things were simply magic. It didn't always serve to search for an explanation.

"Owen's very excited," Wendell said, smiling and climbing over the ledge of the tub to join us. "He's looking forward to meeting your tiger."

"And the others?"

Wendell shrugged. "Fine, calm. Well, Cress is pacing."

I smiled at that, and then Wendell vanished, replaced by a massive white tiger swimming amiably through the water, butting his head against my waist as he passed.

"Are you nervous?" Thao asked.

"A little," I said. Wendell had given me his full record of the experience already, but for all my insistence on this act, I couldn't help but agree with Aric that my transformation would probably be different.

"I'll be as gentle as I can be," Thao said, unusually somber.

I nodded. "It's not the pain I'm nervous for, really." It was everything that came after. If the magic would fail, if it wouldn't, how I might feel as a tiger.

Thao's hands settled on my shoulders, anchoring my toes to the tile floor of the tub. "There's no consequence but getting you healed up if this doesn't work. And Wendell and I will be with you if it does."

I nodded again and then held my breath as Thao bent to kiss my brow.

"I'm ready to work stabilizing charms if they're needed," Aric said softly from the corner.

"And to duck out if I shift," I reminded him, and he reluctantly agreed.

"Ready?" Thao asked.

I probably wasn't, not really. I wasn't frightened, but I wasn't *ready*. We hadn't warned my mother I would be trying this, too afraid it might get to the council, and while I was confident I would be fine, success or failure, there was a little chiming 'if' at the back of my head.

"Ready," I said, because in my experience, taking a risk wasn't something anyone was ever fully prepared for.

Thao took a deep breath, and Wendell's tiger sat down at my back, massive brow against my spine, hot breath caressing me as he held me up.

Thao began to chant in Mennarian, and while my head was too full to sort through the words, I knew what they meant. Prayers to the tiger at the head of his family, who imparted this gift. Prayers to the sea to bless change and transformation. To the earth for steadying the magic and solidifying forms. I shut my eyes, matching my breaths to the slow beat of Wendell's, letting Thao's low voice wash over me, the dizzying clash of the scent of oils making my head spin.

Thao kissed my lips once, briefly, and then water shifted and lapped at my skin. I peeked and found the large orange and black beast before me, nuzzling his head at the top of the water, into the skin just below my ribs. Wendell moved behind me too, standing and turning, and I glanced once at Aric, trying to hide the little flicker of worry I was fighting off. My mage smiled at me, ducking his head, eyes glinting with awareness and the smallest, most faintly challenging smirk curling the corners of his lips. He saw the girl in me who wanted to suddenly run away, and he dared her to go through with the act.

I turned, smiling slightly as Wendell nudged his massive jaw against one breast, and then let me drape myself over his great back.

Thao had asked if he could bite my ass, and without waiting for my answer, the others had all refused to let it be marred. It was kind of flattering, if a little galling too. We'd settled on the back of my thigh instead, a safely fleshy area carefully chosen for the wound so it would miss any major arteries that would be harder to heal. If the magic worked, the bite would heal quickly. And if it didn't...

Hopefully, mine or Aric's magic would make quick work of it. Or I would be left with an uncomfortable seat for quite a while.

Thao and Wendell were both chuffing, trying to soothe me with the happy sounds, and I wondered if they could smell my anxiety through all the oils. A massive, furry chin rested itself on the crease of my bottom, and I let out a little giggle as Thao waited for me to calm myself. I wrapped my arms around Wendell's shoulders and sighed.

"Go on," I said.

Thao licked at the back of my thigh, and my eyes widened briefly, muscles stiffening at the strange drag of his rough tongue on my skin. It was simultaneously threatening and an oddly pleasant touch. Wendell's head lifted, and I pressed my face into his wet fur as Thao licked my thigh again. I wished I was facing Aric, able to see his expression daring me to be brave as Thao pulled away. But perhaps it was for the best. Aric might not have been able to keep the worry out of his face.

There was a rumble behind me, a warning, and then four symmetrical points of pressure around the back of my thigh. Thao's breath rasped over my skin, and my arms squeezed around Wendell's strong shoulders. The pressure was gentle, more a reminder for me to hold as still as I could so Thao didn't tear muscle needlessly when he bit.

And then it was cruel, digging and stabbing, aching like brutal fingers. I buried a cry into Wendell's fur, but when Thao's bite *finally* broke through flesh, there was no volume to my scream.

Stay still. Just wait, I reminded myself, gasping through an open mouth. *Just wait.*

A soft gurgle of pain escaped my throat as incisors dug through muscle, the sensation somehow numb and painful at the same time. And then it was hot, Thao's teeth retreating and the nerves in my skin screaming in answer, grieving for the wounds. Wendell shifted in my hold, and it took me a moment to move my focus away from the bite burning on the back of my leg to remember how to loosen my grip on him.

"Bryony?" Aric rasped, appearing at the ledge of the tub, brow tangled.

"It will take a moment," Thao murmured, back in his human form.

"I..." I blinked, wincing as the heat in my leg grew.

Aric paled as he looked at the water, where red was clouding out around my hips.

Magic was rising in me, but it was my own, cold and furious. It bloomed from my chest, indignant at the injury, and I realized, even as the fire stretched down my wounded leg to my toes, that Aric was right. My magic *would* fight off this assault.

"Do you feel it?" Thao asked me, turning me in the water to face him.

"I feel...hot," I murmured.

"Her pupils are dilated," Aric murmured.

"She's not bleeding out, Aric, give it a moment," Thao said through a tense jaw, his eyes holding mine.

I whimpered, and my eyes fell shut as the magic of Thao's bite spread like a hot iron scratching through me, until there in my core, right in my hips, it struck against my own power. There was a war inside of me—lightning and ice against a smoldering coal burn.

Thao cursed, and Aric began to bark orders to him about getting me out of the water. I wanted to cry—I probably already was, given the agony coursing through me—over the failure. I *wanted* this. It had been my idea, and it was wholly unfair that the Hunger would prevent my transformation.

I yanked on my magic, tugging at it like the reins on a wild horse. Fire rose up into my belly, cold biting magic retreating.

I gasped as Thao tried to lift me from the water. "Wait! Wait, I have it," I cried out, pushing on his shoulder with a trembling hand. "I have it."

Aric had said that the Hunger was the superior of the two magics, but it was *mine*. I controlled it. And I wanted it to stand the fuck down and let me have this.

Thao's hold on me loosened, and I groaned as the fire of the tiger magic grew hotter, higher, scorching through my chest and up into my throat.

"Aric, she's going to shift," Thao said, catching my hands before I could grab and claw at my neck. "You've got to get out."

"Are you—?"

"I'm sure, Aric!"

I was jerking in Thao's hold, some reflex I was trying to bury.

"That's it, Bryony. You're doing beautifully. I will tell you more about Wendell's transformation after this. He threw up right on me," Thao murmured as I trembled violently.

It was the worst in my skull, white-hot and blinding. I was certain that the magic was burning down everything I was, blazing away the girl to make room for the animal. Thao released me, and I had no strength to hold myself up, the water rushing up around me as my legs gave out, and I sank beneath the surface, the warm water no relief for the fire eating me up.

Fur surrounded me, two bodies circling, eyes watching from above.

An empty vessel, ensconced in a pool, staring blankly back... and then—

My claws scratched over the tile beneath me, muscles striking hard. I resurfaced with a roar that thundered over tile, water sloshing from my fur, my head shaking and spraying the—

Cage. Trap. The scent of the air all wet and wrong with other smells. Two males circled me, huffing and butting me with their heads, and I snarled back, clawing them away. They tried first to soothe and then to subdue, the dark one growling in warning, and I gave them my full roar, his ears flattening against his head, even as he braved another step closer. I smacked him hard for his daring. They were small, these two. Small compared to me.

I kicked and climbed my way to the edge of the too-smooth pool, and the pale one slammed himself in my way.

Fine.

I would teach them better.

They were reluctant fighters, trying to wrestle me back, but I was bigger. I was stronger. I would master them later when I was free; they couldn't keep me between them. I bit the pale one on the ruff and wrestled him below the water, the dark one howling and finally daring to bite my side. I subdued him next, finally winning my way to the edge, scratching myself out and free of the water, little human—

Human.

—Trinkets clattering to the floor.

There was smooth reflective water—*mirror*—on the wall, and I caught a glance of myself, massive and grand and exquisite, shaded softly even sopping wet, before I turned and paced, searching for my escape.

The orange and white ones tried to call me back, gentling their tones after our fight. I wanted out, out, out, *out*.

There was a squeak, and I jumped around, crouching and expecting to see prey, another challenger, but instead there was a sliver of light when there hadn't been before. One of the males in the pool howled a warning, trying to scramble out of the water.

My escape.

I nudged the door open—*door, bath*—with a careful claw, stepping into a new space full of...familiar smells. A safe cage, but still a cage, full of more human things.

Aren't I...

Another open door and—

I was knocked sideways with a roar, a jaw clamped around my throat, paws digging hard into my belly. I growled. These fools —*fool men, my men*—wanted to fight me?

They'd learned better already, the pair of them quick to try and subdue me together rather than each on their own, but it was no use. I was stronger, I was better, I wanted *out*, and I would claw and bite when they were too shy. I threw one off of me and toward the light, the other in direction of the boxed flame, and took off running for the open door.

Another fucking safe cage.

I growled as I heard the thunder of those two males following me. I ran for the flat wall, crashing hard against it before turning around to snarl back at them, warning them away.

"What's hap—"

Open door.

I fought my way out, knocking aside the tall human—*familiar, safe*—waiting outside.

"Fuck! Bryony! No one touch her. Get out of the way!"

This was free, or close to it, I thought, with a gleeful kind of clarity, grinning toothily at the two-leggers leaping out of my way as I careened down the hall.

There was a roar behind me, unfamiliar, dangerous.

Predator. A good challenge. Better than the two males I'd left behind. I would play with that new one later.

"Bryony!"

A human name, how dull.

"*Princess!*"

Ugh. Even worse.

My claws skidded over the too smooth ground of the hall, and I slipped at a corner, huffing as I crashed into a wall, a yelp released from the other side of the surface. Following that sound would be fun, but—

There was a smell here...

My snarl was automatic. Familiar. Unsafe. Predator but also prey.

The great beast, big and dark and tall was catching up to me, making the ground tremble as he raced in my direction. But he was slow, and I was bigger than the males like me. Stronger.

I grinned at it as it chased after me, two-leggers close behind, my males following.

A game of chase. No, better. A *hunt*.

I called for them to join me, those males, and one snarled a threat in answer as I took off down the hall. Two leggers appeared with their glittering hard skins and their extra-long claw, but they stepped aside in deference to my beauty, their fear a pleasant appetizer to my hunger.

My Hunger.

I was chasing the trail of sweat and magic, of sex and pain, bounding down slippery staircases and across this great vast free cage, full of familiar smells. Most of them bad.

"Shit, she's heading for Camellia."

"Is it...worth stopping her—"

"Imagine Bryony's reaction if she eats her sister!"

Not eat. Bad meat. Slay. Hunt. Protect my mates.

My Chosen. I couldn't *kill* Camellia. Not like this. But I wanted her to see me. To know she was weak and small and fragile and would fit in my jaws like a snack. That I could pin her down with my great paws, and she would have no strength to make me budge.

"Bryony, stop!"

It was my name, after all. How disappointing.

Pieces of the woman, the human, were returning, my pace beginning to falter and slow. I huffed, and with it came a great taste of my prey, sour and sickly and stained. Bad meat. My hackles rose, and my growl broke free. I was close.

Footsteps chased closer, and one of my memory men skidded in front of me, his face red and eyes so wide I could see the whites. He smelled of anger and fear and magic. Something sweet too, that made the woman in me want to sit on her haunches and preen for him.

"Princess," he growled, and I bared my teeth in answer. "You cannot go in."

There was magic gathering in his hands, and it tasted like flint sparks on my fat tongue. I shook my fur in answer, lowering into a crouch, warning him I would pounce if he didn't move.

"I don't want to hurt you," he warned.

I growled. Threat.

The magic released from his hands, and I leapt up with a roar. It crashed into my chest, but I knew its flavor. It was *my* magic not his. The man dashed out of the way, and I slammed into the doors, wearing magic in my fur as I crashed against its surface.

They parted for me, and I snarled at the first wave. Pain, fear, anger, sex. Bad meat.

Two-legger men, weak and frail and sickly, scrambled out of my way, my men barking orders behind me. The trail was rich in the air, spoiled milk.

Camellia. Sister. Danger. Predator and prey.

The bear, Cress, padded at my side, ready to intervene, trying to push himself in my way, but I was too quick and sleek, and he was too devoted to harm me.

Camellia was on the floor mating, with the flavor of anger dense around her. She screamed at my arrival, scrambling off the man's cock and then kicking him in my direction. She was bone and brittle, so small, and I growled at her over and over, a low and steady rumbling warning as she wormed back until she hit the bed. Human words fell from her lips, garbled and pleading, but no apologies. She was afraid, but only for the moment. Only because she was faced with tooth and claw and strength where she had none. Her magic was there, but it fizzled weakly against me, and she flinched when it bounced away and struck her instead.

"Mistress."

I snapped at Cress when he tried to step between us again, bit his shoulder in warning, although he didn't move.

"Mistress, look how fine you look."

Something soft brushed my shoulder. My shoulders flexed, but the touch wasn't unpleasant. A slow steady rub between my shoulder blades, as if I were a kitten.

A two-legger, one of mine, crouched at my side, ignoring the stench of Camellia as he bowed his head and nuzzled against mine, just behind my ears. Familiar and animal and sweet. Another hand reached bravely for my snarling jaw, fingers scratching into fur as I continued to growl.

"You always have been, and always will be, the finest creature I've ever laid eyes on."

There was another kind of magic, but this wasn't mine. It was gentle, like a blanket, but it sank into me, softening my snarls, soothing my muscles.

"Not like this," Owen whispered in my ear, making me twitch with the tickle of his breath.

"You—you... It can't be," Camellia gasped, staring at me. "It can't."

I roared and lunged, and she screamed and cowered, eyes slamming shut. I laughed, chuffing and pulled back again, watching her tremble weakly.

All the while, Owen petted me. Calm, fearless, patient. My head turned, butting into his shoulder, and he hummed happily, working that strange sweet magic of his to calm me. I was calm. As tempting as it was to bite Camellia—she'd earned it—the tiger in me knew she would taste horrible. And the woman—I, Bryony— knew that I couldn't use the excuse of being a tiger to kill my sister. I was trying to prove that the two-natured *weren't* dangerous, and such an act would undo everything.

Guilt, a purely human emotion, sank uneasily into me, and with it, the tiger stepped back.

I rose, with Owen's help, naked and calm before my sister.

"Are you *insane*?" Camellia gasped, staring up at me with plain horror on her face, body crumpled on the floor before me.

"Luckily for you, I am not," I answered.

"Come, Mistress," Owen murmured, edging away.

Cress stood a man again, his eyes blazing on mine, but it was a mix of anger and love and relief.

"Be careful, sister," I said as Cress took his jacket off and slipped it over my shoulders.

"Of *what*?" Camellia squawked.

I smiled in answer and backed away.

22.
BRYONY

"My...goodness."

I yawned, and the woman, my mother, gasped at the sight of my enormous toothy jaw.

"Now she's just showing off," Cosmo murmured, smirking at me.

My tail thumped against the floor, and my artist grinned and turned back to the grand model of me on his table. It was rough still, but already elegant, powerful. Just as I was.

"Beautiful," my mother murmured.

"You can pet her," Owen urged.

My mother glanced between us, excitement filling her face, but there was a little flavor of fear on the air too. Cosmo huffed as I pushed up from the floor and padded over to my mother, who stiffened. She'd kept safely away from me since I'd transformed for her, and while she seemed her usual delighted by anything self, the nerves in the air were a clear hint to something else.

I resisted the urge to let out a rumble of annoyance even as she stumbled back two steps. There'd been no keeping my new second-nature a secret. Not after I'd gone barreling through the castle on a spree. Or a hunt. Even now that the tiger and I were more unified, I could still recall the flavor of Camellia's terror, sharp and dense and bitter, scratching at me to track her down and snap at her just to hear her scream again. Maybe that was a little bit my own wish.

I sat down in front of my mother, close enough to rub myself against her but waiting for her to grow more comfortable first. Her heart was loud and fast in her chest, eyes wide and fixed to watching. Owen reached out, and I tilted my head to catch his scratching fingers behind my ear, a huff of pleasure escaping. My mother laughed, one trembling hand reaching out slowly. She smelled of men and of magic and the animal in me found something unpleasant in the flavors, but I was trying to prove to her how gentle, how myself I really I was, so I leaned into her touch, lapping my tongue over a spot on the back of her wrist and marking my scent there.

"Oh my." She sank down to her knees in a quick rush that prickled my senses, warned of an attack, but I held those instincts back, blinking at my mother as her face hovered in front of mine. "Oh my," she repeated. "My daughter...is a tiger."

I chuffed as she reached into my fur with both hands, scratching and rubbing pleasantly. She laughed, nearly falling sideways as I rested my chin on her shoulder.

"She's harmless," my mother said brightly.

"She's Bryony," Cosmo said, and my tail thumped at the correction. I wasn't harmless, not at all, but I wasn't wild. Not now at least. It had taken a few practicing shifts with Thao and Wendell before I'd really been able to change and hold onto myself right away.

"Her colors are unusual," my mother said.

I had orange and white stripes, although Thao called me 'pink' when the sunlight hit. I wasn't sure if he was just sore that my tiger was bigger and stronger than his.

"We think it's something to do with her magics interacting," Owen said.

"Does this mean her children will be tigers too?" my mother asked.

Cosmo set his tools aside and lowered himself to the floor. My mother laughed as I slid myself down to the floor to drop my head in Cosmo's lap, exposing my belly to them—it prickled the tiger to do this, but my mother sighed as she ran her fingers through the soft pale fur there.

"If her daughter is Thao's, yes. We're not sure if the magic will carry on from Bryony herself though," Cosmo said.

My mother pulled away then, her hands folding in her lap, face going unusually somber. "It's not the same magic as the Kimmerian two-natured?"

"No," Owen said.

"No. But this will change things."

I shifted back, sitting up and smoothing my skirts around me, my mother's eyes widening briefly at the transformation. "I think it's a good thing to embrace the different kinds of magic that make up Kimmery. I think magic *is* Kimmery's prosperity."

"I'm not sure how the farmers and the merchants would feel about that," Mother said drily. "But perhaps you're right. The council will have to be informed."

"I ran through the castle as a tiger. I suspect they already were," I said.

"You weren't *really* going to eat your sister, were you, darling?" Mother asked, brow furrowing as she gazed at me.

I might've if Owen hadn't intervened. It was hard to read myself as a tiger. My hunt for Camellia might've been a game of chase, or it might've been the intent of a predator. The two weren't so different for the animal.

"Of course not, Mother," I lied.

She sighed happily, and Cosmo let me crush his hand in mine. "I didn't think so," she said. "Now let me see you as a tiger again."

I sat up just as a throat cleared in the doorway. Aric stood there, a folded letter pinched between his fingers. "A note from our friends in the north."

I shot up from the floor before I remembered myself. "Oh, I'm sorry, I—"

"It's fine," my mother said with a laugh, taking Owen's hand for him to help her up. "Another time. I'm glad you made such friends in the north while you were there."

I wasn't sure what my mother would think of Griffin, Sam, and Mistress Sanders if she met them, or what she would think of my being crowned King of Thieves, for all I'd neglected that title. It was better not to find out.

"Another time," I agreed, escorting my mother out of Cosmo's studio and through the suite.

"You've made your changes here," my mother said, admiring the strange landscapes that had appeared on the walls of the hallway.

"My magic did," I said with a little shrug.

My mother's eyes lit up. "Like in the ballroom!"

I blushed, recalling the game Daniel and Aric had made of my first dance, and nodded.

"You know," my mother whispered, leaning in close. "I tried that myself the other night with my Chosen. Nothing quite as impressive, but we did change the drapes. How funny to learn something new about myself after all this time. I wonder what else I've done without ever noticing."

I kissed my mother's cheeks at the door to my suite, barely waiting for the lock to click shut before I whirled around and leapt toward Aric. "Who wrote? What does it say?"

"How did your mother handle your tiger?" Aric asked, holding up the letter high above our heads. I jumped for it, and his arm wrapped around my waist.

"Aric!" I snapped. He arched an eyebrow as the others watched and hid their chuckles poorly. "It went fine, I think. She warmed up to me."

"You're very soft," Aric said, grinning and drawing down the letter by a mere inch. "Although your huffing is louder than Owen's snores."

"I will turn into a tiger right now and bite your hand off if you don't show me that letter," I growled.

"There's my girl," Aric said, and he ducked down, nibbling at my throat as I snatched the letter from his fingers.

"Why are you distracting me?" I hissed, squirming in his arms as he laved and sucked at my neck. I held the letter behind his head, ignoring my rising Hunger from his kisses as I tore it open. "It's from Griffin!"

"Do you two have to do that here?" Morgan called from the corner of the room as Aric's now free hand squeezed my bottom.

"I agree with her, what are you on about?" I gasped as Aric lifted me from the floor, his laugh vibrating against my skin as he carried me backward to the bedroom door. It was an effort to keep my eyes open at his assault, but it was even more of a challenge to focus on the words on the page.

The situation as it stands in your northern court can't continue, Bryony. I'm on my way south to speak with you in person, and this letter will likely arrive at the same time I do. Meet me in the southern thieves court at the edge of the capital on...

"Aric, she's here! She's in the capital! Aric!" I nearly dropped the letter altogether as we reached the bedroom, the door still hanging open behind us. Aric had done some trick of his on the back of my dress, laces unraveling, and his hand was already down in my skirt, clutching and squeezing roughly at my ass.

"If I'm taking you to Thatcher's thieves court, I'm taking you there full to the brim with magic," Aric growled.

"You read the letter? Of course you did. Scoundrel," I moaned, rocking into Aric briefly before my eyes widened. "There are thieves here in the capital?!"

Aric laughed and lifted his head finally. "Princess, there are thieves *everywhere*."

"And Thatcher? That's the king here?"

"Cassius Thatcher is a rogue, a scoundrel, a thief, a king, and a man so dangerous, I am tempted to tell Griffin she can come to the castle if she wants to speak to you," Aric snarled, tugging my dress down my shoulders and roughly over my hips.

I tilted my head and narrowed my eyes at Aric. "That sounds like praise coming from you. It is, isn't it? You like him?"

Aric paused, his arms wrapping around my now bare shoulders, pressing my breasts to the soft linen of his shirt. He kissed the tip of my nose and smiled at me. "I do. He's an old friend. That doesn't mean I trust him with your safety. King's agreement or not."

The king's agreement was a thief code where no king would act against another or encroach on each other's territory.

"I should've introduced myself to him already," I murmured, frowning. "It's what I would've done if I visited another country."

"You're here as the princess, not the king," Aric answered quickly. Which only meant he'd known all along I should've already made my addresses to this Cassius Thatcher. "You'll pay your respects tomorrow evening. Until then..." Aric pushed the fabric of the dress down to the floor and then lifted me up, my legs wrapping around his hips automatically.

"I should close the door," I said as Aric carried me to the circular bench, sitting me at the center platform and kneeling on the cushions in front of me. It was the perfect height for him to slide inside of me. The furniture in our bedroom was well-considered.

"You should call the others," Aric whispered, brushing his mouth over mine as he opened his trousers. "After I'm done with you."

I'D SPENT VERY little time on the streets of the capital, at least outside of a carriage. Wendell and Aric knew their way around much better than I did, not that it mattered much. I had to keep my head down, even with the glamour I wore from Aric.

We'd informed Head Guard Amos that we had an errand in the capital but refused any extra guards. I had seven men who would give their life for me, but more importantly, I had my magic and my tiger. I was my own best defense if it came to any danger, but we traveled through the city on horseback, each of us disguised.

The city was beautiful, especially near the castle and on the main road, but Aric's directions soon veered us in a new direction, away from the main center and toward the western edge where the shipping docks were busy, even so late at night. Buildings bore the brunt of the sea air here, their paint chipped and stripped from the wooden structures. It was loud, many of the buildings appearing to be either warehouses or inns and taverns.

But the loudest, largest, and most weathered building—set away from the docks and surrounded by dark warehouses—was our destination. Aric stopped his horse short, keeping us in the shadow of two silent buildings. I pulled Crescent to a reluctant stop, Cosmo pressed to my back, his arm around my waist.

"We'll tether the horses here. They look a little fine to be waiting outside Thatcher's," Aric said. "I'll charm them safe."

Cosmo and I jumped down together, a quick echo of boots hitting damp cobblestone close behind. It was cold, and I pulled my cloak tighter around me as a sharp lick of sea air snuck its way through the narrow alleyways to butt against us.

"Will you tell Griffin about your tiger?" Thao asked me as Aric tied our horses to the post.

"Of course," I said grinning. "I can't wait to see her, really."

"Her letter was a little ominous," Wendell said, a faint frown on his face as he stared at the bright windows of the massive building we were heading for. It was the only brick building in the area that I'd seen, and even that didn't drown the sound of music and chaotic conversation inside.

I nodded, sliding my hands into the pockets of my simple skirt. It'd been such a long time since I'd been able to dress as I had in the north, and it was nice to be out in the world as Bryony rather than the princess, even if my role tonight was still political.

"Let's go," Aric said, striding to the front to lead our party. I followed without thinking, and a moment later, his steps slowed. "I just remembered I'm not king," he said, turning back to me with a sheepish smile. "You'd better take the lead. It'll be crowded, loud. Cassius will be behind the bar, he always is. He keeps his spies on the floor. Griffin will find us after we've made our introductions."

I nodded and moved into the lead, Cresswell and Aric framing me at my back and the others moving into their own positions. My feet seemed to bounce on the beaten stones as I walked to the noisy doorway. I was excited to see Griffin, but I was even more excited to be thinking about something other than Kimmery's crown for the night.

No one seemed to take notice of us as we entered, or if they did, they were too good at hiding it. The volume was deafening, and the room was dense with activity. There were narrow pathways around small tables packed with too many people, and even more faces overhead on a balcony surrounding the great open room. There was a stage ahead of us with a lively band of players, more shadowy seating beneath the balcony to our left, and a vast and heavily populated bar to our right. Aric said the other king would be behind it, but I couldn't see any sign of a bartender through the crush of bodies.

"Griffin?" I asked Aric, somewhat intimidated by the crowd.

"Just get to the bar," Aric said, leaning in to speak directly into my ear.

I sucked in a breath, stepping bravely forward, and was nearly barreled over by a massive man. Cresswell pulled me back into his chest and then propelled us forward together, his arm firmly around my waist.

"I hate this," Cress shouted to Aric.

"She has more enemies in the castle than she does here," Aric answered back, just a touch quieter.

"They can't get this close to her there."

I'd fisted my hands in my pockets, gathering strength, and marched into the mass of bodies surrounding the bar. I was smaller than my men, more easily able to shoulder my way between the strangers who seemed used to being bullied about. I squeezed my way closer, Cress's hand wrapped tight around my arm like an anchor, until finally, just when the oppression of so many people so close grew to be overwhelming, I broke free to the front, the edge of the bar crashing suddenly into my ribs as two strangers stepped away.

The wall behind the bar was full of bottles, far more colors and shapes than I'd ever seen. Of course! This wasn't just Kimmerian mead and wine, this was alcohol imported from every ship in the harbor. Or stolen from it, in some cases. It took me several moments of catching my breath and marveling at the vast wall before I noticed the man moving behind the bar.

At first glance, he seemed plain, just a man working, and I had to remember that Aric swore this was the southern King of Thieves before I looked again. At second glance, he became handsome. Elegant even. He was graceful as he moved, pouring and passing drinks in almost the same breath, one ear always tilted to the voices calling their orders into his ear, one hand always gathering the coin that landed on the bar before someone else could. I suspected he was tall, although it was hard to tell since he was usually bending and working. His hair was inky black, and there was something not quite Kimmerian about him. Hawkish sharp features and skin just a couple shades too dark. Most of the bar looked to have its fair share of foreign blood really. Perhaps they were sailors, or perhaps this was the look of the people who lived near the docks and met many travelers in their lives.

Cassius Thatcher was making his way methodically in our direction, working his way down the orders of the bar, and it gave me time to study him. He looked clever, if there was such a way to do so, and I never once saw where he put the money, even though I didn't feel the slightest trace of magic in the air.

Aric had pushed his way through the melee to lean against the bar, his hips resting close to mine. I glanced back over my shoulder briefly to see I was safely surrounded by my Chosen, their forms a protective wall around me. When I turned back, I found myself face to face with Cassius.

"Your...Majesty," he said, a smile as slick as oil sliding over his features.

"Your Majesty," I answered with a dip of my head.

"I should've brought her sooner," Aric said.

Cassius didn't look at Aric, his eyes didn't even flick in his direction. Stars, those eyes were almost entirely black. I'd never seen a color so dark. It left me with the odd impression that there was absolutely nothing to be read in his gaze, and his expression was far too smooth to really decipher.

"You're here now," Cassius said, more to me than Aric. His head tilted. "Why are you here now?"

"To meet Griffin," I said without thinking.

I only regretted it for a single heartbeat. Griffin's name seemed to strike this man, the elegant dark mask faltering to reveal genuine surprise and...something joyful. I'd understood Aric's claim of how dangerous Cassius must've been a second before, but now I also knew there was something wonderfully likable about the man.

"Give it away, why don't you," a soft dry voice muttered at my ear.

I spun with a gasp, finding that Owen and Wendell had parted to make room for Griffin at my back. "Griffin!" I cried, wrapping my arms around her.

Griffin stiffened in response, and through the cacophony of music and shouting and conversation, I heard the man behind the bar murmur, "Birdie," in greeting. Over Griffin's shoulder, a friendly and familiar lopsided grin greeted me.

I squealed and pulled away, clapping my hands together. "Scrapper! Oh! And Sam!"

"Your Loveliness," Scrapper said with a wobbling bow. At his side, a nervous but alert Sam dipped his head to me.

"Oh, I've missed you all! And I have so much to tell you and so much I want to hear!" I cried, spinning to face Griffin and laughing at the grimace she was wearing. "I'm sorry, I know tonight is important. It's just so *good* to see you again. We'll sort everything out now that we're together."

Aric's hand settled on my shoulder as if he could contain my excitement, trying to pin me back down to the floor.

"Your Majesty, you have neglected your duties to your court in the north," Griffin said, sudden and biting, her face twisted with anger or... "Your lack of attention to your people leaves me only one choice."

"Griffin?" I murmured, all my joy seeming to fizzle away like steam on the hot coals of her scowl.

"I challenge you, my king."

23.
BRYONY

The hush that followed expanded slowly, seeping from one body to the next as if the quiet were infectious.

"You what?" I asked, even though I'd heard the words perfectly.

Griffin's brow furrowed as if she were pained. "Bryony, I—" She swallowed, glancing briefly around us, aware of the growing silence. "I challenge you to the northern crown, Your Majesty."

Even then, even perfectly aware of what she said, it was as if my ears were full of water, the words not fitting together. My court. Griffin wanted to steal *my* court from—

No, I realized, thinking back to what Aric had said. I might have to give up one crown before I could seize the other. He'd been trying to warn me. I'd taken the northern court by accident. I hadn't wanted it, and I'd tried to give it back to Aric straight away.

But Aric couldn't be the king and my Chosen, and he'd picked his side. I couldn't be Kimmery's queen and the thieves' king. Stars, I wasn't even managing to be a princess at the same time.

"I see," I said slowly, holding Griffin's gaze. She seemed to relax by a small fraction. I *did* see. Griffin had to take this crown from me, I couldn't gift it to her any more than I could've handed it back to Aric. She had to win it in the challenge just as I had. At least she knew what she was doing.

"Do you hear that, folks?"

I jumped at the sudden and boisterous tone of Cassius Thatcher. He was leaning back from the bar, arms raised up at his sides and his voice ringing fully around the room.

"Our Birdie wants a crown of her own!"

The room cheered, and my eyes widened. Damnit, I wanted to be digging gossip out of Griffin more than anything right now.

"Birdie?" Scrapper hissed with a laugh.

"Don't you dare pick it up, Scrap," Griffin ground out of the corner of her mouth.

Sam's lips quirked, glancing between the pair.

"Funny you never asked me for mine, Birdie," Cassius said, falling forward with his elbows to the bar, his voice lowering to just us crowded together.

"I don't need your help, Cass. I just needed the audience," Griffin said, glaring at the man. There was fire in her gaze, his too, I noticed. Ohh, they were absolutely lovers once. I wanted every sordid detail of their history. And I wanted to subject Griffin to the wonderful misery of my pestering her for it all. It would be a act of suitable revenge for her springing this on me.

"You may have whatever you please," he answered, Griffin's nostrils flaring in annoyance at the silky seductive tone of the words. He stood straighter and turned back to the room. "As challenger, Griffin has the right to choose the method."

"No magic," Griffin said to me immediately. "And no blades."

My eyes widened. "What?"

Griffin shrugged, and finally there was warmth in her smile. "I'm not an idiot, Bry. You're too good."

"Flattery and treachery in one go. And I wasn't prepared for either," I answered back, a little tart.

Griffin just grinned at me. "Let's stick to our profession. First of us to steal a precious item off the other's person wins."

I stepped back immediately, and Cassius chuckled, the room quick to follow suit. Griffin's lips pressed together to hide her own smile. I wanted to shout that that wasn't fair at all, I wouldn't even have begun to know what was precious to Griffin, let alone how to take it off her. But it was her right to challenge. And anyway, I needed her to win, didn't I?

Yes, but...

"I'm not going to make this easy for you," I said, glaring.

"I don't need you to," Griffin answered.

"We'd better make this fair," Cassius declared, jumping up onto the bar. "Ladies, gentleman, make an arena."

The crowd was quick, people hurrying out of their seats, dragging away tables and chairs to the edges of the room. Griffin melted into the crowd opposite me, and Aric pulled me away from the bar before we were trapped in the crush.

"You knew she'd do this," I hissed to Aric.

"I knew she'd feel like she had to. I didn't know until her letter arrived if she would go through with it. To be honest, I thought she might wait until our return. Things must be bad in the north." Aric pushed me forward through the bodies, my Chosen a tight cluster around me. "Do you want to keep it?" he whispered in my ear. "If you do, I can—"

I shook my head. "No, this is right."

Aric kissed my temple as we reached the edge of the new ring of open space at the center of the room. "It'll be a bit of a fight. Bit of wits. You'll be the first Queen of Kimmery to have a King of Thieves for a friend."

I smiled at that, leaning into his kiss briefly.

"If you want her to work for it, you let her make the first move," Aric whispered.

I stepped forward into the open space, turning slowly, searching for Griffin in the crowd. I saw Sam and Scrapper together at the edge. Cassius Thatcher was on the stage, seated on a stool as if he might pick up an instrument and start to play. No Griffin.

And then I saw the strange shadow on the floor, my feet narrowly skidding backward before Griffin leapt down from the balcony, landing on bent legs, red hair floating about her face.

"Worth a shot," she said, rising slowly.

"You're supposed to steal from me, not squash me," I answered, surprised when a few voices hooted in my favor from the crowd.

"You said you had lots to tell me?" Griffin said, walking casually around the edge of the ring in my direction.

I mirrored her in a slow opposite pace. "I suppose I'll have to show you later," I said, thinking of her face when she saw my tiger for the first time. The castle was aware of my new second nature, but there was no way the news had reached these parts so quickly, and certainly not Griffin's ears.

"And is it good to be home here in the south again?" she asked. My steps faltered as I thought of everything that had already happened. Griffin paused too, frowning. "I'm sorry," she mouthed.

I didn't know if she meant it about my grandmother. Or about the challenge, or all of the above. I only nodded and danced away.

"And you? How is your homecoming here?" I asked, eyebrow arching.

Griffin shrugged, and half of the audience booed cheerfully, including the southern king, making her roll her eyes. "Nothing around here changes much, as far as I can tell," Griffin said, raising her voice and tilting in Cassius' direction. "Same *old* faces."

I didn't think Cassius looked that old, but he laughed loudly in answer. "Pick it up, Birdie. We can't watch the two of you in your contradance all night!"

"You can take her, Your Loveliness!" Scrapper called from the edge.

Griffin scowled, tossing him a dark look, and I took a chance, in spite of Aric's advice. Griffin was too quick yanking roughly away from me, but I saw enough, noticed the way she immediately pulled her left side away before her right. Whatever was precious to her was somewhere on the left.

Griffin's eyes widened, and she laughed brightly at me, surprised by my daring. "It's there, you know," she said, a little breathless, and I thought she meant her own item until she glanced down on my right hip. "I can see it beating against your skirt, flattening the fabric."

I held myself still, resisting the urge to flinch as she had. It didn't matter. She was right. The dagger Aric had fashioned for me was fastened to my hip as it always was, hidden away in the folds of my skirt.

"We said no blades," Griffin said, arching an eyebrow. "You should've taken it off."

I shrugged. "If I had, there would've been nothing for you to steal."

Griffin glanced over me, head to toe, and then offered me a warm smile. Oddly, I had never been more sure of the older woman's friendship than I was in that moment. She nodded to me, both of us certain I spoke the truth. My most precious possessions were the men watching from the edge of the crowd. If not for the dagger gift from Aric, I would've had nothing for Griffin to steal, not even in my royal finery.

And if she so much as dreamt of keeping the dagger once this was over, I would bite her hand off with my human teeth if I had to.

Griffin jumped forward, sudden and graceful, and rather than back myself to the edge of the crowd, I met her in the middle, my hands grappling at her left side, her eyes widening in surprise. I didn't really stand a chance, but I stood less of one if I didn't make an effort to win, and I'd promised her I wouldn't make this easy.

The room hollered as we wrestled one another, one of my hands catching hers before it reached my hip, twisting it roughly in my grasp and making her hiss. She caught my own hand near her side, our arms crossing and tangling. Griffin's arm in my hand tensed and then whipped over my head, making me stumble and spin, my back to her chest and my arms crossed in front of me held tight in her grip.

I stomped my boot onto Griffin's, my teeth gritted as I tried to shake her off, and she rewarded me with a pained grunt.

"Shit. I did think you'd make this easier," Griffin growled.

"Owen's been teaching me to fight," I gritted out.

And then I bent my knees, using my body and Griffin's grip on my hands to toss her over my head and onto the ground. It pulled horribly on my wrists, but the second her back hit the floor, she released me with a great oof of breath, a bright cry of delight rising from our audience.

"Shit!" Griffin exhaled with a little laugh, and I couldn't stop my grin.

This was absurd, but it was strangely fun too. Danger without terror.

"Bryony! Left back pocket!" Aric barked.

Griffin's eyes widened as I dove down, and with a quick twist from her, I landed roughly against her raised knees, bouncing away and then kicked onto my ass. I cried out as Griffin grabbed my ankles, tugging hard and making me slide across my skirts and onto my back.

Aric's shout was helpful and probably more instinctual than

intentional. I could see the small hint of something in Griffin's pocket now, but I wasn't *meant* to win. Not really.

Still, it wasn't a concession on my part when Griffin's fingers snagged around the hilt of my dagger, yanking hard. I tried to tear her hands away, rolling on my side to try to get back onto my feet, but it was too late. Griffin's tug broke the sheath off my belt and she leapt to her feet, face flushed and bright with victory, my lovely dagger in her grip.

"The king is fallen!" Cassius bellowed over the thunder of cheers. "Long live the king."

"Long live the king!"

Griffin laughed and winked at me, towering over my messy, rumpled form. I growled up at her and then before I could think, I twisted and leapt up, tackling Griffin to the floor. Massive orange and white paws pinned her shoulders down as great gasps and screams went up around us.

"Bryony!" one of my men cried out.

I roared into Griffin's face, watched the blood rush away, her eyes going wide and lips parting in shock. And then I sighed, relaxing back into the woman, sitting heavily down on Griffin's thighs.

"I told you I had so much to tell you," I said, catching my breath as Griffin remained flattened, pale and shocked. "Congratulations, Your Majesty. Let me buy you a drink."

I pushed myself up to standing, smiling at the startled quiet of the room, and then I reached down for Griffin's hand.

Behind me, on the stage, Cassius Thatcher released a belly laugh so loud, I thought it shook the rafters.

THE FESTIVITIES DIDN'T TAKE LONG to pick up again. Griffin recovered quickly from my surprise, taking my hand and letting me pull her up from the floor. Aric and Scrapper ushered us all over to an abandoned table in the far, dark corner of the room, one large enough for the mass of us—Griffin, Sam, Scrapper, my Chosen, and eventually Cassius Thatcher with a massive tray of unusual looking drinks.

"I thought you were about to eat me," Griffin said, eyeing me over the rim of her drink. She'd taken it immediately off the tray without glancing at Cassius, and I expected he'd brought it specifically for her.

"I might've," I said with a shrug. "I'm still getting used to her. I still may if you don't give—" Griffin slid the dagger quickly across the table to me, and I smiled. "Thank you."

"Thank you," Griffin said with a shrug. "You nearly had me."

"You mean I nearly had this?" I asked, twirling the white feather pinched between my fingertips.

Griffin went even paler than she had when I'd roared at her, and I glanced at Sam in the corner, who only smiled. He looked more centered since I'd last seen him and a great deal more solid and healthy. I handed the feather back to Griffin, who pocketed it quickly away. One look at Cassius and I could see the frown on his face and the calculation in his stare as she hid the feather.

I knew it was Sam's. Cassius obviously didn't, and it was clear he wanted the explanation.

Sam, Cassius, Jack McCallum. I counted them in my head, Griffin's odd collection of men. Not that she seemed aware of the fact. I wondered what a thieves' court would think if their king took Chosen like a Kimmerian queen.

"In truth, I'm glad you came and challenged me. You're right, I've done a terrible job," I said, moving easily away from my teasing.

"That's not really your fault," Thao said, shrugging. "A thieves' court is a small burden against your kingdom."

Both Cassius and Aric scoffed at that.

"Martin, this is certainly not a position I ever imagined you in," Cassius said, grinning at his former colleague.

"It isn't one I pictured for myself," Aric said.

"Understatement," I muttered.

"But my princess makes a compelling argument for the finer things in life," Aric said drolly. I glared at him, and he added, "And in a way, Thao is right. I'm helping her carry a heavy duty, one that I sincerely want her to succeed in."

Cassius only looked amused. "How did I find myself at a table full of do-gooders, eh, Scrapper?"

Scrapper grinned, but there was a tightness in his eyes as he stared across the table at the king. "You don't feel the bite as we do in the north, Thatcher," Scrapper said with a soft shrug.

"Do you feel ready, Griff?" Aric asked.

"More ready than I did when you left," Griffin said with a shrug. "But we underestimated Emory's court. It's not your fault," she said to me, ducking her head to meet my eyes. "Thieves don't like to feel they're working for anyone but themselves. Emory did the damage when he cut down Aric. I'll have to create loyalty on my own now. But Bryony, this isn't even why I've come south."

"The challenge was just a bonus then?" I teased, but my eyes slid to Sam, who hovered behind Griffin, almost glowing in the shadows. "Oh. The two-natured. Because of what happened in the mines?"

Griffin nodded solemnly. "I've been trying to keep tempers down. McCallum has too," she said.

"Mac!" Cassius said, leaning forward, eyes fixed to Griffin, who thoroughly ignored him.

"But it's past the breaking point now," Griffin said, lowering her voice and leaning in toward me.

"I've been talking to my mother, trying to make her understand," I said.

Griffin's lips pressed together. "The two-natured are traveling to the capital, Bryony."

My eyes widened. "To fight?" I asked.

"Not if we don't have to," Griffin said softly. "We're going to shift. We're going to show Kimmery the truth, how many of us there really are. Our hope is that it will remain peaceful."

"I'll join you."

"Bryony," Cress growled.

"I will," I said, more firmly, glaring back at my Chosen. "The palace staff already knows what I am. Perhaps I can help keep the peace with my presence."

"Our presence then," Wendell said, covering my hand with his.

I smiled at a glowering Cress. "You'll have to come too of course. My tiger can fend for herself, but a grand bear never hurt." I turned to Cassius next. "And perhaps, Mr. Thatcher, your court can lend support."

Cassius's dark eyebrows raised first, and then his hands from the table. "Your Highness, you mistake me. I am a King of Thieves, not a mercenary. I'm sure there is some of my court who will be there, but that's not my business and I'm not a hired hand."

"Cassius has no conscience to guide him, Bryony," Griffin said, soft and sudden as a knife.

And as if he were struck, Cassius Thatcher rose suddenly from the table, the smooth mask fully in place again. "Birdie is right, as usual. I'll take my leave now and keep my ear out of your business. Good to see you again, Martin. Stop by again if you have anything of interest from the castle."

Aric waved, more in dismissal of the suggestion than anything else, and smiled smugly at Griffin as Cassius disappeared into the crowd. "You could've asked him."

"It's not worth owing him the favor," Griffin snapped back quickly.

"Speaking of favors," I said, pushing Aric back into his chair, "Would you say you owed me one for springing tonight on me?"

"I wouldn't, no," Griffin said.

I ignored her answer. "Because I have something I need you to steal. From the castle," I added when she arched an eyebrow at me.

"I like my hands attached to my wrists, Bryony. What could you possibly want me to take from the castle?"

"A man named Atticus Darby."

Sam shot forward from the shadows, clutching at the back of Griffin's chair, his pale eyes wide. "Atticus? You've—he's still alive?"

I nodded. "But he may be executed for trying to kill Camellia if we don't find a way to get him out. And I'm beginning to put together a plan."

Griffin twisted in her seat to look up at Sam, shrugging in agreement as he stared wide-eyed back at her.

"I could think of better treasures," Scrapper said with a huff.

"She's taken, Scrap," Aric answered, throwing an arm around my shoulder.

"I'll find something lovely for you too," I offered, grinning back at the man.

"What do you need, Your Highness?" Sam asked softly.

24.
DANIEL

It took me a moment of staring into the dark before I was certain Bryony wasn't in the bed. It was hard to tell with so many limbs thrown about, but she'd been slipping away the past couple of nights until one of us would carry her back again.

I found her in the sitting room, one of our trusted guards standing at the door, his eyes just fixed overhead of Bryony, who was curled up in a large armchair by the fire. She moved aside for me without a glance, settling her legs over my lap and her head against my shoulder as she continued to watch the fire. There was a book open in her hand, one of her novels, and I smiled when I realized how long it had been since I'd seen her reading.

"Want me to take over?" I asked, tapping the open page.

"No, I...I haven't really been reading. I tried, but all I can do is sort through possibilities," Bryony murmured.

I turned my head, pressing a kiss to Bryony's brow, closing my eyes as her sigh warmed my throat. "Any concerns?"

"Millions," Bryony answered with a faint laugh. "I can't predict what the council will do, I can't even really predict my mother. I feel like I've sat through the conversations one hundred times already, just in my own head."

If I were Owen or Aric, now would be the time I distracted Bryony with sex. If I were Cosmo, Wen, or Thao, I would reason through the problems with her. But they weren't awake. We'd already worn ourselves out trying to occupy Bryony's body, and I suspected her mind really had run through every scenario by now.

"You present your case, that's all," I said, pulling her a little closer, combing the tangles out of her hair slowly as she nodded.

"And if the case fails?" Bryony whispered.

I doubted it would, but all of us had more faith in Bryony than she usually did in herself.

"You transform into a tiger and bite Lord Thomlinson just for fun," I suggested.

Bryony snorted and pressed her face to my throat to stifle her giggles.

"One way or another, you're giving your mother a great deal to think about tomorrow," I said. "You haven't given up yet, and if the case doesn't go the way we hope, you won't give up then either, right?"

"Right," Bryony said, kissing my neck. "Thank you."

"My pleasure," I said, smiling at the fire. It was the truth. I was easily pleased perhaps, but for all of Bryony's troubles and worries, life with her was strangely...simple for me. She asked very little of me, aside from the care of a lover and friend. After a lifetime of chasing approval, gaining it with so little effort felt almost like cheating.

Bryony's breathing was starting to grow heavy and slow, exhaustion rather than desire, and I pulled the book carefully from her fingers, tucking it into the cushion of the chair.

"Carting me off?" Bryony murmured.

"You'll want your wits in the morning. Better sleep for the rest of tonight."

She hummed and wrapped her arms around my neck, letting me carry her back to bed. Owen had already rolled into my spot, but Cosmo was awake when I headed for the edge, smiling briefly at me before making room.

"Did she fuss?" Cosmo whispered.

"I did not," Bryony mumbled, too tired to sound annoyed, and Cosmo grinned, sharing the work of wrapping her up tightly between us.

⚜

SAM WAS PACING in the staff yard of the castle, in and out of the shadow of the courtyard, high morning sun catching in his hair. Griffin was leaning in a dark archway, and if it weren't for the way her eyes tracked every footstep of Sam's, I would've said she looked careless.

"They're bringing Darby up from the dungeons," I said.

Sam's steps faltered, and I suspected he was seriously considering taking flight for a moment, before he spun on his heel to face me.

"And she—she'll be—?"

"Bryony called the meeting with the council and the queen only. The council might demand Camellia attend when they realize what it's about, but she's not there now."

"Do you want me to come?" Griffin asked faintly.

I pressed my lips together. Griffin wasn't really unwelcome, but she wouldn't do any good at the meeting. However, if it was between her attendance and Sam backing out, the new King of Thieves would have to be there.

Sam stood stock still under the sunlight, eyes blinking down at his own shadow. I wished Owen had come down to fetch him. I'd been too concerned about Sam working his way into Bryony's Chosen instead of me when he'd been left at the Winter Palace, and I didn't have any kind of relationship with the man. Owen was every bit as brotherly with Sam as he was with any of us. He would've been able to soothe him where I couldn't.

"No," Sam whispered.

I held my breath, wondering if it was a refusal to come or just turning Griffin down on her offer.

"No," he repeated, with more strength. "No, I can manage. What can she do, really?"

"Nothing. Bryony's tiger almost ate her. I don't think Camellia would dare with Bryony in the way," I said.

Sam looked up at that, his eyes a little brighter, lips quirking. "And Atticus will be there."

I nodded, glancing to Griffin, "You'll still—"

"Bryony almost ate me too. I also wouldn't dare defy her," Griffin said dryly.

She definitely would, but I had a feeling Sam's excitement to see his former fellow Chosen outweighed any of Griffin's disinclination to help.

"All right," Sam said. He didn't look prepared, his shoulders were still hunched, gaze still skittish, but when I turned back to the doors, I could hear him following.

"We'll come back this way," I called over my shoulder, but Griffin was gone and there was a hawk swooping overhead to perch on the ledge of the castle walls.

The meeting was being held in the council chambers, which was closer to this part of the castle than Bryony's suite.

"What do I need to say?" Sam whispered, following down the kitchen halls to the side staircase that would take us up into the castle proper.

"Only the truth, all of it," I said, glancing back at him. "Hiding your second nature won't matter in a few hours anyway."

Sam nodded jerkily. He looked a little green, but he'd never struck me as an especially solid fellow. I wondered what he was like before Camellia had spat him back out like a cat who'd lost interest in the mouse she'd caught. Or what he would be like now if it was Bryony's choosing ceremony he'd been selected at.

We reached the dark stone hall of the council chambers, the sound of chains clinking ahead of us.

"Atticus!" Sam whispered behind me.

Atticus Darby was escorted between Cresswell and Head Guard Amos, his head down, but maybe his second nature gave him sharp hearing because his head shot up, eyes locking over my shoulder immediately. A grim smile took over his mouth, not happiness but a kind of relief. His wrists were locked together, legs chained just enough for him to walk, and I knew it was more for appearance's sake than any threat Atticus really posed.

"What happened?" Sam whispered.

"He tried to kill Camellia," I said, adding at the other man's gasp, "Head Guard Amos didn't want to set his execution until he knew why, and we've been delaying it since."

"He always said..." But Sam fell quiet as we met the others at the door.

"It's good to see you again, although I'm sorry you had to return for this," Atticus said to Sam.

"Maybe it will be worth it," Sam murmured, and Atticus let out a soft scoff as Head Guard Amos opened the door.

A gentle thread of conversation halted as we stepped inside.

Lord Thomlinson, Sir Weston, and a few other senior members of the council turned to watch us enter. Bryony was at the other end of the table with her mother, their Chosen waiting calmly behind them, and Prince Holden. The man's bruises on his throat had mostly healed, but there were a few marks left, enough to give credence to his story when it was his turn to speak.

"Bryony, what is this about?" the queen asked, eyeing us with a frown, which grew deeper as her gaze landed on Darby's locked wrists.

Bryony stood slowly from the table, the council members hurrying to take their own seats. "I'm sorry for the abrupt call to speak, but I wanted to gather you all so we might discuss, in relative privacy, the extreme risk Camellia's behavior poses if left unchecked."

"Oh, Your Highness, this petty rivalry is too—" Lord Thomlinson began, but his tongue tangled to quiet with the slight lift of the queen's hand.

"Not yet, Thomlinson. I don't believe there is one of us here who is unaware of Camellia's behavior, and I've been concerned it might be growing more volatile," the queen said slowly. "You have proof, Bryony?"

"I have testimony," Bryony said.

"Your Majesty, might I suggest that testimony brought to us by—"

"By my daughter, Lord Thomlinson," the queen said, holding Lord Thomlinson's stare as he swelled and turned red with embarrassment.

"That man in chains was locked up for trying to *kill* the princess, Your Majesty!" Thomlinson spluttered.

The queen paled and turned back to stare across the open table at Darby. "Did you really?"

For the first time since I'd met Atticus Darby, he looked a little ashamed of himself, head bowing briefly. "I did, Your Majesty."

"Then I think we will hear from you first," the queen said.

Bryony let out a little sigh of relief and her hand reached out for her mother's, but the queen only shook her head and Bryony's gesture dropped lamely to her side.

"I take it my daughter hurt you in some way?" the queen asked Darby.

"Not hurt—not..." Darby went pale and swallowed. Sam had this same reluctance to speak, and I wondered if it had more to do with this pain of having to relive, confess to what they were subjected to, than any kind of stoicism or pride. "The princess was...young and demanding," Darby said, and Thomlinson and his cronies scoffed at the far side of the room. "I suppose she was a normal princess, at first, but it hadn't been a few months when her appetite for pleasure became a constant. She had favorites, and when she'd worn them out, she learned she could use her Hunger to force them to...to continue."

There was a blush rising up the queen's throat, but she held her chin high as Darby went on.

"I wasn't a favorite. Only a witness. I saw the way she seemed to burn men up. Paul Kent, Thomas Gensley, Jeremy Gibbens, and others, until they were too weak to eat, even for the Hunger to make use of them. And they'd be sent away."

"All queens have had their enthusiasm—" Lord Thomlinson tried but was quickly cut off.

"None so many as the princess, though," Sir Weston said, bowing briefly to Bryony's mother. "Excuse me, Your Majesty."

"It's true," Queen Peony said weakly, waving her hand and nodding at Atticus.

"Sometimes...she didn't even want sex, she just wanted to fight, to hurt men. Or do the two together." Darby frowned as the queen nodded, some acknowledgment of what she'd already known. "She had her second choosing, and she seemed calm for a time. She made a favorite of...of one of the men, and he revealed he was two-natured. She used to make him fly around the room to entertain her. Made him let her pet his feathers. Then she wanted to pluck them. And then one day, she broke his wings." Darby paused as Queen Peony gasped. "These games of hers piled up, Your Majesty. I don't know how much you want—"

"They were my wings," Sam said, drawing the focus of the room.

I stepped back as Sam moved forward, his stare focused absently on the window facing the city.

"She broke my wings when I asked her once if I could fly at night," Sam said.

"Your Majesty, this man has just revealed that he *hid* his status from the kingdom!" Thomlinson cried, jumping up from his seat.

"And why shouldn't he? Why shouldn't any two-natured?" Bryony called back, cheeks sporting twin spots of angry red. "The two-natured are thrown into horrible labor conditions, or into the army. There are incredible consequences for them to live openly, and *why*?"

"Enough!" Queen Peony snapped, and Bryony seemed to choke abruptly on her words, eyes falling to her lap. The queen's eyes flicked back and forth between Sam and Atticus before finally settling on Sam.

"Is that all?" she asked.

"All?" Bryony mouthed, eyes widening.

"She took me with her to the Winter Palace. I couldn't...I couldn't serve her anymore, I was so...tired. But she left me there and told me I should kill Princess Bryony," Sam murmured, and the room burst into layered arguments.

"I heard her mention as much when she returned," Atticus rushed to say.

"Your Majesty this is—"

"Really, Your Highness, what did you have to promise these men—"

"Outrageous claims!"

The queen remained pale in her seat, seemingly frozen, when a chair screeched against tile and we all flinched. Prince Holden, more or less forgotten in the chaos, seemed to have found his moment.

"I joined your daughter's Chosen only recently, Your Majesty. And while it pains me to say it, that woman is the most unnatural creature I have ever come across in my life," Prince Holden announced. "I was not witness to anything previously mentioned, but I heard whisper of it and much worse. And I was subjected to the same...physical treatment. Perverse games, cruelty, pain. The night of the fencing tournament ball, Princess Camellia dragged me into the hall, used her magic to rouse me, and then proceeded to choke me nearly to death."

Silence followed, and I glanced at the council's side of the table. Even they understood the gravity of Holden's story, and it seemed to sink them lower in their seats.

"I had every intention of returning home and urging my father to declare war on Kimmery in retaliation for the crimes your daughter committed against me, but it was Princess Bryony who pulled me to safety, and it was she who convinced me that you would hear reason and take measures against Camellia."

Bryony pursed her lips together, a slight pinch of annoyance on her brow, but I thought Holden was playing his part admirably. He spoke without the same shame Atticus and Sam had, and his threat was clear. Handle Camellia, or Noren would demand reparations for his experience.

"This is...this is..." But Thomlinson didn't seem to be able to decide what it was, and his stuttering melted back into silence.

And in the silence, the sound of voices filtered from outside, through the closed windows of the room. One of the queen's Chosen turned, staring outside for a long moment as Queen Peony remained staring at each of Camellia's former Chosen in turn.

"Peony...there's something happening outside."

Bryony's gaze met mine as Head Guard Amos moved away from Atticus to go and look out the window. I nodded at her, ready for our moment. Against the wall, Aric was moving slowly in my direction as the rest of the room turned toward the window.

"I think you should stay back, Your Majesty," Head Guard Amos said.

"No, open the balcony, I want to hear them," Bryony said, wiggling through the crowd, Thao and Wendell close to her side.

"Your Highness," Head Guard Amos snapped, but Bryony was already turning the handle of the thin doors, and the roar of voices rushed into the room with the cold air.

Aric traded places with Cresswell, taking a baffled Darby's arm in his hand.

"Wait until—"

"I know," Aric said, arching an eyebrow at Cress.

It didn't matter. The rest of the room was too distracted by the scene outside of the gates, and even Bryony's mother was wiggling her way through the men to join her daughter on the balcony.

Aric's hand covered Darby's locked wrists, and Sam stirred anxiously at my side.

"Your Majesty, it appears to be some civil unrest, surely you should—"

I watched, a little jealous to be waiting inside, as Bryony reached the banister of the balcony and the volume reached a fever pitch outside the gates, drowning out the question Queen Peony asked Bryony, or her answer.

My heart hammered in my chest, and Bryony looked back over her shoulder briefly, through the open doors and right at me. She nodded, smiling faintly, and then turned away again. The woman vanished, replaced by the massive orange and white tiger, soon joined by Thao and Wendell's beasts as well.

"Now," Cress said.

Bryony's head tipped back, and a thunderous roar echoed out, chorused by Wendell and Thao on either side of her. The crowd answered, and then the unified shout of human voices broke apart into hundreds of animal cries. Beneath it all, lost in the chaos, the lock clicked, and Atticus Darby's chains dropped to the floor with a muted rattle.

Aric yanked on Darby's arm, and Sam nudged my back.

"Time to run," Aric hissed.

25.
BRYONY

ime to run, I thought to Wendell and Thao, jumping deftly up onto the edge of the balcony and then down to the roof below with a thump of my paws.

"Bryony!" my mother cried.

"Your Highness!" Head Guard Amos bellowed.

I felt a little bad for not warning the man of what was coming, but it was in the two-natured's best interest for the castle guards not to be prepared.

From one roof to the next, I jumped my way gracefully down into the front gardens. Rabbits and cats and foxes and mice were swirling around the castle gates, not running in but calling to one another. Overhead, songbirds and great massive hawks were flying together. And outside the gates, the great beasts stamped their feet, stags and bears and wild hogs and dogs all howling and growling up at my mother. The two-natured would turn away soon, march through the city together, but first they made the queen look upon them. Hundreds of them.

It was chaotic but careful. The two-natured had promised to do no harm, only wanting to make themselves known, but there was something horrifying about the strange collection of creatures who had suddenly appeared. Animals that would've naturally been hunting one another were now standing side by side. I roared toward the gate, and the animals there answered back, one horse kicking roughly at the metal bars before he was shuffled back by the others, temper in check.

We needed to get to the staff yard, I remembered, fighting off the urge to chase down a bunny leaping past me. I'd promised to meet Cress there and let him accompany me out into the city so he would trust I was safe. I padded around the castle, finding guards rushing out of the main doors, looking wildly about, not entirely sure what to do. Head Guard Amos followed close behind, but his stride was more determined, heading directly for me.

"Your Highness! What do you think you're doing?!"

I jumped out of his reach, racing playfully around him in a circle as Wendell and Thao waited patiently for me. The two-natured were determined to stay shifted until midnight, but I broke back into my human self, making Amos stumble to a sudden stop in front of me.

"I'm standing with my people," I said.

"It's not safe. This is mad. One of these—these *people*, could break into the castle!" Amos yelled.

I frowned at that. "Don't let anyone be hurt, please, Guard Amos. Like you said, they're *people*. They don't want to do harm, they just want to be heard."

"They're breaking the law!"

"They're protesting the law," I said.

His jaw ground, eyes watching the gate, flicking up to the sky to see the birds circling overhead. "It's not safe."

"Head Guard Amos, I am a tiger. I'll be fine. Reassure my mother. Make her listen. I'll be back tonight."

"There could be a mouse assassin in the castle right now—"

It was such a comical but horrifying notion that I couldn't help my laugh. "Aric warded the castle. No mouse shifter, or any other kind, will make it through a door."

I didn't wait for another argument, just hurried back into a tiger, padding quickly away and around the side of the building as Amos barked new orders to his men. Thao moved up to my side, rubbing his head against my shoulder, Wendell nipping playfully at my hip before doing the same. They were too close by my tiger's standards, but I knew they were only keeping their promise to Cress to guard me like a—

Overhead, a hawk screamed. Griffin or someone else perhaps.

We passed a door, and I grinned toothily as Nora raced out of it, Morgan hot on her heels.

"What are you—Oh!"

Nora flashed Morgan a bright smile before leaping into the air, replaced in a shimmery moment by a bright yellow finch which zipped quickly around Morgan's head before settling on her shoulder.

"That's not fair!" Morgan cried, laughing.

Aric was waiting for us in the yard, a massive draft horse saddled, reins in his hand. On the saddle rested a bright snowy owl, and Cresswell the bear stood on Aric's other side, falling forward to his paws and lumbering in my direction.

But where was...

"Honestly, princess, we couldn't have come up with a better disguise if we tried," Aric said, nodding his head to the horse.

Oh! Oh, Atticus Darby *was* the horse. Well...that was convenient.

Owen, Daniel, and Cosmo were waiting in a doorway, and they came out to my side.

"It's madness inside. No one knows what to do, and I think a good percentage of the staff went missing during the shift," Cosmo said, kneeling down and sliding his fingers into my fur. "No going back now, little muse."

I butted my head softly against his chest. I wished all my Chosen were coming out into the city with us, but I wanted someone to keep an eye on the castle while we were gone, and I didn't want them caught up in any danger as humans without magic of their own. It would drive my tiger mad if they got so much as a scratch on them, and that would only lead to serious trouble.

"You'd better go. I heard the council demanding they send in the army," Owen said. I snarled at that, but Owen just ruffled my ears. "Remember that the army is one of the first places they put two-natured to work."

"Sam, go tell Griffin and then come back to find us. We should go," Aric said to me as the white owl took off overhead. Aric hadn't risen into the saddle he'd put on Darby, but perhaps the idea of being ridden was offensive for a two-natured. "They'll send guards around to the back gate soon."

I rubbed up against the legs of my Chosen who were remaining behind, nuzzling my jaw into Daniel's outstretched hand.

"Have fun," he murmured. "Don't get into any trouble."

I huffed at that, and Thao bit lightly on the end of my tail, urging me to chase after Aric and Darby heading for the gate.

There was a winding road through tall outbuildings adjacent to the castle, where carriages and stores were kept, that separated it from the city. We hurried down it now, and I enjoyed the change of scenery. It'd been weeks since we'd been to the beach, and I realized now that I had too little fresh air in my life, cooped up during mourning. The floors in the castle were slippery under my paws, and this gritty road was uncomfortable but an improvement, less likely to send me sliding into walls as I gave chase.

"Stars," Aric gasped as we reached the first break in the narrow road that opened to the city.

The city now overtaken by animals. And in spite of the strangeness of foxes and deer and groundhogs strolling the road, the scene was calm, as if the city had been abandoned in order for wildlife to take over. The only sign of humans were the faces plastered fearfully to windows, staring out of the shops. I wanted to paw at the glass, draw the humans out to show them that we were safe creatures, not monsters, but an enormous strange tiger banging on a window probably wasn't the most effective tactic.

"Griffin said she'd be watching for conflicts from overhead, but if the council is calling on the army, that's where they'll likely break out first," Aric called to us, frowning briefly and shaking his head. "Feel like a zookeeper with you lot looking at me like that. Or dinner."

I grinned at him, not the most reassuring sight in this form, and pushed my way around my shifted Chosen to lean against his side, making him stumble. He reached down, patting at my head, and above us a soft gasp exhaled, a shop girl leaning out of a window with wide eyes.

"My lord, aren't you frightened?" she shouted to Aric, squawking as a squirrel ran along the building ledge past her, chasing after a bird. "One hardly knows if they're real beasts or not."

"How many tigers do you think are roaming about the capital generally?" Aric barked back with a roll of his eyes. The girl only gaped at him, and he shook his head, muttering down to me, "Not sure I enjoy being called milord." He eyed me in silence for a moment, and his frown quirked. "And I'm surprised to find I don't enjoy that you can't talk back at me. I'd expected to savor your silence."

I growled and butted his hip with my head. Truthfully though, I felt strange in this form for so long, especially not being able to communicate in more than animal signals with the others. Cresswell's warning growl as I moved too far ahead sounded more like a threat than concern, and it was a struggle keeping my human brain in control.

And unfortunately, that control didn't grow easier when we found the first instance of violence in the city, and it wasn't even from the army.

I caught the whiff of fear, a horrible warning stench, and hurried around a corner to see four young men crowded around an upturned crate.

"Ughhh, stars, smell that? Look what you made it do!"

"Bryony," Aric shouted as I bounded in their direction, snarling.

Cresswell, Thao, and Wendell were quick behind me, and one of the young men let out a wild screech at the sight of us, the others whirling around.

"Shut it, Cowper, it's just one of *them*," one of the larger men snarled, and he stepped forward with a sharpened stick thrusting in our direction, his teeth gritted back at me. "You'll be put to death if you so much as scratch me, you fucking beast!"

Wendell's back was bunching with tension at the perceived threat to me, and I knew his control must've been as thin as my own. Cresswell was trying to prowl in front of me, but at the thought of him being stabbed *again* on my behalf, I leapt up, not from paw but from my feet.

"And what do you think will happen to you if you scratch your princess or one of her Chosen?" I shouted.

The young men gasped, and one stumbled right into the gutter of the street, falling on his ass. The one with the stick in his hand paled and fell to his knees, or seemed to until I realized he was attempting some strange kind of low and humble bow.

"Begging your pardon, Your Highness, we didn't know you were—"

"What should it matter who I am? You have a fellow Kimmerian trapped under that crate. Release them at once!"

Wendell was still growling, but he eased up as I dug my fingers into the fur at the ruff of his neck.

"But they're just—" The man's argument died on his tongue as he looked between the crate—which reeked horribly and made it pretty clear they'd caught a skunk two-natured—and up to myself.

"You heard the princess," Aric said, looking fierce with one hand on the hilt of a dagger.

"Whatever word you were about to use applies to me as well," I hissed.

"A-a-apologies, Your Highness," the one who'd fallen first whispered, scooting forward and throwing off the crate.

Sure enough, a sweet-looking black critter with its white stripe running down its back appeared and scrambled away from the men, more of its horribly pungent defensive smell appearing. But instead of running to safety, the skunk transformed in front of all of us, revealing a massive, scarred man with dark hair and the characteristic soot marks of a blacksmith.

"You four better fucking watch yourselves," he hissed, the men paling. "Get back inside, you smell worse than your personalities."

They were boys really, and were probably just out of school. I hoped the skunk smell clung to them for days.

The blacksmith turned in my direction, lips quirking. "Never can tell, can you? Would've pegged you for more of a kitten type, Your Highness," he said, with a surprisingly gallant bow that did nothing to diminish the oddly flirtatious feeling that rose up from the comment. He vanished back into a skunk and hurried away.

"I suppose I would've imagined him as something more robust," I mused, watching the skunk's retreat.

"What's that look in your eye?" Aric asked, frowning. I smiled and transformed back into my tiger without answering. "Come on, let's get to the barracks."

Cresswell nipped my shoulder in punishment for hunting down trouble, but I ignored him aside from nudging back. This was why I'd chosen Thao's bite in the first place and why I was so determined to join the march.

The rest of the trip through the city was fairly peaceful, there were even a few scenes of the two-natured interacting with their human neighbors, much to the delight of any nearby children. But I noticed there seemed to be fewer animals out than we'd seen at first, and it wasn't until we neared the barracks—halfway between the castle and the thieves' court we'd visited—that I realized why.

There was a standoff between the army and the two-natured. I was tempted to rise up to my human form again to involve myself until I noticed that the army seemed to be facing off itself at first, at least half of the suited soldiers standing in a line protecting the two-natured.

"Your orders are to stand down!" one general bellowed.

Howls and roars and yips answered back.

Would it come to fighting? I knew the two-natured wanted the day to be peaceful, and the men still guarding them were silent, calm guards. I was still debating how I might be most helpful in the situation when a bright familiar cry tore through the air. From a barracks rooftop, a flash of rust zipped down toward the crowd of two-natured, Griffin spying us in the mass and heading in our direction.

Aric raised his arm for her to land on, but before she'd passed overhead the line of army-aligned soldiers, a net was tossed into the air. I roared as it tangled around the hawk's form, bundling and flattening her wings, weights dragging her down to the ground.

"Shit, she's on their side. I'll—Bryony!"

I was leaping away from my Chosen, around the smaller animals at the back of the crowd, past an odd assortment of deer mingling with bobcats and other predators.

Cresswell roared his frustration, but I ignored him, weaving and slinking and pushing my way through to the front of the crowd. Through the legs of soldiers, I could see flashes of the heap on the ground, no longer small, and with a shade of crimson deeper than Griffin's feathers. She'd transformed back into the woman, still tangled in the net.

One of the soldiers bravely spun to face me, eyes wide but arms outstretched. "No! We promised peace."

I flashed back into my human form, perversely pleased when he looked more terrified by my feminine form than my feline one. "Let me through immediately!" I snapped.

But it was too late, Griffin was surrounded on the ground, one soldier holding a spear over her. She was trying to stand as the men bellowed for her to flatten herself on the ground. I wasn't sure if it was an accident, or intentional, but the spear came down at Griffin's face at the same moment she tried to rise.

"Griffin!" I screamed.

I didn't notice the hands on my waist, pushing me through the line of soldiers to reach my friend.

"Release her at once," I cried.

"Step back from the woman, by order of Her Royal Highness, Princess Bryony," Cresswell echoed.

"Magic," Aric hissed in my ear, jumping forward and tugging two of the soldiers roughly back from Griffin as I marched forward. There was another scream from the air, Sam's white owl landing heavily on the ground next to Griffin before quickly becoming the man.

"Transform," Sam breathed to Griffin, clutching her shoulders.

"No, wait!" I cried, falling to my knees next to them. "Get her out of the net, I can help."

"It's a fuckin' scratch," Griffin said, but her voice was as tight as a pulled string, and there was blood seeping quickly out from between the fingers that cupped her eye.

"Then it's a scratch I can heal," I snapped back.

"Was flying too low," Griffin breathed as Sam and Aric hurried to untangle her. Cresswell barked orders back to the general to take his men into the barracks. I thought I heard him use my mother's title too, but I didn't care.

"You weren't too low. They shouldn't have been trying to *capture* any of you," I said, gathering magic into my palms.

"Just glad it was me," Griffin said, but she whimpered as Aric accidentally nudged her arm.

"Move your arm," I said, reaching out to her face.

"What if my eye falls out?"

I blinked at her. Griffin was exceptionally pale and starting to tremble, and she let out a strange giggle.

"I'll—I'll put it back in," I said, trying not to grimace, sincerely hoping I didn't have to keep that promise.

Griffin bellowed as Aric tore her hand away from her face, and

I quickly slapped my own over the brilliantly red and bleeding wound running down the right side of her face.

"Hold her still," I said to Aric.

"Why—" Griffin's question broke off with a scream as the magic struck.

"Griffin!" Sam reached for me, about to tear me away, but Aric wrestled him back.

"Leave it! Bryony saved your wings, didn't she?" Aric snapped.

Sam groaned, but together the men held Griffin still, her face thrashing slightly underneath my grip, magic pouring out of me as Griffin's blood also wet my palm.

"Oh stars, enough!" Griffin grit out.

I ignored her for a beat, and then finally lifted my fingers up, just a fraction. Her face was smeared with red, bloody tears running out of her injured eye, but it looked as though...

"You're frowning," Griffin whispered up at me.

I tried to smooth my face, smearing away some of Griffin's blood gently to reveal a shiny scar. She blinked, and Aric, Sam, and I all sank back at once with a unified whoosh of relieved breath.

"Eye still attached," I said weakly. "Can you see all right?"

Griffin kept blinking, forehead wincing, but each blink seemed to wash some of the red out of her vision. Her eye was pale now, almost white, but the pupil was still intact, if drooping down a little. Oh stars, had I left her blind?

"What did you do?" Griffin whispered, eyes widening, looking between each of us. She closed her eyes tightly, and Aric handed Sam a white handkerchief, the other man quick to wipe the blood away from Griffin's face.

"I...healed you? Shit, Griffin, did I—?"

Her eyes opened again, head shaking, taking the cloth from Sam's hand and rubbing her face more roughly. "I can see," she said, but there was still something wary in her gaze as she looked between us, and she winced as she glanced at me. "I can see, it's just...still healing probably. I can see."

"Your hawk will be fine," Sam reassured her, and Griffin nodded jerkily.

I glanced behind us. The crowd of two-natured was growing agitated, and Cresswell was still arguing with the general. Another man pushed through the line of soldiers, and in the wildness of his appearance, it took me a moment to realize I recognized him.

"Griff?" Jack McCallum was undone, out of the usual formal dress I saw him in, hair tangled and collar open. He hurried to us in open panic, and I slid out of his way, watching with nervous interest as he took Griffin's face in his hands.

She didn't flinch, but her eyes widened in that startled look she couldn't seem to shake since I'd healed her.

"I'm fine," she said, some of her calm, dry nature returning, although she was gentle with Jack and her bloodied fingers left a brief stain on his wrist.

His lips pressed flat, but he nodded and released her, moving to join Cresswell.

"By order of Her Majesty the queen, and the Southern Council, we order the army to *stand down*," Jack bit out. Jack turned toward the vast crowd, voice raising. "The army's official duty is to protect the peace, including the safety of the two-natured. Her Majesty is making an official announcement at the palace. The gates will be opened."

I landed roughly on my bottom, my gaze drifting to Aric in surprise, his own face reflecting my shock.

"We have to get Darby out of the capital," he said, voice almost too low to hear.

"I'll keep my end of the bargain," Griffin said. "We'll leave with him now."

"You're sure you're all right?" I asked.

Griffin didn't look back at me, her gaze lowered firmly to the ground, even as Sam helped her up off her feet. Jack returned to us, and my Chosen slipped through the crowd, back in their human forms, Wendell's hands holding Darby's reins. The army was finally falling out of their lines, and the two-natured were turning in the direction of the castle, some of them also taking on their human forms.

"The announcement?" Griffin asked Jack.

"Good news, you should come."

Griffin shook her head. "Errand to run. Need to sneak this fellow out of the capital," she said, nodding to the horse standing amongst us.

Jack's eyes widened, glancing at me. "It was my request," I said.

"Well in that case, take my carriage. Stay at Cambell Manor, Griff. Don't be a pest and argue," he said, arching an eyebrow at her as her mouth opened to refuse. "We'll have business to discuss."

"You should rest," Sam urged her.

"Fine," Griffin bit out. "Carriages and manor houses, sure." She pushed past the men, and I stepped back out of her way until she caught my hand. "Thank you."

She looked up at me, a brief flinch in her scarred right eye quickly covered with a soft smirk.

"Good luck, Your Majesty," I said, squeezing her fingers.

Griffin huffed a laugh. "What an awful mess you've left me with," she murmured, but she squeezed back. "Come and see me when you're in the north."

A sudden pang struck me. I didn't know Griffin well, I knew significantly less of her than I wanted to, and now I wondered if it would ever really be possible to grow that friendship. I would be queen. She would be king, funny as it was to say it. Opposite sides of Kimmery, as Scrapper had put it.

"Oh dear, where's Scrapper?" I asked, looking suddenly around for the man.

"Drinking at the bar with the rest of his lot," Griffin said with a roll of her eyes. "S'pose we'll have to pick him up on our way out."

"We're certainly not keeping him," Aric answered wryly. "Come on, princess. Let's get back to the castle to hear the queen's announcement."

I jumped into Griffin's path before she could leave, wrapping my arms around her shoulders and squeezing tightly. "I'm sorry, and thank you, and—and..."

"Goodbye, Bryony," Griffin murmured, patting my back gently.

26.
BRYONY

"You seem awfully solemn," Cresswell murmured.

We were in the crush of the crowd of two-natured, an odd sight and an even stranger feeling. Animals kept brushing up against my skirts, and I wasn't sure if it was because of the close quarters or if it was some strange acknowledgment of thanks or appreciation.

"I feel...it's as if the air is changed," I said, my voice barely audible over the sound of hooves and paws on gravel, of bird cries in the air. "I don't know how to explain it."

"There's this kind of flavor—no, energy, on the battlefield on the last day," Cresswell murmured. "It's the feeling of change, I think. One night, I would fall asleep with the sense that the fighting would never end, and the next morning, I'd wake knowing and not understanding how that it would be the last day. You don't know if you're about to win or lose, you just know it's the end."

"Is that what I'm afraid of? That I'm—that these people are about to lose?" I asked. Because no matter the fact that I could claim a second nature now, it would never change the fact that the moment I transformed back into a woman, I could immediately stop any injustice I might've suffered as a two-natured, and that these people around me lacked that power.

Cresswell stopped us, Aric, Thao, and Wendell butting up against us, letting the parade of creatures continue to pass by.

"Yes, Bryony, that's what you're afraid of," Cresswell said with a small smile, dipping down to kiss my brow.

"And the fear won't change the outcome," Aric said. "So we'd better keep moving."

We could've walked into the palace, gone to find my mother, to hear the words from her first. Instead, we followed the steady path of the two-natured around us through the main palace gates, up the path through the gardens, to stand on the yard beneath the balcony. We were near the back of the crowd, but it parted easily for me, letting me walk forward, my gaze fixed upon the figure at the balustrade.

My mother was so small. Soft and rounded and petite, surrounded by the taller figures of men. It was evening and the sun was setting, but there were lamps resting on the edge near her.

"Do you think the council talked her into stricter measures?" Thao whispered to Wendell, who hushed him in answer.

My mother was searching the faces of the animals and people, and it wasn't until we'd reached the front of the crowd that she found me. There was sorrow in her expression, pain and a little resentment, like how she'd looked at my grandmother when she'd asked why she'd been given the crown so young.

In truth, I didn't know if my mother would ever have been ready to rule. I wasn't even always certain that ruling was something one *should* feel prepared for.

Please, I thought up to her, my heart pounding, eyes burning. *Please do the right thing. For me. For them.*

My mother's hand lifted, and hush sank over the crowd like a blanket, her gaze still holding mine.

"My people, my beautiful Kimmerians," she said, pausing as she stared at me another moment, before lifting her gaze away. "Forgive me. I hear your voices now as if my ears are uncovered for the first time. I see your trials. You have been treated without care or justice.

"No citizen so exquisite should be forced to hide. From this moment forward, the classification of two-natured will be stricken from our legislature. The registries burnt. The laws abolished."

A brilliant scream of victory rose up around us, even Cresswell huffing with shocked laughter. I held my breath instead, watching my mother. Who had given her these words? Jack McCallum? Who'd given her the strength against the rest of the council? Michael? He was there in the background with her other Chosen.

"The only law regarding the two-natured will be one that ensures your place of safety and respect with every other citizen of

Kimmery!" My mother's voice wavered, unused to her own clear tone, the volume of authority. Her eyes widened as the crowd screamed again. We were jostled, my Chosen and I, as bodies surged and celebrated.

My mother smiled briefly, but the sunset caught on the tears tracking down her cheeks.

"We need to get inside," I said to Aric, who was watching the dancing crowd with a smile. His eyes flicked to me, brow furrowing slightly in confusion, but he nodded, catching the attention of the others and pushing me forward to the veranda doors.

"What's wrong?" Cress asked, seeing the tension on my face.

"I don't know. Maybe nothing."

But it wasn't *nothing* I'd seen on my mother's face. I didn't know what that pain meant, only that this victory wasn't as sweetly won as most of my mother's support.

Amos was waiting in the doorway, ushering us inside, a deep scowl carved into his face. He took one look down at my hands, dark with Griffin's blood, and his scowl was wiped away by brief horror.

"I'm fine, it isn't mine," I said, adding before he could recover his temper. "I apologize for leaving you unprepared for today—"

"I know the nature of a protest, Your Highness. You acted recklessly all the same," he said, bowing briefly.

I wanted to argue, but I pressed my lips together. I'd interfered in his duty of protecting me, no matter how right I felt in my own actions.

"Your mother and the council have been waiting on your return," he said, turning quickly and leaving us to follow his swift steps.

Cosmo was waiting for us in the upper hall when we returned, and he charged for me, snatching me right off my feet. "You did it. You did it, Bryony! That's not your blood, is it?"

"No, Griffin's, she's fine, I think. I didn't, not really," I murmured, resting my face against his throat.

"You did, you spoke to your mother enough about everything that two-natured have suffered. The council couldn't shake her, no matter how hard they tried. Well, Jack and Weston and a few others fought back too," Cosmo added, pressing a kiss to my temple. "Come, they're bullying her again, I think, and they've sent for Camellia."

Amos opened the door to the conference room, and my eyes went directly to the balcony. It was a mild night and the doors remained thrown open, the revelry and cheers from the garden still rising up to meet my mother where she stood at the balustrade.

"*You*," Thomlinson hissed, and my shoulders straightened, chin lifting.

Daniel and Owen moved to my side, Thomlinson squeezing himself around the edge of the table.

"Do you even realize what you've done? The consequences of this night? What kind of army will Kimmery have to protect it now? Do you know the wealth of the kingdom relies on those mines?"

"If Kimmery relies on what might be equated to slave labor, then we are certainly failing as a kingdom," I snapped back. "And I sincerely doubt it's Kimmery who relies on the profits of those mines. You own three of them!"

Thomlinson growled, attempting to tower over me. He was a tall man, and very wide, but his intimidation relied on bluster and I refused to be swayed.

"Thomlinson, enough," Weston barked from the other end of the room. "It's done now, regardless."

A few of the other councilmen grumbled in agreement— although most didn't seem happy about my mother's declaration, but their voices only made Thomlinson turn red with fury.

"When Roderick hears about this," he spat out.

I arched an eyebrow. "What will Roderick have to say about your failure in the argument? Listen to your peers, sir, it is done."

"Bryony."

Thomlinson whipped back suddenly at the sound of my mother's timid voice.

I sank into a deep curtsey as she moved slowly forward from the open doors.

"They seem happy, don't they?" she asked me with a tremulous smile, glancing back over her shoulder. "They've turned back to the city for their celebrating."

"Mother, you've transformed hundreds of lives for the better," I said, rising up again and taking her hands in mine, gripping them tightly.

"Oh, Bryony!" Her mouth dropped in horror as she stared down at my grip.

I pulled my hands away quickly, "It's nothing. A—one of the two-natured was caught and injured by a soldier. I healed them."

"Your Majesty, can't you see now? See what it will cost Kimmery to follow in this young woman's volatile influence? Rioting and violence! Upheaval!" Thomlinson cried.

My mother swallowed hard, looking between us, staring back at me imploringly. "I think...I think if so many are so happy, it might be a good kind of change, Lord Thomlinson."

Thomlinson opened his mouth again, taking a great gasp of breath to start another tirade, and I leaned in, keeping my voice gentle but firm as I cut him off.

"I *do* want change for Kimmery, but only to undo the measures that prevent magic and beauty from flourishing here, those laws that cut off the wealth before it reaches *all* our people."

My mother smiled shakily and nodded at me, but my heart sank a little when she looked to Thomlinson next.

"All due respect, Your Highness, but you are very *young*. What do you know of any of this?" Thomlinson sneered.

"Thomlinson! Bryony has taken great pains to educate herself," my mother said, surprising me. "And she has taught me a little of what she's learned too. You forget yourself."

"Apologies, Your Majesty," Thomlinson said with some kind courtly flourish to the word and as much of a bow as he could manage, a hand pressing into the back of a chair to balance himself. "But perhaps you have the natural partiality of a mother? Aha!"

The door to the room opened, and I stiffened at the sight of my sister, glancing quickly to see that my Chosen were safely behind me.

"Your Highness, at last," Thomlinson said through gritted teeth. "We expected you two hours ago."

Camellia eyed me warily from the doorway, flanked by a few of her own Chosen, who passed their hands impatiently over her skin. She was dressed decently, which was rare lately, and someone had made an obvious effort to make her look flush with health, although the stain on her cheeks really gave her the appearance of a shabby doll.

My mother's hand reached out, squeezing mine as she stared at Camellia.

"Darling, are you well?" Mother asked.

"Fine," Camellia snapped, flashing a glare at Thomlinson. "What do you want?"

It might've been comical, the obvious annoyance Thomlinson wore at Camellia's tone, her total disinterest at managing to play the part she'd been given, but I knew she was here now for a reason.

"Your Majesty, you have two heirs, two possible queens to lead Kimmery. I beg of you, Your Eminence," Thomlinson all but moaned with another labored bow, "choose the successor who will do her duty to Kimmery, and not prevent your most dedicated council from doing theirs as well."

"Thomlinson," my mother ground out, her hand tightening around mine, "both of my daughters possess the Hunger. That's been made quite clear."

Thomlinson only smiled, and I realized my grip on my mother's hand was just as tight as hers. "Of course, Your Majesty. But only one of them is making the effort to get with child."

My gasp escaped, too quick to swallow, my eyes growing wide as Thomlinson pulled an innocent looking cloth sack from his pocket.

"Princess Bryony has been taking great care to *avoid* such a circumstance. The kitchen prepares her a tea every morning to ensure she does not conceive."

"What fucking business is that of yours?" Aric bellowed, but I could see that even Sir Weston, one of my best allies, looked startled by this revelation.

My mother's hand pulled free of mine. "Bryony? You don't want children."

"Of course I do," I said, perhaps too quickly. I swallowed hard and met my mother's wounded gaze. "I *do*. I only wanted time first. With my Chosen. Time to know that I would be safe, a child would be safe. And time to...to act for Kimmery as I did today. To heal the kingdom before producing an heir."

But I knew already that my mother wouldn't understand. Not right away, not with me fumbling my explanation in my panic. We should've been more careful, should've made the tea ourselves, but I'd never realized what a powerful secret I'd left lying out, practically in the open. It was *my* body...

But my body belonged to Kimmery too if I was to be queen.

"Please," I whispered as my mother only gazed thoughtfully back. "I would never deceive you in this."

My mother's eyes softened, but only for a moment.

"Mother."

I flinched at Camellia's delicate tone, glaring at her out of the corner of my eyes. She had her arms crossed protectively over her stomach, although if she meant to make herself look as though she was protecting a swollen belly, I thought it was fairly obvious how incredibly thin she still was.

"I have been trying, and I do think it's possible—"

"You're lying!" I cried out without thinking, and Camellia's attempt at wide-eyed innocence faltered with a wicked kind of glee.

"Obviously, Your Majesty, continuing the line of the succession *must* be considered of the utmost importance," Thomlinson droned.

"There's never been a member of the queen's line who *failed* to produce an heir, Thomlinson," Sir Weston snapped.

"But has there ever been one intentionally *preventing* the act?" Thomlinson tossed back.

"How would you know? You're a *man!* What business is this of yours?" I shouted.

"Enough!" my mother snapped.

I stumbled back, and Owen's hands cupped my shoulders firmly, drawing me into his steady warmth, right as my knees felt as though they might crumple beneath me.

"Your Majesty, an heir—" Thomlinson started again.

"I said *enough!*" my mother yelled. Her head whipped around, and one of her Chosen stepped forward immediately, wrapping an arm around her shoulder for her to lean into him.

Camellia, having certainly performed her duty—feeding what I suspected was a massive pile of shit to my mother—curtsied low and hurried out the door, the council members including Thomlinson backing away and heading for the exit as well.

"Mother, she doesn't even look *well*," I whispered.

"Oh, peace, Bryony!" my mother snarled, a hand raising to rub at her temples. "You put me through *two* trials today, isn't that enough?"

Michael stepped forward quickly, placing himself between us, shooting me a warning look. It wasn't aggressive, just cautionary. My mother was past the point of agreeing to please anyone. If I pushed one more word into her ear I might risk everything.

One by one, everyone but my Chosen and I left the room. Outside the open doors, I could still hear the city celebrating. And on the table, staring at me, Lord Thomlinson had dropped the bag of herbs he'd taunted me with. Proof of my one failure, a little personal selfishness that might cost me everything.

27.
BRYONY

"Point," Thao gasped, jogging quickly backward and away from me as if he thought I might chase after him with my sabre after getting my winning point anyway. "I need a break. Farraque, your turn."

Daniel, also suited head to toe, stepped forward, and I considered accepting the match. The pair of them had been taking turns sparring with me, trying to help me burn off the temper that boiled in my veins, but it was only a temporary distraction.

I was gasping for breath too, my muscles burning, and I shook off the urge to push myself into a collapse. I waved my hand at Daniel.

"I can't," I admitted, ignoring the irritating sting that rose in my eyes.

Both Daniel and Thao sighed in relief.

"Finally," Cresswell grumbled from the sidelines, standing from his seat and walking quickly over, digging his fingers into the padding of the jacket to try and soothe my trembling muscles.

"Keep your clothes on! Innocent maid entering!" Morgan hollered at the doors of the training room.

I huffed out a laugh in spite of my foul mood and rolled my eyes. "No, I don't see Nora with you."

"Ha!" Morgan laughed, grinning at me, but she walked quickly.

"News?" I asked.

It had been two days since my mother had dismissed us all from the argument of succession, and she hadn't left her suite. Wendell was relentless against Thomlinson in a council meeting the following day, but he couldn't lie to me and it was obvious that my contraceptive tea had shaken some of the council's faith in me. The shifter march probably hadn't helped.

"Your presentation of Camellia's crimes certainly came at the right time. From what I could dig out of the maids, any attempt made to try and make the queen choose Camellia as her successor has been rebuffed for many of those reasons. At this point, I think she's trying to just...avoid making a decision," Morgan said.

"Typical," I muttered, scowling. "And Camellia?"

Morgan took a brief deep breath, eyes widening. "They just sent a midwife and doctor in."

"Oh!" I nearly dropped the sabre in my hand, but Thao was quick to catch it, moving it over to the attendant for safekeeping.

I was halfway to the door when I heard the running footsteps. Wendell entered the training room, hair rumpled and out of breath, but he was wearing a smile.

"You did it," I gasped running and jumping into his arms.

"I think it's a good sign Thomlinson fought so hard," Wendell murmured. "But Sir Weston secured a trustworthy woman. Thomlinson likely knows the news won't favor him."

"It shouldn't matter even if it *does* favor him," I hissed. If Camellia were pregnant, it still wouldn't make her a good queen, and it was absolutely horrifying to think of her as any kind of mother.

"I know," Wendell said, kissing my temple and setting me back on my feet. "One thing at a time, love. Jack gave me news for you too."

I stiffened, and Wendell nodded. That meant news from Griffin or at least news regarding Atticus Darby. "And?" I asked, pushing gently on his chest.

"Everyone is on their way safely to Rumsbrooke," Wendell said.

I sighed. We'd been honest with Amos regarding Darby's sudden vanishing, and while *he'd* certainly noticed, the council and my mother hadn't really taken notice of the man.

"He's free," Wendell whispered. "Jack also said Griffin's eye really is healed, and that Scrapper's been telling her it will raise her in the court's estimation for having a scar like that."

I snorted and sagged into Wendell's chest, the others moving in closer. "Then all we need to deal with now is Holden and the conduit. Aric's with the mages today. Simon is convinced, so I think they've ganged up on Nathan."

"Nearly there," Daniel murmured, offering me a smile.

But we were still all tense. Nothing was promised. Not after my mother's shock at Thomlinson's revelation. An uncomfortable twist of shame sometimes wormed through my belly now, and drinking the tea in the morning made me nauseous. I was certain that I'd made the right choice for myself, but doubts about whether or not it was best for Kimmery were beginning to creep in. I did *want* children. If it secured the crown...

"Bryony."

The queasy feeling in my stomach vanished as I looked up over Wendell's shoulder, Aric marching fast down the hall, Owen and Cosmo fast behind.

"The queen has called for an audience," Aric said.

I stood frozen for three full heartbeats, stunned by the announcement. I'd expected my mother to remain sequestered, even to perhaps reemerge and pretend that there had been no conflict in the first place.

"Oh, come on!" Morgan barked from behind us. "Don't you want to know?"

I wasn't sure that I did, but her shouting did the trick and I hurried forward, Wendell's hand clutched tight in mine.

"Where?" I asked Aric.

"Throne room."

I sucked in a breath. A real audience then. Had she already made her decision? I wasn't sure if that boded well for me. But no, Morgan had said she'd been resisting the efforts to persuade her to name Camellia. There had to be hope still.

My heart was pounding faster and louder in my ears than our footsteps on the tile. The halls weren't empty, they grew thick with courtiers the closer we got to the throne room. It was one of the oldest rooms in the castle, part of an older building with darker stone, and I could only recall seeing my mother and grandmother in it once or twice before. It was where coronations took place, significant proclamations.

Ones like which of two princesses would be named successor.

Thomlinson was already there at the front of the room, but my mother had ten of her Chosen around her, ensuring he couldn't bend to her ear in this moment. Her eyes met mine as I walked up the center aisle of the room, galleries of seating on either side, filled with nobles. I wanted to feel hope at my mother's look, but there was an uncharacteristic blankness, steel even, so I bowed my eyes and reached her dais, sinking into a deep curtsey, feeling the shadow of my Chosen bowing at my back.

"Your Majesty."

"You may stand," Mother said delicately, and her hand gestured to my right, opposite Thomlinson and Sir Weston and some of the other councilmen.

The air seemed thick around me, my movement sluggish, and I wondered if everyone in the room could hear the labor of my breath as my Chosen and I moved to the side. Wendell had a hand on my elbow, steadying me. Thao gripped my waist, reminding me to stand tall. Cresswell stood ever so slightly in front and to the side, prepared to leap in as a shield. The others were close, their touches grazing my back, the waistband of my fencing pants, reminding me of their support.

My mother's eyes remained forward, watching the doorway, and it wasn't until Camellia appeared, thin and ghost pale, eyes red and a rosy pink dress nearly hanging off of her, that I realized I'd been holding my breath.

Camellia's stride was quick and stiff, her shoulders pinched in close to her ears. There were men at her back, but they seemed as little aware of her as she did of them, as if they only followed out of force of habit.

"Do you think this summons interrupted the doctor?" Daniel whispered, but none of us knew the answer.

Camellia's curtsey was quick, head bowing, a murmured greeting passing through clenched teeth.

"Daughter," my mother said again and I thought she would dismiss Camellia as she had me, but she sat forward on her throne. "Do you want the crown, Camellia?"

Camellia blinked at my mother, head jerking back a little. "Of course."

"Tell me why?"

The whisperings of the court died. Neither my mother or

Camellia were bothering to lift their voices, and the entire room held its breath to listen.

Camellia's gaze flashed to the council first, and then to me, narrowing. She forced a smile for my mother, an imitation of simpering that was more of a grimace. "To serve Kimmery with the great strength of my Hunger, Your Majesty." She curtseyed again, and perversely, the room clapped for her.

My teeth ground together at her answer. It was what we'd been told our entire lives, but it meant *nothing*.

My mother nodded and finally gestured for Camellia to stand aside. Camellia shifted anxiously as she moved into position, one of her Chosen leaning into her gravity, only to be pushed away with a clawed hand.

"Bryony," my mother murmured.

I stepped forward and even though I'd just heard the question, it still took me a stunned moment when my mother asked it again. "Why do you want the crown?"

My mother smiled slightly, but there was a shuttered look in her eyes. Had I already lost? Simply for wanting to be a queen who put her focus on the state of the kingdom first, for wanting to be a mother who had *time* to look at her daughter, to make actual conversation with her, care for her?

"Because as I grew up, I loved Kimmery, and I wanted to do my duty as a woman of the queen's line. I wanted to provide prosperity and joy for the kingdom," I said, and my mother's smile tightened, so I pushed on, my voice rising. "And because now that I have *seen* Kimmery, I understand that love and Hunger, which I possess plentifully, are still not enough.

"I want the crown because if I want Kimmery to feel wealth, there must be changes made so that wealth travels beyond that fist clenched around it greedily. If I want the fields to grow rich with their harvest, I must touch them myself too, gift my Hunger to the ground so it might gift my people with its feast. I see Kimmery's strength being stifled, and I want to break those cages that seek to trap and smother our people's magic so that it can flourish. I want the crown so that I might rule Kimmery by serving it with every last breath I take."

The words wobbled, broke a little as I gasped for air. My

mother was crying, one hand over her heart, but she was smiling too. For real this time.

There was a whoop from Owen, but the note had barely died when the polite clapping returned, a little more enthusiastic than before. Nobles were not my audience, I knew that. But there were other men and women, like Sir Weston and Jack McCallum, whose hearts were as wrapped up in the good of Kimmery as my own, and they cheered for me at my back now.

My mother nodded, rising slowly from her throne and reaching a hand out for me.

I was breathing unevenly at the relief of speaking my mind and almost stumbling forward, but I clutched her hand and brought her knuckles to my lips for a quick kiss before following her tug to stand at her side. I couldn't see the room, blind to the faces in front of me, but I turned my head and my focus cleared at the beaming smiles of my Chosen, my men. My love for Kimmery had been empty before, the notion of a princess raised to think in a straight line. It was brilliant and staggering now, and entirely bound up in those men.

My mother's voice raised high, cutting through the murmuring voices and the fading applause. "There's been a question of succession. I think it is clear now. Her Royal Highness, Princess Bryony, is eldest. She not only possesses the Hunger, she transforms it. She has Chosen. And she is my rightful and *deserving* heir."

I'd been calling myself the crown princess for months, but it had never felt certain until this moment, and the resolve surged through me, a little like sexual ecstasy.

"Your Majesty!"

Oh, fuck.

Joy soured, and I opened my eyes to find Thomlinson marching forward, scowling right at me.

"Your Majesty, the princess may be eldest, but she seeks to *undo* Kimmery. To destroy the council. This is impossible!"

"I don't want to destroy the council, I want the council to serve the kingdom rather than its own members!" I answered, taking another breath but holding it when my mother's fingers squeezed mine.

"Lord Thomlinson, my decision is final," my mother said, just a little too gently.

"If you want an uprising, girl, that's exactly what you'll see," Thomlinson hissed at me, eyes glinting. "Kimmery will have a civil war, and what good will your scrappy farmers and thieves and *beasts* be to you against Kimmery's army?"

My mother gasped, and Thomlinson grinned but only for a moment.

I giggled.

The older man's eyes widened at the sound, and I lifted a hand to cover my grin but another giggle escaped.

"Forgive me, my lord," I said, not meaning it in the slightest. "But I think you forget who serves in Kimmery's army. Those *beasts,* as you call them, have their queen to thank for their recent celebrations, and you think *you,* a man who sought to cage them in camps from the start to the end of their lives, will call them to arms against the crown?"

Thomlinson blinked at me, and the councilmen to my right stirred and stared at one another.

I took a deep breath and stepped away from my mother, sharp magic stabbing at my palms, building like flashes of lightning in my veins.

"Men like you have been sucking Kimmery dry for generations, but it is *women* who made Kimmery powerful, and we will do so again," I said, my fingers sizzling brightly at my side.

Thomlinson gasped as the old stone floors of the throne room trembled. I planted my feet beneath me, forcing my magic down, and then smiled at the man in front of me. Roots broke through stone and several women screamed, but the bryony vines wound harmlessly up the walls, white flowers blooming. Bushes of deep red peonies sprouted around my mother's throne, and dark violets carpeted the ground, the air shimmering with floral perfume and magic.

"Kimmery will no longer remain pinned beneath your boot," I growled. "I will make certain our kingdom grows stronger than ever."

A high, agonized screech tore through the stunned audience.

Camellia, I realized, and with the thought of her name, pale pink camellia blossoms joined the white bryony blooms.

"Bryony!" Aric bellowed.

That same saccharine shade of pink was racing toward me, and I was still flooding the stone with magic when my sister tackled me to the floor.

"Cam—" My voice cut off with a choke, Camellia's thin fingers wrapping around my throat like iron, my lips parted on a cry as she squeezed.

She was screaming, eyes pressed shut, and little spots appeared in my vision at the same moment I realized she was screaming in *pain*, not anger. Our Hunger was scratching at one another, my magic pulsing around me, making her writhe even as her fingers tightened. I couldn't call my tiger out with our Hunger in the way, I could barely even *think* with the clashing chaos wracking through me.

My dagger burned at my hip, and my fingers found the hilt easily, drawing it out of its sheath and up to my sister's throat. She shook me, my vision blacking briefly as my head slammed against the stone again. My lungs were burning, legs kicking, and there was a thin trickle of Camellia's blood running from my dagger down to my hand and wrist.

Men were shouting, but even Aric couldn't reach us in this violent bubble of magic, the electricity of our fractious power flickering around us. Or maybe that was just me running out of air.

The energy rippled on the dagger at Camellia's throat, the rest of the room, the world, going fuzzy at the edges.

No, I thought.

And it wasn't because she was my sister. Or that I knew her rage belonged to the Hunger she'd let grow and squat inside of her like a parasite.

I didn't want to carry Camellia with me for the rest of my life. I didn't want to kill her and wake up at night with her face in my mind like I did with Emory, wondering if I might've made a different choice.

My hesitation cost me, the dagger dropping out of my fingers, landing against my numb chest. I released my magic too, eyelids fluttering at the brief relief when the scratching, clawing, burning feeling dissipated.

"Bryony!"

"Get her off!"

Weight lifted, but my eyelids were still too heavy to open, and pain surged, sudden flowers of color blooming and exploding behind my eyelids.

28.
BRYONY

There's no better proof of living than pain.

I woke with a breath, my eyes growing wide at the fire in my throat and lungs, the throb of my head.

"Don't move," Aric whispered, cold fingers landing delicately on my burning throat.

Even that was too much, my throat too bruised, and I whimpered, clutching soft fabric beneath me. Bedsheets.

A moment later, the excruciating ache eased, just enough for me to feel the moment that the swelling gentled enough for me to catch a solid breath.

"Oh," I moaned, the sound frayed.

"Shh," Aric said, still frowning, his brow tangled with deeper lines than ever, a little sweat dewing there.

Why did I hurt in so many places? Had Camellia kicked me as well as strangled me?

Camellia!

I made to sit up, and a strong hand pinned me down.

"Damnit, girl, don't you listen?" Aric barked.

"Gentle," Cresswell growled, his fingers digging into my shoulders in contrast to his warning at Aric.

Aric huffed, and cold magic continued to trickle into my throat, soothing some of the headache. I swallowed and it *hurt*, but Aric sighed in relief.

"Take a break," I mouthed.

I didn't expect him to listen to me, but Aric sagged back with a brief nod.

We were in our bedroom, which surprised me. Cresswell's tense hands slipped beneath my shoulders, helping me to sit up.

Cosmo was quick to hurry forward, sliding in behind me, his arms wrapping around my chest but leaving room for Cresswell to press to my shoulder.

I pointed around us, and Aric leaned forward, pressing his head to my breastbone, his shoulders shaking. I wasn't sure if it was exhaustion or relief or something worse. I looked to the others, and it was Wendell who finally licked his lips and spoke.

"Aric used magic to keep your heart beating. And Camellia had cracked your skull on the floor, so healing that was next. He got you breathing before we brought you up here, but we weren't...we weren't sure if—"

A throat cleared from the doorway, Nora there with Morgan, both their faces pale. "We'll go and tell the queen."

"I'll do it. I have to go anyway," Aric grunted, pulling back.

My hands flew up to reach for him, and Aric paused, his breath catching and his hands covering mine where I'd grabbed for him low on his neck.

It was gratitude, that look in his eye. He'd lost Charlotte, I remembered, and now he was just grateful he hadn't lost me too.

"Go?" I asked, just breathing the word to keep from straining.

"They have Camellia in a cell. I'm going to make sure she can't get out of it," Aric said darkly.

"A cell?" I winced slightly, and Aric moved one of my hands to my own throat.

"I'm running low," he said, and I drew up a little of my own magic so Aric could guide it to healing me. I was also running low, having foolishly wasted some on that display in the throne room. It was the first time in months that I felt that hollow ache in my belly, and Aric and I both drew away quickly.

"Camellia's...her attack on you was treason, Bryony," Cresswell murmured. "Your mother ordered her contained. Amos chose the dungeons."

"We told them to post two-natured soldiers, but I want to be certain Camellia won't be able to use her Hunger to grab onto any guards or to free herself," Aric said. He drew my hands up to his lips and pressed firm kisses to both my palms, breathing me in for a moment before releasing me and moving off the bed. Owen took his place.

"Wait," I said, rising up to my knees. I wobbled a little, sore and shaken, gazing around at each of them. "It's...done?"

I'd been named successor, and Camellia had...she'd tried to kill me. She was imprisoned, and I didn't think there was much hope for her if she was cut off from men to feed her Hunger.

"The council pressed the doctor and the midwife," Wendell said, one hand reaching beneath my skirt to stroke my calf. "I think perhaps they were hoping you wouldn't...Anyway, Camellia isn't pregnant. The midwife said she didn't think your sister could conceive in her state."

"It's done, Mistress," Owen said, smoothing strands of my hair back.

It wasn't how I expected to feel. I'd thought I would feel victorious, happy at least. Relieved even.

Perhaps there was some relief. Mostly though, I felt tired and heartbroken. I looked down at my wrist, and there was a smear of rust-red there, as if someone had tried to wipe Camellia's blood off my hand and only succeeded in rubbing it in. But I hadn't killed my sister when I had the chance.

She hadn't killed me either.

"Rest, I'll be back as soon as Simon and I have a solution," Aric said.

"We'll bring tea. And broth. And ice water," Nora rattled off, dragging Morgan from the door.

Aric leaned in again, despite his words of leaving, kissing my forehead and resting there. He let me clutch his collar, one of my arms spreading out, and soon I was enveloped in arms and muscle, lips and hands grazing every bit of my skin my Chosen could find.

We'd succeeded, and it wasn't joyful or celebratory, but it was done.

❧

I STARED in the mirror at the purple and green bruises smeared around my throat the next morning. Aric had returned to our suite late in the night, pale and weary. I'd spent most of the day in and out of sleep, Cosmo reading to me, Thao and Wendell washing with me in the bath, every hour strangely clouded in my head.

It was clearer now.

I was the successor. Thomlinson had publicly threatened a civil war. Camellia had tried to kill me.

"Heal those," Cresswell rasped, stepping up behind me, tying up the back of my dress before bending to meet my eyes in the mirror.

"Not yet," I said. My voice was a little raw and cracking still, and it hurt to speak, but it was a reminder with every swallow.

Camellia had wrapped her hands around my neck and I'd put a dagger to her throat and neither one of us had succeeded in killing the other.

Cresswell scowled at me, one hand cupping gently over half the bruises. His head turned, and he grazed a careful kiss over my pulse.

"Heal them by tomorrow morning," he said, a little iron in the words this time.

We were about to meet with my mother and with the council and the royal guard. The bruises would be a potent reminder, although I didn't think anyone was prepared to forget what had only happened yesterday afternoon.

I nodded, rubbing my cheek against Cress's, and he sighed, stepping back and holding out a hand for me to rise. I picked up my golden snake and resisted the urge to flinch as I brought it up to my throat. It slithered gently around my collar bone, below the bruises, an eerie ornamentation, but one that made the dark colors imprinting my skin stand out more starkly.

Cress's hand was tight around mine, leading me to the front room of the suite where the others waited. Cosmo grimaced at the sight of me but stepped forward quickly, taking my chin in his hands and pressing a firm kiss to my lips. There was a little flavor of chocolate lingering on him, and for no clear reason, it almost brought tears to my eyes.

"Ready?"

I nodded, and together we traveled to the council meeting room where I'd presented my case against Camellia, and where my mother had announced her decision regarding the two-natured.

The room was quiet as we arrived, and I was surprised to see Nathan and Simon, the royal mages, as well as the castle physician in attendance. The members of the Northern Council were in attendance as well, including Lord Roderick and few of my old enemies, but I noticed that Roderick and Thomlinson weren't at the head of the table now, but shuffled down to the ends.

"Bryony!" My mother jumped up from her seat as I stepped inside, her eyes fixed to my throat.

"Your Majesty," I croaked, sinking into a curtsey. My mother's breath was shaky and gasping, eyes filling with tears.

"May I say, Your Highness, what a great relief it is to see you recovering," Sir Weston said from the council's end of the table. There were murmurs of agreement, but Thomlinson's nostrils only flared and Roderick had his back to me.

"Thank you, Sir Weston," I said with a dip of my head, moving for the large open seat at my mother's side.

"Your Majesty, Princess Bryony, I hope it is not too presumptuous of me to begin this meeting by expressing the council's sincere shame and grief for yesterday's events," Sir Weston said, and my mother, who was sitting in the lap of one of her Chosen, began to hiccup with weeping. "Specifically and especially, the opinion that was shared regarding the choice of succession made by Your Majesty. Lord Thomlinson's expressions were given by himself alone and without the consensus of the council as a whole. We certainly have no intention of seeking to influence or change your decision."

I reached a hand back to my shoulder and held my breath as Daniel's touch met mine, anchoring me in my seat. I stared down the length of the table at the men there and realized there was genuine fear in many of their eyes. I'd been so busy thinking of Camellia, but of course, it had been Thomlinson who'd tried to threaten to turn the army on me. He was as guilty of treason as she was, and it was obvious now how desperate the other members of the council were to distance themselves from what he'd said.

"Lord Thomlinson has agreed to step down from the council, and we will hold an election for our new head soon, provided Your Majesty is still comfortable with our continued efforts to assist you," Sir Weston concluded with a respectful bow.

My mother only wept harder, and it was several minutes of her crying, of the men at the end of the table waiting for her to swing an axe down on them, before I broke the silence.

"Gentlemen, I don't believe either my mother or I would be able to accomplish our goals in Kimmery without the support of a council of loyal citizens," I said slowly. "It is only great relief to know that words spoken in anger yesterday were a reflection of a smaller voice on the council."

My mother was gathering herself, dabbing her eyes with a handkerchief, watching me with a slightly puzzled frown, but she didn't try to interrupt me.

"Lord Roderick," I said, watching the man in question stiffen in his seat, head turning slowly to meet my gaze. "You and Lord Thomlinson were great allies."

"I—I believed so, Your Highness. However, I would never—"

"And it was you who first arranged to have my Chosen Daniel Farraque join my service as steward to spy on me," I said, squeezing Daniel's hand and feeling the reassuring answer of his touch.

"Your Highness," Lord Roderick said, but his mouth remained open and empty of anything to add.

"You also expressed great prejudice against Kimmery's two-natured citizens. You called them beasts, if I remember correctly."

"You do," Jack McCallum chimed in, his glare focused on Roderick.

"Your Majesty, I have served Kimmery for *decades*," Lord Roderick gasped out, turning to my mother, his hands pressing down flat on the tables.

"Bryony?" my mother murmured.

"I have concerns regarding Lord Roderick's leadership in the north," I said softly to my mother, one hand raising up and resting briefly on the bruises on my throat. I'd spoken more just now than I had since being strangled and was starting to regret not letting Aric heal me a little more than he had, but my mother's eyes flashed down to my fingers and her eyes began to well again.

"What should we do?" my mother asked, brow furrowing.

The room was still, and I could feel the pressure of the dozens of eyes on us. It hadn't been intentional on my mother's part, she was *used* to taking advice. She'd been doing it with the council and my grandmother for the two decades she'd been queen. And now she had just revealed to everyone in the room that she would take mine.

I turned back to Roderick's stare, a strange thrill rushing through me at the power I suddenly possessed. Roderick and I had been butting heads since the moment we met. He'd had Emory at Aric's throat, and regardless of how it had turned out, he'd pressed Daniel into my life as a spy. With any control left in his hand, he would fight me at every opportunity.

But tearing him from the council would leave the other members feeling insecure, and insecurity would breed disloyalty. I had time to eliminate Roderick from their number, but it was possible I wouldn't have to.

"I trust the council to mediate themselves. I only ask that their continued goal is to carry out the *crown's* interests," I said.

Roderick's eyes narrowed at me, lips pressing together in irritation, and I knew I'd made the right choice. The council had favor to gain from me now that I was named successor. If I balanced myself carefully with them, Roderick would topple in their ranks quickly, especially if he wasn't cooperative.

"Wisely considered, Your Highness," Sir Weston said, lips twitching with a smile, which faded quickly. "Now onto a more unsavory discussion."

Weston nodded to Head Guard Amos, who stepped forward from his post by the door. My mother's tears started up immediately again, and it was my eyes that Amos's met. "Princess Camellia is being kept in a cell in the north wing. We did...we did have to bind her hands. The royal mages have warded the room to prevent the influence of magic, but—"

"It's not a perfect system," Nathan interrupted quickly. "The queen's line power is... It has more influence on magic than magic does on it and—"

"But why is she bound? Why warded?" my mother cried out.

I ducked my head as the men in the room all gaped at her.

"I don't—I don't mean why is she in a cell," my mother said. "I just—Oh, this is all terrible!"

Her sobs broke free, the arms of her Chosen bundling her closer.

"I think there are concerns that if Camellia is able to use her Hunger, she might convince a guard to release her," I said carefully, watching my mother.

I ached for her in a strangely resentful way. My mother didn't like making decisions, and she didn't like making people unhappy. Choosing me over Camellia for the crown had to have been difficult enough, but for what came next...I didn't think she'd have the strength. And yet I wanted some acknowledgment of care from my mother. Just like Lily's attempted assassination, my mother hadn't come to see me while I recovered yesterday. She hadn't asked how I was today. She took her comfort from her Chosen, and that seemed to be where she expected me to receive mine.

"She is contained," Aric said, moving up to the arm of my chair. "Her Hunger is...festering is the word for it, I think. Princess Camellia's appetites have exceeded beyond a body's natural ability to consume."

"Her crimes against her Chosen went unchecked too long," one man on the council spoke up. "It is one thing for our queen's line to do what they like with Kimmerian commoners, but with lords' sons? With foreign *princes*? The risk of conflict is too high. And now that there is treason in the mix, she will have to be—"

His voice stopped abruptly at my mother's broken moan.

The castle physician stepped forward, hands clasped in front of him. "Gentlemen, Your Majesty, Your Highness, I had wished to speak to you yesterday, but events prevented this until now. I attended Princess Camellia yesterday morning over the matter of pregnancy, which quite frankly was an impossibility in her state. Having seen her now after just one night in a cell away from access to Chosen to feed her Hunger, I'm afraid...Your Majesty, Princess Camellia is dying."

"What?" I gasped, sitting forward.

My mother sat up too, one hand clapped over her mouth, staring wide-eyed at the doctor.

"She's malnourished, dehydrated, sleep-deprived, her body is failing. If there was something sustaining her this long, it was the magic of her Hunger," the doctor said.

You're not surprised though, are you? a dark voice whispered in my head.

"Dying?" my mother repeated.

"Naturally?" Sir Weston asked, frowning and rubbing his jaw.

"As naturally as one can under the circumstance," the doctor said with a soft shrug.

I thought of the early days of my Hunger coming in, giving into hours and hours with Cosmo and Owen until we were all too tired to continue. And even then, the Hunger had craved for more.

And Camellia was such an impulsive, selfish personality. She'd thought the Hunger made her powerful, and after visiting the Winter Palace, after I'd *threatened* her, she'd probably foolishly believed that feeding hers would make her stronger than me.

A sliver of guilt wormed its way into my heart, but rather than fight it or sink into the feeling, I simply let it find its place there, amongst the tangle of anger, relief, and sorrow that had already taken up residence.

"Is she in pain?" I asked.

"Acutely, yes," the doctor answered.

"Can anything be done for her relief?"

"A sedative, perhaps."

"Your Highness are you considering...measures to heal your sister?" Jack McCallum asked. "I don't mean to be insensitive, but is that wise?"

"Can she be healed?" my mother asked, eyes widening.

"Physically...it's unlikely," the doctor said. "Her state is deteriorating too quickly."

"In my personal opinion, the Hunger is eating away at the princess now that it's not being fed," Aric said.

"I'm not sure why it should matter, considering her actions yesterday are grounds for execution," another council member muttered with his head down.

I expected my mother to start weeping again or to cry out and object. To insist Camellia was saved, as if we might somehow find our way to peace after everything that had happened. She did neither, although there was a soft catch of breath from her throat before she stood at the end of the table.

"I would like to go and see her in her cell. Bryony?"

"Not a—" Cresswell growled from the back, but one of the others hushed him.

I stood slowly, and my mother reached out a hand for me. "Yes, I'll come."

⁂

CAMELLIA'S CELL was similar to Lily's, a decent room in a sunny corner of the north wing. Not quite the dungeons, but just above them. The windows were high and barred, a small fire in a secured grate keeping the small space warm.

"It's...there's less in here," I whispered to Head Guard Amos.

"She was volatile yesterday when we brought her in," he answered.

I couldn't see her through the narrow slitted window of the door, but her ragged breaths and pained whines were clear.

"She's... The physician is right. She's failing quickly it seems," Amos added. "Are you sure you should go in? I can't go with you."

My dagger was at my hip. I didn't know if I would need it, or if I would make the same choice not to harm my sister again, but I looked back past Amos to my Chosen. They would only be feet away, and nothing would stop them from running in if I was in trouble. I had my tiger too, and I could shift quickly if Camellia tried to attack. I'd be ready this time, and I wouldn't let her touch me.

"Open the door," I said, nodding.

The key turned in the lock, every thump in time with a beat of my heart, and my mother stepped inside first. I hesitated for a moment, considering going in as my tiger, but already the scent of sweat was strong, bile too. My mother's gasps came quickly, and I finally followed for her sake alone.

Camellia was in a stained nightdress on the bed. Aric had fashioned some kind of binding for her hands, arms crossed together, that looked gentle enough to keep from hurting her as she pulled and twisted on the mattress. She was pale and trembling, lips broken from her own biting, eyes zipping between our entrance and the window and the door. She tried to sit up and I tensed, but then she groaned and sagged. The doctor was right. There was nothing to fear from Camellia. She was dying, and she was doing it quickly.

My mother, on the other hand, backed away from the bed toward the wall. "The Hunger is doing this to her?"

Her lack of control is. Her lack of discipline. Our habit of ignoring her misbehavior. I bit my lip on all the possible answers that rose up.

"You..." Camellia hissed.

I stiffened, but it wasn't me she was looking at.

"You came—" Her voice broke off into a whine, body arching and eyes squeezing shut, thin tears leaking out of the corners of her eyes. Agony clamped her in its teeth, and Camellia tried and failed to catch a breath.

My mother pressed her hands over her mouth, watching in horror, and I swayed in place, torn between running out of the room, running to Camellia, or simply standing and watching like an idiot.

Camellia finally snatched a great gasp and collapsed back to the bed, air rattling in and out of her chest. Slowly, step by step, I moved closer to the bed. Her eyes flicked in my direction, narrowing, and her head winced away slightly, but she didn't speak or mock or laugh. She just watched me sink down to the stone floor, just out of reach. Her eyes were shockingly red, pale blue irises standing out eerily, the skin shadowy all around. Her cheeks were hollow and pale now, instead of flushed with arousal.

She was not what she ought to be to me, a competitor rather than a sister. Just as my mother wasn't what she ought to be to either of us.

"I can't do this," my mother whispered.

I kept my eyes on Camellia, not certain if her Hunger might see an opportunity to challenge me. "Can't do...? Mother, I'm not sure there's anything we *can* do for her."

"No. I can't rule."

Camellia's eyes were falling shut, her breathing fit apparently too much effort for her. I watched her brow furrow and smooth, her tongue licking out over her bottom lip but failing to leave any moisture behind.

"I don't know that I ever wanted to be queen. I wanted my Chosen. That was all. Everything else has been so...so hard."

Camellia's eyes opened again, already focused on me. We were part of that everything else, me and my sister.

"You'll have to take the crown," my mother said.

"Fine."

"Soon."

Camellia whimpered again and began to squirm, her thighs pressing and rubbing together, arms pulling at the strange sleeve she'd been trapped in.

"Bryony."

"Yes. Soon. And Camellia?"

Camellia groaned, senseless to the conversation, panting and then seizing without being able to take a breath.

"Mother?"

I turned my head and found her standing with a blank and empty look, her head shaking slowly. "I can't. I wash my hands of it all."

When did you ever get your hands dirty? I thought, pressing my lips into a hard line to keep from speaking it aloud. It didn't matter, she was already on her way out of the cell, footsteps echoing, Camellia's breath stuttering.

"Your Highness?" Head Guard Amos called.

"An announcement should be made declaring Princess Camellia having taken ill," I said, watching my sister watch me in return. The courtiers had seen her attack me. Everyone would assume Camellia was killed. Just as Sir Weston and the other lords assumed that previous sisters in the queen's line died off by one another's command. Maybe they had. Or maybe they'd gone like this—eaten up from the inside by their own power when misapplied.

"I'm sorry I didn't do anything decent for you sooner," I said, although the words didn't quite fit on my tongue. They weren't a lie, but Camellia and I weren't close either. Even prior to her Hunger developing, we'd always been kept separate. Probably with the understanding that one of us was unnecessary in the long run.

Camellia groaned and twisted away, and I couldn't tell if it was a physical complaint or just irritation at my pity.

Boots scuffed on the stone, Aric's hands settling on my shoulders. "The physician is on his way with a sedative."

I nodded, counting the sharp knobs of bone that ran down my sister's back, the outline of her ribs. Neglect. She'd been neglected, perhaps even more so than I had. I hadn't done anything to repair that, hadn't reached out to her, too busy soothing my own loneliness in the pages of books.

"What would...what would I do, normally, in this situation?" I asked.

"There's nothing normal about this, princess," Aric whispered.

"I know, but...as sisters? What would a sister do?"

His fingers smoothed over the top of my head. "Would you like to sit with her?"

Camellia's body was starting to strain and stiffen, tension coiling, and I reached back to push Aric toward the door, nodding.

"Yes, I'll stay."

"I'll call for Morgan and Nora. We'll wait for you."

Camellia moaned and rolled as the door shut behind Aric, facing me again, breaths gasping, brow sweating. I took one long look at her, brittle thin and hands bound, goosebumps and sweat and trembles, and then I rose from the floor. Could she really hurt me like this? I didn't think so.

I sat gingerly down at the edge of the bed, and Camellia rolled face down at my side. Her hair was growing thin too, I realized, and thick tangles were rooted at the nape of her neck. My hand hovered over her spine for a moment, surprised by the heat rising off her when she was shivering so fiercely. She moaned once more, and I gave in to the urge, pretending I was Owen trying to calm me, circling my palm over her back.

"I didn't want the crown either," Camellia rasped, words almost entirely muffled against the mattress. Her head turned a little, eyes squeezed shut, back rising and falling unevenly under my hand. "I just didn't want you to have more than me."

There wasn't anything to say to that. She'd tried to humiliate me for years. Tried to take Owen from me. Wanted me dead. Wanted to let the council have its way with Kimmery just for the sake of defeating me. And yet for the first time in months, I wasn't angry with my sister.

"I think I understand now," I murmured. "I wish I had earlier."

Camellia just grunted. I would be angry with her another day.

It would come up in mourning anyway, Grandmother's death had taught me that.

I circled my hand over Camellia's bony spine, feeling her shivers tremble up through my wrist, and waited for the doctor to come.

※

"Bryony?"

I woke with a groan. My back was stiff and aching, my arms numb from holding my head as a pillow. My throat was dry, and my head was pounding. I leaned into the tender fingers at the back of my neck and twisted to find Cosmo bent behind me.

The fire was still burning in the grate, but the room was dark. My legs were numb too, pins and needles pricking in my muscles as I shifted from my seat on the floor.

"It's time to go," Cosmo whispered, one hand reaching up to cup my cheek.

I leaned into his palm, sighing at that sweet rich scent of him I knew perfectly. "No, I should—" My head turned, and my voice died abruptly.

Camellia was on her side, eyes open, and she was empty, peaceful. It was the peace that made it clear. She'd been heaving with breaths for the last hour I'd been awake, gasping and then going still until the next one would come. There was no struggle in her now, but no life either.

"It's done now," Cosmo whispered, turning my face back to his.

"Oh."

Camellia and I hadn't spoken again, but she hadn't tried to kill me and there was something almost soothing about sitting at her side, trying to keep her calm and comfortable as pain wracked through her. Hideous and heartbreaking, but not full of our usual animosity.

"I'm so sorry, muse," Cosmo said, his voice cracking. He leaned in, kissing just above my nose and staying there.

I sank into him, my arms circling his shoulders, my body pushing itself into his. There were no tears, I was too tired or my emotions regarding Camellia were just too complicated, but there was *need*. The demand to be held closely by someone safe. My Chosen, Cosmo and all his depth and empathy especially.

Cosmo lifted me up from the floor, hooking one arm beneath my knees and cradling me as he moved steadily for the door.

"My mother is giving up the crown," I whispered.

"We heard. She'll have to wear it for the night at least," Cosmo answered. "It's time for us to sleep."

I glanced over his shoulder, watched Head Guard Amos move quietly into the cell, drawing the thin sheet up and over Camellia's body, leaving only shadow and firelight in her place.

29.
BRYONY

"You don't have to do this today, Mistress," Owen murmured as I paused in front of the mage's office. Inside, the conduit pulsed like a heartbeat. "Aric said he could manage the work."

"He did, but I am faster," I said, stroking my hand over Owen's forearm to reassure him. "The coronation preparations are being made, and we can't expect Holden to wait much longer. None of the other Chosen even waited for her funeral."

Not that Camellia's funeral had been much to speak of. Officially, Camellia's illness had been lumped in with my grandmother's, and the burial had been a small affair. It looked shameful, that was what I thought as if we were trying to hurry through the event and move on from Camellia quickly.

Owen was still frowning so I added, "Anyway, it helps me to keep busy."

He relented at that, as I knew he would. It was the truth too. I was glad my mother had decided she could only tolerate one round of mourning in a year, even though carrying on in life as if everything were normal was just another injury against Camellia's memory. My sister would be a footnote in our line, like all the other sisters who had died in some far off castle. On days when I burned with anger, that felt right. Other days, it made me queasy and sad.

Owen opened the door to the mages' workroom just as Simon and Aric bustled out of opposite doorways, heading for the conduit. Surrounding the great crystal prism on the ground were deep crates of pennies and crowns and quarters. This wasn't my first day pulling magic from the conduit, pushing it into crystals to be buried throughout Kimmery, but it was our last opportunity to finish the work. We'd leave Kenneth and Holden a little pool of magic to work with, enough to frighten Kenneth but not so much as to allow Holden to go to war.

"Princess," Aric said, eyebrows lifting briefly. He looked me over, studying my expression, and then nodded. "Good. You know I hate heavy lifting."

My lips quirked, and I considered running into his chest to push him roughly and kiss his cheek. Aric seemed to understand best of all my Chosen my need to *keep moving*.

"Well stocked?" he asked.

I thought I might've blushed, which was kind of silly really, considering I'd spent almost a year enjoying my Hunger with my men. I glanced at Simon, who looked amused and more than a little curious.

"Yes," I said simply. I was well stocked on my magic. I'd spent the morning in bed with Owen, Cosmo, and Cress. And then another hour or more in the bath with Daniel, Thao, and Wendell. "Do I really need to be if I'm pulling from the conduit?" I asked.

Aric shrugged. "Can't hurt. Come here, there's an open spot."

"Where are Kenneth and Nathan?" I asked, moving to the other side of the conduit, where crates had been pushed aside to make room for someone to stand directly in front of the conduit's frame.

"Nathan's keeping Kenneth busy. And truth be told, I don't know that Nathan would approve of this exact method of magical distribution," Simon said, grinning down at the coins.

"It is safe, though?" I asked, glancing at Aric.

"Safest I can think of, princess," Aric said, hands circling my waist to steady me. "Metal's more resistant to taking magic on and tougher to pull it out of."

I nodded and rolled my shoulders. The pulse of the conduit was a little overwhelming from this close, but while Aric and Simon had sorted out a way to draw the magic out, it tired them in a way it didn't with me. I took one deep breath, reached both palms out, fingers splayed, and felt the brief curious tug from the conduit at my own magic before grabbing fistfuls in my grip, yanking with all my might and concentration, then bending to thrust them down to the coins waiting in the crate.

Metal rattled as if the pennies were wriggling in excitement, and the shaking grew stronger until the wooden crates were thumping and bouncing in place. I released the magic and stood, blinking down at the instantly still coins.

"Two down," Simon said.

"Doesn't even feel like a dent in the conduit though," Aric said, frowning at the prism over my shoulder.

"Then we do it again," I said, standing straighter, taking another breath, and reaching out to the magic of the queen's line.

◈

THAO'S orange tiger prowled around the rose garden, and my own itched to join him.

"We could seat the countess of Amonsbury with the Duke of Pemony," Morgan said, making a hasty scribble.

"Ah, no. Their families were cousins and there was a great falling out," Wendell said, fingers working almost aimlessly at the tense muscles of my shoulder as I traced patterns in the fine gravel of the pathway. "Seat her with Lord and Lady Sandimon."

"Urghh! Where is Nora? I *hate* this sort of nonsense," Morgan growled, scratching repeatedly at the marks she'd just made. We were planning the seating for the feast after the coronation. Well, the others were. I was resting my head on Wendell's thigh and enjoying the sudden warm spell of the day.

"This sort of nonsense is valuable if you want to work with the council," Wendell said, and I could hear his smile and the laugh he was trying to restrain.

"Then fuck the council and I'll join the mages," Morgan muttered.

"We won't have you," Aric answered easily.

I hid my grin against Wendell, nipping his muscle briefly through his pants as he tugged a strand of hair on the back of my neck. He grunted, and his fingers clasped the back of my neck in a commanding grip that made me think Wendell and I would be moving inside shortly.

"There you all are!"

"Nora McCallum, get your ass over here and solve this abominable puzzle of decorum!" Morgan shouted.

Wendell tapped the base of my neck, and I sat up, accepting his helping hand to move up to the bench, resting on his lap. Nora was hurrying to us from the double doors, a wide and shallow box in her arms.

"In a moment, I have a gift for Bryony first," Nora said, her cheeks flushed and smile wide.

"A gift?" I asked, glancing at the box she carried, a little spark of excitement bubbling up in me. I didn't receive gifts very often, and for some reason, it was even nicer to know this one was coming from Nora. I had not only allies in my ladies-in-waiting but actual friends too.

"It's for...well, it's from the two-natured," Nora said, passing the box into my hands. "For the coronation, if you want it."

My eyes widened as the box weighed down my hands, an unexpected heft to it. "The coronation?"

Most of the time, it felt as though we were speaking about someone else. My mother hadn't made much of an effort to speak to me since Camellia's death, and our conversations were usually strained. She'd insisted on abdicating the crown to me as soon as possible, accelerating every plan for the event.

It was less than a week away now, and I hadn't wrapped my mind around it yet.

The box was wrapped in layers of shimmering, delicate tissue, and I hunted down within the tucked-in folds of paper, trying to unwrap it with care.

"Just rip it," Morgan muttered.

Thao moved closer, rising into his human self, and Cosmo abandoned his sketching to join us until my ladies and all my Chosen surrounded me.

I lifted the lid, my fingers sliding inside to brush against something soft and silkily sharp. Thao lifted the lid impatiently away, and I gasped. Inside the box, tucked thoughtfully in more tissue, was a cape in pale shades of white and cream and pink and blue. There was a heavy shoulder armor, embroidered with stones and cording and threads of silver, but the rest of the cape was cascading white feathers.

"The two-natured?" I asked as Daniel leaned in, lifting the shoulders up out of the box. I ran my fingers over the feathers. Some were fine and downy, others long and broad and hard like blades. My mouth parted as it sank in.

Nora was bouncing on her toes, hands wringing together in front of me. "There's a few of my own. The milliner asked for permission to strip the color out and I think it looks—"

"Beautiful," I breathed.

This wasn't just a purchased gift from the two-natured, it was their actual feathers. I remembered Griffin keeping Sam's feather in her pocket and knew that this was *meaningful* to them, even if I didn't understand it fully.

"A token of gratitude and of confidence," Nora said softly as I blinked rapidly, trying to fight tears.

"I don't know how to say thank you," I whispered.

"You already have, Your Highness," Nora said.

"Stand up and try it on," Owen urged.

I shook my head quickly. "No! No, not until the day."

"Not long now," Wendell murmured, kissing my jaw.

❦

DANIEL'S FINGERS were stroking around my sex, teasing, his mouth alternating at my breasts, as Cresswell thrust against me, his breath panting on my back, hips snapping against my ass.

My fingers combed through Daniel's strands, moans stuttering with Cress's rhythm, but my grip turned tight as Daniel focused his touch directly on my clit. I came with an exhausted cry, and Cresswell's landed heavily against me, the clutch of my orgasm drawing his on. I was sandwiched between my two Chosen, Cresswell plastered to my back as he bucked deep and quick through his finish.

Daniel was still swirling his touch on me, and I reached down to still his wrist, shuddering through the aftershocks, his chuckle vibrating against my breast.

"Enough," I pleaded.

Cresswell sighed into the nape of my neck and twisted, lowering us gently to the bed, Daniel sitting up and smiling at me, his fingers lifting to his lips. I closed my eyes to ignore the tempting sight of that red tongue licking away my taste, and Daniel laughed.

"Give her a few minutes to recover at least," Cresswell said. "For my ego, if nothing else."

"More than a few minutes," I said, opening one eye as Daniel settled himself on his side. I'd already enjoyed them both twice. I felt I'd earned a decent nap.

Daniel didn't disagree, but he leaned in, pressing feather-light kisses over my throat and collarbone, and I knew that in a few minutes, I'd be pushing his face between my thighs and starting all over again. He probably knew that too, and Daniel liked to see how far he could go before I really pleaded to be left alone.

Thankfully, or maybe unfortunately because his kisses were divine, there was a knock on the door.

"Her Majesty is here to see you, Bryony," Morgan said quickly through the door.

Daniel grunted and sat up grinning. "You're free," he said, head tilting as I started to scramble out of the bed, Cresswell growling at the interruption. "You're nervous?"

"A bit," I admitted. "She hasn't reached out much, and the coronation..."

The coronation was in two days, and sex with my Chosen had been a necessary tool to fight against my anxiety—along with its usual benefits.

Daniel scooped me up and carried me off the bed, Cresswell following after us. I cleaned myself up quickly, finding a simple dress to wear as Daniel and Cress hurried into pants and shirts to join me.

When we reached the sitting room, we found my mother unattended, and my heart pounded in my chest.

"I'd like to speak alone if that's all right," my mother said.

Daniel started to return back to the bedroom immediately, but Cress's fingers squeezed my shoulder and I nodded to him. "Go ahead." They left together, wearing frowns.

"Can I get you anything?" I asked.

"No, come sit."

Unease swooped through me as I moved to join my mother on the couch, facing her. "You've changed your mind?"

It was the only thing I could think of that she might want to speak on, and there was an unexpected sense of relief at the idea. Certainly, I knew I would be a stronger ruler than my mother had been thus far, but the coronation was looming, more daunting by the day.

"What? No." My mother frowned and looked at me out of the corner of her eyes. She was subdued, and it was a bit shocking to see her here alone. "Have you?"

"No," I said, and it came more easily than I'd expected, given all my worries. "I want to be queen."

My mother nodded and sighed. "Everything is ready now. I only came to say..."

I held my breath. Would she...apologize? For being an indifferent mother and queen?

"I think I will go north with my Chosen after you take the throne. Just for a little while. I am badly in need of a...a break from all of this."

I turned away from her, staring absently at the doorway, counting the names of my friends and my Chosen in my head as a means to keep myself calm. Of course this was what she wanted. And part of me didn't blame her. She'd lost her own mother and a daughter, had her failings as a queen laid out before her. I could consider it an improvement she told me at all. I pushed aside the hurt for the moment, I could unpack it later with someone like Cosmo or the others, and fixed a smile to my lips.

"I think you will enjoy the Winter Palace. In spite of its name, it's beautiful this time of year, and I found it a wonderful place to relax," I said. Which was true, in spite of the council and Emory and fighting with Aric.

My mother sighed and her own smile bloomed, but it was more wobbly than it had been months ago. "Yes, yes I thought of that."

"And Lady Prudence is a wonderful woman. I'm sure she and the staff will be thrilled to have the palace busy again," I continued. "I'd like to spend the winter there next year, myself. We left not long after the snow fell. Thao will whine, but..." I waved my hand through the air, a frail smile wiggling on my lips. I liked Thao all bundled up and constantly trying to cuddle up with one of us for warmth.

"You'll make a good queen," my mother murmured, nodding to herself.

I would. I was determined. But my mother's words were a little empty, so I thought of my grandmother and what she'd said to me as she died. That she was *glad* I would be queen. My heart fisted around those words, clung to them. I was ready, ready enough.

"I'm glad you came. There's something I wanted to ask you about the coronation ceremony," I said, straightening and turning to my mother. "I've had an idea."

30. BRYONY

"You look beautiful, regal," Cosmo corrected with a half-smile.

I stood in an adjoining chamber to the throne room, my feet frozen and gaze fixed unseeing out the window. There was a mirror behind me, reflecting the long pale feathered cape I'd been gifted from the two-natured, and my hand smoothed over the gauzy skirt of the dress I'd created to match. Aric's snake was resting around my throat, the gifted dagger at my hip, and the bryony blossoms in my ears.

My feet seemed to be sinking into the floor, weighted there by my own heavy thoughts.

"It hasn't even been a year," I said.

"Hm?"

I turned to Wendell and blinked. "It hasn't even been a year since my choosing ceremony. Almost, but I can't believe...I can't believe how much has happened."

"I can't believe it either," Aric said with a little laugh.

I stared, eyeing him up and down. He was in a red velvet waistcoat, silver hair smoothed back, and boots polished to a deep brown leather. He looked like a king, but certainly not the King of Thieves he'd been the day of my ceremony. In fact, the only one of my Chosen who really still seemed unchanged was Thao, and that was only because he was wearing his beautiful Mennarian military uniform. He was every bit the humorous and generous man I'd grown to love and lean on.

"I remember when you called up my line and I stared at you in your seat, prim and contained with your jaw grinding," Aric murmured, moving in and stroking his thumb over my jaw. "I hated you."

A laugh escaped. I'd known as much probably, but I hadn't expected to hear it at this moment.

"I thought you might've been the worst of your line, simply because you could control your Hunger in a way Camellia didn't bother with," Aric continued, frowning a little. His lips quirked.

"I thought you looked noble and principled, so I guess we were both wrong," I answered, arching an eyebrow.

Aric grinned and kissed my brow. "Mm. I think I was proved wrong first. You were too sweet when you greeted us all. Too nervous and shy. I hated being proved wrong, and you were the prettiest and most tempting puzzle I'd ever met."

I smiled and let my eyes fall shut as he kissed his way down my nose to my lips. I might've argued his point. He'd managed to be pretty disinterested for plenty of time, but I liked the compliment too much to refuse it.

"I thought you'd shuffle me out of your Chosen once you'd found your footing with Owen," Cosmo said.

I drew back from Aric and whipped around to face him. Cosmo shrugged, and I shook my head. "Never. I may not have had the Hunger the day of my choosing, but I had divine luck when I met every one of you."

"We were worried too," Wendell said, glancing at Thao.

"To be honest, I held my breath until you finally had her writhing on your tongue the night of the festival," Thao said, winking at me as I gasped.

"I knew you'd be queen the moment you cut Sir Hubert down to size," Cress said.

"And Lord Roderick," Daniel added.

Owen just grinned at me. "I never had a doubt."

My heart split at its seams in that moment, sharing itself with each of my seven men, and yet still pounding in my chest. They'd given me as much, if not more, in return and there was no one else I trusted with myself.

A knock on the door echoed in the room, and I jumped, suddenly remembering why we were here and what we were waiting for.

Morgan opened the door, her hand over her eyes. "Stop whatever it is you're doing."

"Nothing, you mean?" Aric asked.

Her fingers parted, and she sighed. "Oh good, it's time for you lot to wait by the dais."

I considered briefly running and slamming the door shut on Morgan in order to hole up inside the room with my Chosen, continue to let their faith in me bolster my own, but it was too late. My men were ready for me to be crowned, even if I wasn't quite sure yet.

Aric cupped the back of my neck, pulling me closer and pressing a firm kiss to my temple. "Princess."

"You'll have to stop calling me that," I said, laughing nervously.

Aric smirked. "I don't think I will. I never meant it as your title."

He'd meant it to tease me, calling me spoiled. Or maybe he'd meant that I *should* be spoiled and cared for, treated delicately and teased terribly. I would be queen soon, but that wouldn't stop Aric from correcting me when he felt I was wrong or commanding me when I needed someone to put a path in front of me before I lost my way.

He squeezed my fingers and headed for the door. One by one, they kissed me, wished me luck, and left the room. Owen and Cosmo hovered as the others left, waiting until we were alone.

"I wish you could make that walk with me," I whispered.

"You don't need us," Owen said.

I caught my breath and shook my head. "I do. More than anything. But you're right, not for this."

Owen wrapped his arms around me, disregarding my fine gown and my carefully arranged hair and the feathers of my cape as he drew me to his chest and pressed a firm kiss to my lips.

"I love you, Mistress," he said.

I sighed, reaching up between us to cup his jaw and kiss him again. "I love you, my Chosen."

He squeezed me and headed for the door, and Cosmo quickly took his place, mouth against my ear and one hand cupping my throat.

"I was born for you, little muse," he whispered, and shivers ran through me at the ache in the words and his breath on my skin. "And you were born for this."

He kissed my cheek, and then I was alone in the room.

Stillness returned, but this time it was calm, the seconds ticking loudly by on a small clock on a window ledge.

Tick, tick, tick...

A heartbeat for each of my Chosen.

Tick, tick, tick...

One for each of the women of my line whom I'd conquered in my own way to gain the crown. My grandmother and her prejudice against me. My mother and her ignorance. Camellia and her greed.

And when the trumpets and the strings blared to life beyond the door, my heart hammered fastest and loudest in my ears. For Kimmery.

I'd rehearsed the ceremony so many times, I knew it by heart. I knew my route out of the antechamber up to the aisles between gallery seats, where the visiting nobles all stood watching somberly, likely remembering Camellia's attack on me just weeks ago. There were still flowers climbing the walls and violets bordering the stones of the floor.

My steps moved in time with the music, and time seemed slowed and warped, my mind a little too distant from my body. Feathers whispered behind me as I walked up to the dais, the voice of the two-natured urging me gently forward. My mother was there, her Chosen waiting behind her throne, a golden crown on her head, old and heavy and beautiful. The same crown that my ancestor had taken from the head of a king barely anyone remembered.

They'll remember me, I decided. Not for battles or for hardship, but for the golden age of Kimmery I'd been told I'd help create since I was a little girl. I would fashion it with my own hands if I had to. I would march through fields and plant seeds myself if that was what it took.

My mother rose from her seat, a soft smile on her lips, shoulders loose with relief. My Chosen were waiting in the wings to the side of the dais, watching, their eyes like pillars shoring me up. My mother's hand extended to me, and I dipped my head to kiss the back of it.

"Bryony of Kimmery, Daughter of the Queen's Line, why do you stand before me today?"

"To carry on the mantle of Queen of Kimmery," I said, surprised by the strength of my voice, the way it carried up to old wooden arches, bounced against dark stone.

"What is in your heart?" my mother asked.

"My love for Kimmery." The answers were my own, although I was sure I hadn't been the first woman to say something like them.

"What is in your hands?"

"The lives of my people."

"What is in your blood?"

"The strength of the queens who came before me," I said, thinking of my grandmother.

My mother paused and smiled, and I wondered what her answers had been.

"What is in your mind?"

I hesitated. I had too many answers for this question. All my plans for Kimmery's betterment. Acts of change and promises of improvement. But I didn't know how to fashion it all into a single answer until the words fell from my lips.

"My own voice."

My throat tightened, breath freezing. It was a risky answer in a way. Probably not reassuring to the council, and a bit of a slap to my mother and her habit of listening to everyone else, but it was the truth. I'd learned to trust my own conscience.

My mother only blinked. "Kneel, Bryony of Kimmery."

I sank, releasing a silent, wavering sigh.

"Do you swear..." There was more, questions to answer in the affirmative, old promises someone had written hundreds of years ago. But that part was easy and a little mindless. "...and to live your life in service of Kimmery and its people?"

"I do," I said easily, in a bit of a daze and nearly forgetting that I'd just sworn to my last promise. It struck me, and I looked up, my eyes on my mother's. She was calm, and I suspected, relieved.

"I surrender unto you my crown," she said, raising her hands up to her head and taking the crown in her grip, lifting it carefully away, "Bryony, Daughter of the Queen's Line, Queen of Kimmery."

The metal was warm from her head, sinking into my hair, and I closed my eyes as my throat squeezed shut. The crown settled easily, heavy enough to be a reminder of what I'd just taken on, but reassuring too.

"Rise," my mother said, gently, taking my hands and helping draw me back up from the floor. One hand remained held in mine as she stepped carefully to the side of the throne, leaving me in the center. Behind us, men shuffled away, my mother's Chosen making way for my own.

I looked at her, and she nodded, magic sparking between us. I guided it for her, down into the stones, up into the rafters, pushing it into the ground and the sea and the sky. There was a whisper of breath, expectant from the audience, but the transformation was small. Behind me on the throne, the peonies vanished, roots crumbling down back into the magic I'd made them from. Bryony flowers took their place, white and shy and delicate, vines curling over the great old wood, coiling and digging themselves deeply.

"Good luck, daughter," my mother whispered, and her hand pulled free of mine, leaving me alone. I stepped back once and took my seat on the throne, deaf to the clapping, the cheering, my gaze full of the future.

❧

I GIGGLED, tossing a fistful of charmed coins into the street, seeing the shimmer of the metal catching the sunlight before leaping hands claimed them from the sky. The carriage bumped along the main road of the capital, crowds packed together. Flowers were tossed over the heads of the guards marching alongside us, just as my Chosen and I threw coins back into the hands of my people.

"My people," I murmured, suddenly stunned, staring into one face and then the next as they cheered at our passing.

Large warm hands wrapped around my waist, drawing me back until I was seated on Cresswell's lap. Cosmo took my place at the edge of the carriage, and I caught my breath, watching the glitter of coins in the sky, the roar of voices in my ear. Then a soft pair of lips pressed in closer.

"You did it, my queen," Cresswell said, voice gravelly and dark, my eyes falling shut and a slow smile stretching over my lips. "Are you happy?"

Camellia came first to my thoughts with a pang, my grandmother too, every ache of the journey to this point rising slowly up in my chest. Becoming queen hadn't been simple or sweet, and I wasn't the girl from a year ago. Kimmery wasn't the kingdom I'd imagined while growing up. But it would grow and heal, and so would I.

"I am," I decided, twisting on Cresswell's lap and helping myself to his heady kisses, sinking into him as his hands mapped my form beneath the feathered cape.

"Save it for the ground blessing," Aric called to us, laughing from the opposite bench of the carriage.

"As if she couldn't have both," Cress grumbled, but he turned his kisses into pecks along my jaw, back up to my ear, and turned me back to the others, steadying me as I stood in the wobbling carriage and grabbed another two fistfuls of coins.

"We don't know how far these will go," I said to Aric, tossing them into the air, watching the crowd hurry to catch them.

"We don't," Aric said, looking wickedly pleased with the notion. "But it's fair to say there's more magic going into Kimmery than going back to Noren with Holden and Kenneth. A little magical commerce might do the kingdom good."

"To magic and commerce then," I said, throwing another shower of charmed coins, adding a little extra boost of magic to them and grinning as they transformed into bright yellow and copper butterflies, drawing gasps from the crowd.

"To you, Bryony," Aric said, wearing a half-grin.

❧

THE MOON WAS high and so full in the sky, it almost looked as though it might burst above us, but it lit the large tent in the field that had been erected for the blessing.

I was grateful for the cover of night because just looking at the space made me blush.

"Are you nervous?" Owen teased, ducking to bump his head against mine.

"A little. I know I've never been the *most* modest, but it's very... transparent, isn't it?" I asked. "The one at the festival at least had proper curtains."

There were bonfires erected past the four corners of the tent, an odd collection of nobles, officials, and commoners gathered together around the field to observe the ceremony. If it could be called that.

Aric pushed the door of the carriage open and leapt down first, Daniel following just after him, their hands outstretched in offering to help me down.

"I think between the seven of us, we can safely guard your modesty," Aric said.

"You liked being watched at the ball," Daniel added, smirking just a little.

I swallowed hard, but I didn't deny it.

"Forget the audience, muse. Forget the magic and Kimmery too, for that matter. Just take tonight to celebrate what you've achieved," Cosmo said and then grinned. "With us. Naked."

Laughter burst out of me, and I shook off my nerves, accepting Daniel and Aric's hands and stepping down to the cool earth. We'd ridden in the carriage for most of the day, north out of the capital and through the towns that bordered it, until we'd reached farmland. I didn't know if the magic we made tonight would reach all the way to the north, but it would ensure that the soil here in the heart of Kimmery would be rich and ready to be seeded in the coming weeks.

Clapping and bright cries rose up as my Chosen and I stepped out of the carriage. There was a carpet laid down that led to the gauzy, waving curtains of the tent, and my feathered cape whispered softly as I accepted Wendell's arm to escort me to the entrance. Eager eyes watched from every corner and around every border, and I couldn't quite shake the feeling that this was a performance to these people. It was one thing to be spinning in a crowd of dancers as Aric and Daniel toyed with me, but it was quite another to put on an orgy for an audience.

I reached a hand up to the curtains as we reached the tent, letting my fingers graze the fabric, magic racing out of my hand.

The crowd gasped and oohed as the gauze darkened in strange

patterns and tableaus, figures tangled in erotic embraces, flowers vining like pillars, shooting stars and racing animals. It was still transparent in places, but it would at least do a better job of distorting what went on inside and gave me an illusion of moderate privacy.

"Very clever, my love," Wendell said, and then he scooped me up from the carpet and hauled me inside.

There was a low platformed mattress in the center of the tent, large enough for all of us, but a little cozier than the bed in our castle suite. A table in a corner was dressed with plates of fresh fruit and bread and meats, as well as several bottles of wine and mead. I considered going there first, but Wendell carried me directly to the mattress, climbing on top to great cheers from our audience and settling me over his lap.

"Oh stars, are they going to do that the whole time?" I hissed as a voice hollered in approval.

Wendell just wrapped his arms around my waist and rested his forehead to mine, Cosmo joining us on the bed and unclasping my cape, scooping it up from around me and passing it to Owen to set aside.

"To be honest, they probably are," Wendell said, kissing the bridge of my nose. His hands settled on my thighs, stroking but nothing more. Behind me, Cosmo kissed a steady path back and forth over my shoulders, his fingers playing at the buttons of my dress.

And my Hunger stirred.

Apparently, it didn't mind the audience.

I sighed and relaxed on Wendell's lap, closing my eyes as he peppered kisses over my face and Cosmo's hands stroked my bare arms.

"I suppose I'll get used to it," I murmured, arching my neck in invitation. Wendell chuckled but refrained from further comment.

The bed dipped as Wendell's kisses feathered over my shoulder and Cosmo's fingers worked a button loose. I had a brief warning, a nose against mine, and then my lips parted for a kiss. Wine, tart and rich, touched my tongue, quickly followed by a tongue stroking against mine. I moaned, familiar with Thao's thorough, starving way of kissing, and pulled away to swallow, blinking up at his grin. He put the goblet to my lips, and I took another sip before he had one of his own.

"Dress," Wendell murmured, and Cosmo pushed one shoulder off, Wendell quickly ducking to my breast, taking it with his mouth before it could even be exposed.

I gasped and rocked over his lap, eyes widening, and then Thao ducked down to consume me with another kiss.

A moment later, a hot firm hand was sliding beneath my skirt to grip and massage my thigh, fingers calloused. Owen. My Chosen weren't going to give me a moment to be self-conscious.

"So this is your plan for me?" I asked, sucking in air as Thao lifted away again. I blinked and realized Cress and Daniel and Aric were already on the bed too. It would be impossible for anyone to see me surrounded by my Chosen this way. "To keep me so caught up between all of you I can't even think?"

I caught Aric's grin before Cosmo had pushed the other side of my dress down and Wendell switched breasts, just moving aside enough for Daniel to take the other. The contrast of their mouths, the scratch of Daniel's beard and his love of licking versus Wendell's smooth mouth and hungry sucking, made me gasp and stiffen. I rocked desperately, eyes shut again, grinding on Wendell's lap and searching for Owen's hand to slide closer to where I wanted it.

"That would've been smart of us, but to be honest, princess, I think we're all just desperate to have you," Aric said.

"Queen," I corrected, a little triumphant at the claim.

Aric took my chin in his fingers, stretching my throat and pulling my head back. "You're *my* princess, and you always will be."

My dress wadded around my waist, and my men seemed to reach a consensus to pull back as one, dragging it quickly off me.

"Share your magic with me," Aric growled.

I was low, but I wouldn't be for long, so I lifted a hand to wrap around his wrist and gave him everything left in me. A moment later, my Chosen were nude.

Owen's fingers were on my clit, and Wendell was pressing his length into me as I moaned. There was a roar from the audience, but Daniel had been right. Their joy fed my arousal. This was who

I was, and if I could make my people happy by fucking the men I loved, there was really no downside to be found.

I giggled at the thought, and Cress growled. "She's not far gone enough yet."

"Thao, fuck our lover's ass," I gasped out as Wendell started a slow, steady, glide in and out of me. Thao would make him race, and I loved when Wendell gave way to the animal inside of him.

"Lower her, arched, just like that," Cosmo breathed.

I was held in seven pairs of hands, stroking over my breasts, on my sex, Thao gripping behind my knees to spread me wider for Wendell. Cosmo held my head, upside down, half-hard cock approaching my open mouth as he dug into the muscle at the back of my neck. I licked his head, and he groaned, fingers tightening in my hair as I sucked him down.

Aric and Daniel teased at my breasts, one pair of fingers twisting, another mouth soothing the ache, back and forth. Cress kissed my belly, and Owen worked my clit. It was crowded and clumsy and so wholly consuming, there seemed to be nothing else in the world. Just touch and cock and kisses.

There would be magic in a moment. Kimmery to manage in the morning. The council to keep in their place, diplomacy and balls and all of the nonsense I'd fought so hard to take on.

But for a few minutes, there were only flesh and heartbeats and pleasure with the men I loved. My blood pounded in my veins until it drummed in my ear, my muscles taking all their cues from my Hunger to rock and twist and arch for more. Mindless desire rose until it blocked every other thought from my mind.

Cosmo pulled away gasping before I could finish him off, and he ducked down, kissing me crookedly. Aric had one of my nipples in a gentle pinch, and it created an electric line directly to where Wendell was rocking and grinding against my clit. My magic was impatient, and I could almost feel the ground calling, pulling on my Hunger as my men dragged out my orgasm.

I came with a gasp, Cosmo releasing me from the kiss as I cried out. Candlelight flared in our tent, and outside of it our audience gasped with the roar of rising bonfires. It was beyond me to notice whether or not the ground was trembling when I was clawing and shuddering in the arms of my Chosen, but the following cry of applause and cheers from outside was enough.

"Seedlings are sprouting," Aric huffed out before taking my breast in a devouring kiss.

Owen pushed forward, his forehead resting against mine. "Pace yourself, Mistress. We won't let you sleep tonight."

"You know I'll only want more," I answered, moaning and twisting to meet Wendell's now rushing thrusts, arching for Aric's mouth. "When I'm with you, I only ever want more."

"More it is," Cresswell said, stroking his palm over my stomach. "Forever, Your Majesty."

The door to our suite had a squeaky hinge. The staff kept trying to oil it, and Daniel kept chasing them away for me. I liked the sound, especially at night. I counted it in the evenings, waiting for the last squeak that told me we were all together again.

Creak.

I sat up in bed, roused from a brief grip on a rare bit of sleep. Owen's arm was slung over my waist, thunderous snores still sinking heavily into the pillow, but Cosmo sat up with me, smiling in the candlelight. From the bathroom, Daniel appeared, a towel slung low around his waist.

"You're not going to race out?" Cosmo asked.

"I can be patient," I answered, and when he and Daniel shared a humored grin, I shrugged. "Fine. I'm too tired to race."

I didn't have long to wait. The door to our bedroom opened, and Wendell stepped inside with a sigh.

"There's a sight for sore eyes," he said, pausing.

"How was the council meeting?"

"Fine, uneventful, if you don't count Morgan calling one of the others a cotton-brained traditionalist. Which I don't at this point," he said with a shrug, not moving from the doorway.

I arched an eyebrow. "You're late."

Wendell grinned. "That's because I've brought you a surprise."

He stepped aside, and three achingly familiar figures moved into the room.

"Oh!" I didn't care how tired I was, *now* I was absolutely racing. Owen grunted as I accidentally kicked him aside, scrambling my way to the edge of the bed.

Aric and Thao met me halfway, arms snapping around me, their faces lowering at the same time to kiss me until we all ended up bumping our noses together. Aric caught a peck, and then Thao demanded more. I fought the urge to cry and simply let them bundle me tighter between them.

"How'd you manage to bring them both back at once?" Daniel asked.

"I helped," Cress said. "Met Aric halfway with a change of horses so we could make a rush of it."

"The ship caught a good wind this week," Thao said, easing up so Aric could take his fair share of kisses too.

I whimpered between them, fingers digging into their shoulders. Thao had been gone for nearly a month, finalizing the details of a new trade treatise with Mennary, and Aric had spent the past two weeks at the royal magician's college. Most of the council still thought my Chosen spent too much time out of my bed, meddling in the kingdom for me. I didn't agree, but there were times where I hated having them away from me. The past weeks with both Thao and Aric gone had been especially hard.

As if to remind me why, a soft cry rose from the bassinet, and Thao and Cosmo both hurried over. Aric stayed, his arm wrapped around my waist, fingers smoothing my hair back.

"You look tired, princess."

My lips twitched, he'd never given up the nickname.

"Managing Kimmery isn't half as challenging as your daughter," I said, arching an eyebrow at the bassinet.

Dahlia was burbling in Thao's arms, pressed to his chest and drooling onto the shoulder of his satin jacket.

"Mm, she takes after her mother then," Aric said, grinning, resisting me as I tried to playfully push him away. He kissed me once more and then hurried over, smoothing a hand over Dahlia's pale hair and kissing the back of her head, he and Thao both taking a deep whiff of her.

A moment later, like clockwork, she began to fuss.

"She wants you," Thao said, frowning with what I suspected was a little bit of offense. He was determined to be her favorite, if such a thing was possible at two months old.

I shook my head, crossing my arms over my chest. "Not me.

Cosmo," I said nodding at the man who had already taken up position in the rocking chair. "She's not hungry, she just likes his voice as far as we can tell."

"How are the nurses taking it?" Aric asked, kissing Dahlia once more before sitting down on the bench and kicking off his boots.

"They think we're perverse for trying to do everything ourselves," Daniel said.

"You should see their faces when I nurse her," I huffed out, rolling my eyes.

Thao kept a greedy grip on Dahlia, trying to bounce her gently into submission, but eventually her cries rose higher and more desperate. I was immune by now, but he relented, passing her into Cosmo's arms.

I tiptoed closer, settling next to Aric on the soft bench and tugging on Thao's coat to pull him closer to my side. Fall was closing in, even in the south, and we'd be leaving the capital soon for the harvest festival and our stay in the Winter Palace. My mother and her Chosen would return south to keep an eye on things and to avoid the worst of the snow on the mountain. I was looking forward to the privacy of the north again, I wanted more moments like this one with my family.

"Hello, little love," Cosmo cooed as Dahlia settled, those great doll eyes of hers blinking up at him. I wasn't really sure which of my Chosen might've contributed to her making, she looked a little too much like me, but there was something in her eyes, an innocent and knowing quality that reminded me of Owen.

"You could sleep now, you know," Cress said as Cosmo chatted softly with Dahlia.

"I know. I think I get as much comfort from listening as she does," I admitted with a sheepish smile.

"I'm getting partial to storytime as well," Wendell admitted, settling down on Thao's other side, slouching into the bench and resting his head on our prince's chest.

"Once upon a time, there was a princess in a beautiful castle at the edge of the sea," Cosmo murmured. Owen moved from the bed to sit behind me, Daniel and Cress moving in to join us all. "She had a pretty room and a pretty garden, but she was all alone, so she made friends with the characters in the books she read."

"Oh, not that one," I gasped, realizing Cosmo was telling my own story.

"It has a happy ending," he teased, smiling at me as Dahlia reached up to slap his chin for more.

"It has the best ending, but parts of it are too..." *Painful*, I thought, Camellia's face in my mind. Emory's too. Daniel's as I left him on the floor of his office. Aric's as he turned away from me in the orchard, eyes flashing with anger. His hand squeezed mine now, and I sighed, falling back into the moment with my family.

"Mm. Fine then," Cosmo said with a nod, closing his eyes to think. "Once upon a time, there was a beautiful little princess, born in a castle by the sea, to the most wise and powerful and fair queen in the world, and seven very loving and lucky fathers."

"Bryony doesn't approve of this one either," Thao said, nudging my cheek as tears coursed down.

"If she has a story, it means she'll face trials," I sniffled.

Cosmo chuckled and tilted his head at me. "Muse, we all face trials."

"She's so little!" I cried.

"I think it's time for our wife to be taken to bed," Aric said, stifling his own laugh as I scowled at him.

"She'll have us," Owen said to me. "We'll face her trials with her until she can slay them herself."

"It was always going to have a happy ending, little muse," Cosmo promised me. "One every bit as beautiful as our own."

I sighed and closed my eyes. I was a *little* hormonal lately, and it was only a story after all. "Very well. Continue."

"Start from the beginning again," Daniel said.

"Once upon a time, there was a princess..."

The End.

ALSO BY KATHRYN MOON

COMPLETE READS
The Librarian's Coven Series
Written - Book 1
Warriors - Book 2
Scrivens - Book 3
Ancients - Book 4

Summerland Series
Summerland Stories, the complete collection plus bonus content

Standalones
Good Deeds
Command The Moon
Say Your Prayers - co-write with Crystal Ash

The Sweetverse
Baby + the Late Night Howlers
Lola & the Millionaires - Part One
Lola & the Millionaires - Part Two

Sol & Lune
Book 1
Book 2

Inheritance of Hunger Trilogy
The Queen's Line
The Princess's Chosen
The Kingdom's Crown

SERIES IN PROGRESS

ACKNOWLEDGMENTS

Thank you to my author world, full of incredible friends and encouraging readers and outstanding authors. I'm so lucky to be a part of the microcosm I've found and so grateful for the hundreds and thousands of amazing women making it richer with every word!

Now specifically onto the people who keep me on track and in the best possible shape-

Gorgeous cover compliments to Covers by Combs for the exquisite work on the cover!

Proof-reading amazingness thanks to Bookish Dreams Editing!

My alphas - Desiree and Momma Moon for helping me organize my thoughts and see this to the bittersweet end!

My beta babes who absolutely devoured and protected this story; Jami, Ash, Kathryn, and Helen - thank you so much for all of your input and for helping to shape my stories!

My author pack - most notably my babes Lana, Chloe, Aleera and Crystal

And thank you, lovely reader, for taking this journey with me, Bryony, and her Chosen. I hope this happily ever after sees you satisfied!

ABOUT THE AUTHOR

Kathryn Moon is a country mouse who started dictating stories to her mother at an early age. The fascination with building new worlds and discovering the lives of the characters who grew in her head never faltered, and she graduated college with a fiction writing degree. She loves writing women who are strong in their vulnerability, romances that are as affectionate as they are challenging, and worlds that a reader sinks into and never wants to leave. When her hands aren't busy typing they're probably knitting sweaters or crimping pie crust in Ohio. She definitely believes in magic.

You can reach her on Facebook and at ohkathrynmoon@gmail.com or you can sign up for her newsletter!